About

J. H. Fletcher is the author of two historical novels, *Claim the Kingdom* and *The Burning Land*, both set in Australia. The best-selling *View from the Beach* was published by HarperCollins to both critical and popular acclaim in 1999. The author's plays for radio and television have been produced by the BBC and the South African Broadcasting Corporation, and many of this author's stories have been published in Australia and throughout the world. Fletcher also writes regularly for the *Singapore Straits Times*.

J. H. Fletcher was born and educated in the U.K. and travelled and worked in France, Asia and Africa before emigrating to Australia in 1991. Home is now in a small town on the South Australian coast.

Other books by this Author

Claim the Kingdom
The Burning Land
View from the Beach

Keepers of the House

J. H. FLETCHER

HarperCollins*Publishers*

HarperCollins*Publishers*

First published in Australia in 2000
by HarperCollins*Publishers* Pty Limited
ACN 009 913 517
A member of HarperCollins*Publishers* (Australia) Pty Limited Group
http://www.harpercollins.com.au

Copyright © J. H. Fletcher 2000

This book is copyright.
Apart from any fair dealing for the purposes of private study, research,
criticism or review, as permitted under the Copyright Act, no part may
be reproduced by any process without written permission.
Inquiries should be addressed to the publishers.

HarperCollins*Publishers*
25 Ryde Road, Pymble, Sydney, NSW 2073, Australia
31 View Road, Glenfield, Auckland 10, New Zealand
77–85 Fulham Palace Road, London W6 8JB, United Kingdom
Hazelton Lanes, 55 Avenue Road, Suite 2900, Toronto, Ontario M5R 3L2
and 1995 Markham Road, Scarborough, Ontario M1B 5M8, Canada
10 East 53rd Street, New York NY 10022, USA

National Library Cataloguing-in-Publication data:
Fletcher, J. H. 1934- .
Keepers of the house.
ISBN 0 7322 6740 4.
I. Title.
A823.3

Cover: Arthur Streeton, *The old inn, Richmond, Hawkesbury River*, 1896.
Oil on canvas, 40.7 x 35.5 cm.
Gift of Howard Hinton 1932, The Howard Hinton Collection,
New England Regional Art Museum, Armidale, NSW.

Printed in Australia by Griffin Press Pty Ltd, Adelaide
on 50 gsm Ensobulky

7 6 5 4 3 2 1   00 01 02 03

*To Elizabeth
as always*

It gives me great pleasure to acknowledge publicly what I have long acknowledged in private, the debt I owe to my agent Selwa Anthony, for her friendship, encouragement and unfailing support in times both good and bad. To say nothing of her super-glam looks, efficiency and finely-honed commercial skills.

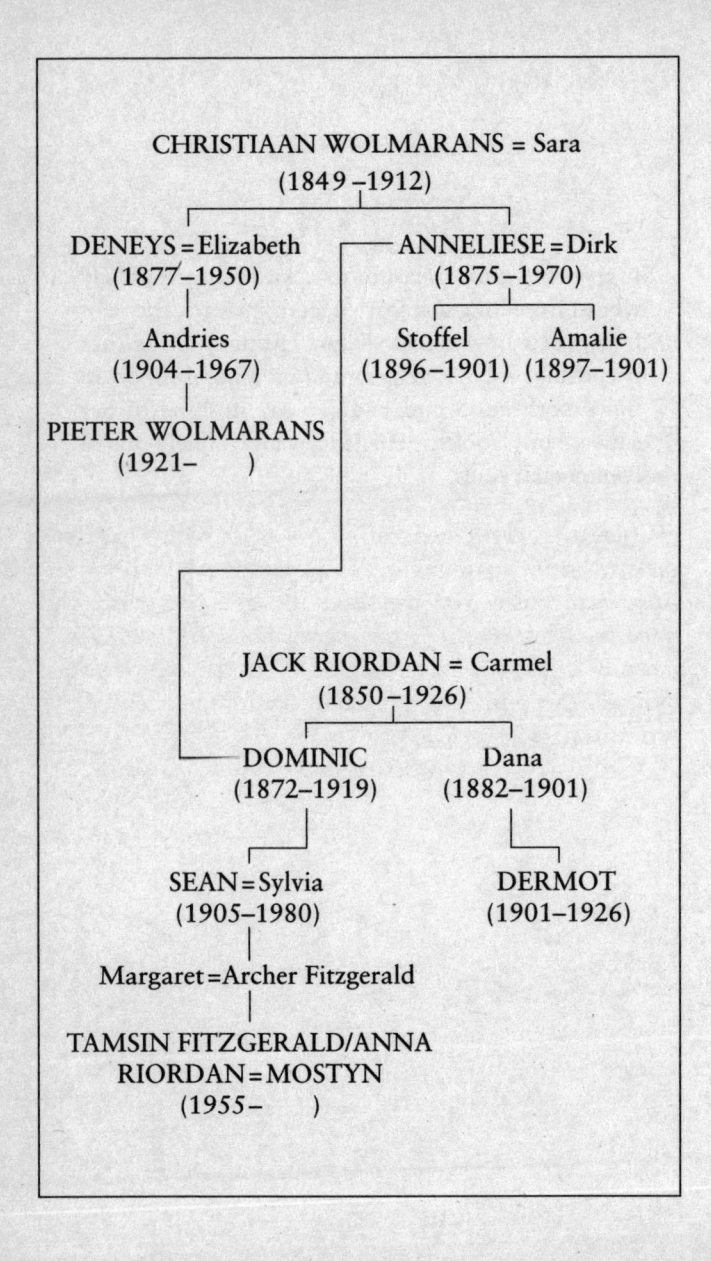

```
CHRISTIAAN WOLMARANS = Sara
         (1849–1912)
    ┌─────────┴─────────┐
DENEYS = Elizabeth    ANNELIESE = Dirk
(1877–1950)           (1875–1970)
    │                 ┌─────┴─────┐
Andries            Stoffel      Amalie
(1904–1967)       (1896–1901)  (1897–1901)
    │
PIETER WOLMARANS
(1921–    )


         JACK RIORDAN = Carmel
              (1850–1926)
         ┌─────┴─────┐
      DOMINIC        Dana
     (1872–1919)   (1882–1901)
         │              │
   SEAN = Sylvia     DERMOT
   (1905–1980)     (1901–1926)

Margaret = Archer Fitzgerald
         │
TAMSIN FITZGERALD/ANNA
RIORDAN = MOSTYN
     (1955–    )
```

PRELUDE

I saw it once in a painting by Arthur Streeton. Ever since I have held its image in my heart. It is weathered, sprawling, unpractical, totally lovely. There is a dried-up creek bed before the door with a rickety-rackety bridge spanning it. All around is the glory of the Australian bush. You can hear the birdsong, taste the underlying silence. It is my dream house. More; it is a metaphor of the longing for fulfilment that lies in every human heart and I, keeping faith with my vision of the future, am its keeper.

— Ruth Ballard (*View from the Beach*)

ONE

The first thing that Anna saw when she came into the house was the envelope propped foursquare against the crystal vase on the table in the entrance lobby. She turned it in her fingers, frowning. Mostyn's handwriting. Her heart went pit-pat. Her thumbnail broke the seal. She took out the single sheet. Read it. Pain sliced.

Dear God.

The envelope slipped unnoticed to the floor. On numb legs, letter still clasped in her hand, she walked through the lounge to the terrace that ran across the rear of the house. She rested her hands on the stone capping of the wall and looked out at the manicured lawn, the flowerbeds that now, in the second week of December, were bright with petunias and antirrhinums, the scented heads of roses. Beyond the garden, the blue water of the harbour. The Manly ferry, toy-sized, trailed its wake as it tossed through the chop towards the city. The water was white-flecked, the air crackled with salt. The house unfolded its wings behind her.

Home.

It was here she had planned so many of her triumphs in recent years. To it she had returned to lick her occasional wounds; who, in the savage world of business, had not known a few of those? It had comforted her, cosseted her, protected her. Her safe stronghold. No longer. Now, with Mostyn's note, the walls had been breached.

In the house the telephone started ringing. Anna did not move. It was probably Hilary with the latest production figures from the new factory in Geelong. They could wait. For the moment she was not up to Hilary's obsessive pedantry, her accountant's voice scratching dust over all Anna's bright visions.

The phone stopped as the answering machine cut in. Released by silence, Anna walked down the steps to the grass. The turf yielded beneath her boardroom shoes. She had an urge to chuck away not only the shoes but everything they represented: the structure of deals and treasons, lies and promises, minutes and financial statements that for so many years had constituted her life.

All that, she thought, so that one day — today — I can come home to an empty house and find that my husband of thirteen years has walked out on me.

She was still holding Mostyn's letter. She looked at it again. Behind the written words she could hear his voice, hot and spiteful, listing all the faults he claimed to have found in her in recent years. Yet the letter contained nothing of that; he had never been one to commit himself in writing if he could avoid it.

I've had enough. I'll send for my things.

Just that. Not much to end a life with its attendant pains and joys, its hopes and plans and companionship.

Its love.

Because there had been love, surely? To count no triumph complete without sharing it. To feel warmth at the sound of his voice. To know contentment and peace in his presence. What were these if not love?

They had found this house together; like excited kids had run through its rooms, sharing their vision of its potential, its place in their future. They had eaten Sunday morning breakfasts on that terrace, crumbs and newspapers and the hot, strong smell of coffee. They had laughed together, wept together, clung together. Silly, trivial things.

Of course, there were other, less delightful memories. Of rows and more rows, particularly lately. And now this.

I've had enough.

The crash of her collapsing world reverberating in her head and heart, Anna Riordan climbed the steps to the terrace and went back indoors.

She looked in the kitchen. Mrs Casey had left a cold meal in the fridge. Mrs Casey was no doubt the reason Mostyn had taken care to seal his note. Meats, salad, cold potatoes, the remains of a fruit flan.

You will not think, Anna said, as adept at giving orders to herself as to others. You will eat and then you will have a bath. Only then will you decide what has to be done.

Half an hour later, wreathed in steam, she lay in the hot scented water and, for the first time, brought her mind to bear on her situation.

She supposed she should have known a break was on the cards. The good times, the shared delight in each other, the enmeshing of minds and bodies had all ended years ago. For a long time they had not even made love, had been no more than two strangers sharing the same accommodation. Yet, in truth, she had not expected it. It was what happened to their friends; never once had she thought it might happen to her.

Now this.

She stirred restlessly in the bath, running her hands over a body that at forty-one was still taut and firm.

We had something precious but were so tied up in our piffling careers that we never bothered to take care of it. Never even realised that care was necessary. Now it is dead, from indifference and neglect. And we are supposed to be so smart.

Damn, damn, damn.

One question remained. What had happened to cause Mostyn to make the break?

Another woman?

She supposed that, in this situation, it was the first thing all women wondered. It was certainly possible. Mostyn's eye had wandered often but she had always been careful to ask no questions, had not permitted herself to care too deeply; always, the moments had passed. She thought she would have known had Mostyn involved himself seriously with someone.

No, not that. What, then?

Only one thing seemed possible. Over the last few years Anna had had the Midas touch; all her ventures had turned to gold. Because of her flair she had been invited to join the boards of some of the largest companies in the land; political connections had caused her to be offered — and accept — a seat on the prestigious State Economic Strategies Committee.

By contrast Mostyn's own career had topped out. No one could call him unsuccessful. He was executive director of a merchant bank, had a hatful of other directorships and enough cash to indulge his whim of investing in premium vineyards, both in Australia and overseas. It would have been more than enough for most men. Yet, somehow, his career had lacked the sparkle of her own.

He had known it and resented it. Small signs that, in retrospect, had been significant: a determination, ever more frequently expressed, that Anna's career should be subordinate to his own; unreasoning anger when their schedules clashed and she was unable — or unwilling — to put off her arrangements to suit his.

Recently had come what might have been the final step in bringing him to the break. Some weeks earlier, Anna had been invited to lunch at an unfashionable restaurant by one of the main power brokers in the party. He had spoken ambiguously, yet to someone like Anna, who understood the language, his words had been unmistakable. People had been wondering, he said, whether she might be interested in a place, a very senior place, in government. If one happened to become available. If she should by chance be interested in a political career. No need for a decision right away, he had told her. Think about it.

She had gone home ten feet off the ground, bursting to share the news with her husband, who knew well that politics had been a source of unending fascination to her ever since the early eighties when she had spent two years as aide to Jack Goodie, at that time shadow Trade Minister.

Mostyn had been unable to handle it.

'I'd as soon mix with the Mafia as that riffraff. At least you know where you are with the Mafia.'

'Just a chat. They're not committed. Neither am I.'

'No such thing as just a chat with those blokes.'

He was probably right. She had not committed herself but knew she probably would, had felt the tingle of excitement that for her always signalled the lure of a new adventure.

'Isn't business enough for you?' The genuine astonishment of a man to whom the acquisition of money was the world.

'Probably not.'

For some time she had felt restless at the prospect of spending the rest of her life making nothing but money. Such a limited ambition ... Whereas politics would give her the opportunity to stretch herself, perhaps even do some good in the world.

For some time she had become involved in a number of issues, women's rights and third world matters among them, telling herself they were no more than sidelines.

Perhaps, with the cautiously worded invitation, it was time for them to move centre stage.

Had that caused the final rift? Probably. Since that conversation, if you could call it that, Mostyn had never stopped bitching about how her career was taking over both their lives, had made it clear that if she wanted him to play second fiddle she was in for a disappointment.

'You needn't expect me to trot along behind you ...'

And then, two days ago, the Premier himself had phoned. An election was due next year; it would be helpful if he had an idea of her plans.

Even then she had not committed herself. She had not said no, either, as she had admitted when Mostyn questioned her. Some husbands would have been proud; he had been furious, had told her that she thought only of herself, that his career meant nothing to her.

It was nonsense and she had said so, angrily. It had ended in a terrible row, recriminations flying like bullets, and the spoiled brat she had married thirteen years earlier had stormed out in what she now saw had been a rehearsal for today's main event.

Envy, she told herself, a petty, petulant reaction from a petty, petulant man. The thought made her feel better, if not much.

She stood up, body glowing from the hot water, mind clear. She reached for a towel and began to rub herself dry. Envy, pure and simple. Except that envy was never pure and seldom simple.

She knew Mostyn so well. He had always been a hatchet man, even had the nickname to go with it. Hatchet Harcourt, they called him in the city. If he fell out with you, people said, look out. Anna had never thought she would have to worry about that — her *husband*, for heaven's sake — but now was not so sure.

She tossed the towel into the laundry basket and walked naked into the bedroom. Theirs, it seemed, no longer.

She would have to watch her back.

She put on a deceptively simple linen dress in a tone of dusty pink that suited her colouring. She had bought it in Genoa the last time she had been in Europe; it was one of her favourites for a summer evening when she didn't want to get too tarted up. She brushed her dark hair — no grey so far, although after this episode who knew what she might find in the morning? — and put on the dab of lipstick that tonight was her sole concession to the conventions of make-up.

As she did so, she thought deliberately about what she had to do. Speak to Maurice Steyn, first of all, if she could get hold of him. He was her lawyer and would have to be told, much as she hated the idea. She would check the answering machine for messages, return Hilary's call, if that was who it had been. She might phone Monica; it was what friends were for, wasn't it, to lean on in times of trouble? The idea of leaning on anyone was so bizarre that she found herself smiling at her reflection in the dressing-table mirror.

Perhaps the shock of all this will make me cuddly, she thought. But doubted it. Loving, yes, that might still be possible. But cuddly? Never.

Apart from sitting on the phone for an hour, she had no plans for the evening. Tidy up the bits and pieces, eat her supper on the terrace, have a glass of wine and watch the lights come up in the city on the far side of the harbour ... She could have done all that in a dressing-gown. In nothing at all, come to that. The idea of sitting in the nude, clutching the phone and discussing her marital problems with the dignified Maurice Steyn brought the smile back to her lips. How the idea would have horrified him!

So why go to the trouble of dolling herself up in her favourite Italian dress to make a few phone calls?

Because I must, she told herself. Suddenly she felt like tears. Resolutely she fought them down. I have to prove to myself that the show will go on. My show. However much I want to lie down and scream my heart out, I shall not do it. I shall not allow him to destroy me.

Purposefully, as presentable as she could make herself, Anna walked down the stairs to her study.

Let's get on with it.

Two hours later Anna, plans for a quiet evening blown out of the water, sat with her friend Monica Talbot eating Chinese food at a harbourside restaurant in the Rocks.

Monica had been less surprised by the news than Anna had expected, had at once suggested that they should go out and eat together.

'*Cheong Wah's*,' Monica had said. 'Eight o'clock.'

It was nice to be bossed for a change.

Monica was bowstring-taut, angry-eyed and neurotic. She'd been through two husbands and now blamed the world — or at least the male part of it — for them both. One had been wealthy, pleasant. After five years she had caught him making up to a woman she had regarded as a friend. The second had been a dealer on the stock exchange who relieved stress by drinking. When he drank, he used his fists. The first time, Monica had warned him; the second, she had packed an overnight case and walked out. Anna had sheltered her on that occasion; now she was returning the compliment.

Not that Anna needed it. She could look after herself and said so.

'Don't you believe it. Your husband's no different from the rest of them. They're all bastards.'

'Mostyn's not the bash 'em and mash 'em type.'

To Monica, Mostyn was male, the enemy. 'I wouldn't put it past him.'

'He's probably home already,' Anna hoped. Or did she? She couldn't be sure.

'Reckon there's someone else?' Monica asked.

'Thought you might be able to tell me that. They say the wife is always the last to hear.'

Above their heads the bridge's familiar girders loomed against a rash of stars, but here, on the cobbled waterfront, her new situation had made all things strange. It was like finding herself in a new, incomprehensible world where the signs were back to front. I don't understand this new place, Anna thought. I don't want to understand it. Bruised ego or not, she wished with desperate fervour that everything could go back to how it had been three hours ago. Futile, no doubt, but knowing it did not stifle the wish.

Monica was not into wishes where husbands were concerned. 'It stuck out a mile. You were bad for his ego. A wife more successful than he was? No way he would put up with that.'

Her own thoughts; yet she disliked hearing them from anyone else. Absurdly, she found herself defending the indefensible. 'He's not that bad –'

'If he's so marvellous, why aren't you home with him instead of sitting here with me?'

Monica was right, of course. His place was here, with her. They'd dined out a lot together, once. Had fun together. Once.

'He certainly chose his moment. The first free weekend I've had in yonks and he messes it up.'

'Only if you let him.'

That was true, too. For the first time in thirteen years she could do what she liked without thinking about anyone else. She could walk the beach, stay in bed, get on a plane. She could do anything she wanted. If she wanted anything.

Oh Moss, she thought, how could you?

If he'd turned up that minute, she would have thrown herself at him. Open arms; open legs, too, no doubt. You make me sick, she told herself.

Belatedly, something that Monica had said a few minutes earlier struck her.

'I would hardly say I was that successful,' she said.

Monica laughed in disbelief. 'Australian Businesswoman of the Year?'

'Doesn't mean much.' Though she'd been delighted at the time. 'What's the point of it? I've worked my butt off all my life. For what?' To be like you, filling lonely evenings with food and bitterness? Somehow, she managed not to say it.

'You started with nothing. Now look at you. How can you say you're not successful?'

It was true, she supposed. She'd picked the tree she'd wanted, had climbed damn near to the top. It was a bit late to start wondering if it had been the right tree.

She was in shock, she told herself. That was why she was thinking like this. It would have been remarkable if she'd felt nothing, after all.

Out in the harbour, islanded in darkness, a brightly-lit ferry headed somewhere unknowable, like a metaphor of her life.

'Love is a mistake, isn't it?' Anna said. 'It makes you vulnerable.'

Vulnerability was a new experience, yet now it had arrived it seemed in no hurry to abandon her. Later, at the house that no longer felt like home, it tightened like a clamp about her heart. Lying alone on the tossed sheets in a bedroom that was suddenly far too big, far too small, every creak of the house jerked her out of the doze that was the nearest she could get to sleep. Afraid Mostyn would come home after all; afraid he would not.

He wouldn't; she knew him too well to believe anything else. The ego that had driven him away would make it impossible for him to return so quickly. She hoped, all the same. Unavailingly.

At last, after a dozen lifetimes, the dawn. The harbour as serene as on the first day.

I can't stay here all weekend, Anna thought. I'll go ape.

She showered, wishing she could scrub her mind as clean as her body. She arranged a few clothes tidily in a case — not even a broken marriage, which was what she supposed it was, could break her addiction to order — spread a croissant with jam, drank one cup of black coffee. She went out to the garage, stowed the case in the Porsche, and headed north.

Past Broken Bay she found a beach with a pub at the far end, a lake behind a scattering of houses. Miraculously, being a fine Saturday, it had a room. So small the bed almost filled it, a rickety, dark-stained wardrobe jammed against one wall. At the end of a bare corridor, the shower and lavatory were as drab as a public toilet. It was a long time since Anna had stayed anywhere like it but the very discomfort eased her. Here everything was different. She had a name for resilience, for permitting nothing to faze her. Very well. Now was her chance to prove it. Here she would start to forget.

She gave it her best shot. She walked the beach; when she was sick of the sea she crossed the dunes and followed a sandy track shaded by trees until she reached the lake. Watched a man with a dog, a father and mother surrounded by a joyous scream of children.

I should have been like that, she thought, knowing it was nonsense. She had never been cut out for a housewife. A week of it and she'd have been climbing the walls. She imagined packing hubby off to work, the kids off to school. Cleaning the house, doing the shopping, building her own little kingdom in her own little home. Nothing wrong with any of it. Admirable, even, but not — most emphatically not — for her. If everyone were like I am, she thought, the human race would have died out long ago.

Which at the moment did not seem such a bad idea.

It grew hot. She returned to the beach. Luckily, she had thought to slip on some bathers beneath her clothes. She peeled off shorts and top, baring white city skin to the cancerous eye of the yellow sun. Much she cared about that. She rubbed on sunscreen, lay on the stinging sand, plunged periodically into the tepid Pacific as it lapped along the shore. Later, when she'd had enough sun, she found a scrap of tattered shade, sat and stared at the water.

She wasn't used to doing nothing. It was an art, like everything else, and she had never thought to acquire it. All her life had passed in a rush. She wondered what was the point of it.

Don't start that again.

But there had to be a point. Simply to function mindlessly, with no object in view — that was scary.

Surely there was merit in the generation of wealth, not simply for herself but for tens of thousands of others? People better off than they'd have been without her? Of course there was. Then why didn't it seem enough?

Damn you, Mostyn. I never had doubts before.

Except that she had, which was why the political option had seemed so attractive. Now she found herself wondering even about that.

She wasn't going to walk out on her present life, make any rash decisions. She had to give herself time. It was less than twenty-four hours since she'd got the letter. Besides, what else could she do? She wasn't the sort to sit on her bum and do nothing. She was used to seizing problems by the throat and shaking them to death. Not being able to do so now made her uncomfortable. Like the drying, powdery sand, frustration itched her skin.

Give it time and it will pass, she told herself. I only wish it would.

She wondered if Mostyn had been trying to contact her. It pleased her to think of the phone ringing in the empty house, him listening to her metallic voice on the answering machine. She liked to imagine his indignation at discovering that she was not available just because he wanted her to be. Of course, the chances were he had not tried to get in touch with her at all.

Once again she thought back over their relationship, seeking the defining moment when the balance between Mostyn's options — to stay or go — had finally shifted. She remembered one of their more recent rows. At the time, she had barely noticed it. It had been simply another in what now she realised had been a crescendo of rows.

If only I'd taken more notice, she thought. If only I'd listened. If only ...

But she hadn't.

Now she saw that it had been remarkable only because Mostyn had come closer than ever before to expressing his real feelings, the core of his resentment of her and their life together.

Mostyn's voice, battering the living room walls. 'You've always wanted to keep up with me but you couldn't hack it. Envy — that's your problem. It's become a kind of mad game, hasn't it? How many directorships, how many TV appearances?'

'I don't see anything wrong with being well-known.'

It was true that most businessmen favoured a low profile, but Anna had always enjoyed the limelight. She knew how to manipulate the media, with its politically correct cringe towards any woman who achieved prominence or notoriety.

Mostyn topped up his Scotch without offering her one, took a ferocious belt. Given half a chance he would have devoured her too, and her independent ways.

'All this palaver about human rights ... In the old days it was South Africa. Now it's Northern Ireland, the United States. Australia too, of course. Why do people like you always pick on their own side? Softer target, I suppose. As for this feminist garbage ...'

On and on.

Anna, maliciously, said nothing, knowing that it would make him madder than ever. Which it did.

'Bumped into Donald Jeffreys last week, at the SCG. Know what he said?'

No, Mostyn, I do not know what Donald Jeffreys said. No doubt you are about to tell me, though.

'Asked if I'd burned any bras lately.'

And down, yet again, went the Scotch.

'Good work if you can get it,' Anna said, contempt hot as flame. 'Right up Donald Jeffreys' street, I'd have thought.'

Mostyn had already told her about Andy McKillop and his chuckles over Hatchet Harcourt's feminist army. *Better not call 'em women. They don't like that.*

'Don't you see how embarrassing it is when my friends start talking like that? Doesn't do my image much good.'

'You've no idea how I despise your friends,' she said.

Mostyn glared savagely. 'They put bread on your table, though, don't they?'

Which was true, too, if irrelevant.

None of which had anything to do with the real problem, what Mostyn called buttering up the pollies.

'You don't get the nod in the boardrooms of this city by playing footsy with the ALP.'

Had that been the moment when the balance — to go, to stay — had finally shifted? Probably not; from what Anna had seen of other people's bust-ups, one isolated episode seldom made the difference; it usually took a series of events to cause the break.

None of it mattered, now.

She meandered back to the hotel, forcing herself to take her time. She had a shower, washed her hair, determined to make herself as sparkly as possible. Not to attract anyone — heaven forbid! — but for her own sake.

If I have to make a new life, let me get on with it.

That night, iron bedstead and lumpy mattress notwithstanding, she slept. Woke, romantically, to the first rays of sunlight shafting through the smeared window. Discovered that in the night she had come to a decision.

I shall do nothing until after the New Year, she thought. Give myself time to work things out. She had two board meetings that week. The Christmas break meant there would be nothing after that until mid-January. In past years she had worked through the holiday but this year Hilary could handle it. She had not had a real break in years; now she would.

She spent the day in the hills, had a bite at a fancy-pantsy restaurant, felt herself beginning to come back to life. Driving back to Sydney that evening, she wondered how her great-grandmother would have reacted to the situation.

She laughed, ruefully. Anneliese had been dead for twenty-six years yet, in a sense, had never died at all. Her strength and willpower had been a role model to Anna all her life. She could feel her right now, beside her in the car.

The ferocious old lady would probably have gone for Mostyn with a shotgun, Anna thought. How she had been influenced by her! — even to the extent of changing her name from the Tamsin Fitzgerald she'd despised to an Anglicised imitation of her great-grandmother's name.

What would I have been like without her genes in me?

She tried to imagine herself as placid and easy-going, a cow chewing the cud in her own particular paddock. A preposterous idea; she laughed and felt better.

Anneliese Riordan had died in 1970 at the age of ninety-five, when Anna herself had been fifteen. Her will had been diamond-bright until the end, eyes focused resolutely upon the twin objectives of her life: never to relinquish her heritage; never to forgive the past. She had lived sixty-seven years in Australia yet never for a moment had she allowed her hatred to grow dim.

As long as Anna could remember, *Ouma* Riordan, as she had liked to be called — Granny Riordan — had told her tales of her life in the years before she had been forced to leave Africa.

Such tales. Of her first husband and the two children they had made together. What had happened when, after nearly three years of war, her own home burned, she had returned to *Oudekraal*, the farm that had been the centre and focus of her childhood.

Anneliese's guttural voice had drawn pictures in the air: *Oudekraal*, with its steeply-pitched roofs, its white walls gleaming in the moonlight, the central gable rising over the front doorway; the *stoep* along the length of the building, the oak trees to shade it from the fierce suns of summer.

Tamsin, as she had then been, had seen it so clearly, had felt herself as much a part of the great house thousands of kilometres away as if she had been born in it herself.

'My brother Deneys came to terms with the English,' Anneliese had told her, spitting hatred. 'Something I would never do. Yet without him they'd have had me, sure enough.'

For a moment she was silent, her eyes seeing every grain of soil, the terraces of vines climbing the hill behind the house, the valley enclosing it. Tamsin saw it, too; had heard about it so often that it was hard to believe she had never been there herself.

'I wrote once to an attorney in Stellenbosch,' Anneliese said. 'He told me my great-nephew has it now. Pieter Wolmarans. By rights it should have been mine.'

Anna's memories faded but later, back in the house overlooking the harbour — no messages from Mostyn on the answering machine — they returned. She remembered the last time she had spoken to the old woman.

In the bedroom Anneliese was fighting her final battle. Echoing voices, a confusion of memories, death with its hand already upon her. Her voice rose and fell, gasping, barely coherent.

'I was twenty-eight when I came to this country. Already I'd had children of my own. *Ja*, and buried them. My first husband dead. No, I was no longer a child.' She cackled. 'Surprising your great-grandfather would have me. But he was a wild one, too.' Her eyes were lost in distance as she remembered. 'Dominic,' she said. 'And fire, the curse and cleansing gift of God.'

And for a time was silent. Eventually she came back. Outstretched fingers clutched at the past. 'Two hundred years,' she muttered. 'Two hundred years since the first of the Wolmarans carved his farm from nothing. *Oudekraal*. A garden where before had been only a wilderness of stone.' The wandering eyes focused again on Tamsin. 'My land was stolen from me. You know that?' Spit rattled urgently in the ancient voice. 'My life has been a life of blood. Some from my heart, some on my hands. There are times when I can hear the screams ...' Again she drifted, again returned. This time the old note of purpose was back in her voice. She stared up at Tamsin, leaning forward over the bed. '*Oudekraal* is mine. You will recover it. Never forget. You will reclaim my house. Our past. It is your destiny. I can see it in your face.' She tried to sit up a little but could not, and lay back again, panting. 'The book on the table beside the bed ... Is it there?'

'Yes.'

'You know what it is?'

'It's a Bible.'

'Take it in your hands.'

She waited until Tamsin had done so.

'It is not like the one we had when I was your age, with brass hinges and the names of all the family from the beginning written inside the cover, but the word of God, all the same. There is something in it that I want you to remember. For me and for yourself.' The claw fingers tightened on Tamsin's wrist. '*Oudekraal* is mine. I want you to swear to get it back for me. The Bible says it. *In the days when the keepers of the house shall tremble ...*' The dark eyes probed, as fierce as a hawk. 'Keep my commandments,' Anneliese said.

On Monday morning Anna sat in her office on the twentieth floor of the building overlooking Darling Harbour. She thought long and carefully before at last picking up her private phone to dial a number in the city.

'*Reporter.*'

'Mark Forrest, please.'

'Please hold.'

'Mark Forrest's office.'

People who called her had to fight through a similar ring of defences.

'This is Anna Riordan. May I speak to him, please?'

'Mr Forrest is not available. So sorry.' She didn't sound sorry at all.

'You mean he's out or in a meeting?'

Ice chinked at the end of the line. 'I mean he's not available.'

'Do yourself a favour. Tell him who's calling, right?'

What a bully! Anna thought, not worrying about it. She had grown used to bullying. At times, as now, enjoyed it.

Silence as again she was put on hold.

'Anna?' Laughter as well as astonishment in his voice.

Even after so long there was no mistaking him.

'Hi.'

'What did you say to my secretary?'

'I asked her to put me through to you.'

'Was that all?'

'More or less.' She shared his laughter. 'Why?'

'You seem to have got up her nose.'

'Oh dear.' Not in the least repentant.

'What can I do for you? After all these years?'

'I want you to have lunch with me.'

'Today?' He sounded doubtful.

'If you can.'

'Let me grab my diary ...' A pause as he considered. 'I could maybe re-schedule a couple of things ... What time?'

'Twelve-thirty?'

'Where?'

'There's a place in Darling Harbour called *Hugo's*. I've heard good reports about it.'

'I don't know it.'

'Neither do I.'

She had thought to suggest *Ristorante Venezia*, where they'd shared their last meal all those years ago. She had been there again in recent times and found it as good as ever but, for this meeting, somewhere without echoes would be a wiser choice.

'Look forward to it.'

She cradled the phone. He had not asked if her business were important. She liked that. It was like saying that anything involving her was bound to be important. The implied compliment gave her a warm feeling, as his voice had given her a warm feeling.

She indulged the luxury of thinking back, something that her own inclination and monstrously busy schedule rarely permitted. Her brain juggled dates. Fifteen years since they'd first met. Good heavens. That meeting, startling as it had been, had at first been a good deal less than friendly, although almost at once the atmosphere between them had changed. Then, later, it had changed back again. How it had changed! At that time it would have seemed ridiculous to imagine that they would ever choose to meet again. Yet here they were, fifteen years down the track, going to have lunch together. At her invitation. The wheel turning in a world where it seemed nothing was ever definite, nothing final.

Despite everything that had happened since Friday, she found herself looking forward to the lunch with more than warmth, even with a touch of gathering excitement.

Re-visiting old times ...

TWO

The finals of the 1981 Australian Tennis Championships. Afterwards there was a party for players, officials and selected hangers-on, of whom Anna was one.

She had been working for Jack Goodie for six months. Opposition spokesman for Trade and Economic Affairs, Jack had poached her from the accounting firm which she had joined after qualifying. She was a high flier, a partnership had been only a matter of time, but Jack had built a career out of getting people to see his point of view. He had introduced Anna to his vision of the big world and she had moved to Canberra.

'I won't be able to pay you as much as you're getting now,' he had warned her. 'Nothing like what you're worth.'

'That's not important.'

Even at that age she had known that for her there would always have to be more to a job than simply making money; had been confident enough to believe that aspect of things would eventually take care of itself. What Jack had been able to offer her, what she had seized with eager hands, had been the possibility of influence, of having a say in how things were done. Even more exciting, of how things might be done in future.

She had never regretted it. She loved the cut and thrust of politics, the interplay of minds and personalities, the trick of getting her own way. The first seductive — and addictive — lure of power.

Jack was mad about tennis and had taken her to Melbourne for the last three days of the championships. Not that there was anything between them but Jack liked to have his aides around him and Anna, who two weeks before had dug up the ammunition that had enabled him to shoot holes in the Government's trade policy, was flavour of the month.

She was just coming out of the Ladies. A sudden blur of movement, an almighty collision and she was sprawling on the floor.

Half-stunned, a quick fury heating her blood, she looked up at the tall man of her own age bending anxiously over her. She had an impression of long black hair and vivid blue eyes. Then she was on her feet. Screaming.

'Why don't you look where you're going?'

'You all right?'

'No thanks to you, you moron!' Nursing a bruised elbow. Bruised ego, too, with everyone staring.

He was fussing around her, would have dusted her down if she'd let him.

'I'm really sorry –'

'For God's sake leave me alone.'

His eyes cooled. She realised that this was a man who did not apologise easily.

'I said I'm sorry. You want me to crawl?'

Some instinct for the incongruous made her laugh. 'Why should I be the only one?'

And, as easily as that, it was all right.

'Aren't you Mark Forrest?'

'Afraid so.'

'I used to be one of your top fans.'

He grinned ruefully. 'Used to be. That'd be right.'

His Aussie accent was overlaid with a hint of American. He was rangy and broad-shouldered, fit-looking under his suit.

'Why did you quit?'

'Not good enough.'

'How can you say that? You got to the semis in your first Aussie Open. If you'd kept going –'

'Not to the top. McEnroe, Connors ... I was never going to be as good as those guys.'

'Even so –'

'If you're not going to be number one, there's no point.'

She could relate to that. 'What are you doing now?'

He smiled at her. 'Let me get you a drink and I'll tell you.'

'Okay.' Amazing herself.

He was a journalist or trying to be, determined to attain the success that had eluded him on the circuit.

'Sports reporter?' she guessed.

'No way. When I quit, I quit.'

'Why?'

'I saw it when I was still playing. Has-beens hanging around the edges of the game, trying to be mates with the players.'

'What's wrong with that?'

'I saw what it did to their pride. I swore I'd never be one of them.'

He was arrogant yet she found herself admiring him for it. If the time ever came for her to quit Canberra, she'd make sure she did the same. In or out: nothing between.

'What, then? If you've turned your back on sport?'

'Foreign affairs. I'm based in Africa at the moment.'

Her interest sharpened. A question about Africa had come up recently at the office; Jack might be interested in having a word with this man.

'Whereabouts in Africa?'

'I got home from Cape Town a couple of weeks ago.'

'Going back?'

'Next week. I'm taking over the bureau there.'

Throwing the words away as though they meant nothing. But was proud, she could tell. Perhaps this time he really would make the top. She found herself hoping so and wondered briefly why she cared.

'Are things there as bad as we hear?'

'They're not good.' Which was not what she'd asked. 'You have to see it from the African point of view and that's not easy.'

'I'd have thought the riots made it plain what they thought.'

'Riots can be rigged.'

'Are they?'

'Quite often.'

She was intrigued. 'That's not what we see on the telly.'

'We see what they want us to see.'

'They?'

'The media.'

She could not resist the opening. 'Shouldn't that be "us"? You're the media, too.'

The blue eyes challenged her: fire and ice. 'I try to be objective.'

'Pretty unusual in your game.'

'In any game.'

Which was fair enough, she supposed.

'I work for Jack Goodie. I think he might like to meet you.'

She saw she had no need to explain who Jack Goodie was and was pleased.

'Why should he?'

'He'll tell you that. If he wants to.'

Jack, when they ran him to earth in a corner of the bar, had no inhibitions.

'This business of sanctions ... People are beginning to ask if they serve any purpose.'

'I'd say so. But you really need to go there yourself to understand the situation.'

'If I go, I'll see half a dozen government blokes and that'll be that. No point.'

'Mark says we need to see it from the African point of view,' Anna told him.

'How can I do that?'

'You can't.' She took a deep breath, went for it. 'I could, though.'

Jack stared, first at her, than at the journalist at her side. 'You two an item?'

Only Jack would have had the brass to say such a thing, she thought. Yet found she didn't mind.

'Sure,' she said. 'After all, we've known each other for all of ten minutes.'

'I've known it happen.' Jack was watching her thoughtfully. 'Didn't you tell me once your family came from South Africa?'

'My great-grandmother. Way back.'

'But you've still got people there?'

Jack's ability to retain even the most trivial information was a legend throughout Canberra.

His question conjured memory. Once again Anneliese's voice drew pictures from the air, again Anna saw the moonlit gleam of the white walls, the central gable rising above the entrance, the *stoep*, the oak trees. *Oudekraal*.

Instinct made her belittle the image. 'No one important. Some vague cousin. I've never met him.'

After Anneliese's death she had thought to write to him, to find out about this cousin whom she had never seen, but the impulse had died. She had not thought of Anneliese's great house for a long time now.

'Maybe this could be your chance,' Jack said.

By now she knew him well enough to read his thought processes. He viewed everything from the same perspective: what was in it for Jack. Sanctions might be important; a lot more important was where South Africa was heading, which side was going to come out on top. And when. The international implications were enormous. Know the answers and Jack would have a head start when it came to choosing the next Foreign Minister.

He looked at Anna. 'I'll have to clear it with Bill first. But if you went you could, couldn't you?'

'Could what?'

'Get to meet your cousin.'

'Did he mean it?' Mark asked later.

'He's probably forgotten about it already.'

But Anna wondered; she had seen that speculative look in Jack's eyes before. She guarded her thoughts, smiling at Mark across the table.

After what had happened at the reception, it had seemed only natural for them to finish off the evening by having a meal together. They had gone to an Indian restaurant in a shabby inner suburb. Anna did not know where they were and didn't care; anything was better than traipsing off alone to that depressing hotel.

'How come you knew about this place?'

'Came once or twice when I was playing.' Grinned. 'At least this time I can have a glass of wine.'

Or two. They would be using a taxi; it seemed a pity to waste the opportunity.

The food was hot and delicious, the wine a robust red that went well with it. They talked about themselves; found that despite their different lifestyles they had a good deal in common. Neither of them had started with any money; both were in a fair way to remedy that. Neither had commitments or, for the moment, any plans.

By the time they'd finished the wine it was ten o'clock; too late to do anything else, too early to call it a day.

They looked at each other.

Mark said, 'One thing I always wanted to do ...'

'What?'

'Hire one of those horse contraptions. Go for a drive in the park.'

She had seen the carriages trundling through the city streets, the horses stepping proud. At this time of night, the clip-clop of hooves would echo from the silent buildings.

'Let's do it,' she said.

She was immersed in impressions: the musty smell inside the carriage, the worn upholstery, the night streets unrolling slowly past the window, the clop of hooves and rumble of wheels. The man sitting at her side.

Never spoken to him until tonight, she thought. Now we've had a meal together, drunk wine together, we're sitting in this carriage together with the darkness outside, the fairy lights in the trees. Insanity on top of insanity, there's even a possibility we may be going halfway around the world together.

Africa. She thought about that. The prospect ought to have been romantic: the Dark Continent, David Livingstone and Stanley, lions roaring in the *veld*. She waited, but the tingle did not come. Even the prospect of seeing *Oudekraal* at last failed to excite. No matter. There was excitement enough right here. More than enough.

She turned to Mark, seeing only the outline of his face in the darkness. 'I would like to have gone to St Petersburg in the old days, ridden in a *troika* through the frosty night with the stars snapping overhead.'

It wasn't like her to think such things, never mind say them, yet there the words were, shining in the darkness.

Where has all this sprung from? she asked herself incredulously. *Africa*? What have I to do with Africa?

It wouldn't happen, of course it wouldn't, but if it did ... It would be for only a few weeks, yet the prospect still made her uneasy. It would be simple enough to go, to find out what she could and come back again, yet she had a hunch that it would be asking for trouble, that the person who came back from Africa might not be the person who had gone there.

She didn't need that. Her career was on the move. A couple more years with Jack and then, with his backing, a safe parliamentary seat. After that, the sky. No, she thought. My mind is made up. If Jack says anything, I'll tell him I don't want to go.

Throughout the ride Mark made no attempt to touch her. Her hand lay disregarded on the seat between them and she told herself she was glad.

The ride finished and they climbed down, returning to the mundane, twentieth-century world. They walked to her hotel. At the marble entrance they stopped. Anna felt her blood, her heart beating.

'You reckon he will send you?' Mark asked.

'Not a chance.' She was very positive about it.

He grinned. 'Indispensable, eh?'

'Something like that.'

There was a hole between their words. A succession of holes. They looked at each other. Down the street the fairy lights shone in the darkness.

'I hope you're wrong,' he said.

She felt the warmth, spreading. 'Why?'

'Because I'd like you to come.'

He was close, looking down at her, eyes seeking.

She laughed, shifting gear. 'Jack gets these mad ideas. They hardly ever come to anything.'

'Talk him into it.'

'Why should I do that?'

'Otherwise ...' He gestured helplessly. 'Ships that pass in the night.'

His words ran like blood through her veins. She reached out, wound her fingers around his. Smiled. Her answer said itself.

'No one said anything about passing.'

Up in the lift together amid the hum of the mechanism, the soft whisper of air. Anna stared at her reflection in the bronze doors and wondered what she was getting into.

I don't do this. Never. One night stands ...

She had never been in the least promiscuous. She'd had only one other relationship in her life; it had ended in failure, although she had hoped for better things at the time.

You two an item?

The veined eyes, the knowing smile. She had almost laughed in Jack's face. An *item*? Do yourself a favour.

Now this.

The corridor, endless. The succession of doors. Cards hanging from the handles. *Do Not Disturb*. Dear God.

If anyone had told her that morning that she would be doing this, she would have thought them mad.

They reached her room. She could feel his physical presence behind her as she turned the key in the lock.

They went inside. Behind them the door closed, pincering out the light. They were alone in darkness. She felt him raise his hand, seeking the switch.

'Leave it.'

The better to hide from his eyes, from herself.

She walked across to the window and looked out. Far below, the street was empty. She left the heavy curtains undrawn and turned back into the room. Where he waited.

'This way we'll be able to see each other,' she explained.

See and not be seen.

She was alone with him, yet not with him. She sensed the beating of her heart, the tick of her life's slow clock. The seconds drew out like hours. Still he did not move. A moment's exasperation; did he expect her to make all the running? Suddenly, passionately, she wanted to end the tension stifling them both, this hovering upon the brink of what might happen, might not. By answer she reached up to caress the side of his face. Without warning her hand took charge, did something totally different and unexpected. She took hold of him. Tightened her grip.

There.

She woke once in the night. For a moment she remembered nothing; then memory flooded back. She put out her hand, tentatively, felt him sleeping peacefully beside her. She was glad that he had stayed and not cheapened her and what had happened by sneaking away while she slept. She lay still, eyes closed in the darkness, remembering.

The muscled body, hard yet gentle. The hair springing on chest and loins. The heat. The light from the distant streetlights gleaming in his eyes as he found her. And again found her. She waiting. She sharing. She filled by him, by the moment, by the wonderful togetherness. By the surging explosion of delight. Again, and again.

Now was a time for tenderness. The tenderness of heart and loins, of memory sharpened by joy. She had to share the moment, could not bear to be alone while he was there. She woke him gently.

'Love me,' voice and body urgent, 'love me now.'

Back in Canberra Anna found that Jack Goodie had spoken to the party leader, got the green light for what he wanted. Early in the new year, Mark Forrest beside her, she flew to Sydney on the first leg of her journey to Africa, to the country that her great-grandmother had left seventy-nine years before.

THREE

Heat. Smoke. Dust. The stink of Africa.
Anna stood at Mark's side with the other media people and looked past the protective screen of blue-overalled riot police at the chanting, swaying mob spilling across the dusty square of earth that passed for a football field.

This is what I came to find out, Anna thought. Exhilarating but, God, frightening too. I'm a Sydneysider. What has this to do with me?

Somewhere there was burning, a building maybe, the acrid smoke heavy in the still air.

The crowd was shouting, a continuous, chanting rhythm that swelled and crashed like the sea. She couldn't understand the words but it didn't matter. You didn't need words to recognise the meaning.

Fury.

The so-called peaceful protest was getting out of hand.

The mob drew nearer, black eyes taunting the police. She could smell the stench of sweat and dust driven up by the pounding feet.

The first stone hurtled through the air and skittered across the ground between two of the cops. The police line stirred as an order was barked by the captain standing on top of the armoured vehicle at the end of the rank.

'They're letting them get too close,' one of the media men muttered. Tension was a wire tautening his voice

Anna thought so, too. She glanced at Mark apprehensively but he was busy with his camera and did not notice.

More stones, a clattering fusillade of them. More orders. Two men loped forward out of the police line. Their arms swung in unison. Tear gas grenades popped at the feet of the dancing demonstrators. Grey clouds of gas billowed out. The crowd fell back.

A few whiffs of gas came back to the newsmen. There were some coughs, and a couple of the guys were busy with their handkerchiefs. Anna's eyes were smarting, too, and again she glanced at Mark. Again he took no notice, squinting through the viewfinder of the Nikon, its motor drive whirring.

Again she felt the exasperation that, with passion and tenderness, made up so much of her feelings for him, but there was no use complaining; he hadn't wanted her to come at all.

'It'll be hot, filthy. Quite likely dangerous, too.'

Anna's mind had been set on it. It would make her look good if she could tell Jack she'd seen at first hand what was going on. She had kept on and on until at last Mark had given in.

'You're mad. But if you really want to ...'

He had even written out an accreditation card to show the cops, if it came to that.

She had her own camera; if they were going to stand here, she might as well use it. She raised it, focusing through the viewfinder.

A posturing, grimacing man, clenched fist held high,

fingers closed, symbolically concealing the white skin of his palm. Only black was beautiful here.

Click.

A girl, no more than fifteen, frizzy hair tightened in braids across her scalp, throwing out her hips mockingly as she danced.

Click.

Behind them a sea of faces, one hundred, two — figures rhythmically chanting and swaying in the shuffling dance that had become commonplace on television screens across the world.

Thanks to the international press corps; thanks to Mark Forrest. It was the first time she had really understood what his work entailed.

Click.

Mark had told her he came here often to run the tennis clinic he had started with the help of one of the local teachers. He'd spoken of tin shanties and bare brick houses, of dusty alleyways and corrugated iron fences. Of chickens, scrawny dogs, children in the streets. None of that today. Today the mob was a surf of anger pounding against the rock wall of the waiting police.

I wouldn't want their job, she thought.

Mark had shifted half a dozen paces to one side. She followed, not wanting to be separated from him, and saw that he was taking pictures of the police line. Little more than boys themselves, Anna thought, but their faces belied their age. Eyes watchful, mouths tight beneath trim moustaches, faces grey with dust and tension. They held their rifles across their chests. Pointing at nothing, for the moment, but there nonetheless.

Click.

More yells. More stones. The tear gas thinning now. A stone flew high over the police line and fell close to the huddled journalists, who shied like nervous horses. Too close, as the man had said.

Anna stared down at the stone. More than a stone. It was a great chunk of paving. Whoever threw that must have a wrist like a tennis champion.

One of Mark's pupils, maybe.

And grinned, despite the circumstances.

Another chorus of yells. Stones. In the dusty air, rage as potent as dynamite.

The police line stirred again. She could feel the tension. Trouble coming.

Mark obviously felt it, too. He turned towards her.

'I wish you'd get out of here.'

She shook her head. 'I'm staying.'

A wry half-smile as he shook his head, yielding to her stubbornness. 'Please yourself . . .'

He turned once again to watch the mob. She studied him, seeing the dust and sweat on his upper lip. One or two of the journalists were already scurrying for shelter; she knew he'd be happier if she left with them but she wasn't going to do that. This was what she'd come to Africa for (*wasn't it?*), and she wasn't going to run away at the first sign of danger. At least he wasn't badgering her.

What a man he is, she thought. Perhaps I'll be luckier this time.

A few metres to her right Mark was moving again, bringing the rioters and the police together in the viewfinder, a weaving pattern of confrontation.

Click.

There were dogs now. German shepherds, trained for the work, held by their handlers on long chains.

All of a sudden, on no order that she had heard, the dog teams charged the crowd, the dogs snarling and leaping, yanking at the steel leashes. The blacks fled a dozen stumbling yards out of range, terrified of the dogs. And who could blame them?

One man somehow avoided the charge and danced up almost to the line of cops. Red T-shirt, dirty jeans, upraised finger jabbing the air derisively under the nose of the nearest policeman.

She saw Mark move closer, hands busy as he focused.

Click.

One for the front pages, she thought.

He came back to her; she felt his tension, as hot as flame.

'What is it?'

'I want you to stay here for a moment. I won't be long.'

'Where are you going?'

'Just to get a couple of pics. I want to try out a different angle.'

'I'll come with you.'

'No.'

'I don't see why –'

'No.'

His voice said, *No argument.* He stood watching her until at last, reluctantly, she nodded.

'Take care,' she said.

'Sure.'

Cautiously he edged away from the group of journalists, the protective police screen. Now he was exposed to the demonstrators but they, too, were preoccupied and nobody took any notice of him.

She watched as he crossed the road bordering the football field. He ducked down one of the side lanes between the houses and was gone.

FOUR

Take care, she'd said.

Mark thought, If I wanted to be careful I wouldn't be here at all.

He took one final look over his shoulder. A police officer had clambered on top of the armoured car. He'd met him several times at township demonstrations. Captain Scholtz was a hard bastard, although better than some. Now he was speaking into a microphone held close to his mouth, eyes on a section of the crowd on the far side of the field. Far too preoccupied to pay any attention to Mark.

Excellent.

Swiftly he crossed the last few metres of the football field and eeled his way into the confusion of alleyways leading back between the small houses, the corrugated iron fences. He knew the area vaguely, had driven this way lots of times on his way to the tennis clinic he had arranged with the headmaster of the nearby school. Abraham Qwele, quietly-spoken, a courteous man with a closed face.

The tennis court had been a joke, lines scratched on the open ground, but someone had found a net and there'd been no end of kids interested. Boys in grey shorts, girls in black gym slips. It had turned out well, and Mark had enjoyed himself.

Now his knowledge of the area might come in handy. Everyone was familiar with the images of rioters seen over the shoulders of policemen. The dogs, the tear gas grenades. What was needed now was something to freshen the world's jaded imagination. If he could work his way around to the back of the crowd through the narrow lanes, he might just manage it.

People said Mark Forrest would always go that extra yard for a story, a picture. It was true; it made him feel good, knowing it. But he knew, too, that they shook their heads, telling themselves that he was living on borrowed time. Take the chances he did, one day there'd be a reckoning.

Hell, man, it's only a job.

They were probably right. Except to Mark it had always been more than that. If you lacked the talent to be grand slam tennis champion, maybe you could still be champion of something. You still had something to prove, didn't you? To yourself, if no one else? That you weren't the bum your old man had been. Not the bum your ex-wife had always said you were, either.

Mary-Lou Aspinall.

They had been on the circuit, both of them talented, but she, in truth, better than he. Both of them so much in love. A marriage made in heaven was what the papers had said. The way it had turned out, more like a marriage made in hell. They'd broken up months before Mark had pulled out of the tennis circuit and gone home. No doubt she had been as glad to see the back of him as he had been to leave. If she'd minded enough to care, one way or the other.

Why the hell do I always think of her at moments like this?

The sound of yelling was fainter now, blanketed by the buildings. Mark hurried down the lane to the end. There was refuse everywhere, the ripe stench of decay. The smell of fire was stronger, too, the crackling swirl of black smoke staining the sky over to his right. Not a building, after all; the fire wasn't big enough and the smell was wrong. More like a bus. Probably the mob had torched it on its way through. It was what mobs did. Maybe he'd have a chance to get some pictures of it later.

A black face appeared suddenly in a gap between the houses. Mark's heart leapt. The face vanished as suddenly as it had come and he heard the scuff of running feet.

A child. Thank God.

He went on, running now. No time to spare. That demo was set to explode any minute and, if he didn't get a move on, he'd be too late.

The lane ended at another road. He flicked a cautious eye around the corner. Nothing. No peace-loving residents on the streets today. He went left, running easily, Nikon swinging from the strap around his neck. He turned into the next lane and sprinted along it towards the football field, the sound of the mob growing louder as he ran.

The field opened before him. The crowd, backs to him now, still faced the police line. Mark saw at once how the situation had deteriorated in the few minutes he'd been away. The police had raised their rifles and were pointing them at the demonstrators. There were a lot more dogs and the anger in the mob's voice had notched into hatred. The explosion was only a spark away.

Mark crossed the field towards the back of the crowd. He passed a scattering of hangers-on, people who'd come to watch rather than take part. He got some unfriendly looks but nobody tried to interfere. They were too interested in seeing what was happening at the front of the crowd. 'Watch a mob' — great spectator sport. People never seemed to realise that the guys at the back were almost as much at risk as the ones in front. Flying bullets had a way of finding you, wherever you were standing.

And you? he asked himself. Reckon white skin gives you immunity, maybe?

The crowd was a lot bigger now. For their own safety, the cops would have to make a move soon. And when they did ...

It could become another Sharpeville.

If he'd been around to take photographs of that riot, when all those demonstrators had died, his name would have gone around the world.

The crowd stank. Black or white, all crowds did when tensions ran high. The stink was different, that was all.

Yelling, chanting, stamping, eyes blood-red in the black faces. Mob frenzy was taking over. The killing mode.

Perched on top of the armoured car, Captain Scholtz was shouting through a loudhailer. Mark couldn't hear a word; the voice of the mob drowned him out.

The tension was jerky, orgasmic. It needed only a spark —

A crack, like a stick breaking. One of the cops stumbled. Mark saw him sag, rifle thudding on the bare earth, before he realised that what he'd heard had been a shot.

Someone in the crowd had opened fire on the police.

The mob realised it at the same moment and surged forward with a triumphant roar.

Don't! Mark wanted to scream the warning. Didn't they realise what would happen next?

The police line took one step forward, rifles pointing. The crowd hesitated. Cross-tides of confusion ripped through it and the police charged, a furious rush of men and dogs.

The demonstrators broke and ran.

Mark ran with them.

On the far side of the field they felt the pursuit slacken and stopped, looking back at the police. Not everyone had been fast enough; some had been cut off. The cops had been badly frightened. One of them had been shot, maybe killed. Now they were angry, determined to repay that solitary bullet. Wooden batons rose and fell as the victims were beaten systematically into the dust of the football field. Their blood stained the earth, as Mark had foreseen.

Click.

The crowd rumbled, reformed, started hesitantly to move back, but the police line was still intact, the guns still raised. The impetus was gone. The police charged again. The crowd retreated and began to break up. The police stopped. The rifles swung up. They fired into the mass of people.

Screams. Men and women going down around him, eyes wide in horror and disbelief as the bullets bit home.

Mark was caught in the milling mob. He managed to focus the camera as the second volley came. More cries, more people falling. Blood.

Now the dog teams came in, harrying the fragmenting crowd.

Click.

They were off the field now, dispersing down the alleys leading into the heart of the township. They would be safe there. The cops wouldn't follow them into that maze but they'd been thrashed and knew it. Now they were angry, looking for a victim.

Mark sensed the change. Until now, mob consciousness had protected him. Now he was a potential target, white amid a sea of black.

He edged away, hoping to be invisible.

How the hell do you manage that, white man?

Most of the crowd ignored him, confrontation over until the next time, but here and there knots of youths still held together. That was where the danger lay. For them Mark was a target to dream about, a solitary white man where nobody, including himself, wanted him to be.

He saw one group watching him. Half a dozen of them, about eighteen years old. The most dangerous age.

Mark grinned at them, a shit-eating grin, easing himself away. Nobody grinned back. He was white, they were black, there was nothing more to be said. To be white here was to be dead.

The group split, heading his way. Mark ran.

Anna had been tempted to follow him but had promised and would not break her word. She was frightened, too — not only of the mob, although certainly that, but of being a burden to Mark in whatever lunacy he was up to now.

The chanting of the crowd had become a menacing accompaniment to fear. With Mark's departure she felt terror, raw and absolute, for the man, lover, stranger, whose presence could still evoke in her such disbelief and astonishment. More than terror, there was outrage that he should endanger so carelessly the relationship, passionate and consuming, that had sprung up between them.

Emotion was a scream within her head. Never mind your damn *story*. What about us?

Watching, almost paralysed by fear, she caught a momentary glimpse of him crossing the open ground behind the crowd. He ducked between two buildings and was gone.

Now only fear remained.

Time passed. Five minutes, ten. She waited and cursed and hoped, balancing on a knife-edge of terror that brought the acid taste of vomit to her throat. Then, between one moment and the next, the world went mad.

Out of nowhere, men and dogs charged, scattering the crowd as anger turned to terror. Batons wove their rhythmic pattern of violence, the sound of the blows a sickening counterpoint to the screaming of the crowd. Then all other sound was stilled by the staccato rattle of the guns.

Hand to her disbelieving mouth, Anna watched as fleeing figures crumpled and fell. Time stopped, became an endless, appalling present in which some figures crawled, others were hauled away, heels and heads dragging, others still lay motionless, their blood soaking into the bare and thirsty ground.

Of Mark there was no sign.

There remained only a stillness, a capsule of horror and disbelief within which her own questions ricocheted like bullets.

Where? Where has he gone?

I don't know.

You were with him, weren't you?

Yes.

He knows it's against the rules for anyone to go off unaccompanied. He could be killed. Doesn't the fool see that?

Yes. No. I don't know.

Where did he go? Why? *Answer me.*

At last, silence.

Unreality remained. Disbelief separated her from what was happening around her. The return journey in the guarded vehicle. The city with its illusion of normality. The cottage, peaceful at the end of its driveway. The mountain leaning in serene beauty against the blue sky. The room with the bed upon which she fell. Familiar and irrelevant. A dream.

In her head was the only reality. One question going round and round, a bird trapped and frantic within her skull.

Why? *Why?* WHY?

A yell and the youths were after him, hunting him down. Shrill laughter giggled in their voices as they called to each other, believing him helpless. This was their home ground. No one would help him here. They were between Mark and the sanctuary of the police line, driving him ever deeper into the township's alleys. They were young and fit, they could run like the wind but were in no hurry.

Plenty of time to enjoy the chase and kill whitey, too.

How could he hope to get away from them?

He ran, thanking God he was pretty fit himself. The camera bumped against his chest. He thought of dropping it, but would not. The pictures in there were his passport to success, to fame, even. He would not abandon his future.

Future? What future?

He rounded a corner. The streets had emptied fast. Hardly anybody about now. Thank God.

There certainly wasn't much else to be thankful for. Twenty yards back, the pack of youths still followed, not hurrying, but not going away, either. Wearing him down. It was the fun of the chase, the anticipation of getting something of their own back when they finally caught him.

If, he told himself fiercely, breath beginning to catch in his throat. Not when. *If*.

Another corner, another alley, and there was an opening to the right, a narrow pathway between two buildings. He followed it, praying it wasn't a dead end, flogging himself onwards over the bare earth.

Cut me off here, I'm dead.

Another turning, another alley. Breath getting difficult now. They were still there. He'd heard them shout to each other only seconds earlier. Pathways led off the alley but he daren't take them, afraid they led nowhere.

A corrugated iron fence appeared, six feet high, flanking a two-storey building with no visible windows. Mark skidded to a stop, grabbed the top of the fence and felt the edge of the rusty metal hack into his palms as he hauled himself up and over. He dropped with a thump to the ground. Looking about him, he could see no one. He crouched behind the fence, fighting for breath, joints loose with fear now he'd stopped running.

If they'd spotted him getting over ...

The pad of running feet. He froze, hearing the sound of their breathing. If they stopped ... They didn't.

Relief sighed in his throat, yet he knew the respite was only temporary. They'd be back as soon as they realised they'd missed him. Somehow he had to get back to the football field, to the police. Easily said. After all the twists and turns of the chase, he hadn't the slightest idea where he was.

He knew he had to move, even so, and take advantage of the few seconds he'd won. He placed his hands gingerly on top of the sharp-edged fence, for the first time seeing the blood in his palms where the iron had cut him.

Go septic if I'm not careful. An ironic grimace through bared teeth. If I live long enough.

Heart pounding, he levered himself up and over. The

alley was deserted. He fled back the way he had come and reached the road at the end. Still nothing.

Which way? He'd no idea where he was. There were too many roads, too many alleys, too many buildings all looking exactly alike.

He remembered going as a child with an older boy to watch trains. Did kids still collect train numbers? They'd had a quarrel and he'd walked home alone, only to find out when it was too late that he didn't know the way. He'd never forgotten the feeling: the unfamiliar streets, the people he'd been too scared to approach, the terror of being lost.

Those youths hadn't gone home. Any minute one of them might come round the corner ...

Stop it. *Stop it.*

The question remained: if he didn't know where he was, how was he going to get out?

The smell of burning hit him, and he hesitated in midstride. The column of smoke was still rising over to his left. It hadn't been far from the football field. All he had to do was head that way until he saw something he recognised.

The panicked child of memory receded. He walked quickly towards the distant column of smoke.

The pack of youths erupted out of a side street thirty yards away and skidded to a stop with an exultant yell. They flung themselves towards him. Mark turned and fled once more, terror pounding to the frantic rhythm of his feet.

They'd almost lost him, playing games, and would not make the same mistake again. The football field was too far.

Fifty yards ahead, a beat-up Valiant came out of a side street and turned towards him. Mark watched it as he pounded down the road, sweat stinging his eyes, breath tearing at his throat. Would the driver help him? Or cut him off?

The car stopped. Above the sound of his breath, Mark heard the whine of the differential as the driver slammed the car into reverse. It swerved backwards into an alleyway, rear bumper clanging against an overflowing dustbin, hurtled back the way it had come and disappeared around the corner.

You couldn't blame him. But if only he had stopped, if only, if ...

Useless thoughts.

The footsteps of the youths hammered the ground behind him. Mark ran on, going nowhere, yet running all the same because the only alternative was to give up, and that he would not do.

A bitumen road crossed the one he was on. A few shops. A petrol station. Suddenly hope. He knew where he was. He drove past here every week. The school where he gave the tennis classes was just around the corner. If he could make it.

He was running flat out now, trying to put as much distance as possible between him and his pursuers.

Qwele's house.

He'd almost passed it before he recognised the building with the tin roof and red-painted walls where he'd been to talk about tennis lessons. He skidded to a stop and looked back along the road. His pursuers were still there, no longer shouting, but running with dogged purpose. He hammered on Qwele's door, knowing he could run no further.

If he won't open to me, I'm dead. If he's not there, I'm ... He hammered again, frantically.

Come on!

They were not more than thirty yards away, now.

A voice behind the closed door. 'Who is it?'

'Mark Forrest. The tennis coach.' His voice was edged with panic, but he couldn't help that. 'Please, Mr Qwele ...'

The latch clicked. The door opened an inch and Mark saw the chain. The teacher's eyes gleamed in the darkness.

'Mark Forrest? What are you doing here?'

'There's a bunch of blokes chasing me.'

'Ah.'

Qwele unclipped the chain, stepped onto the street, and saw the situation at once.

'Get inside. Now!'

He pushed Mark into the house, closing the door between them.

Mark leant against the wall, fighting to suck air into his lungs, listening. He could hear Qwele's voice on the far side of the door and others, low-pitched and surly, answering him.

Get their hands on me, they'll kill me.

The voices stopped. The door opened. Mark braced himself, but Qwele was alone. 'I've sent them away,' he said.

Just like that.

Weakness swamped him. 'I must thank you ...'

Qwele hadn't finished with him. 'Are you mad? What are you thinking of, walking around here in the middle of all this trouble?'

Mark gestured weakly at his camera. 'Taking pictures.'

'And for this you risk your life?'

Qwele was short, plump, gold-rimmed glasses on his stubby nose. He glared up at Mark, all six-foot-four of him, and dominated him completely.

'If you had gone to any other house in the whole of Guguletu, you would be dead by now. You understand that?'

'I know it.'

Ten years old again, in front of the angry teacher.

'Photographs? Haven't we seen enough of those?'

'These are different.' Ten years old or not, Mark would let no one disparage his pictures.

Qwele regarded him severely over the gold rims. 'In what way are they different?'

'The cops fired on the crowd. I took some pictures. From the crowd's side.'

Eyebrows like elevators. 'From the crowd? How?'

Mark explained.

Qwele watched him, thoughtful now. 'These pictures, they will come out well?'

'No reason why not.'

'And they show the police firing on the crowd?'

'And the dogs.'

'Wait here.'

He turned, went into the inner room and closed the door. Mark heard the low murmur of voices. He hadn't thought of anyone else being in the house. The voices stopped. The door opened.

Qwele said, 'There is someone here wishes to meet you.' He stood aside, and Mark walked into the inner room.

Even seated, the black man looked huge. He was tall, with massive arms and chest, a shaven head, small, neat ears, eyes almond-shaped, the whites a little yellow. A strong man. Thirty, perhaps a little more. Strong in other ways, too. Outside, Qwele had dominated. Here, this man was in charge.

He looked at Mark expressionlessly. 'You have been taking photographs of the police?'

His voice was deep. He spoke English with the word-by-word precision of the educated African.

Mark nodded. 'Right.'

'Why?'

'My job.'

'Tell me about your job.'

Here was a man used to handing out orders. No one was going to explain to Mark who he was, that was obvious. All the same, it was Qwele's house.

'Okay if I sit down, Abraham?'

Qwele made a fussy gesture of assent, subdued in the other man's presence. Mark sat, eyes on the other's face. 'I'm a journalist.'

'We know about journalists.' The man tasted the word contemptuously. 'So many killed. So many injured. Fifty people arrested. Ten necklaced. You keep the score. Like a football match.'

Bloody know-all.

'Not like any footie match I've ever seen.'

'You watch. You take pictures. The police protect you. You never get involved. Exactly like a football match.'

Mark remembered his terror, the frantic chase through the blind streets. 'I wouldn't have said so, myself.'

'A stupid thing to do. Are you stupid, Mr Forrest?'

Mark flushed. 'I don't think so.'

'Why do it, then?'

'I want people to know what it's like to be in a riot. Really in it. The pictures you usually see, the police are chasing *them*. My pictures, it's the police chasing *us*. You were complaining we don't get involved. I just did.'

'You will publish these photographs?'

'Of course.'

'The police shooting? The dogs?'

'The lot.'

'The authorities will not like that.'

'What can they do?'

51

'You saw them shoot into an unarmed crowd and you ask that?'

'They're careful with the press. They know it'll come back on them if they try anything with us.'

The man stood and took two steps to the window. Standing, he was like the side of a house.

'Why did you come here? Why today?'

'To save my neck. That bunch of *tsotsis*, I don't reckon they were planning to kiss me, do you?'

The man had turned so that his back was to the window. His eyes gleamed in the shadow cast by his body. 'You arrive on the doorstep claiming you were chased by a group of hooligans. *Tsotsis*, as you call them. Naturally, we believe you. We have the evidence of our eyes, do we not? So we take you in. And all the time ...' The eyes did not move from his face. 'You know what they say, Mr Forrest. The South African police are everywhere.'

Mark stared. 'You're saying those blokes might have been *cops*?'

'Chasing you but strangely never catching you. It would be logical, if you happened to be a police spy yourself.'

Bloody hell!

'You know what happens to police spies, Mr Forrest?'

Mark tried to laugh, was not sure it came out too well. 'You've got a suspicious mind,' he said.

'Trust too easily, a man dies.' A pause. 'How do I know I can trust you?'

'You don't.' He tapped the camera. 'Except that I ran the risk of taking these pictures so that the rest of the world will know what happened here today.'

'You took them so you'd have a story.' Still the contempt.

'Of course. That's my job. But it will do your cause a bit of good, too.'

'What do you know about my cause?'

'It's obvious. Perhaps I can help you another way, too.'

'Help me? How do you imagine you can do that?'

'Australia is thinking of lifting sanctions.'

'I do not believe you.' For all the arrogance, there was concern.

'Believe what you like. There's someone over here right now, looking into things.' Mark paused deliberately. 'I could probably get you a meeting, if you like.'

'If he's here officially, the government will know all about him. A meeting would be impossible.'

'They don't know anyone's here. No one knows except you and me.'

The heavy lips curled. 'How is that possible?'

'Because this person and I are friends.'

The man watched Mark steadily for a long time. He said, 'Comrade Qwele recognised two of the boys who were chasing you, so perhaps you were speaking the truth, after all. But you are still in my hand, Mr Forrest. I am sure you understand that.'

'It won't help you to kill me.'

The man bared his teeth. 'It would mean one white man less.'

'And you would lose your interview.'

Mark watched as he thought about that.

'Very well. I shall arrange for someone to take you back, in case any more of our comrades are waiting for you outside. As far as this man from Australia is concerned, you will hear from us.'

'I've a good mind to place you under arrest.' Captain Scholtz was furious, pale blue eyes sparking in the thin face. 'Wandering off like that ... Part of my job's looking after you people. Someone kills you, *skollie*, I get the blame, heh?'

'Pretty thoughtless of me,' Mark said.

'How come the blerry kaffirs didn't get you, anyway?'

'Maybe they decided I'm harmless.'

'You're white, my mate. That's all that matters here. What were you doing, anyhow?'

'Poking around.'

'Taking pictures, more like.'

Scholtz's eyes sharpened on the camera around Mark's neck. He stuck out his hand. 'I'll take that.'

Mark placed his hand protectively on the Nikon. 'Why d'you want it?'

Scholtz blazed. 'So we can check it. That's what blerry for.'

'You'll have to give me a receipt for it.'

'You think I carry a receipt book to a fokking riot? You'll get it back when we've finished with it.'

'And the film?'

'We'll have to see, won't we?'

He had no choice. Refuse to co-operate and Scholtz would confiscate the camera, too. He handed it over.

'When do I get it back?'

'You can come to headquarters tomorrow.'

'And the film?' Anxiously.

'Like I told you. We'll see.'

Scholtz turned and looked across the deserted square. From the cluster of blue-overalled men around the armoured car came the sound of laughter, the smell of cigarettes.

He sighed. 'I wonder if these dumb kaffirs will ever learn,' he said.

They were bloody good. Mark sat in the empty office and stared exultantly at the photographs spilled across his desk. The arrogant, capering figures. The profiles of the police, mouths grim, jaws determined. The savour of confrontation.

He'd managed to catch something more: the abyss between the two sides, the hatred, fear, contempt.

I hate, therefore I am.

It was the hardest thing in the world to capture on film but Mark looked at the pictures on the desk and knew that he'd done it.

Apartheid. It was there in the fluent, capering forms of the demonstrators, the unmoving rigidity of the police.

They'll love these, and the rest of them, too: the smoking rifles, the fleeing crowd, the expression on the face of the man shot from behind, as he fell towards Mark's camera, the dogs.

It was the truth of what had happened. No selection, no bias. A demonstrator's view of confrontation.

He sat back in his chair and looked through the pictures once more. The best work he'd ever done. He still had to write the story, but that wouldn't take long. As far as possible, he would let the pictures speak for themselves. The important thing was to get them off fast. The cops wouldn't be happy when they discovered he'd switched films. They would probably come a-calling, looking for the original. He had to get them away before then.

An hour later, it was done. Now they could do what they liked. He had a bottle of Scotch in his desk, a good journalistic tradition. He wasn't much of a boozer but reckoned that tonight he had something to celebrate. He poured a generous shot, added ice and slugged half of it in one gulp, excitement beating in his blood.

He remembered the photograph that Frank Capra had taken, the death of a Republican soldier in the Spanish Civil War. That picture had made Capra famous. These pictures, today, might do the same for him.

Now for the next item on the agenda, to find out who the mystery black man was. They kept a small photo morgue in the office, so he started digging through it. Half an hour later, he struck gold.

It was eleven by the time Mark got home. Anna had been waiting, mounting dread in her heart. When she heard the car she was so relieved that she almost burst into tears. She ran to the front door of the cottage and flung it open, catching Mark on the doorstep with his key in his outstretched hand.

At sight of him, her fear and anguish became fury.

'Where the hell have you been?'

'At the office. Look, I'm sorry —'

'Sorry? You disappear in the middle of a bloody riot —' She didn't swear much, as a rule, but *God* — 'And then I hear nothing till bloody midnight, and you say you're *sorry?*'

Her voice was climbing the decibels, like a monkey up a tree.

Mark said, 'You want to fight, let's go indoors, eh?' He shoved past her into the cottage. She slammed the door and went after him. In the bedroom he was chucking his denim jacket down on the bed. He turned to face her.

'Look, I said I'm sorry. Okay? Now it's late, I'm just about buggered. Can we leave it for now?'

He looked exhausted, true enough, but Anna did not feel in the least forgiving. 'One phone call. That's all.'

'I told you. I'm sorry.'

'I've been worried sick.'

'I was going to phone, but I was flat out. I just didn't get around to it.'

'You forgot.'

'No.' Irritation was leaking in.

'Didn't bother.'

'Bloody hell ...' He seized her by the forearms and drew her to him. Even now she resisted, her body shaking yet board-stiff against his. 'Don't you understand? If I'd phoned, it would have risked everything.'

'Rubbish!'

'I really am sorry,' he said.

He tried to kiss her but she twisted her face away. 'No!' she said. 'That's too easy.'

'I was wrong. I admit it. But it was one hell of a day. Let me fix us both a drink and I'll tell you about it.'

She sat apart from him, pointedly ignoring the drink he'd given her. All the same, she listened as he told her about the photographs he'd taken.

'The best I've ever done. Honestly.'

'And afterwards? After the police fired?'

'Then things got tricky.' He told her of the heart-stopping chase through the township, of the man he had met at Qwele's house.

'Adam Shongwe. One of the ANC's young guns. I read about him at the office.' He hesitated. 'I think he might like to meet you.'

'How does he know about me?'

'I told him. You want to hear the African point of view, he's the guy.'

'You say the police took your camera?'

'I'll get it back. It was the film they wanted, not the camera.'

'How did you stop them getting it?'

'Put in another one. Kept the one they wanted in my pocket.'

'You made a fool of that captain. He'll be furious.'

'Nothing he can do about it.' He grinned at her cheerfully. She could see he believed she'd forgiven him, told herself she wasn't going to let him off the hook quite so easily. Yet relief was drowning anger.

He came closer, still grinning. She did not move. His finger traced the line of her eyebrow, gently. She could have slapped his hand away, but did not.

She had changed out of the jeans and military-style shirt she had worn earlier — what the well-dressed woman wears to a riot — and had put on a cotton dress. Now Mark cupped her breasts through the material, staring at her. Again she did not move. His fingers moved to the line of buttons. Step by step, things followed their accustomed path, and she did nothing at all to stop him.

At last, lying together in the narrow bed, she breathed furiously in his ear. 'Do that again, ever, I'll kill you. Hear?'

Then passion engulfed her and there were no words at all.

In the morning, as it was getting light, Mark went out to get the papers. Anna got up after he had left. She drew the curtains and looked up at the grey-green bulk of the mountain. The sky was pellucid, the streets quiet in the dew-fresh dawn.

God, this was a beautiful place.

She was wearing a skimpy pair of panties, nothing else. She ran her hands down the length of her body, feeling the silky texture of her skin. After the traumas of the previous day, she felt good, at peace with herself and the world.

Then Mark got back and the sense of peace was gone. 'There's a police Landrover around the corner.'

Alarm. 'Are they coming here?'

'What do you think?'

'I'd better get dressed.'

'They're not interested in you.'

But she was already grabbing at clothes. The doorbell rang. Mark went to open it. Tugging a comb through her reluctant hair, Anna heard voices.

'*Meneer* Forrester?'

'Forrest.'

'May we come in, please.' It was not a request.

Mark came back into the room, the policemen on his heels. There were two of them, a sergeant and a constable, in short sleeves, cotton trousers tucked into polished brown combat boots, pistols in canvas holsters on their hips. They seemed to fill the cottage.

Under the peaked caps, flint-cold eyes inspected her.

'And you are?' asked the sergeant.

As though she were a thing. Her chin went up. 'Anna Riordan —'

Mark intervened. 'An Australian journalist. A friend of mine.'

Friend ...

The word hovered, ambiguously. But it seemed the cops were not interested in her, friendly or not. The gun muzzle eyes switched back to Mark.

'You gave Captain Scholtz your camera yesterday,' the sergeant said.

'Brought it back, have you?'

A spark of anger in the hard eyes. 'The film had not been used, *Meneer*.'

'I must have just changed it.'

'Did you tell Captain Scholtz you had just changed the film?'

'I didn't know what he wanted the camera for.'

'Where is the other film?'

'The one I used before, you mean?'

More than a spark of anger, now. 'In Guguletu, yes.'

'I developed it. I sent the pictures to Sydney last night.'

'You have dispatched them already?'

'Sure. After you blokes dropped me off, I went to my office, developed the pics and filed the story. Have to, sport. Don't do these things straightaway, they're useless. Must have been gone ten, time I finished.'

Mark was smiling at them, candidly. See how co-operative I'm being? All the corroborative details. Not that it would fool anybody.

This was a dangerous business. Anna held her breath.

'You knew why Captain Scholtz wanted your camera.'

Mark shook his head. 'He never said.' Smiling and smiling, determined to tough it out.

That was the secret, Anna thought. Make up a story, never mind how dumb it was, and stick to it. I bet they just love dealing with foreign correspondents. She could see how furious they were now, knowing that Mark was giving them the run-around and unable to do anything about it.

As they left, the sergeant leaned towards Mark, almost but not quite touching him. No phony courtesy now.

'You try to take the piss out of us, you're making a big mistake. We can be good friends but we make blerry bad enemies, believe me. You should maybe remember that, *Meneer* Forrester.'

He sounded mean, dangerous, but it was too late for diplomacy.

'Forrest,' Mark said and followed them to the door.

No brownie points today.

FIVE

Mark came back, cheerfully. 'That gave them something to think about.'

But the threatening presence of the police had stained Anna's day. Beyond the window the sun had shifted, leaving the mountain's mass dark and threatening. On impulse, she turned on her heel, marched into the bathroom and locked the door behind her.

I need time to think, she told herself.

There was certainly plenty to think about. She was here as a tourist. If the authorities found out the real reason for her visit there would be hell to pay. That phony press card for starters. And now Mark had told the police — the *police*, in a country like South Africa — that she was a journalist. Passing yourself off as something you were not, that had to be an offence, surely? One phone call was all it would take.

They're not interested in you, Mark had said. It wouldn't take long for that to change, if they started digging. They would discover what her real job was in Canberra, hear the name Shongwe ... She could see the headlines:

AUSTRALIAN SPY UNCOVERED

Assuming they didn't chuck her in jail instead. Back home the government would love it; they'd been dying to nail Jack Goodie for years. As for her, they'd probably *ask* the South Africans to keep her in jail.

It didn't bear thinking about. She decided to think about Mark, instead. Not much joy there, either. Last night she had been so relieved to see him that, after her initial fury, she had let him talk her around. Now her anger re-surfaced. It was time they sorted a few things out.

She marched out and flung the words at him:

'I still reckon you could have let me know when you got back to your office.'

He sighed, too obviously. 'I've told you already. I couldn't.'

'That's crap!'

He moved swiftly, taking her arms in his strong hands, glaring down at her. 'It was out of the question. Don't you see that?'

This time she would not be fobbed off so easily. 'No, I don't! Why was it out of the question?'

'Because the phone's tapped.'

She was in no mood for fairy tales. 'Don't be paranoid.'

'It's the same with every correspondent. They listen to all our conversations.'

She stared.

'It's true, I promise you.'

A shaker. She gestured at the phone on the side table. 'This one, too?'

'Of course.' An apology for a laugh. 'Don't go phoning Jack Goodie, will you?'

Which was exactly what she'd thought of doing.

Still she wouldn't let it go. 'Half a dozen words, that's all. So what if they heard? Where's the harm?'

'Because they'd have known I was at the office. At that time of night they'd have wondered why. Might have paid me a visit. Certain to, once they found out about the film. I had to get those pictures away, don't you see? Had to.'

Anna was trapped in a world of nightmare. She did not know what to believe. Phone taps, police raids ... It all seemed too fantastic. Perhaps he was making it up. Yet she could not bear to think it.

Please God, she prayed, don't let him be lying to me.

'I hate this country,' she burst out. 'Hate it.'

'You've only seen one side of it. Politics apart, it's a great place.'

'The SS probably said the same about Auschwitz.'

It was nonsense and she knew it, yet the shock of yesterday was still poisoning her every perception. She stared at Mark, and there was a tightness in the air between them that had not been there before.

'You know what I think you should do?' he said. 'That cousin of yours ... Got his address?'

'I got it before I came over.'

'Why don't you give him a call, go and see him? Go back to your roots. You never know; it might give you a completely different idea of the place.'

'I shan't forget what happened in the riot ...' She said it threateningly, as though afraid she might.

'But it'll help put it in perspective.'

'Will you come with me?'

Mark shook his head. 'Family's everything to these old timers. He'll never open up if I'm there. In any case, I must hang on here in case Shongwe tries to get in touch. Don't mention him,' he cautioned her. 'Not to anyone. Under South African law, he's a criminal.'

'What are South African jails like?' she wondered.

'Not good, I imagine. Why?'

'The way things are going, we've a good chance of finding out.'

The old man came out through *Oudekraal*'s big oak door and walked to the end of the shaded *stoep*. There was a rocking chair and a small table beside it with a bit of cloth, so that a drink could stand on it without marking the surface of the wood. It was Pieter Wolmaran's special place. He went there for pleasure or, as now, whenever he was tired or troubled.

He was sixty-one years old, with grey hair that had once been yellow and blue eyes in a face weathered by years of storm and sunshine. It was a farmer's face and the strong body with its powerful arms and shoulders was a farmer's body. When he stood, he was well over six feet. When he sat, he filled the chair.

He sat down now, heavily, and the chair creaked and rocked beneath his weight. Both table and chair had been in the same position for more years than he could remember. From the chair he could see across the valley with its neat rows of vines to the distant fence of white palings that marked the end of the property. There were trees along the boundary, great oaks that had been there for over a hundred years, although none as old as the patriarch that leant heavily over the courtyard and that tradition said had been planted by the founder of the family almost two and a half centuries before.

Every evening when he had finished his work, he came and sat in this chair, the table with a tall drink upon it, and watched the sunset. Today was different, though, because he had much to think about.

Early that morning, with the sun barely above the eastern mountains, he had received a telephone call. *Soos 'n bliksemstraal uit die helder lug* — like a bolt from the blue — a young woman he had never heard of, claiming to be his cousin from Australia.

The violent leap of his heart had left him breathless.

As far as he knew, no one had ever heard from Anneliese after she had run away. Now, seventy-nine years later, this stranger was claiming to be her descendant.

Well, perhaps. One read about people claiming to be what they were not. So he had been cautious.

'And what cousin might that be?'

But he had known, oh yes. Something in his body's response told him that this caller was genuine.

'Anneliese Wolmarans was my great-grandmother,' the strange voice said. 'She married Dirk van der Merwe, and then, after the Boer War, came to Australia and changed her name to Riordan. She died in 1970, when I was fifteen. I was with her the day she died.'

Pieter's wits were scrambled by shock but he could recognise the truth when he heard it. Not that it made him feel any better; hearing all this was like bringing back a world that he had hoped was gone forever. Like many old bachelors, he spent a lot of time thinking about the past, but as an observer or the reader of a book. Listening to this strange woman talking about her great-grandmother, it was as though Anneliese herself had returned from the grave.

Family legend had made much of the woman who, at the beginning of the century, had fled South Africa with her Irish lover, one step ahead of the law. That had been just after the Anglo-Boer War and Pieter supposed allowances had to be made for the times; even so, it was hardly an episode to boast about.

'And why are you phoning me?'

Of course, he had known that, too.

'I'm in South Africa on holiday,' Anna said. 'Anneliese told me so much about *Oudekraal* and the family. I wonder if it might be possible to come and meet you?'

Pieter was not a man who was easy with strangers, particularly foreigners, but did not see how he could refuse.

'When do you wish to come?'

'Today? If it's convenient?'

One of the family albums had a photograph of Anneliese at the time of her marriage to Dirk van der Merwe. After he had put down the telephone, Pieter went and dug it out.

He studied it thoughtfully. She had been a spirited girl, that was obvious, with a mouth that said *watch out*. Even an old bachelor like himself could see how she would have had no difficulty in drawing the eyes of men, or in getting her own way when she had done it. Of course, that had been before all the troubles that had engulfed her later.

He thought for a while, then went into the room he used as a study and took down from a bookshelf the bound copy of the journal that his grandfather Deneys had written about those years.

Pieter had not read it for a long time but knew that the journal set out everything that had happened to Anneliese and her children and the crime she had committed afterwards.

'If this Australian wants to discover her roots,' Pieter told the room that had seen all these things, and many others, in its time, 'she may as well hear the whole story, while she's about it.'

He took the leather-bound journal, and the photograph, and went back outside to wait. An hour or two later, Anna arrived, driving along the dirt road from the main gate, dust blowing from the wheels of her car.

With Anneliese's ghost beside her, Anna drove along the narrow road that wound across the valley floor. Many things would have changed since Anneliese's day — the bitumen road, the pattern of vines extending far up the flanks of the hills — but much remained. The white tongues of the jetting streams, the stands of oaks as stalwart as the earth itself, the mountain crests flourishing their stone signature against a brilliant sky — all were as Anneliese would have remembered.

Other things, too. Anne remembered everything that Anneliese had told her about this place, the living memory of all that had happened here. In one sense Anneliese had never left this valley at all, yet in physical fact she had left it seventy-nine years before, and what Anna was seeing now was not the setting of the tales with which Anneliese had peopled her childhood. The valley she could see about her was as remote from those stories as Anna herself. It was like visiting an unknown country equipped only with an out-of-date guide book. Anna was glad; to be too close to those traumatic memories might have been unbearable.

Yet echoes remained. Changed or not, this was still the setting of Anneliese's early life, of her father Christiaan and brother Deneys, of all the tragedies and triumphs that had marked the history of the Wolmarans clan. All had been played out here and in the great stone house that she had come so far to see.

She drove around another bend; surely she must be almost there by now? She found herself waiting with tight breath for the first glimpse of the house, yet still could see only the terraced vines, with the blue and moss-green face of the mountains beyond them.

On the far side of a spinney of oaks, a river flowed silently beneath the trailing fingers of willow trees, its placid surface reflecting the willows' pale green light.

Anna thought, This must be the river she told me about, where the owner of the store saved the coloured woman and her child from the flood. Unbidden, the man's name came to her: Sarel Henning. And the woman's name had been Hendricks.

The alien sound of the names was like a sudden discord in a piece of music. The land itself, so peaceful, was strangely familiar, and then the harsh bark of the Dutch consonants reminded her that here everything was foreign.

Once, on a visit to England, Anna had rented a small yacht and sailed along the coast of the English Channel. Each night she had put into a different port. Now she remembered one such occasion: a small yacht harbour protected from the sea by massive stone groynes, the town spread across the slopes of the enfolding hills. It was evening; she picked up a visitor's buoy close to the shore and tidied ship. When she finished, she sat in the cockpit and drank the one ceremonial whisky she permitted herself at the end of the day. Darkness came sifting down. The yellow lights of the town emerged stealthily about her.

She had sat in the midst of the little town that she had never visited, in which she knew neither building nor person. To be in a place yet not in it ... It was an impression that Anna had never forgotten.

Now, driving down this valley that was so familiar that she might have been born here, the feeling returned, a sense that she was re-visiting a place that she had never seen before.

She rounded yet another corner, and there it was.

Before her, rising amid still more oak trees, she saw the white walls of a great house, the carved pediment framed by the wind-fluttered spread of leaves. Anneliese had told her that the oak tree beside the house was over two hundred years old, like the house and the family that had owned both all that time.

Generation upon generation of Wolmarans had moulded and changed the land, even as the land, inexorably, had moulded and changed them.

She remembered Anneliese's voice, cracked with age, death's grasp upon her throat. '*Oudekraal* is mine ...'

Was that why she had come? To live out the fantasies of an old and dying woman? To reclaim something that had never belonged to either of them? To seek roots the lack of which had never troubled her?

Mark had suggested this visit as an antidote to the traumas of Guguletu, but was that the only reason?

Certainly this valley with its spreading vines, its trees and rivers and mountains, the house itself amid its screen of leaves, was as far in spirit from the dusty violence of the township as it was possible to be.

She turned in through the tall white gate posts bearing the name that had become so much a part of her childhood, and drove along a gravel drive past a succession of oaks until, at last, she arrived at Anneliese's house.

Whatever her motives might be for coming here, perhaps she was about to find out.

She parked, switched off the engine. For a moment she made no attempt to get out of the car, but sat remembering Anneliese telling her of something that had happened in this place over a hundred years before.

The snow-covered peaks, the ice-bound wind, the breath of the mounted men smoking in the frosty air as Anneliese's father reads from the Book. From the verandah of the house two children and their mother watch as the commando rides out, a dying clatter of hooves up the trail to the distant pass. When, a day and a night later, the men return, the burghers gather in judgement, the flares streaming in the wind, the men's faces as stern as the rock from which both land and men are made. The caterwauling of the prisoners as they are led away.

Here. On this spot. Anna blinked, staring at the old house drowsing in the summer heat. For a moment, she had been in that world that had vanished over seventy years before she was born. Now she had come back, yet the past lingered, adding perspective to the scene before her.

She got out of the car and a man came and stood on the verandah of the house. She looked up at him. Pieter Wolmarans did not move as she walked across the driveway to the house. At the bottom of the steps she paused.

'Good morning, Mr Wolmarans.'

He nodded, barely, saying nothing.

'May I come up?' She was careful not to do so without permission.

Again the nod. Up the steps she went, with the old man staring down. She stood on the verandah. Anna was not short, yet the level of her eyes barely reached this man's shoulder. He would be about sixty, upright and massively built, with no sign of fat on him.

'Welcome to my house,' he said.

My house ... Anna wondered if the words were deliberate.

He led the way to a small table, with two chairs beside it, that stood at one end of the *stoep*. A leather-bound book was lying upon it.

'Be seated ...' Pieter said, unsmiling.

They sat on either side of the table and looked at each other. Now she was here at last, Anna found she did not know what to say.

'You said you were in South Africa on holiday? Why have you come here? To discover your roots?'

His tone was inquisitorial, unfriendly, but it unlocked something in Anna's head. Suddenly she knew that, yes, that was precisely why she was here.

'Something wrong with that? My great-grandmother told me so much about this place.'

'About *Oudekraal*?'

'And the valley. Everything she remembered. The good things and the bad.'

'There was a lot of bad in her life. She was a murderer, of course. Did she tell you that?'

Anna blinked at the hostility in the old man's voice. 'She did not put it like that.'

'No doubt.'

Anna could not decide whether this man's anger was directed at Anneliese and the past or at herself, a foreigner, for bringing back to life something best forgotten.

Too bad, she thought rebelliously. He invited me; he must have known why I phoned him.

'Anneliese told me lots of things. What happened when she was a child, and later. I was remembering one of her stories now, how her father Christiaan rode after the escaped prisoners and brought them back here, to face judgement.'

His expression did not change. 'Is that what they are to you? Stories?'

Confrontation would get her nowhere. She decided to change her approach. 'They are my past, too. As they are yours.'

She felt the weight of his eyes assessing her silently.

'Why?' he said at length.

'The way she talked ... My great-grandmother made this place part of my childhood. Of my life.'

'You could have written,' he said.

'I intended to, when Anneliese died. But ...' She raised her hands, helplessly.

'But did not.'

'I was fifteen. I had never been outside Australia ...'

The apologies sounded lame, terrible. Her voice petered out.

'We never heard a single word in all those years,' he told her. 'Not from Anneliese. Not from you. Not from anyone. My grandfather Deneys saved her neck, yet she never even wrote to say she was safe. And now you come here, with your questions —'

Anna decided she'd had enough. 'You are telling me I shouldn't have come.' She stood abruptly. 'Very well. I shan't bother —'

'Wait.'

She stared down at him, her hand resting on the back of the chair.

At last he sighed, gesturing at the chair. 'Please ...'

She sat again, but warily, on the very edge of the chair.

Once more he was silent, then stood in his turn and walked to the railing of the *stoep* and rested his hands — heavy, outdoor hands, she noticed — upon it. She watched his back as he stared out across the valley.

'Every day I think of what has happened here over the centuries,' he said. 'How my family built this place after Colin Walmer first came from England to settle here. My ancestors are my family. I talk to them just as I talk to you. I shall never leave this place while I live and, when I die, I shall be buried in the graveyard behind the house, become part of the land that made me.' He turned, walked slowly back to the table and sat down again. 'You are an Australian. What do you know about such things?'

There was weariness in his voice but also anger, as though he feared that he had already revealed too much of himself to this stranger. She thought he was prepared to resent her because of it.

'I know very well,' Anna said. 'It was Anneliese's dying wish to be buried here, too.'

Pieter dismissed the remark. 'She chose to leave.'

'They would have hanged her, otherwise. But her last thoughts were of *Oudekraal*.' She decided to make one final appeal. 'I know that I am a foreigner but I am a member of your family, nonetheless. I want to find out something about my ancestry. If you will tell me.'

Pieter Wolmarans sat silently for a long time; then, apparently, he came to a decision.

'This is what we shall do. I shall show you around the farm. I shall think about what you've said. Then we shall come back here and I shall tell you what you want to know.' For the first time there was the hint of a smile, yet with the ice still in it. 'Or not. Agreed?'

Anna saw it was the best offer she was going to get. 'Agreed.'

They went in an open jeep, Pieter driving with an elan she would not have expected across shallow fords and up the slopes of hills.

'Over three hundred metres here,' he shouted above the rush of wind. 'The cooler air is good for the Chardonnay.'

Down the opposing slope they roared, over a narrow wooden bridge that drummed beneath their wheels and up a track winding between trees to the crest of a hill. Pieter switched off the engine. Silence came swooping.

They got out. Below them lay the estate with the rest of the valley beyond. In the distance was the azure glint of the sea.

'Two hundred hectares,' Pieter said.

Anna had done her homework before coming here. 'The biggest estate in the valley.'

'That's right.' He pointed. 'A few years ago we built the big dam. We pump water from the river in winter and use it for spray irrigation during the dry months.'

They got into the jeep and drove back down the hill. They visited the wine cellar where Anna inspected maturation casks of oak with brass spigots and crests carved deep into the ancient wood.

'A hundred and fifty years old,' Pieter told her.

'How much do they hold?'

'Seventy thousand bottles.'

They passed through a door into a different century. Rows of stainless steel tanks looked more like an oil refinery than a wine cellar, with pipes and walkways everywhere. The floor was tiled, and over everything hung the thin sour smell of maturing wine.

A young man came to meet them. Anna saw shorts, an old tee-shirt, sturdy and sun-bronzed arms, an open and pleasant face.

'Nico Walsh. My winemaker.'

The two men spoke technicalities for a while before Pieter took Anna back to the house.

'He's young,' Anna said.

'Knows what he's doing, though. Graduate of both Stellenbosch and Geisenheim, in Germany —'

She cut him off, for the moment uninterested in how Nico Walsh had become a winemaker. 'You said you would show me around and think about what you were going to do.'

His eyes met hers. There was none of the hostility she had seen in them at the beginning, but still he said nothing.

Enough, she thought. Either he will or he won't. 'Mr Wolmarans, are you going to tell me about the past or not?'

After Anna had left, Pieter Wolmarans fetched himself a glass of wine and went and sat again at the cloth-covered table.

'I am going to trust you,' he had said. He had handed her Deneys Wolmarans's journal. 'Take this away and read it. It will tell you something of what you want to know. When you have finished, bring it back and perhaps we shall talk some more.'

She had handled the leather-bound journal with awed fingers. As though it were something precious, he thought, and was pleased. Precious it was, indeed, and good that she should be aware of it.

'I am honoured that you are willing to lend it to me.'

'Take good care of it.'

'I shall guard it with my life.' And meant it.

'You'd better.'

She had gone and he had wondered if he had done the right thing, then dismissed the doubt. She would indeed guard it with her life; in the short time she had been here, he had seen enough to know that.

He thought about this out-of-the-blue cousin. A good woman, he decided, genuine — which was why he had been willing to lend her the book. Yet it was another matter that troubled him now.

She could not be expected to know it, but her visit had created a problem for him. He had never married, had always intended to leave *Oudekraal* to Johannes Verster, his friend and neighbour. Now he knew for certain that there was surviving family, this would present a difficulty. Johannes would be the first to agree that land should remain within the family, yet surely this must be a different case.

Anna was an Australian, had never set foot in Africa until a week ago. You could not expect her to have any real feeling for the land. For the family, either, for all her talk. It made no sense to leave *Oudekraal* to her.

Yet the rule was iron-hard. This place had been in his family for two hundred and forty years and Wolmarans land should be left to Wolmarans blood, as long as a member of the family survived to inherit it. Yet to leave it to one who did not care, who would probably sell it in any case ...

A problem, indeed.

Sixty-one years old or not, he was as fit as a flea yet his visitor had brought to mind something that he had perhaps been too ready to ignore: that he, like all men, was mortal and, like all men, should do what was necessary to ensure the dignified arrangement of his affairs.

To die in violence was one thing. No one could blame anyone when that happened. But to leave things in a mess through neglect, to give someone else the trouble of sorting things out, was another matter entirely.

No one liked to think of the world going on after they were no longer in it but death, after all, was a fact of life. Five years or ten, he thought. Twenty, even, if the good Lord permits. But the day will come when I, too, shall be gone from this place. The last of the Wolmarans, after more than two centuries.

Except that now he was no longer the last of the Wolmarans.

The chair shifted beneath him, seeking the comfort they had shared for more than a generation. Beyond the trees, the valley fell away until it reached the line of purple hills that filled the western horizon. On the other side of the house, the vines again, running steeply up to the foot of the mountain that closed that end of the valley.

I had believed I was the last one, he told himself. Now I know differently, but last or not last does not matter. What matters is that we have been here since 1742, when Colin Stephen Walmer came to Africa and established the first farm in the valley — Colin Stephen Walmer, from Devon in England, who changed his name to Cornelius Stephanus Wolmarans, which must have been quite a mouthful for him, in honour of his new land. His sons and grandsons, in their turn, had cultivated the soil, adding to the buildings, developing the property. Nicholaas, Barend, Willem and all the rest. Their names are there in the family Bible. Within my own memory, my grandfather, my father and now me, Pieter Cornelius Wolmarans, and so finally an end to it all.

Because even if this young Australian woman inherits, she will never sit here as I am sitting here, never look out at the land with the love and anguish that the land brings to those who own it.

There would be bitterness in being the last to look across this land and call it his own, a sadness to rot the heart. The last days, the last evenings, the last sunsets.

He thought: It is strange to think of this place being owned by another person, someone from a different land, even. I have never been outside this country or thought to go. What is here has always been enough for me, as it was for my father and his fathers before him. Until the present generation and all the troubles of these last years, none of the Wolmarans ever wanted to leave their land. They are all buried here in the little graveyard at the back of the house. That has always been our way, to return to the soil those who have worked it, within the sights and scents and sounds that were familiar to them in life: the eagles above the mountain, the sweet smell of the spring grass with the flowers bright in it; the lowing of cattle, the call of voices, the noise the press makes in the vintage; the sharp tang of juice running from the crushed grapes. The breath of a living farm.

It was strange how land differed from other things. He had heard of men who had spent their lives building up a business, a shop or factory or engineering works, who could sell and walk away without a second thought, their money in their pocket. The land was different.

In truth, you never own the land, he thought. It is not your possession or anyone's. It is the other way round. In time, as you work it, it comes to own you. I know of no one who has lived on land that his family has worked who has not left it, when the time to leave has come, without something of death in his heart.

That is how I feel now. This Anna Riordan's visit has caused it. Yet in truth it is not fair to blame her. It all started seventy-nine years ago when Anneliese Wolmarans was forced to flee from the wrath of the English. Nowhere in this country was safe for her; she had to go as far as Australia to find sanctuary, yet now Anna says her heart remained here always.

From what my grandfather told me, there were some folk hereabouts who said she had not been right in the head, that her brain had been turned by hatred and suffering. And indeed she suffered greatly. Everyone knew of the terrible event that drove her out. I remember my own mother talking about it, hush-voiced, and indeed Anneliese was much to blame for what happened. Yet in my heart I can sense her dreadful, empty grieving and wonder what I myself might have done had I the misfortune to be in the same situation.

They were terrible times. I have thanked God often that I was not alive to see them — although, of course, I have felt their impact down the years; the legacy of hatred and vengeance come down to us from those days. Everyone, at the time and since, has been changed by that war.

As for this Anna Riordan ... After my initial uncertainty, I took her around the farm, did my best to make her feel at home, listened to her, watched her. She had said she was here on holiday, but I wonder. Once she relaxed she began to talk, as people do: about justice and the important man for whom she worked in Australia who wanted to know the truth about this country. Which made her a sort of spy, I suppose.

She asked me what I thought about sanctions. I told her the truth: that I know nothing about them or wish to. Nothing to do with politics is worth a *tickey* in comparison with the things of real value, the land, the work that nurtures it and brings it to fruitfulness, the love that makes all things — earth and water, man, woman and child — whole and pleasing to God.

I told her so, she with this nonsense about sanctions and some story about a riot in Guguletu. What was she doing in such a place, and she a stranger to the land and the people, black and white, who inhabit it? She went away very down in the mouth, I can tell you.

Yet I lent her my grandfather's book because, despite all her nonsense, I found that I trusted her. She will read it and come back. Then, we shall see.

Since I watched her little car drive away, I have been telling myself that her visit changes nothing, but her blood remains my blood and that is something I cannot ignore. God indeed moves in mysterious ways and if they sometimes seem perverse that must be a weakness in my understanding, I suppose.

In the meantime, I sit here with my memories. It is strange to look at the vines and the mountains at the back of them and think of the generations that have worked to make this place what it is today.

There are two types of history: the type you read about and the type you know because you were there or knew someone who was there. I have read and loved books all my life, but nothing can beat the knowledge that comes from personal experience, your own or someone else's.

Colin Walmer took out the first title. That I know. His son and all the later generations developed the land, planted the oaks, put their roots deep into this soil. I know that, too, yet for me the real history of the farm started ninety-nine years ago, in 1883, when the escaped convicts murdered the Wessels family and my great grandfather Christiaan Wolmarans set off after them at the head of the local commando.

SIX

Christiaan Wolmarans came through the front door of the big house and strode to the head of the brick steps. Below him, on the expanse of open ground, twenty mounted men waited, coats drawn tight about them, breath pluming the air.

It was dawn, the last day of July 1883, and lamplight shone through the windows of the house. It was a morning of bruised skies and an icy wind bringing the threat of snow from the dragon-backed mountains that surrounded the valley.

Christiaan ran down the steps, cinching his belt tight about his brown leather jacket. He wore no top coat yet was warm despite the weather, excitement and a hunger for vengeance like fire in his belly.

Two weeks earlier five convicts had escaped from the Cape Town breakwater, fifty miles away. The previous day the band had arrived in the valley and broken into the first house they found — the Wessels place, an isolated farm high on the mountain. Johannes Wessels was out. They locked the wife, her ten-year-old son and the maid servant in a bedroom while they ransacked the house. Wessels returned unexpectedly. No doubt frightened of being sent back to jail, they cut his throat and then, panicking, killed the wife, child and maid before making off with some rifles and all the food and ammunition they could carry.

The field hand had been away looking for a stray calf. When he got back that evening and found the bodies, he took the farmer's horse and galloped to the next farm to raise the alarm. Like a firestorm the news spread through the valley and now the local commando had gathered outside Christiaan Wolmarans's house to track the killers and bring them to justice.

Christiaan drew on his leather gauntlets as he reached the foot of the steps. His horse was waiting for him, its black coat gleaming, the butt of the rifle protruding from the holster behind the saddle.

'Good morning, *my baas*.'

The twelve-year-old child who was acting as groom touched his forehead and looked up at him with big eyes, overawed by the man who was known to every human being in the valley and for miles beyond.

'Good morning, Jacob.'

Christiaan knew all his people, adults and children alike, but this morning, unusually, did not return the shy smile. It was an ill-omened day, and his face was grim.

He swung himself into the saddle and trotted forward to join the other members of the commando. He had many horses, but Jupiter was his favourite. It was a huge beast, eighteen hands, and as black as the pit of hell. He needed a big horse to carry him. He was a giant of a man, six feet five inches tall and as broad as a barn. He had a hard, strong face, vivid blue eyes, yellow hair hidden now beneath a broad-brimmed black hat, and a yellow beard that spread across his chest. He wore a full bandolier over one shoulder, a pistol in the holster buckled to his belt and a skinning knife in his boot. He had lived in the valley all his life, as his ancestors had before him for over one hundred and forty years.

In the big house he had left behind him his wife Sara, a daughter aged eight and a son two years younger. He was master of *Oudekraal*, richest and oldest farm in the district, and elected *Kommandant* of the burghers of the valley. If the day went according to plan, tonight or maybe tomorrow he would teach his son something of what that responsibility meant.

He reined in, facing the assembled men. He did not greet them but took a well-worn book bound in black leather from the saddlebag behind him. They did not have their own dominee in the valley. It was Christiaan's job as *Kommandant* to read the words before he led them out.

He turned the pages, knowing exactly the passages he was seeking.

The icy wind stiffened his face as he began to read.

'"Anyone who strikes a man and kills him, he shall surely be put to death."' He turned the pages. '"Let God arise, and let his enemies be scattered: let them also that hate him flee before him. Like as the smoke vanisheth, so shalt thou drive them away: and like as wax melteth at the fire, so let the ungodly perish at the presence of God."' His voice rose above the thin keening of the wind, the stamping and snorting of the horses. '"I am the Lord your God who brought you out of the land of Egypt."' He closed the book. 'Hear the voice of the Lord.'

'Amen,' the men said.

Christiaan replaced the book in his saddlebag, put his hat back on his head and watched as the members of the commando followed suit.

They were granite men, features reddened by the cold, sidearms ready, implacable in their determination to hunt the killers down. Christiaan, like the rest of them, was confident they would do it. The night had brought more snow to the mountains and the convicts would have been unable to get out of the valley.

'Good,' he said. 'Let us ride.'

He wheeled his horse and led the column of men at a canter along the trail that wound through the valley and up into the mountains. Snow lay in frozen drifts in the gullies and quickly grew thicker as they climbed. For the first time they saw the footprints of the men they were pursuing but soon they came to fresh snow and the men's tracks were wiped out.

Spurs to remote farms led off the main trail but Christiaan did not bother to check them. The convicts' priority had to be to get over the mountains as quickly as possible. Once across the pass they would be safe. Fail and they would be doomed, whatever they did.

Perhaps they had crossed the pass before the snow had closed it, but he didn't think so. On foot they would not have been able to make it before dark, and at night the temperature would have plummeted to well below freezing. To stay out in the open was to die; they would have been forced to hole up somewhere.

The question was where.

'Elephant Cave,' he said out loud, and his mouth grew tight in his cold face.

Every man and boy in the valley knew Elephant Cave. For the convicts it would be ideal: deep and warm enough for them to survive the worst blizzard, a stream to give them water. To the pursuers it had less to recommend it. The only way to get to it was along a narrow shelf with no cover at all and a drop of several hundred feet to one side. Yet there was no choice. The commando could not overnight on the mountain; try that in this weather and they would all be dead by morning.

Yet snow in these mountains never lasted long. If they went back down the mountain, there was no guarantee the convicts would still be here by morning. No, open ground or not, they would have to go in at once, before it got too dark to see.

A frontal assault over five hundred yards with no cover, against five desperate men with rifles ... A daunting prospect.

They rode on. The wind blew sharp enough to cut, the cold froze their breath about them and the clouds seemed almost to touch their heads.

It was late afternoon when they reached the place. They dismounted in the shelter of a rock face that concealed them from the cave as well as protecting them from the wind.

Christiaan turned to Hernus Klopper, his second-in-command.

'Take the ten best shots,' he said. 'Spread them out on the slope of the mountain to cover us when we go in.'

Klopper nodded expressionlessly and turned to give the order.

'Wait!' Christiaan said, voice suddenly sharp.

A fragment of white came spinning out of the grey-bellied clouds. Another, then a third.

Snow.

Christiaan grinned and slapped Klopper on the shoulder. 'Let's wait a few minutes, man. Maybe we won't need covering fire, after all.'

The snow grew thicker. The danger now was not rifle fire from the cave, but straying off the track and plunging down the side of the mountain into the tops of the pine trees three hundred feet below.

'Let's get on with it,' Christiaan said. 'Wait any longer, we won't be able to see where we're going.'

They formed up, rifles ready, breath steaming in the cold air. He took a deep breath and stepped out into the storm.

The wind seized him. A suffocating curtain of white snatched the breath from his lungs. Ice particles scoured his face, bringing blood from a dozen tiny cuts. The force of the gale made him stagger, feet groping for the invisible path. Within seconds, his fingers, even within the stout leather gauntlets, were numb with cold. He turned his head to look behind him. The figure of the next man, Willem Meyer, loomed through the snow.

'Hands and knees,' he yelled, trying to raise his voice above the howling wind. 'We'll never make it, otherwise.'

Meyer's beard and eyebrows were crusted with white. Dark eyes gleamed momentarily through the snow. He shouted something, the words swept away by the gale.

'What?'

'We'll never make it at all in this.'

Christiaan shook his head even as he felt the wind trying to prise him from the narrow path. 'We must. At least in this they won't be able to see us. Without it they'd have picked us off like shooting ducks off a wall.'

He didn't wait for further argument but turned, sank to his hands and knees and began to grope his way forward.

Nearer the ground it was easier. Easier to breathe, easier to hold his eyelids open against the cutting force of the gale. The outline of the path was a snow-covered scrawl across the slope. The snow soaked and chilled him, the rocks bruised his knees.

He shut his mind to pain, cold, fear.

Don't think of five hundred yards, he told himself. That is too far. Rather think of one yard. Do that, then go on to the next.

His fingers groped. One knee moved. One hand. Again. And again. Inch by inch, yard by yard, minute by minute, he progressed. His groping hand found a large chunk of rock. He put his weight on it, felt it shift. It bounded away into oblivion, the noise of its fall swallowed by the wind. Despite the cold, sweat started beneath his leather jacket. He took a deep breath and went on.

The path was gone now, blanketed by snow. The world was reduced to a wilderness of howling white. Fingers, cheeks, even legs were numb. He had no idea how far he had come, could not even tell if the commando were following him or not. Yet he knew his men. They would be behind him still.

Slowly, painfully, he went on.

After what seemed hours, a shadow loomed out of the snow. He stopped, breath shuddering. He had reached the cave.

He waited until Willem Meyer emerged from the blizzard behind him. Christiaan gestured silently at the indistinct outline of the cave mouth twenty yards away. He brought his mouth close to Willem's ear.

'Where are the others?'

'Behind me. I suppose.'

'I'm going in. It won't be easy but at least in this they probably won't be expecting anyone. If we wait until it clears, they'll spot us before we can get at them.'

Christiaan looked at his Mauser. It was saturated. He wouldn't be able to rely on it. Never mind. He still had his revolver. And his knife.

Willem asked, 'Can you see the path?'

'No. But it must run straight ahead.' He remembered the rock he had dislodged. Any obstacles would be buried in the snow. Loose stones, fallen rocks, uneven ground — any of them could throw them over the edge. The drop to the right was still there, steeper than ever at this point, he remembered.

Think about it too much, we'll never move.

He got to his feet, feeling the precipice suck at him.

I'm not even sure I *can* run. One way to find out. 'Let's go.'

He was running, after a fashion. Staggering, knees stiff. He stumbled over a hidden rock and felt the world tip under him. Somehow regaining his balance, he ran on, the cave mouth looming now, and in the entrance ...

... Men.

Breath harsh in his throat, Christiaan flung himself up the last ten yards of the path and into the cave.

A figure in the opening raised a rifle, pointing it at him. There was a crack, a wave of air slapped his ear, but he was inside the entrance before the man could fire again.

He did not try to fire his own rifle but seized it by the barrel and swung it horizontally with all his might. The man leapt back. The butt of the gun did not connect but Christiaan's hand found the knife in his boot. Following up hard he drove it to its hilt in the man's belly.

Before the man had even begun to fall, he had spun round to face the others, the bloodied blade ready in his hand. There were three, no, four other men. Two more rifles he could see. He charged them, brandishing the knife. They broke before him, panicking, and fled into the darkness of the cave at their backs.

He followed up hard. Another of the men turned and raised his rifle. He was only three yards away but three yards was too far to reach him and at that range the man, however panicky, could not miss. He flung himself sideways and felt the bullet smack the air.

Within the cave, the sound of the shot was shattering. Christiaan was on his feet again. Before the man with the rifle could fire a second time, he had flung himself at him. Again he felt the knife sink home. The man screamed and fell away, rifle clattering on the rocky floor.

The remaining men had gone to ground behind the rocks that littered the rear of the cave. Christiaan threw himself down behind another rock before the last rifle could fire on him. He put his knife to one side and drew his revolver. With his left hand he picked up a fragment of rock and tossed it underarm into the depths of the cave, his eyes alert for movement.

It clattered off the walls. A flicker behind one of the rocks. He fired at once and missed, the bullet screaming as it sprang off the rock. The echo of the shot reverberated, died.

Christiaan felt a presence at his back and turned his head. Gert Raas. 'Where's Willem?'

Face grim, Gert jerked his head at the cave entrance. 'Back there.'

'You mean ...?'

'Between the eyes.'

Rage smote Christiaan like a flail. A widow and two orphans to add to the butchers' bill. And for what?

Without thinking, he leapt to his feet and charged deeper into the cave, Gert beside him.

'No!'

The three men were on their feet, cowering, no fight left in them. A crash as the last rifle was thrown to the floor. The men backed away, hands in the air.

'We give up, *baas*! Don't kill us!'

Silence in the cave.

Christiaan covered them with his revolver. 'Throw down your arms.'

A moment's hesitation, then three knives and a revolver clattered to the ground.

'That the lot?'

'Yes.' The man who had spoken before nodded eagerly. 'That's all, *baas*.'

Without turning his head, Christiaan said, 'Search them.' Gert came forward and searched the prisoners roughly.

The cave was filled with the men of the commando. Now the fighting's over, Christiaan thought savagely, all of a sudden there's no shortage of them.

A sudden exclamation. Gert had found another knife. The culprit cowered. Christiaan stepped forward and swung the barrel of the gun hard against the man's temple. He dropped.

The remaining men had nothing, were squawking like chickens as they felt the weight of the commando's eyes upon them. 'Please, *baas*. Don't kill us, *baas*. We won't give no trouble.'

He eyed them coldly. Two men, two women, one child dead because of them. It could have been more. They'd had two shots at him. Only by God's will had they missed. Out there, in the blizzard, the whole commando might have perished.

'We won't kill you,' he said.

Not yet.

The snow had eased but it was too late to get off the mountain before dark. They spent the night in the cave and, in the morning, the sun shining and the sky a gentian blue over the white peaks, they made their way down into the valley.

Christiaan sent riders ahead to tell the people that the men who had killed the Wessels family had been captured. A message also to the Meyer farm. As soon as possible Christiaan would be calling on the widow himself; an unhappy task, yet necessary.

They made good time, but it was late afternoon when they got back to *Oudekraal*. Behind the house the mountain peaks gleamed in the setting sun yet, in the valley, shadows were gathering as the men rode in with their prisoners. They were tired at the end of two long days but proud that their mission had been accomplished. Their heads were up; some carried their rifles loose in their hands, barrels projecting over the pommels of their saddles. Their severe faces stared unsmiling over the heads of the crowd that had gathered to see justice done.

Most of the valley was there. Even some of the people from the outlying farms, men normally seen only at the monthly *Nagmaal* gathering, had come in, too.

The commando reined in before the house, the prisoners with their feet bound beneath the bellies of the horses that carried them.

Christiaan dismounted. Back straight, shoulders squared, he walked slowly up the steps to the *stoep* where his wife Sara waited to greet him. The children stood on either side of her, their hands clasped in hers. The lights of the house shone yellow in the gathering darkness.

Sara looked up at him. It was a formal business, welcoming the head of the house on his safe return, and she did not smile. At the back of her dark eyes there was something of a smile, perhaps, but for the man, not for the leader of the commando. Not for the crowd, either.

'Thanks be to God you are safe home,' she said, her voice raised for the crowd to hear.

'Thanks be to God,' he agreed gravely.

'Amen,' the crowd said.

Christiaan bent to greet the children, then straightened. 'Take Anneliese indoors,' he told his wife. 'Stay with her.'

From here on it would be men's business and she did not argue.

'Deneys?'

'Stays here.'

He waited until the door was closed behind them, then turned once again to face the crowd. In his hand was the book he had taken from his saddlebag, and when he spoke, his voice carried to every one of the men gathered on the open ground below him.

There were lighted torches among them. They fluttered in the wind, casting pools of darkness and yellow light upon the faces, the eyes and the barrels of the rifles. Above them the white peaks of the mountains caught the last rays of the sun amid the gathering dark.

Christiaan opened the book.

'"The voice of him that crieth in the wilderness,"' he read, and his deep voice rolled over the people, filling the place where they stood. '"Prepare ye the way of the Lord. Make straight in the desert a highway for our God."'

He closed the book.

'Bring them forward.'

Full dark, now. Rifles ready, four of the commando led the prisoners forward and turned them to face the crowd. No one moved or spoke and the light from the flames ebbed and flowed over them, as fluid as water.

'See the men we have brought back to you,' Christiaan said. 'Sentenced to prison for their crimes. Escaped. They came into the valley, not to seek refuge. Not as an escape route to the interior. They came to steal. And to kill.'

The crowd stirred.

'People are dead who would otherwise be alive. Women and children mourn who would otherwise have been glad. These men' — he thrust out his hand — 'broke into the Wessels's farm. They stole food. Weapons. Ammunition. But they were not content with that. One by one, they killed the members of the family and their maid servant. They could have tied them, stolen what they wanted and gone. They chose to kill them instead. Four deaths. For nothing. Yesterday, when we caught up with them, they fired on us. Now Willem Meyer is also dead. His wife is left a widow, his two small children fatherless. People of our community. People who had the right to look to us for their security but did not find it.'

The crowd murmured louder and the sound was ugly.

'"Prepare ye the way of the Lord,"' Christiaan quoted. '"Make straight in the desert a highway for our God."' He raised his voice. His clenched fist smote the air. 'Is this how we make God's highway straight in the desert? To let such as these kill the innocent? Is this how we discharge our responsibility to our flock? Who among us can hope to stand before the Judgement and say he is innocent when the blood of the victims cries unavenged from the ground?'

Silence, as though the valley held its breath. Then:

'They shall be punished,' Christiaan said.

'Yes,' the crowd shouted back at him. 'Let them be punished.'

'Does anyone disagree?'

Silence.

It was cold now as the frost came down. The mountains were hidden, without even the faintest glimmer of light from the snow. Behind the house the shape of the mountain loomed black. The torches streamed flame and the eyes of the men made deep holes in the pallor of their faces. Shadows flew like bats against the walls of the house and the breath of the people hung silver in the air about their heads. And everywhere the mutter and murmur, the occasional shout, the crowd angry at the bound men and what they had done.

Christiaan said, 'We can keep them safe until the snow is clear from the mountain. We can feed them while they sleep easy at our expense. Keep men from their work to guard them. Then we can return them to the prison in Cape Town or hand them over to the authorities in Stellenbosch, where they will be hanged for what they have done.' Pause. 'Or we can deal with them ourselves. Now.'

'Deal with them ourselves,' the crowd cried.

What a clamour of protest from the bound men! They threw themselves about on their horses, screaming and shouting, knowing the decision meant death.

Christiaan's voice overrode them. 'Take them from here and do with them as you will. But remember, you are doing God's work. Therefore let it be quick, without unnecessary pain. And if it is wrong, I shall answer to God for it.'

His hands dropped and his shoulders. He turned and went to his son and crouched down before him, holding the little chin in his strong hand.

'Remember today,' he said, and his voice was soft, his words for the boy and not for the crowd. 'This is what it means to be master of *Oudekraal*. One day you will be the one to lead them. It is the place God has given you, and you will have to do it. Put your faith in God and his Book. Then all will be well with you and the people you lead.'

Deneys's eyes were wide in his pale face. 'Will the people kill them?'

'Yes, my son. The people will kill them. Not out of anger or hatred, but for what they have done.' He straightened. 'You will remember this night.' An instruction, not a question.

He took his son's hand and went with him into the house, walking as a man does who carries a great weight upon him. The door shut behind them, leaving a silence among the crowd as though the people were asleep. With the bang of the door they woke, looking about them and at each other in a dazed, puzzled way. Quietly, without fuss or discussion, they took the men, still protesting and screeching, and led them away into the darkness.

There were lights on the slopes of the mountain, too far for sound, and, after a while, the lights went out and darkness lay over all.

SEVEN

Elizabeth Grant was not a tall woman. She had the bluest eyes that Deneys Wolmarans had ever seen but it was her hair that he noticed first: as gold as wheat and so heavy that he thought how it would weigh in his hands when he lifted it. Not that there was any question of anything like that when he first met her, of course.

In those days there was no chapel in the valley. The burghers used to come in once a month from all the outlying places to hold *Nagmaal*, or Holy Communion as they called it in English, and the dominee travelled from Stellenbosch to conduct the service.

Deneys's father had set aside a big field especially for the purpose. In his time he never permitted it to be used for anything else, because it was a place dedicated to God. After the Anglo-Boer war that practice fell away, like so many others. The *Nagmaalvlakte*, or Communion Field, as they called it, became covered in vines, as were the lanes, white with summer dust, along which the burghers had brought their wagons.

The women used to pick the wild flowers from the verges and weave them into garlands for the wagons and the mules. Some of the young girls wore flowers in the bonnets they used to cover their hair, although not when they were going to *Nagmaal*, in case people should accuse them of vanity.

Some of those old-timers were very hot on things like vanity and *Thou Shalt Nots*, quick to shout about sacrilege and blasphemy and all such matters, but neither Deneys nor his father could see any harm in it. It was all innocence and lovely to see although after the war nobody did that any more, either. They had heard that some churches used flowers and there were those who spoke against that, too, but to Deneys it always seemed a good custom. Almighty God created the flowers of the *veld* as he created all things, and to bring them into his presence as an act of worship — how could there be anything wrong in that?

People came from all over the valley and even further, from places deep in the mountains. Some of the farms were very remote and the owners would be on the road for two days or even longer to come to the *Nagmaal* celebration. Not that distance stopped them. They always came, except perhaps in winter when the snow was too thick to get through.

It was not just for the service. They came because it was the one chance they had to meet their neighbours and find out what was going on in the world, or as much of the world as they cared about.

The farmers used to *outspan* their mules for two or three days. There was no trading on the Sabbath, of course, but the next day was different. The farms were self-sufficient in most things, but not in powder or the lead they needed to make bullets, nor in coffee and such things as spectacles for those whose eyes were aging along with the rest of them. Those they had to buy and the *Nagmaal* gathering was the place to do it. People brought livestock with them, too, and produce, and a fair bit of trading took place before the farmers *inspanned* their mules and headed back once more into the mountains.

Andrew Grant had a farm at the far end of the valley. The Grants had never been rich but farmed their land well, followed the customs of their neighbours and generally lived in a civilised way. Andrew Grant was from Scotland, a settler who had come to the country twenty years before. He had married an Afrikaans woman, and his only child Elizabeth had been brought up according to Afrikaner custom, but to the people living in the valley both he and his daughter were English and would be so until they died.

When Deneys was nineteen, the Grants came to *Nagmaal* as usual. Deneys was carrying out some errand or other for his father. He came past the place where the women from the wagons were drawing water for the cooking and came face to face with the seventeen-year-old Elizabeth Grant and fell in love with her there and then.

Afterwards Deneys always claimed it was that wonderful wheat-coloured hair that first drew his eye, but that was impossible. All the women wore big cloth *kappies* with brims that came down over their faces to protect them from the sun and the eyes of those who should not have been looking, and their hair was tucked up out of sight. Anyway, whatever he saw or fancied he saw, that was Deneys hooked and it appeared Elizabeth was in the same state, because later she told him so herself.

That same day, not one hour later, Deneys went to his father in the little room that was used as an office at *Oudekraal* and told him he intended to marry Elizabeth Grant.

Christiaan Wolmarans came to his feet, big fists bunched, expression incredulous.

'Elizabeth *Grant*? You will do no such thing!'

Deneys quailed but fought to conceal his fear. 'Please, father ...'

'Andrew Grant is a nobody. He has nothing but his farm. He —'

'That's all we have.'

'*Oudekraal* is the biggest and richest property in the valley. Grant has a few acres at *Doornbosch*. There's no comparison and you know it.'

'I would not be marrying her for the farm.'

'You won't be marrying her at all.' The bright blue eyes dug into him, sharp as porcupine quills. 'When did you meet her?'

Deneys avoided his father's gaze. 'Today.'

'Have you spoken to her?'

Deneys shook his head. 'No.'

Christiaan let his relief show. Speaking to a girl without permission could cause serious trouble. 'Thank God for that.'

He prowled to the window and looked out. Sunlight lay like honey on the leaves of the oak trees. The noise of the people in the *Nagmaalvlakte* came faintly to them. Christiaan turned, shoulders heavy beneath his light shirt, and stared at his son.

'You don't know her. You never set eyes on her until today. You haven't spoken to her and now you've decided to marry her. Is that what you're saying?'

Deneys tried to stiffen knees like jelly. 'Yes.'

Christiaan turned back to his desk and sat down. 'Out of the question,' he said dismissively. He picked up his pen; the discussion was over.

No, Deneys thought. I won't let him send me away like a ... like a servant. He willed confidence into his voice. 'Why?'

Christiaan lifted his head and stared at him. 'Why what?'

Half expecting his father to order him from the room, Deneys said, 'Why is it out of the question for me to marry Elizabeth Grant?'

'I have just told you. The Grants are nobodies. They have no money —'

'*Doornbosch* is a good farm —'

'It'll never amount to anything. Andrew Grant does his best, but it's too small. It's too high for grapes and too far from *Oudekraal*.'

Deneys remembered his glimpse of Elizabeth, her slight body stooped to lift the water pail, her blue eyes looking up at him from beneath her cloth hat. Frustration moved like heat through him. Why did these old people think only of money? There were other considerations in life.

'That's not the only problem,' Christiaan said. 'Elizabeth is English.'

Deneys forced an angry laugh. 'That's ridiculous —'

'Her father's from Scotland.'

'Her mother's from Stellenbosch. Elizabeth was born here, for heaven's sake! She comes to *Nagmaal* with the rest of us. She's no more English than I am!'

'That's not how people around here see it. You live in a community, you have to abide by its rules.'

'*You* don't.'

'I am master of *Oudekraal*.'

His father's arrogance infuriated him. The fact that it was unconscious made it worse.

'One day I shall be master, too,' Deneys said, greatly daring.

'God willing. Which is why the woman you marry must be someone the valley will accept.'

'If you're master, surely people have to do what you tell them?'

'People don't like being told. The trick is to get them to do what you want without telling them. Let them think it's their idea, that's the secret.'

'You mean I should be persuading you it's your idea that I should marry Elizabeth Grant?'

Christiaan laughed. He leant back in his chair and studied his son, tapping his teeth with the end of the pen. 'I'll tell you what I will do.'

'What's that?' Eagerly. Oh *please*, father, *please* ...

'I'll think about it.'

Deneys's face fell. 'Is that all?'

His father raised his eyebrows. 'Many would say I'm foolish to promise as much.'

'How much time will you need?'

Christiaan was not to be pressed on this or anything. 'As long as it takes. Now let me get on with my work. And remember, stay clear of Elizabeth Grant. For the time being, anyway.'

Alone in the office once more, Christiaan Wolmarans laid his pen on the desk and sat back in his chair.

Well, now.

He had been expecting something of the sort for some time. Deneys was nearly twenty. Anneliese, his other child, had married at sixteen, five years before, and gone off with her husband to his farm near Lydenburg in the Transvaal Republic. Time now, for Deneys, too, to be thinking of marrying and settling down.

To the right woman, of course.

He would have reacted with fury whoever Deneys had mentioned. Fathers, not sons, decided marriages, and it was as well to remind him of the fact. Strange, though, that he should have chosen Elizabeth Grant. Christiaan had thought about her himself more than once.

He thought about her now.

It was true that the valley wouldn't like *Oudekraal* wedded to an outsider, but Deneys was right. The girl was Dutch in everything but name and blood. Both were important, of course, but less so than custom or language. People would soon forget her background once they were used to the idea.

As for her lack of fortune ... It would be a problem whomever Deneys married. Apart from himself, there were only three large landowners in the valley. The van Rensburg girls were married already. The Brands had no daughters. The only possibility was Hernus Klopper, who had a niece of the right age and had hinted, more than once, about a possible link between the families, but Klopper was a *slimmerd*, a sly fox. He wanted Deneys in his family because that would bring him closer to *Oudekraal*. That was his real target, and Christiaan would go to war to stop him having it.

Christiaan selected a cheroot from the pottery jar on his desk and leant back, blowing a thin stream of fragrant smoke into the air. One thing in Elizabeth's favour was the English blood he had allowed Deneys to think he despised so much. He didn't despise it at all. The Wolmarans had English blood themselves — much diluted, certainly, but there. Perhaps the time had come to strengthen it a little.

There was trouble coming up-country. Sooner or later the Boer Republics and the British Empire were going to war. The Boers had no chance. They were tough and determined, but could muster at most forty thousand men. The Empire had ten times as many. Twenty-five years earlier, the Confederate States of America had shown the world that determination alone could never win against such odds.

What would the Cape burghers do? Many had family up north, but Christiaan thought the majority would stay neutral. They had too much to lose to get involved in lost causes. He certainly had no intention of getting involved himself. His fighting days were over. He had never been an admirer of Paul Kruger, in any case. No, he would stay at home and mind the farm, whatever happened. All the same, it wouldn't be a bad idea for the family to strengthen its English links, just in case.

He smiled around the cheroot, eyes fixed contemplatively on the smoke swirling in the air above him. Deneys had been plucky enough about it. Impetuous, too. How long had it taken him to make up his mind after seeing the girl? Not even an hour. But that was Deneys all over, to make up his mind and act without further thought.

At least he had the guts to stand up to me, Christiaan thought. Facing my disapproval, not realising I'd planned the whole thing.

What had he told Deneys?

The trick is to get them to do what you want without telling them.

There was no reason for Deneys ever to know that he had sent him on that errand to Grant's wagon on purpose. Let him believe it had all been his own idea. He stood up, stretching, and stubbed out his cheroot. Outside the window the sound of voices was dying down. *Nagmaal* was over. He would have a word with Andrew Grant before he went back to his farm.

Two months later, the betrothal was announced of Deneys Wolmarans and Elizabeth Grant. The news created quite a stir.

Briton and Afrikaner kept themselves apart from each other. In the Cape, passions ran a good deal lower than in the independent nations of the Transvaal and the Free State. The two races had lived side by side for three-quarters of a century and had grown accustomed to each other. Still, the idea of a Wolmarans marrying an *uitlander*, particularly one who was not wealthy, created a lot of ill-feeling.

Elizabeth Grant might have been a Hottentot, the way people talked.

Hernus Klopper was full of it, muttering about slaps in the face to the leading families in the valley and people marrying beneath them. Sour looks all round.

Christiaan Wolmarans didn't give a damn about sour looks but in a little while there was sour talk, too, of people maybe having to get married in a hurry, and that was different.

Andrew Grant was fit to be tied. He wanted to challenge Hernus Klopper to a duel, and to hell with the law. 'I'll not have anyone talk about my daughter like that, by God,' he said.

'Leave him to me,' Christiaan said. 'I've known him all his life. I'll handle him.'

And did.

He invited Klopper and his wife to dinner. After the meal, when the men were alone, they talked.

'This marriage ... There has been talk of a child. If it were true I would have Deneys out of this house today, only son or not. And Andrew Grant would kill his daughter. But it is not true. It is a lie, made up by those who should know better.'

Klopper smiled. 'If you say so.'

Christiaan's eyes raked him. 'I do say so.'

'You know your own family better than I do. You say there's no truth in the rumours, that's fine by me.'

'I'm glad. Because I've invited you here to tell you something. I shall track down whoever started the rumour.' Christiaan's blue eyes, hard as steel, watched his guest. 'When I have found him, I shall speak to him, as a warning. In friendship. After that, anyone spreading such lies I will kill.'

He waited for an answer. A light sweat beaded Klopper's forehead. He forced a laugh. 'No need for such talk, surely?'

Christiaan smiled grimly and echoed his guest's earlier words. 'If you say so.' He stubbed out his cigar. 'There will be a wedding. You may be sure of that. You are of course invited.'

A fat lot Deneys cared, either way. He was nineteen years old, Elizabeth was seventeen and they were marrying for love. To hell with the lot of them.

Things had to take their course. No slipping away for an evening's stroll by the river. Any woman who did that would have been up in front of the dominee double-quick; any man would have been in danger of a bullet from the girl's father, never mind who his own father happened to be.

There was conversation between the families and eventually Deneys was permitted to get on his horse and ride three hours to the Grants' farm. That was not the end of the frustration but rather the beginning of it. For one hour he was permitted to sit on the Grants' *stoep* with Elizabeth, her mother always in attendance, and exchange polite conversation. Elizabeth still wore her hat so the famous hair remained hidden, and he was not allowed to touch her in any way. Then it was back on his horse and three hours home again, the whole thing to be repeated a week later.

After a few visits like that, Deneys was fit to burn up the whole farm with Elizabeth's mother still inside it. He could not abide anybody standing in the way of what he wanted to do and what he wanted at that minute was to marry Elizabeth Grant and to hell with all the nonsense.

Elizabeth felt the same but it did not matter what either of them thought. They had to wait because, if they didn't, they would have to leave the valley and neither of them wanted that.

Six months later, when even Mrs Klopper had stopped hinting about a child, Deneys Wolmarans and Elizabeth Grant were married at *Oudekraal*.

The wedding was held at *Nagmaal* because that was the only day they could get the people together and the dominee to come out from Stellenbosch.

The whole valley was invited. After the ceremony the bride and groom stood up on the hay wain they used for weddings, clean and shining and its wheel spokes painted. Flowers aplenty and a black horse for good luck, with its coat brushed until the sunlight ran golden all over it, with flowers, too, in its bridle. The wain did a stately circuit of the *Nagmaalvlakte* while everyone cheered and fired off their guns. Powder only, of course, because bullets were precious.

Afterwards Deneys remembered only one thing, of being scared out of his wits that the wheels would hit a bump and throw them both out on their heads.

Elizabeth's memories were different. She remembered her husband standing beside her, laughing and waving, his arm around her at last, the sunlight bright on his face and his blue eyes shining. She looked up at him, the veil off her face and blowing in the wind. He had a little scratch under the corner of his jaw where he had nicked himself shaving. She remembered that particularly.

She thought how strange it was to remember so small a thing among so many more important matters, but that was how it was.

Then came the food: the beef and lamb, the wildebeest, the impala, the sausages and hams, chickens and ducks, the *bobotie* and *denningvleis*, *melkterts* as big as wagon wheels, mountains of fruit and vegetables and thick slices of bread baked in the ovens behind the house. And the drink ... Beer, cordials for the children and barrels of wine, red and white. Brandy, too, so that by the time it was over the servants were giggling and useless and half the guests were walking sideways as they made their way back to their wagons.

All the time people were smiling at the married couple, winking and thinking the hot thoughts that people think at weddings. It would have been as far from Elizabeth as the moon to discuss such things with a living soul but she was untroubled by what was to come that night. She was a country woman. Like everyone she knew, she lived her life to the rhythms of birth and harvest and death. She had grown up with the beasts and knew how such things were. She was above the beasts because, like all humans, she had been touched by the forefinger of God but did not believe, as some townspeople did, that babies were brought in paper bags. Such nonsense.

Afterwards, in the big bedroom of *Oudekraal*, there was quietness and a touching of hands, eyes bright in the candle flame, and stillness together and a lifting down of the heavy, wheat-coloured hair.

Two weeks after the wedding, Doctor Leander Starr Jameson led a scallywag bunch of raiders into the Transvaal.

The English always said that the Anglo-Boer war was fought about gold and maybe, for them, it was. Certainly it was the discovery of the main reef on White Waters Ridge, *die Witwatersrand*, that made the leaders of the British Empire decide to steal the independent Boer republics. For the Boers the fight was about freedom and justice.

Freedom and justice. Words that meant a lot or little, depending on who was saying them. To the English, freedom meant being able to mine the gold, control the country, control the continent. To the Boers, freedom meant being left alone to run their own lives in the way that suited them best, which meant basically to go on living as they were, to change nothing, to shut out the outside world.

Freedom and justice were words like love. They meant anything people wanted, but were a clarion call to the young. If anyone had asked Deneys to go and fight for the South African Republic he would have asked why. If he'd been told it was to keep the gold mines away from the English he would have laughed outright. But when he heard the words freedom and justice, it was a different story. And of course he believed, as did a lot of young men who had never seen war, that there was glamour attaching to it too.

Freedom and justice and glamour made a brew so potent that even the mildest of youths would have had problem resisting it. Deneys did not try very hard. He loved his wife very dearly but it was not enough. He had a wife, a place in the world, a big farm that one of these days would be his and that his father needed him to help run. The quarrels of the up-country Boers were not his quarrels. President Kruger meant less than nothing to him. Yet the bugle sounded in his ear and Freedom and Justice and Glamour did the rest.

Christiaan did not want him to go. Worse, he *forbade* him to go, which was a mistake, given Deneys's nature. Elizabeth did not want him to go. What sensible woman would? There was no sense at all in his going.

Nevertheless when the Anglo-Boer war began on 12 October, 1899, off to fight Deneys Wolmarans went.

EIGHT

In August 1901, after two years of fighting, Kommandant Lammers sent Deneys and a few others of his commando east to find out what was going on in that part of the country.

Things were certainly going very badly in their area. Many burghers had surrendered or simply given up and gone home. Even some of the generals had put up their hands. One of them, General Cronje, had formed the National Scouts to fight on the English side.

Now the English soldiers were burning the farms, destroying the crops, driving off the livestock. Perhaps things would be better in the east.

At first Lammers had not wanted Deneys to go at all but he had pleaded for permission. His sister and her two children — Stoffel, now aged five, and Amalie, a year younger — were on the farm outside Lydenburg. Her husband was fighting with Louis Botha and the English had been reported in the area. Deneys wanted to make sure they were still all right. Anneliese was a lovely girl, tall and dark-haired, two years older than himself, but she was also light-hearted, a little careless. He wasn't sure she'd be able to handle the war with her husband away.

Eventually Lammers agreed.

They rode in a big circle around Pretoria, where the English army was now strongly established. There were few other towns but, such as they were, they avoided them too. The enemy was master of the towns and roads, so they kept to the open country.

Open and terrible it was. For two days they rode through a nightmare landscape of blackened ruins and trampled fields, desolate and totally deserted.

'Jesus, will you look at that?' Dominic Riordan's pale eyes were shocked in his sunburned face. 'So they've been doing it here, too.'

Dominic Riordan was someone out of the ordinary among the Boers. He was not Dutch at all but Irish and had come to the war from Australia. Others had come from that country, but nearly all to fight for the English. For that reason people had been suspicious of Riordan at first but soon it had become obvious that there was nothing to be feared from him on that score. Whatever the reason, his skinny body held such hatred for England and the English that its ferocity scorched everyone who had anything to do with him, and every incident throughout the long and bitter campaign had only made things worse.

'God and his holy angels! Not a blade of grass in sight!'

They reined in their horses at the top of a low rise. Eyes shaded beneath the brims of their Terai hats, they stared into the distance. The stench of ashes filled their nostrils. As far as they could see, ruin, with here and there the broken shells of buildings presiding over a wilderness of burnt fields.

No crops, no animals, no people. The devastated land extended in silence to a distant horizon. Here and there the wind stirred spirals of ash that rose half-heartedly into the air and subsided again, as though even the wind had been destroyed by the passing soldiers. Nothing else moved.

Deneys swore softly, turned to the others. 'I would never have believed it ...' He dug out his battered Bible. 'We should pray.'

Something he would never have thought to do in the old days, but war changes all things and Deneys was changed.

'Pray that they shall all be destroyed.' Dominic Riordan again. 'Pray that the Lord shall scatter his enemies. I'll join you in that. Let's be having no talk of forgiveness, mind.'

Deneys looked at him and at the broken countryside, the ashes stirring in the wind. He was his own man and would read what he wished. He opened the Book, turning the pages until he reached what he wanted. He raised his voice above the keening of the wind.

'"They that wait upon the Lord shall renew their strength. They shall mount up with wings as eagles; they shall run, and not be weary; they shall walk, and not faint."' He turned the page. '"How beautiful upon the mountains are the feet of him that publisheth peace —"'

Dominic jerked as though the words had stabbed him to the heart.

'Didn't I just say let's not be talking of peace?'

Startled, Deneys's horse danced a little. 'All of us should pray for peace,' he said.

Dominic's face was flushed with rage. He stabbed a furious hand at the devastated landscape. 'With that in front of you? Well, Dominic Riordan's having no part of any talk of peace, I can tell you that.'

Deneys sat taller in his saddle. 'Do not pick and choose which part of the Book you wish to hear. It is all the word of God. All!'

'From which I suppose a man may choose what he wishes to read,' Dominic said. 'What about the bit that says they have sown the wind and shall reap the whirlwind?' He stood in his saddle and raised his clenched fist in the air. '"Let God arise and let his enemies be scattered." Read *that*.'

Deneys felt for him with all his heart but would not give way. Softly, without looking at the Bible that lay still open in his hand, he quoted, '"Break forth into joy, ye waste places, for the Lord shall redeem Jerusalem."'

Dominic's face was wet with tears. He rubbed his cheek with the back of his hand and turned away. The ugly flush had gone from his face; that at least. He stared across the devastated land.

'Redeem Jerusalem?' he repeated softly. 'We shall never see it.'

They moved eastwards past torched farmhouses and empty, trampled fields. No crops; no animals; no people.

'Where is everyone?' Kaspar Pieterse wondered.

That was indeed a question and with no one to answer it. With every mile Deneys felt more and more frightened for his sister and her children but, two days later, at long last, they came out of the burnt land.

There were many small hills with valleys running between them and the trees were filled with a wonder of birds. Streams ran everywhere and the countryside was lush and green. After what they had seen it was like paradise and Deneys's heart lifted. Perhaps Anneliese and the children would be safe after all.

At sunset on the following day they reached the farm. Deneys had never seen it but had heard much; climbing the wooded slope to the house was like coming home. He could see the buildings long before they reached them.

Perched on its hilltop, the house would command a view over the entire valley. No doubt that was where its name had come from. *Uitkyk*. In English, Lookout.

They reached the summit and Deneys's heart turned to water. Nothing stirred. No sign of livestock; no smoke from the chimney; no dogs barking at the strangers. Before he turned the corner of the building he knew what he would find.

Like all the rest, *Uitkyk* had been burned to the ground.

A one-armed doll, lying abandoned.

Deneys sat his horse and stared at the ruins. Thought of the days of happiness, achievement and sorrow burned up in the flames. Of people's lives. All gone now. Nothing but a broken doll lying in the mud.

Dominic spurred his horse to Deneys's side. Stared with hating eyes. 'The Lord shall redeem Jerusalem, is it? Can you look at that and tell me you believe a word of it?'

'I have to believe it,' Deneys protested. But felt himself lost in saying it. 'There has to be a resurrection, surely?'

'I'll give them resurrection. "I shall visit the sins of the fathers upon the children unto the third and fourth generation,"' Dominic said. 'That's what I believe. And, God willing, I intend to be alive to see it.'

After dark Deneys rode into Lydenburg. There was no moon but the stars were bright and, from the top of a neighbouring hill, he looked down at the thatched buildings straggling along the solitary dirt street. A church gable gleamed white. An owl called, otherwise there was no sound. Lydenburg lay still under the stars.

He left the horse and stole softly down the hill into the town. Not softly enough. A dog barked furiously. A door opened and a rectangle of light leapt across the dust. Deneys drew back.

'Who is it?' A man's voice, sharp with fear. The Dutch words stabbed the night.

Deneys walked forward, making sure his empty hands were in plain view.

'What do you want?' The voice had gone up a notch.

'I am enquiring about Anneliese van der Merwe,' Deneys said, 'of the farm *Uitkyk*.'

'Not here.'

The door was closing.

'I thought you might know where she was.'

'Who wants to know?'

'Her brother.'

'Her *brother*?' The man's expression changed. He looked quickly up and down the street. 'Inside with you, man. Quick.'

The house was small and open to the thatch. Dung floor, bits and pieces of furniture, a door leading presumably to another room. A few sticks burned in the hearth, a black cauldron hung from a hook. Beside the fire a woman, staring. The man locked the door. Dragging his right foot, he limped into the middle of the room. He was stockily-built, about Deneys's age, with a bitter, brooding look about the eyes. His collarless shirt was grubby, dark hair unkempt; he looked like someone who had lost all respect for himself.

'You are mad to come here.' Wet lips gleamed in the firelight. 'This place is alive with Tommies.'

'I know about Tommies,' Deneys said. 'I have killed a few in my time.'

Bravado was not his way, but the man's fear was like a sickness in the room and it was necessary.

'I came to ask about my sister, that's all.'

'The farm is burnt,' the woman said.

'I know. I have come from there.'

'All the farms are burnt,' the man told him. 'We live dangerously in these parts.'

Deneys looked at him. 'Not only here. There is not one farm standing between here and Pretoria.'

The man glared suspiciously. 'If you are Anneliese van der Merwe's brother, you ride with Lammers.'

'Lammers is far from here. I am alone.'

'We want no commandos in Lydenburg.'

'I am not even armed.' He had a pistol under his coat and a knife in his belt, but never mind.

'They shoot people for sheltering Boer fighters.'

Deneys was sick of it. 'If you can tell me about my sister, good. Otherwise, I'll be on my way.'

The woman came forward from the fire. Her dark skirts brushed the floor. 'Not until you've eaten.'

'That won't be necessary.'

'It is necessary. My man is right,' she said, speaking as though he were not in the room, 'they have shot people for less. But you will not go through that door until you have eaten.'

'Tell me at least if she is alive.'

'The last we heard she was.'

'Not her husband, though,' the man said. He brandished the news bitterly as though it gave him satisfaction. 'But you will have heard that.'

'I had not heard. When did it happen?'

'Six months ago, at least. Where have you been, man?'

Deneys stared him down. 'Fighting. And you?'

The man flushed angrily. Before he could speak, Deneys turned back to the woman. 'Where is she? Do you know?'

She shook her head. 'Food first.'

A small square of coarse bread, a scrap of home-made sausage, a mug of harsh black coffee. One plate; they were not eating with him.

'You will say a blessing,' the woman said.

Obediently Deneys gave thanks. He wondered how big a hole he was making in their stores by accepting, but knew he had no choice. It was the only dignity left to them, to offer hospitality to a stranger.

He finished the food, polished his plate carefully while the man and woman watched. 'I thank you,' he said formally.

'They took your sister away when they burned the farm,' the woman said. 'With the children.'

He tried to visualise it. 'What happened?'

'We did not see it, you understand. Only what we heard.'

He did not ask who had told them; in war you did not ask such things.

'The soldiers were tired and dangerous. No doubt they had done more of the same that day. They ordered everyone out of the house. Then they searched, to make sure no one was left. They rounded up the livestock while other soldiers guarded your sister and the children and the maid servant who lived in the house.'

'The English are so frightened they need to guard babies?'

'I am telling you what I heard,' the woman said. 'One of the soldiers took a big copper kettle from the house.'

'I remember that kettle,' Deneys said. 'It came from my father's house in the Cape.'

'He was going to steal it, you understand, but the sergeant made him put it back. He said they were not thieves but on their King's business.'

'Some business, to destroy good farms and make women and children homeless. What happened to the kettle?'

'It was burned up with the rest. The children were crying. The maid, too. But your sister stood like stone until the flames had taken everything.'

'I would sooner the soldier had kept the kettle,' Deneys said. 'That way at least it would be some use.'

'Lammers would kill you for saying that.' The man smiled maliciously. 'Giving aid to the enemy ...'

'A kettle?' Deneys said. 'What enemies does a kettle have?'

'You might say the same of the land we stand on. If you weren't still fighting, your sister's farm would be standing along with the rest.'

'A man is more than a kettle,' Deneys said. 'And we have burned nothing.'

'Louis Botha said he would burn the house of anyone who surrendered. What is the point?' the man demanded furiously. 'We will never beat them.'

The woman looked at him, as at a slug. 'Not everyone has given up, if you have.'

'Oh, let us keep going, by all means. Let us destroy the whole country rather than bow our necks. You were right about the kettle,' he told Deneys. 'Maybe you should stick to kettles and leave the country to the rest of us.'

'Maybe you should bite your tongue,' the woman told him angrily. 'You want Lammers to come with his commando and burn the house over our heads?'

'Burn and be damned.' Dark eyes blazed. 'Everything is finished, one way or the other.' And flung himself furiously across the room and through the inner door, which slammed to shake the house.

The woman ran her hand over her face and Deneys

saw how tired she was. 'Take no notice,' she said. 'He was brave, once. You see how he walks? Shrapnel it was, at Spion Kop. But the shrapnel took more than his foot.'

'He sounded glad my brother-in-law's dead.'

'He is not glad. He can't handle it any more, that's all. It is what war does to you. People think of the injury they see, the foot, the hand, but they are nothing. The injury to the mind is what matters. What he told you was right. If the soldiers find out you've been here, they will burn the house. It is hard to be a man, waiting and not knowing.'

'It is the same for a woman.'

'A woman is used to waiting. Carrying a child, she waits. When her man goes to war, she waits. It takes courage, certainly, but not a man's courage. A man makes a child, he goes away. In war, he kills or is killed. No waiting. Courage also, but of a different sort. When a man has to wait instead of going to fight, it does something to him. Believe me. I live with it every day.'

Deneys did not want to talk about it. 'My sister ...?'

'They put them on a train. There were hundreds of them, women and little children. Old folk, too. They took them to the concentration camp at Koffiekraal.'

'Concentration camp?'

'Where they put the women and children after they have burned the farms. There are many of them.'

Deneys nodded. 'Good. I am glad.'

She stared. 'Glad?'

'At least they will be safe.' He walked to the door.

'Let me first make sure the road is clear.' The woman opened the door and went outside. In a minute she was back. 'Nobody,' she said.

'I must thank you,' Deneys said again.

'You wish to thank us, don't come back.'

He nodded and walked outside. The night was still. The darkness could have concealed a thousand eyes. The woman stood with the door half-closed behind her, the light drawing a line across the dust.

'My man brought you into the house. A coward would not have done it.'

'I'm sure you're right.' Looking up and down the street, anxious to get away.

'You see?' she said. 'Waiting is not so easy.'

'It is stupid to stand here. If a patrol comes —'

'One more word and you can go.' Her voice was troubled. 'I am frightened of these camps.'

'Frightened?' He looked at her.

'You saw what the war has done to my man? Not his foot, I mean, the other. I think the war has done something to the English, too. Once they would not have burned the farms. The war has made them angry.'

'What about it?'

'Unlike us, they have the power to take their hurt out on others.'

'Surely never on the women and children? That would be madness.'

'So is burning the farms.'

'If they do that, the war will never end. We will fight them to the death.'

Her smile was like the baring of a skull. 'What are you doing now?'

'But this ... I will not believe it.'

'Pray God you are right.' She put her hands on his shoulders. 'Go with God, then. And remember the brave man of Lydenburg who took you into his house.'

She went back inside. The door closed.

They put Anneliese and the two children into a train and took them to the camp outside Koffiekraal, three hundred miles south-west of Lydenburg. They were not alone; the train — a dozen cattle trucks — was packed.

It was a weary journey. Twice a day the train stopped and the prisoners were allowed out for food and water and to relieve themselves. There were no toilets, but a lot of the people had known nothing but the *veld* in any case, so that was no problem. Then back into the trucks while the train went on.

In between stops there was no food or water. No *veld* either and, with both young and old aboard, the stench soon became so thick they could have sliced it.

It took five days, the train trundling slowly across the burning plains. For one whole day they passed the Drakensberg Mountains. They floated like dreams on the horizon, but no breath of coolness came from those far peaks. Anneliese clutched the slatted side of the truck and watched through the cracks as long as they were in sight. She and her husband had gone that way to the farm when they had first married. Green hills, steeply-forested valleys set with waterfalls, the *drifs* across the streams with the water cold and clear about the wagon wheels, the clean freshness of the mountain air ... Memory was like a plague, but still she had to watch.

All too soon the mountains were gone. The truck groaned and swayed. Dust and heat buried them. Now through the slatted sides Anneliese saw only the empty *veld* burning beneath a brazen sky.

She thought, I have lost my husband and my farm but still I have my children. I still have hope.

The camp consisted of bell tents set in lines, far too few for the number of prisoners they packed into them. There was a wire fence patrolled by soldiers, a central kitchen, latrine trenches set in rows, visible to all who cared to look. The tents had no groundsheets or blankets so all the prisoners had to lie on the bare earth. There were no washing facilities, no protection from heat or dust, no medical attention of any kind. There was nothing to do but sit and look through the wire at the *veld* stretching treeless to the horizon.

Into this place the English put them. A thousand to begin with, then more than a thousand, all of them brought there from the burned farms, the stripped countryside.

They would have improved their own conditions if it had been possible, but there was nothing they could do. They needed better food, clean water, some medical attention, at least, but there was none to be had. They complained, but no one did anything.

Many of the people had no idea of even the most basic hygiene. On the farms, when they had needed to relieve themselves, they had squatted where they were. When they were finished, they went on. There it hadn't mattered. In the camp it was death.

Waste fouled the ground. Its stench fouled the air. People, first the youngest and then the older ones, began to die.

Two other women and eight children shared the tent with Anneliese: Ella Joubert, thin and nervous, dark hair drawn back from a scraggy neck, frightened eyes; Margaretha Koch, fat and blonde as her two boys were fat and blonde. To begin with, at any rate.

One day Ella's oldest child awoke in tears, complaining of a sore throat. Her body was hot with fever and the back of her throat was coated with a grey film.

'An infection of some sort,' Margaretha said. 'She's young. It will pass.'

It did not pass. It grew worse. Next day the child complained of double vision. She had difficulty swallowing, and the film at the back of her throat had grown thicker. After the fourth day she complained no longer but lay still, limbs stiff, eyes half-closed and unmoving, breath so faint they could hardly see her chest rise and fall as she lay on the ground inside the tent.

'I'll get help.'

Anneliese went to the wire, called one of the guards.

'One of the children is very sick.'

Her English was rusty, but it served.

The sentry's face was red and dripped sweat beneath his white helmet.

'So?'

'She needs a doctor.'

'Ain't no doctors 'ere.'

'She tried to take hold of his sleeve through the wire. 'Please. I am afraid for her.'

He shook himself free. 'I told you —'

'Please,' she said again. She could hear herself pleading and hated herself for it. The enemy. But what else could she do? She heard herself say, 'I'll do anything ...'

That stopped him, at least.

He stared at her consideringly. 'What's wrong wiv 'er, then?'

'Some infection.'

It was the worst thing she could have said.

'*Infection?*'

He made off down the wire, Anneliese following him, arms out-thrust, tears streaming down her face.

'*'N klein kind, meneer*. A little child ... Surely you cannot let her die? What kind of man are you?'

He turned savagely. 'I'll tell the sergeant. Okay?'

It was the best she could hope for.

'Thank you. Oh, thank you ...'

She went back to the tent. Heat and the stink of sickness was like a blow in her face.

'He's getting the sergeant.'

Margaretha said, 'You could have saved your effort. *Die kleintjie is dood*. The kid is dead.'

The soldiers did nothing.

Two months later, two hundred children and thirty-seven adults had also died.

Ella Joubert. Her remaining daughters. Her son.

Cornelia Erasmus, whom Anneliese had known in Lydenburg. Her two children.

One hundred and ninety-three children and thirty-five adults whom Anneliese did not know.

Her own daughter Amalie. Aged four.

All dead.

The soldiers did nothing.

Anneliese closed her son's eyes and went out of the tent.

The sun was setting. The tent cast a long shadow across the bare earth. Beyond it more tents, more shadows marching like soldiers to the wire. Beyond the wire, the *veld* writhed with heat.

She sat on the ground, feet stretched out.

Emptiness was a chasm.

Her children dead. Her husband dead. Her farm dead.

Margaretha's voice blubbered somewhere. 'Last week it was Amalie. Now Stoffel. Who will be next, Anneliese? Who will close my eyes? Who will close yours?'

Strength rose in her. Hatred was a dark fire in her heart.

'No one will close my eyes. I shall not permit the English to kill me. I shall walk out of here. I shall keep the memory of this place alive. In my heart and in my head. Forever.'

An anthem of hatred, overwhelming and eternal. Her blood carried it, her brain burned with it, her heartbeats echoed it. She neither screamed nor wept.

She said, 'Before God I curse the English and those who have helped them in this war. The scythe of God is in my hand. I swear on the bodies of my children that I shall do to them everything they have done to me. And more. While I have breath I shall never forgive them, never forget.'

On her deathbed, Anneliese had told her great-granddaughter, 'I never did. Never, to this day. I shall hate them and curse them until the moment I die. And afterwards, God willing. They will never be rid of me.'

At fifteen Anna — or Tamsin Fitzgerald, as she had been then — had been appalled by the old woman's undying hatred. Was about to turn away, to run from this room of death, but Anneliese's cracked voice forestalled her.

'They forced me to leave my home, my family, my country. They made me come here, to wander the roads of this land that has never been mine. But one thing they could not prevent: not one mile, not a single step has passed without my curse upon their memory. And before I had to leave I made them suffer. Oh yes.'

Two days after Pieter had lent her his grandfather's journal, Anna once again drove north-east out of Cape Town along National Route 1 until she reached the turn-off to Stellenbosch and the valley lying in the mountains beyond. Oleander trees ran down the middle of the four-lane highway; the tyres of passing trucks hammered the concrete; it was difficult to imagine the existence of a world that had witnessed all the happenings that she had heard about from Anneliese, had read about in Deneys Wolmarans's journal.

The world goes on, Anna thought, gaining no satisfaction from the platitude, but it carries too much of the past, the evils never forgotten, the lust for vengeance that keeps wrongs alive forever.

Even now as she drove, she too was carrying with her the freight of the past: Deneys, riding through a desolation of burnt homes, ruined pastures; Anneliese rail-bound towards the fate that awaited her children and herself in the living death of the Koffiekraal concentration camp.

It was the most terrible of all the tales that Anneliese had told her; had told her, moreover, not simply to share the past but to ensure that her own hatred did not die with her but would remain to poison one more generation, and the next, and the one after that. Forever.

How wrong it was, how self-destructive! Yet could she in all honesty claim that in Anneliese's situation she would not have felt the same? Humanity's inhumanity, Anna thought. Dear God, what a terrible thing it is. Yet if we do not forgive, what hope is there for the world?

An hour after taking the Stellenbosch turn-off, Anna sat with Pieter Wolmarans on the *stoep* of *Oudekraal*. There was a bottle of wine upon the table and two glasses; the atmosphere between them was very different from how it had been at their first meeting.

Pieter admired the contents of his glass. The wine shone as red as rubies in the warm and shadowy air.

'Our own wine. Pinotage 1967; a good year.'

Ceremoniously he raised his glass. 'To *Oudekraal*. And the Wolmarans.' He looked at her thoughtfully. 'You are not married?'

'No.'

'You need a child. Children. All of us need that.'

'Not everyone would agree with you.'

'Children are eternity. The only eternity, I would say. Not that the dominee would agree with me.'

They sat side by side, the half-full glasses on the table between them. Above them leant the great oak tree that Colin Walmer had planted two hundred and forty years before. Beyond its green embrace, the rows of vines ran away until they joined the terraces stitching the slope of the mountain.

'You never married,' Anna said.

'The time never seemed right. A mistake. Now it is too late.'

'You're not so old.'

'Too old for a young wife. For any wife, perhaps.' He smiled ruefully. 'Over the years a man gets used to having his own way.' He sipped his wine, turning his head to look at her across the table. 'Don't make my mistake.'

He stood and refilled her glass. She smiled up at him, feeling completely comfortable with him now.

'1902,' she said.

'What about it?'

'When your grandfather came back from the war. At the end of his journal he mentions his homecoming, the big party they had, but he doesn't go into any details.'

Pieter laughed as he resumed his seat. 'There was a party, all right. Right over there, where the grapes are growing now. The field they called the *Nagmaalvlakte*. He told me about it himself.'

NINE

Deneys Wolmarans came home from the war in 1902, after they had signed the Peace at Pretoria.

He had sent word that he was coming. The telegraph service had been extended rapidly during the fighting and now covered most of the country. The commandos had cut the wires many times but the English had always patched them up and now, with the fighting over, the service was soon back in full working order again.

The trains were running as well. In theory Deneys could have come home by rail but there were tales of Boers being forced off the train in the middle of the desert to walk or die, as they chose, so he decided to come home as he had left, on the back of a horse.

The whole valley was waiting for him. They were afraid he might turn up in the middle of the night and catch them unprepared, so they set a team of small boys to look out for him along the road and send word as soon as he appeared. There were only the two roads in and out of the valley, so that part of it was easy.

Deneys had been at the war for almost three years, a long time in the life of a small boy who had not known him that well to begin with, so when, at four o'clock on the winter's afternoon, the first lookout saw a tall man riding up the trail over the pass, blonde beard over his chest and rifle butt sticking up from the saddle holster behind him, he wasn't sure if it was *Baas* Wolmarans or not.

Quite a responsibility for a child of eight. If he sent word and it was the wrong man, the people in the valley would skin him. If he said nothing and it turned out to be the right man after all ... He daren't imagine that.

The only thing to do was ask the stranger who he was, but he had never spoken to a stranger in his life. And from outside the valley! A big fierce man with a rifle who would shoot a small boy as soon as look at him, perhaps.

The boy watched as the rider drew near, riding slowly as though he had come a long way. He was sitting well back in the saddle, his feet in long stirrups. He wore a broad-brimmed black hat with a band around it and his clothes were covered in dust. The boy could hear the creak and jingle of the harness, the sound of the horse breathing.

There was nothing else for it. Heart pounding, he stepped onto the trail.

The rider reined in his horse and looked down at him. 'Who are you?' Unsmiling but with a quiet voice. He did not *sound* like a man who shot small boys.

Emboldened, the lookout said, 'Samuel, *baas*.'

One foot on top of the other, bare toes twisting into knots in the mud.

'Good evening, Samuel.'

'Good evening, *baas*. Excuse me, *baas*, are you *Baas* Wolmarans from the farm *Oudekraal*?'

A ghost of a smile touched the corners of the hard mouth. 'I am.'

They waited, looking at each other, the horse steaming gently in the chilly air.

'Did they send you to look out for me?'

Too much to answer such a question. The boy stood still, toes working, and said nothing.

The man smiled. 'Very well, Samuel. I will bid you good evening, then.'

He raised a gloved hand to the brim of his black hat and rode on. The boy stood, listening to the fading clop, clop of the hooves in the mud, then ran as hard as he could up the *koppie* behind him. The valley was swimming in dusk, the trees and hills grey in the fading light. Two hundred yards away, another small hillock stood out among the trees. Samuel's cousin was on duty there. Samuel waved and could just make out an arm lifted in acknowledgement. The *baas* had come just in time. Any later and it would have been too dark for the signalling system to have worked.

He clambered back to the bottom of the hill and started to run down the track towards the distant farms. The problem with being the smallest of the team was he had the furthest to run to get home again. When he was bigger, if the *Baas* decided to go off and kill anybody else, it would be someone else's job. He would see to that.

At *Oudekraal* all was ready.

Even for those who had stayed at home, things had not been easy. More than one family had received letters from relatives in the Transvaal, reproaching those who left kith and kin in the lurch while living off the fat of the land at home.

Christiaan's own daughter had lived in Lydenburg with her husband and their two children. His son had been in the war. Yet his land was here and it was the land that had settled it. God had given him *Oudekraal*. It was a sacred trust and he would not turn his back on it. So he stayed but his mind remained troubled. Divided loyalties can drain a man and by the end of the war Christiaan had aged a great deal.

Now the son at least was coming home safely. Not a scratch, after three years. Never mind that the war had been lost. Never mind that the son had been fighting against the English, who ruled in the Cape. Christiaan was determined that the return would be celebrated in a style that no one in the valley would ever forget.

First, the bonfire. Twenty feet tall, of shavings soaked in oil to get it started, then small sticks and branches broken into little pieces, then bigger branches and finally massive tree trunks to burn all night and half the next day as well.

The food, next. Pies and puddings and tarts and *konfyts* and chutneys. Snoek fish and lobsters from the coast. Salted pork and beef, ready in the pans. Apples and pears and pumpkins. Lemons, but no oranges; oranges grew in the Transvaal and there had been none since the war started. Broths to warm against the cold winter night. An ox on a spit over the fire and another smaller fire with a whole sheep turning above it. Wine and *mampoer* by the gallon, in barrels and jugs and buckets, to drink the health of the son and husband who had gone away and returned safely home.

If he turned up.

Christiaan, who three years earlier would never have troubled his head about such things, worried about the ox and sheep cooking over their separate fires. 'What if he doesn't come tonight?' he wondered.

'He sent us a telegraph from Worcester to say he'd be here,' Sara pointed out.

'But what if ...?'

'If he doesn't arrive, we will eat what we have tonight and do the whole thing again tomorrow.'

Of course she and Elizabeth had been ready for hours, both in their best bib and tucker and nothing to do but wait. They couldn't even interfere in the kitchen for fear of getting grease on their clothes. Besides, all had been taken care of, long before.

So they stood around and fussed and got in the way. It must have been quite a relief to the servants when the word finally came that Deneys had been spotted at the top of the pass and they could clear the pair of them out of the house and get on with things.

Everyone who lived in the valley had been invited, as always, but it was too far for the farmers over the mountain, not knowing whether Deneys would turn up or not. The new dominee was there, though. The old man who had objected so much to coming out from Stellenbosch had taken his final journey while Deneys had been away, and his place had been taken by Theunis de Wit, a young man with a great love of God's people and His church.

Christiaan and Theunis de Wit had decided to hold the party in the *Nagmaalvlagte*. One or two eyebrows had been raised over that, people who thought that a field dedicated to the service of God should not be used for a welcome home party, particularly where there was a distinct possibility that a fair amount of liquor would be consumed. But as the dominee said, Deneys's safe return after three years of war was a reason to praise God and what better place could there be for that than the field set aside for the monthly communion? Christiaan said if they didn't like it they could stay away, which would mean all the more food for everyone else, and that put an end to their nonsense.

So there was a big crowd around the bonfire that night. The ox and the sheep were turning on their spits, and the light from the fires flickered on the leaves of the trees and the faces of the people. Enough drink had been provided to keep people warm and interested, but not so much that they were likely to fall down before Deneys arrived. Sparks rose into the velvet sky along with the murmur of voices, the occasional cry of a child. The air was heavy with smoke and the smell of cooking meat.

Christiaan pulled his watch from his waistcoat pocket and inspected it. An hour since Deneys had been spotted at the top of the pass. If he came straight — and where else should he go? — he would be here in fifteen minutes.

He climbed slowly up the steps, feeling the muscles in his legs, and went inside the house. He was only fifty-three and his belly was as flat as ever, but his body was beginning to remind him of the passing years. In the *voorkamer* Sara and Elizabeth were waiting. Very smart they looked. Full skirts of grey silk descended to the floor from tight waists; fitted bodices were tucked and pleated and worn high to the throat; their hats, massive confections of bows and feathers, stylishly aslant. Christiaan himself had put on a three-piece tweed suit, stiff white collar and cravat. He wondered what Deneys would think, after fighting for so long against the English, to come home and find his family all dolled up in the latest London fashions, but at once put the thought out of his head. Fashion was fashion. It had nothing to do with patriotism.

'Fifteen minutes,' he said. 'Time to light the bonfire.'

The three of them walked down the steps. Christiaan went to the ox fire and thrust a long piece of dry wood into the hot charcoal. The carcass of the ox leaked fat, its skin brown and shining, and the heat and smell of the meat assailed him. He stood, left hand raised to protect his face, until the wood was well ablaze, then walked across to the dark shape of the bonfire where the two women were waiting.

He pushed the brand firmly into the base of the bonfire. The kindling caught at once. Christiaan stepped back. Flames crackled and began to work their way through the structure of the bonfire. Amid the oohs and aahs of the crowd, sparks rose in orange clouds into the night.

Christiaan got hold of a couple of the servants.

'Champagne,' he ordered. 'And bring out the wine and *mampoer*.'

He scrambled up on a table and raised his hands. An imperfect silence fell, broken by the excited cries of children, the roar of the bonfire.

He raised his voice to be heard in every corner of the shadowed field. 'My son will be with us shortly. They are bringing wine and brandy. Rum for those who prefer it. There is plenty for everyone. The food will be ready soon. In the meantime drink deep, enjoy yourselves and join with us in celebrating my son's return.'

There was a rowdy cheer, repeated as the servants staggered out with the barrels and set them out in rows, well away from the fires. Christiaan had seen what happened when a barrel of spirit caught fire — he'd heard that Cecil Rhodes's own brother had died when a keg of rum exploded in his tent — and was going to have none of that at *Oudekraal*.

Men and women queued to take glasses brimming with liquor from the servants. The bonfire roared, casting flickering patterns of black and red across the figures of the guests. Everywhere was the sound of voices and laughter. A mounted figure appeared between the flares burning along both sides of the driveway. Suddenly all was still.

There was a lump as big as an apple in Christiaan's throat. He stepped out of the crowd of waiting people. The firelight rippled across his white hair and beard as his son came cantering down the last fifty yards of his long journey home.

Then Deneys was out of the saddle, the horse still moving, and the two men were hugging each other close while cheers erupted about them and Christiaan felt the hot tears wet upon his cheeks.

More muscle than when he went away. Thinner; I'll swear he's grown taller, too. Although he's still got some way to go to catch me.

'Return of the prodigal,' Deneys murmured in his ear.

'We have the fatted calf waiting for you,' he answered.

Three years of waiting, he thought, and the first thing we talk about is food. And smiled to himself, knowing it was to do with a great deal more than food.

Deneys freed himself and turned to his mother and his wife and then Christiaan was up on the table again, with everyone banging their glasses and shouting for silence, and slowly the hubbub died.

Christiaan looked down at the faces. He heard the crackle and roar of the bonfire, saw the tables covered with food, smelt the meat cooking over the fires. He had planned to speak of the war that was ended, the loss and the tragedy of war. Of the men who would not be coming home, their own grandchildren and son-in-law who had died, the daughter who had gone no one knew where. Now the moment had come, he found he could say none of it.

He threw his arms wide. 'My son has come back to us. I will ask the dominee to give thanks.'

Theunis de Wit climbed up on the table beside him. He smiled at Christiaan. 'Will it hold us, you think?' He turned to the people and raised his voice. 'Let us give thanks to our Lord God for having vouchsafed that Deneys Wolmarans should have returned safely to his family and to us all.'

'Amen,' said the crowd, faces lowered.

'Let us pray that the enmity that has divided this land will pass with the return of peace.'

'Amen.'

'Let us pray that those whose sons will not be returning, those who have lost friends and relatives, may find peace and consolation in the love of God.'

'Amen.'

'Let us pray that we may all live out our lives for the betterment of our fellow men in accordance with the teachings of our Lord Jesus Christ.'

'Amen.'

'Let us say together. Our Father ...'

At the end of the prayers, both men got down from the table and the party began. It went slowly to begin with, the sound and weight of the prayers sober in people's minds, but soon grew more lively. There was eating and drinking, talking and shouting, laughter and a little crying. There was even some dancing, impromptu and not well executed, but fun for those who tried it and pleasurable to those who liked to have something to grumble about.

All the food went, amazingly, and the drink and, eventually, the people.

The fires burned down. One by one, the flares sputtered out. The servants removed the plates and scraps of food from the tables, then the tables themselves were taken away. Christiaan and the rest of the family went into the house. The lights went out and a light rain began to fall on the trampled field. Dawn broke with no trumpets for the returned warrior but grey and chilly, with heavy cloud over the mountains.

Side by side in bed, as they had been nearly every night of their married life, Christiaan and Sara held each other briefly, sharing the emotions, the relief and sorrows of the day.

'I'm too old for these late nights,' Christiaan grumbled.

Sara smiled in the darkness. 'Whose idea was it to have the party?'

'You think we should have let him sneak in the back way, like a thief?'

'I don't care which way he sneaked in, so long as he's home.'

He could hear the smile in her voice. 'It wouldn't have suited me,' he said. 'Or the neighbours. Or Deneys. Or you, if the truth be told.' He looked up at the ceiling, loving her as he had for over thirty years. 'You know how much that dress and hat cost me, woman?'

'I knew you would never be satisfied with anything less than a huge party,' she said comfortably. 'How could I not dress for it?'

They both smiled, together in the darkness.

'So much hatred,' Sara said softly, and he knew she was smiling no longer. 'All those dead. Will things ever go back to how they were?'

'After so much blood? Impossible. I can forgive the loss of the men; that is war. But the women and little children I shall never forgive.'

'Our own grandchildren.'

Suddenly she was weeping, her face buried in his shoulder. 'We never even saw them.'

He held her gently, grieving with her.

And our son-in-law, he thought, but did not say. In comparison with the death of the children, the father's mattered less. In the end, it was blood that counted, nothing else.

'At least Deneys has been spared.'

'And Anneliese? What of her?'

Again silence, both knowing that they might never see their daughter again.

'Each day I pray to find the power to forgive them,' Sara said, 'but in my heart I know I never shall.'

In their own bedroom Deneys and Elizabeth were talking, too.

'I prayed. Every day. I find it hard to believe that you are here at last.'

Her hand lay open on his thigh, but quietly. She was shy of this man, after so long apart.

'I tried not to think at all,' he said. 'Everything — you, *Oudekraal* — was like a dream, something I'd had once, but lost. It was too painful to think.'

'Something you had once but lost,' she repeated. 'That is not true, at any event.'

'Thank God.'

She took his hand, playing softly with his fingers.

'Is it over?' she asked.

'The fighting, yes. But for some the war will never be over.'

'Anneliese,' she said sadly.

He did not deny it.

'I wrote when I heard. She didn't reply.'

She had survived the camp, that was all they knew. No one had heard from her since she was released.

'If I were in her place, I would feel the same,' Deneys believed.

'Why doesn't she at least let us know she's alive? What happened is not our fault. She has no business blaming us.'

'I think, at the moment, she blames the whole world for what happened.'

'God help her, then. God help us all.'

'Amen.'

They were silent for a while, then she turned on her side to face him. 'You will be tired after your long journey.'

'Yes.'

'It is very late. You need to sleep.'

He began to smile in the darkness. 'That, too. Presently.'

'Presently?'

He ran his hands through her hair, feeling its silkiness between his fingers. 'I have come a long way. Not just this journey; I mean all through the war.' He felt the weight and weariness of that journey as he spoke. 'I'll tell you about it, sometime. But for now —'

'Yes?'

'I want to be home again.'

'You are home again.'

'Not quite.' Again he ran his hands through her hair and over her body, and it was like coming back from a far place so that he could not tell which was real, this or what had gone before. She lifted her face to kiss him and he touched her again, very gently, and little by little Deneys and Elizabeth Wolmarans came home again together at last.

A month later, trudging on broken boots, there arrived at *Oudekraal*'s front door the Irishman Dominic Riordan, who had been with Deneys on the long journey into the scorched devastation of the Eastern Transvaal.

Deneys was not pleased to see him. Dominic had been a good comrade — turbulent and undisciplined, it was true, too much inclined to go his own way — but they had fought side by side for two years and in those circumstances a man forgives much. His reservations came from a different source. He wanted nothing in his life to remind him of the horrors of the past three years and Dominic brought with him the stench of the war that Deneys had sworn to forget.

Dominic was trouble; from what he had told him during the long nights when they had been on commando together, he had been so all his life. It ran in the family, apparently.

'It's why I'm here at all,' Dominic said. 'In 1849 my grandfather, God save him, killed an Englishman in County Clare and got away with my grandmother to Australia. My father was born on the journey, so I was the first member of my family to be born there, on the opposite side of the world from Ireland which still holds my heart and always will, although I have never seen it.'

When Dominic was grown his father — a wild and harsh man, seemingly, of whom Dominic spoke with great affection and respect — went into the horse-breeding business. As soon as Dominic was old enough, he joined him.

'Times were hard; indeed, when weren't they hard for penniless Irish immigrants? From time to time there were ill-wishers willing to swear that some of the beasts in our yard had no business to be there at all.'

Dominic had laughed uproariously until hushed by the others, afraid he would be heard by the English patrols who were thick on the ground in those parts.

'And what of that? If a horse strays, I'd regard it as an act of Christian kindness to give him a home and some of the fences in our part of the country were purely terrible.'

All the same, horse-stealing was a grave offence, so the Riordans had to watch their step. The police never managed to catch them, although Dominic spoke of nights when he lay out in the timber high above their selection — 'it means farm,' he explained to the others — with half a dozen horses in tow, while all hell was breaking loose in the valley below him. In the end things got too hot for them so they moved up into the high country. When they got there they found their reputation had preceded them. After that it was a case of moving on to survive at all. Survive they did, by the skin of their teeth, with one or two days of excitement thrown in but, as Dominic said, a bit of excitement never harmed a man, did it now?

Eventually Dominic's Da picked a site just below a ridge at the top of the range. They built a wooden house and lived there like eagles above the timbered valley — his parents, sister and himself — until 1899. In that year, when Dominic was twenty-two, word came that there was a war for the asking over the sea in a place they called South Africa. They were calling for volunteers to go to fight for Queen and Empire, and several of the Riordans' neighbours were hot to join.

Once again Dominic laughed. 'I'd as soon stick a bayonet up my arse as fight for an English queen, but I was mortal sick of living the way we were, hand to mouth with the squatters and the police down on us at every turn, so when I heard there were one or two fellows being sponsored secretly by the Feinian Society to fight for the other side — and how else could it have been but secretly? — I let it be known I might be interested.'

He went to Sydney where he met a fellow who said he could arrange things for him. Dominic knew his Da wouldn't like it, and him with the business to take care of, but his mind was made up. Next thing he knew, he had a ticket in his pocket and was off to fight for Johnny Boer.

Who suspected him to begin with, wondering what an Irishman from Australia was doing fighting against the Empire, but they saw soon enough that he was as hot for the fight as the best of them. Things were all right after that.

Dominic grew up in that war, like everyone else who survived. He saw things he would never forget or talk of, things that he knew would haunt his dreams for the rest of his life. The journey he made with Deneys in 1901 to the Eastern Transvaal was one of the worst. It marked a turning point in his life. He had been brought up to hate the English but, in fact, had never known what real hatred was. Until he went to Lydenburg the war had been no more than a game, a scrap with himself on the receiving end more often than not, but nothing to take too seriously. On that journey he learned the real meaning of hatred.

In the last days of the fighting, he took a fool bullet in his shoulder. He was in the hospital in Middelburg when word of the surrender came through. There were several there who could have blown their brains out at the news. But didn't, of course.

After he was discharged from the hospital, Dominic had to decide what he wanted to do. The Transvaal had nothing for him now, red-coats everywhere he looked, but he had no wish to go back to Australia either. He even thought of Ireland, but no one was handing out free tickets to go there so that was out.

In the end he headed south-west, to the Cape. Deneys had told him a lot about that part of the country and to Dominic it had sounded a wonderful place, all lush and green and as different from the Transvaal as could be.

There had been no fighting there, either, and after three years of nothing else he thought he could do with a break from fighting.

The Cape was a thousand miles from Middelburg so it took a while, but he made it in the end. He found his old comrade, sure enough, and a little after that certain other things happened and Dominic found that he had not managed to put the war behind him, after all.

Deneys had been home for six months when Sarel Henning and his family moved into the district. He bought the little store from Isaak Kok's widow and in no time was making a good thing out of it. He was a good-looking man, thirty years old perhaps, tall and well-set, with a neat cap of curly brown hair and an open, smiling face. Always neat, always polite, and his young wife and two little girls were the same.

They did not say where they were from. Nobody asked; there were too many tragedies in people's lives to ask questions like that, but the Hennings had the accent of the Transvaal so everyone assumed they came from there. At least they hadn't been burnt out; those people had nothing and the Hennings had money enough to buy the store and stock it, too. Not that it mattered. Only Dominic Riordan looked at him and then again, frowning.

'I know that face from somewhere,' he said.

It was a cold, wet year. Rain fell for days on end, and on the high ground snow lay from June right through until late spring. Everywhere was mud and water. The rain found holes in the roofs where no one had known they existed and inside the houses the air was dank. Even the biggest fires did little to keep the damp out, and clothes went mouldy in the cupboards. Torrents poured from the mountain and the river rose until it was a sinuous mass of brown water heavy with silt and tree branches and drowned animals. Silent except for the occasional slip and slide of clay falling from the banks, it powered its way through the valley, a distant stranger to the chuckling stream of summer.

In mid-August, after it had rained non-stop for a whole week, the river burst its banks and spread far and wide through the valley. The bare branches of the vines stuck imploringly above the flood like the arms of drowning men. The footbridge that had spanned the river as long as anyone could remember was washed away. The *drifs* had been impassable for weeks and now, with the bridge gone, there was no communication between the east side of the valley and the west.

And still it rained.

High up the valley on the far side of the river was a tongue of land with a cottage housing Avril Hendricks, his wife and child. The land was too high for grapes so the owners ran sheep instead, and Avril Hendricks was a shepherd. He was up the mountain with the flock and his wife and baby were alone in the cottage when the river came over the tongue of land. The next thing they knew, it was inside the house and still rising.

It happened at night and nobody knew anything about it until early next morning, when cries were heard by some labourers. It was barely light when Deneys was told that Mrs Hendricks and the child were marooned on the roof of their house with the water halfway up the walls. He rode up there at once. Early though he was, a few others had beaten him to it, Sarel Henning and Dominic Riordan among them.

They looked at the raging river, a hundred yards wide now, then at each other. With neither bridge nor boats, they could do nothing.

The cottage was still there but, as they watched, one of the walls started to go. The roof settled wearily into the water and the next thing was rushing away down river, the woman still on it, the child in her arms. She did not cry or call out as the water swept her away; perhaps she was too wet and cold for that.

'Is there a rope? A long rope?' Sarel Henning with his hard Transvaal accent.

Several of the men had ropes with them. 'What do you want with them?'

'The big pool,' he said.

They understood him at once. In normal conditions the river formed a deep pool a little below his store. Here the water slowed before hurtling down the valley to the rapids at the far end. Assuming it had not already fallen to pieces, there was a chance that when it reached the pool the roof might be pushed out of the main flow of the current — in which case it might be possible to save them after all.

'Come,' Sarel urged and come they did, riding pell-mell down the bank. They reached the pool and reined in, staring at the floodwaters. It was not an encouraging sight. The river gnashed its teeth as it rushed between the branches of the trees that lined what had been its banks. What was left of the roof was indeed floating in the pool, but on the far side of the stream where no one could get at it. In mid-channel the current cut a sinewy line as it headed for the rapids. The roof lay low in the water, turning lazily as it drifted inexorably back towards the stream. Once the current had it, the disintegrating roof would be swept into the rapids. If that happened, God himself would be unable to save them.

Sarel Henning turned in his saddle, gesturing. 'Give me the rope.' With one end secured to his saddle horn and the rest of them paying it out behind him, he rode into the water.

At first the horse made good progress but, in midstream, things became difficult. Although Sarel had aimed well up-river, the current carried them down so fast that it looked as though they would never be able to cross at all.

To make things easier, he slipped off the horse's back and swam alongside it, one foot in the stirrup and his hands clasping the saddle horn. All the men could see were the two heads straining above the brown flood as horse and man swam on, the rope like a drawn bow behind them. On the far side of the channel, the roof was sinking lower and lower in the water while the rain continued to pour down. No one could see how Sarel Henning could hope to make it but eventually he did. The two heads appeared beyond the line of the stream and, in no time after that, they had reached the roof.

As soon as he had secured the rope to one of the roof trusses, the watchers on the bank lashed their end to a team of horses and set them in motion. Snorting, necks arched, they began to haul. The rope came clear of the water, droplets of water springing from it as it drew taut. Slowly the thatch began to move. As it reached the current it tried to get away down river but somehow, slipping and blowing, the horses held it. The rope was wire-tight, its thin shriek like a needle in the ear. Still the horses hauled, moving step by step away from the bank. Around the roof a lick of dirty foam showed where the current continued to fight it, yet still it came on.

The song of the rope grew higher until, when the roof was two-thirds of the way to safety, the roof truss pulled out.

The horses were down on their knees. Still lashed to the wooden truss, the rope catapulted towards the bank. It crashed with the force of an artillery shell into the trees.

The roof disintegrated. Bits and pieces of thatch were snatched away by the current. The woman was hanging onto the bridle of the horse with one hand, the other desperately clasping the child. With agonising slowness Sarel shoved her up on the horse's back. The watchers on the bank, less than thirty yards away now, could see that both he and the horse were exhausted after struggling so long in the icy water. The woman's head drooped against the horse's neck. It was quite possible that the lot of them would drown before they could reach the bank.

Then they heard Sarel Henning shout hoarsely at the beast, urging it on. Miraculously, the horse gathered its muscles again, fighting its way through the water until at last its hooves touched bottom. It gave a heave and shudder and dragged itself and its human cargo into the shallows.

The child slipped from the woman's grasp and fell into the river.

She screamed. The baby gave one mewling cry, and the muddy water covered it. Sarel slapped the horse's flank with all his might and, as the animal staggered, swaying and shivering up the bank, dived beneath the water.

He could see nothing. It was futile. He knew it, was furious at the river, the stupid bitch of a woman, at himself. He gave up, returned gasping to the surface.

You're a fool, he told himself. And dived.

Came up again, just avoiding the branches of a tree as it swept past.

Give it up, he thought. The brat is gone. And dived.

The air like daggers in his lungs now. Are you trying to drown yourself? Dived, for one last time. Again, for one last time. Again, the cold and lack of air deadly now. And found the child.

It was chance, a blind groping of the hands in water that was too thick for sight. He brushed against something, felt the roughness of clothing, lost it. Dived deeper, lungs screaming, blood pounding in his head, and found it. Brought it up to the light.

It is certain to be dead, he thought. So long underwater. It will be dead.

He brought it to the bank. Hands snatched it from him. He lay in the shallows, too exhausted to move. Willing arms hauled him out. He lay on his back in the mud, heart thundering, breath surging in his chest, his whole body shaking fit to break.

'We must get him into a bath of hot water,' Deneys said. 'And quickly, too, or he will die on us.'

At Deneys's voice, Henning's eyes opened. He tried to speak but was shaking so badly that no one could understand his words. He tried again. 'The ... the child?'

'Will be fine.'

And so, incredibly, it was. Half the night in freezing rain, dragged through the icy river on the back of a horse, underwater for what had seemed hours. Now fit and well, screaming fit to burst. Not six months old. Some children, Deneys thought, are born to be indestructible.

The woman came to Henning's side as he lay there. She knelt in the mud beside him and took his cold hands and chafed them between her own, while the tears ran down her brown face. 'Thank you for my child, *meneer*,' she said.

'He needs the hospital,' Deneys said to Dominic Riordan.

And Dominic stared at him with sudden awareness. He clicked his fingers. 'Hospital,' he said. A wild beast looked out of his eyes. 'That's where it was.'

The next day Dominic Riordan rode over to *Oudekraal*. Deneys saw him coming and his heart sank. Instinctively he knew that the gaunt figure was bringing trouble but smiled, hiding his feelings as Riordan dismounted.

'Morning, Dominic.'

The Irishman's eyes were hard, lines like razor slashes in the hungry-looking face. 'I'll be having a word with you, Deneys, if it's not an intrusion.'

'Of course.'

'Sarel Henning.'

'Better, thank God. And the woman and child.'

'I've been thinking where I saw him before. It was when you said he should be in the hospital that I remembered. You mind I was in hospital myself, at the end?'

'Yes.' Watching.

'That's where I saw him. In uniform.'

Deneys frowned. The Boers had never worn uniform, unless it was bits and pieces of English uniforms to cover their nakedness when their own clothes fell to pieces. 'What uniform was that?'

Dominic's breath hissed like a snake in his throat. 'Cronje's Scouts.'

The arch-traitors, the *hensoppers* who had not merely given up but fought for the English against their own flesh and blood.

Deneys had known it must be something of the sort. He had seen how Riordan had smiled, with teeth, when he had finally remembered where he had seen Sarel Henning before. Yet now felt only weariness that even here, far from the fighting, the war had once again laid its blight upon them.

'The war is over,' he said, knowing it was not.

Pale fire in Riordan's eyes, then. 'Your brother-in-law is dead. His children are dead. Your sister is lost, perhaps dead with all the rest. And you tell me the war is over?'

'We took the oath. Both of us.'

'So I could keep my rifle. So I could fight them again the first chance I got!' Dominic's eyes blazed. 'Your niece and nephew dead because of people like Henning. That means so little to you?'

'The war is over,' Deneys repeated heavily. 'We all fought as our consciences told us. Some on our side, some on theirs. Now it is finished. Let us have no more killing.'

Riordan spat. 'Of course, you have an English wife.'

One stride and Deneys had his hands in Dominic's shirt below his chin. He lifted him on his toes. 'Meaning *what*?'

The pale eyes glared; Riordan was half-choking but not ready to back off. 'It's the truth.'

'You say that to me? After all we've been through together?'

Deneys dropped him like a sack of offal and turned away.

Behind him, Riordan said, 'For some of us, the war will never be over.' He sneered. 'Fat Edward ... I'd as soon swear allegiance to a pig. The oath means nothing, I tell you. Nothing.'

'It means something to me.'

Deneys did not turn and presently he heard the clip-clop of hooves as Dominic Riordan rode away.

TEN

Two days later the Wolmarans were having tea in the drawing room. It had been raining heavily again; now, at four o'clock in the afternoon, it was already dark and the servants were lighting the lamps.

Christiaan and Sara sat close to the big fireplace, their bodies soaking up the heat. Deneys and Elizabeth had joined them for tea, as they did most afternoons, but sitting further from the fire. Deneys had taken over the running of the farm since he had come back from the war and this ritual of the tea was often inconvenient, but it meant so much to his parents that he kept to it whenever he could.

A housemaid appeared in the doorway. 'Madam . . .'

On the vine terraces Deneys might be in charge, but in the house Sara was still queen and not about to let anyone forget it. She looked through her spectacles at the maid's uncertainty. The girl hadn't been with them long and was still not fully trained.

'What is it, Hester?'

'There is a madam to see you . . .'

'What is her name?'

The girl shook her head in confusion.

Deneys stood up. 'I'll see to it.'

By the front door, a woman like a bundle of sticks in a shabby black dress. A small cloth bag lay in a puddle of water at her feet. Everything about her — clothes, bag, the white hair, long and untended, that lay like rats' tails about her face — was soaked by the rain that Deneys could hear drumming on the thatch.

He walked forward. 'Can I help you?'

A hand, skeleton-thin, groped towards him. 'Deneys...?'

He stared, eyes wide. 'My God!'

Two strides. He folded her in his arms. She leant against him, sobbing. She was cold, so cold, and inside the wet clothes there seemed nothing to her at all.

Anneliese van der Merwe had come home to *Oudekraal* in the rain.

No wonder he had not recognised her; her appearance shocked them all. Her face was drawn and haggard, all grey skin and sunken temples. She was bone thin and her hair, which had been dark and lustrous, with chestnut fire in it, was white. Feverish eyes, too large for the face, burned in shadowed sockets.

My sister, Deneys thought. Two years older than I am. She looks older than my mother.

She told them she had caught a train to Worcester and thence to Stellenbosch.

'How did you get here from Stellenbosch?' Deneys asked.

Her grin was ghastly. 'I walked.'

Fifteen miles through the mountains in the pouring rain.

Overjoyed though they were to see her, there was awkwardness. She had been away so long and endured so many terrible experiences that she had become a stranger. Their minds were full of the concentration camp, of her dead husband and children, but she didn't mention them and so, nervous of her and her grief, neither did they. Instead they prattled on about homely things: the problems of the house, the servants, the farm, prices, the latest fashions in Cape Town, the weather.

They offered her food but she shook her head, saying she could eat nothing. She sat in their midst, perched on the edge of her chair, shoulders tense beneath the stained blouse. And all the time the huge eyes, too bright in the wasted face, prowled the corners of the room, the shadows, watching and watching.

Until at last, none too soon, Elizabeth took her away in search of a bath and bed in the room she had not seen these many years. Later, back in the living room, Elizabeth reported that Anneliese was asleep.

'Did she say anything?'

A shake of the head. 'Not a word.'

Next day Deneys was in the office he had built at one end of the wine cellar, checking the paperwork for a shipment of wine that was scheduled to leave that afternoon.

The war had spawned a gigantic bureaucracy whose sole purpose seemed to be to create work by increasing tenfold the pieces of paper that had to be filled in and sent to Cape Town. These forms covered every aspect of the farm's existence. Returns of this. Records of that. Acres under which cultivars. Numbers of workers, condition of housing, medical records ... Inspectors, too, who descended without notice to check who knew what. No end to it.

'Tell them to go to hell,' Christiaan growled, but Deneys never forgot that the authorities knew he had fought against them. He had taken the Peace Oath and meant every word of it, but could not be sure that they believed him. He hoped that dutifully completing their idiot forms might be one way to convince them of his sincerity. Whatever the Dominic Riordans of the world might think, Deneys Wolmarans wanted no trouble.

The office's stone-flagged floor was bare. There was a plain wooden desk, a couple of upright chairs, shelves crammed with papers. A plan of the farm hung on one wall, showing the areas under cultivation and the types of grape produced in each. There were timetables for spraying and weeding, and over everything hung the sour thin smell of the wine.

'This is new.'

Anneliese stood in the doorway.

'I had it put in. There's too much paperwork to keep everything up at the house.'

'Keeping our masters happy,' she said.

She moved restlessly, picking up this, inspecting that. Eventually she turned and smiled without humour, eyes as hectic as ever in the wasted face.

'Well ...'

He couldn't bear the way they were all ignoring the one thing that above all others they had in their minds. He went to her and took her hands in his, feeling her fingers like sticks between his own.

'I'm so sorry ...'

Her eyes scoured his face. 'Sorry?'

He gestured helplessly. 'About everything.'

She freed her hands and took a couple of steps away from the desk, the heels of her boots going click clack on the stone flags. Restless fingers picked at pieces of paper, put them back. 'Everyone's sorry.' She moved again. Click clack. In the lamplight, her shadow reared against the whitewashed wall. 'You're sorry.' Click clack. 'Father and mother are sorry, even though they can't bring themselves to say so.' Click clack. 'Even the damned English are sorry.' She turned to him, mouth tight, eyes violent. 'You know what happened at the end, before they let us out? This senior officer addressed us. There were about six hundred of us by then, where before there'd been over a thousand. They'd killed the rest. And this man with a moustache like a paintbrush standing up and telling us he was sorry. He said these things happen in war and we must all put it behind us. Start again, he said. From now on we shall be friends.' The dark eyes flamed. 'Look at me,' Anneliese said. 'I'm twenty-eight years old and I look sixty. My husband is dead. My children are dead. They burnt my home. Everything I care about is gone. I have no life in front of me, nothing at all. And that man says he's sorry.' Her dry eyes glittered in the lamplight. 'Well, I'm sorry, too. But it won't bring them back. Nothing on God's earth will do that.'

Deneys watched her helplessly, his heart bleeding as hers was bleeding. But could do nothing.

'I'll tell you something,' Anneliese said, lips ferocious. 'Something this war has taught us. Never again shall we permit anyone to stand over us. Never! Anyone tries, we shall cut them down. There will be no more dead children in our story.'

Deneys watched his sister, the lamp casting flickering shadows across her face. Darkness on darkness, he thought.

'What will you do?'

'Stay here, I suppose. If you permit,' she challenged him.

Patience, he told himself. 'This is your home. Where else would you go?'

She lifted her hands, dropped them helplessly at her side. 'I went back to *Uitkyk*. There was nothing there.' Now the blackness shadowed voice as well as face. 'Natives live there now. You people,' she accused him, as though everything that had happened had been his fault, 'you don't know what it was like.'

He was indignant. 'I was in the war, first to last. No one ever saw me with my hands in the air.'

'The war . . .'

She dismissed it.

He was annoyed. 'We lost a lot of men, too.'

She smiled unpleasantly, letting her eyes trail around the sturdy cellar, the racked bottles of wine. 'You seem to have done all right. No fires here.'

'I'm sorry if it disappoints you.' Stiff with sarcasm.

She gave nothing. 'You men went off to the war like it was a game. No woman wanted it. We got it, though. And it was our children who died.'

'Not just your children. Stoffel and Amalie were Dirk's children, too. And he also died.'

'He *wanted* to go.' As though that cancelled all the later suffering. 'We didn't.'

Who had suffered most — a futile argument.

'They even took their bodies from me,' Anneliese said.

Deneys frowned. 'How?'

'I don't know where Dirk is buried. I never saw him dead. They could have lied to me. Maybe he never died at all. Maybe he just ran away.'

'Why should he do that?'

'To get away from me?' She laughed, something like a chuckle bubbling wildly beneath the laugh. 'Could you blame him?'

His heart turned, choking in his throat. 'God, Anneliese —'

'I saw the children die, though. Oh yes. I closed their eyes.'

She rounded on him. 'You are so proud you fought in the war. What do you know about *that*?'

There was nothing he could say. He eyed her helplessly, in silence.

'They put them in one grave. All. There are hundreds there.' She stood in a shadowed corner of the room, the lamplight just touching the wet of her eyes and mouth. 'Tell me, soldier,' she whispered from the dark corner. 'You who fought so bravely in the war. Tell me what I have to do to bring my children back to *Oudekraal*?' She raised her voice. 'Dig them up? Is that what I do? Dig them up and work out which ones are mine?'

He had no words. He stood and opened his arms. She hesitated, swaying, then the black hatred faded from her face and she ran to him. He held her close. Then, at last, she wept.

'Even dead they have taken them from me,' she whispered. 'Even dead.'

Pain shuddered in her voice. She clung to him, tears streaming down her face. Then, suddenly, still clasped in his arms, she sighed and was at once asleep, her head on his shoulder.

Gently, Deneys laid her down on the scrap of carpet before his desk. He placed his woollen coat over her. She did not stir but lay like one dead, the breath sighing in her breast.

He looked down at her. What she had said was true. He had fought all through the war. He had known death and suffering; through the long years had inflicted both. He had listened to the woman of Lydenburg, seen the stark and blackened skeletons of the torched farms. He had known nothing.

He went and sat again at his desk. He stared at the papers arranged so neatly on its surface, at the darkness puddling the corners of the cellar. His sister's chuckling laughter filled his ears.

Later that evening, after Anneliese had gone like one drugged to her bed, his mother, drawn with worry, found him.

'How is she?'

He shook his head. 'I wonder if she will ever be whole again.'

Daggers in his mother's eyes. 'She is tired, that is all! With rest, with love, she will recover.'

'I hope so. Perhaps.'

He did not say what he was thinking: that from some forms of tiredness no recovery is possible. Yet his mother seemed to read the thought through his silence.

'Those damned people ...' It was the first time he had ever known her to swear. She stared into the guttering candle flame and he saw the light dancing red and golden in her eyes. 'They had half a million men. Guns, too. They could have taken the Republics a dozen times, but that was too easy. They had to kill the women and children too.'

Groping, Deneys sought words of consolation. 'It was the war.'

'War?' Sara laughed without smiling, eyes on the flame. 'They have taken everything from her. Her husband, her home, her children. All she has left is her hate. Well, I will join her in that, I believe.'

His mother, who had never hated a soul in her life.

'Kitchener and Milner are to blame,' Deneys said. 'They will burn in hell for it. God will see to that.'

'If there is a hell,' Sara said, 'Apart from here. If there is a God.' She clenched her fists and raised them in the wine-scented air. 'My own grandchildren. Whom I shall never see. I curse the English for what they have done to this family, this land. I curse them from my heart.'

'It is a strange business,' Pieter said.

There had been other journals that Deneys had written during the years after the war. Anna had not been aware of their existence but Pieter had produced them, a conjurer opening the magic box of history or at least one man's version of it. He had read sections aloud, articulating each word with care, his sense of language and of the events that the journal described combining to bring the past shining into the present.

'These books have lain here all my life. I read them long ago but for years I have never looked at them. It never occurred to me there was any need. I took it for granted that everything in them was set fast in my brain. In my heart, too, perhaps. Yet talking about it with you now, reading bits and pieces, has made me realise how much I had forgotten. Not the facts — they are nothing — but the feelings behind the facts, the knowledge that the story of Christiaan and Deneys and Anneliese, everything that happened to them, forms a tapestry of my family's life that leads right here. To me.' His clenched fist smote himself softly on the chest and his face was full of wonder. 'It reminds me of what I am, a part of everything that has gone before.'

'Not only that,' Anna said. 'Those things are part of you, as well.'

'That is true. I have to thank you,' he said. 'If you had not come here with all your questions, I might have died not knowing how much of myself I had forgotten.'

'Why did he write in English?' Anna wondered.

'I asked him that, once. He said because English was the language of the future. It may have been partly that, but he loved the English language for its own sake, I think. There are shelves of books in his study, all of them well used, most of them in English. To speak English in those days was not an easy thing, even here in the Cape. The war was over but for some people, and Anneliese was one of them, it would never be over. To this day there are those, particularly in the north, who will not speak English if they can avoid it.' He sighed. 'I think sometimes that there are people who will go on waging war in their hearts forever. Because they have forgotten or maybe never knew there is an alternative.'

'The first day I came here,' Anna said, 'I wondered whether you might be one of them.'

He laughed. 'Lucky for you I'm not.'

She shared the laugh. 'I can look after myself.'

'Good. I am glad to hear you say it. This is a land where one needs to be able to do that.'

Inside the house the phone rang. Pieter went to answer it, in a minute returned. 'For you ...'

She walked, frowning, to the phone. Picked it up. 'Hullo?'

Mark's voice, very formal, mindful of ears that might be listening. 'I've heard from our friend. He wants to see you.'

Her heart bumped. 'When?'

'Tonight.'

'I'll come straightaway.'

She walked back outside. Pieter was sitting in his chair, one of Deneys's journals in his hand. He was not reading but looking up past the rows of vines at the mountains, and she thought he was once again tying his present to his past, renewing the unity of everything that had happened in this place.

He turned his eyes towards her as she walked along the *stoep* to join him.

'Something's come up. I have to go, I'm afraid.'

'You will come again?'

'Tomorrow. If you'll have me.'

The blue eyes watched her keenly. 'Perhaps you, too, are getting something out of our talks,' he suggested.

She was, more than she would have thought possible, but was shy of admitting it. 'It's just that I'm running out of time. I have to be back in Australia very soon.'

From his expression she knew he believed there was more to it than that. '*Oudekraal* has become part of your life,' he said.

Driving back to the city, Anna wondered if that were true. Coming here had certainly brought her a new sense of unity, an extra dimension that until now she had not even realised she was missing, but whether it would survive her return to Australia was another matter.

Time enough to find that out, later. In the meantime, there was Shongwe.

They met the contact shortly after dark, as arranged. They had been warned the security arrangements would be elaborate and so they were.

They were searched, not roughly but thoroughly.

'What are they looking for?'

'Guns. Radio transmitters. Who knows?'

They switched cars. A black man at the wheel, another between them, they drove through the darkness. No one spoke. Another car joined them as they entered the township. The headlights kindled ghostly images: broken-down cars, iron fences, a succession of box-like dwellings.

At length they stopped outside one of the houses. The car door opened. A black face looked in at them.

'Please get out of the car.'

Anna stepped out into the alien night. A second later Mark joined her and they were escorted swiftly up a narrow concrete path and into the house.

Shongwe, at last. Anna studied the man she had come to see. He was big, heavy in the neck and shoulders, the muscles of his arms fluid beneath the dark skin, yet her first impression was not of size. His aura of power was brutal in its intensity yet this, too, was not it. What struck her most was an overwhelming sense of loneliness and grief. More: the anger of a man imprisoned by circumstance and his own nature in a cage from which only violence offered a prospect of release.

His expression was coldly furious. He looked her up and down, taking his time about it, then shifted his eyes to Mark. 'Why do you bring this woman here?'

Contemptuously, as though she were of less account than a bag of old clothes dumped in a corner.

'Now just a minute —'

Mark spoke through her, his hand on her arm. 'This is the Australian I told you about.'

'They send a woman to talk to me? In Australia they think the ANC is maybe a knitting club?'

Now she ignored the restraining hand. She spoke clearly and emphatically. 'In Australia they think that sanctions are *maybe* serving no purpose, that *maybe* they should be abolished. When I tell them about you and the way you have just spoken, they will *maybe* do just that.'

He eyed her intently, in silence. But still would not accept her. 'You are wasting my time,' he said to Mark. 'Better you should take her back to Cape Town.'

Again Anna spoke, also to Mark. 'That settles it, then. Sanctions go.' She turned away. After all the performance ... Back outrage-stiff, she stalked to the door.

For a moment Mark hesitated. He stared at Shongwe who looked back at him, as cold and hard as black ivory.

'I do not understand you,' Mark said. 'She would have helped, if you'd let her. She has a lot of influence ...'

Shongwe dismissed his words loftily. 'Women do not sit in council with men.'

'Maybe it's time they did.'

He turned and followed Anna out of the room. No one tried to stop them.

Adam Shongwe sat alone in the empty room.

I do not understand you. No, he thought, you do not. How can you? You know nothing. If I had been able to explain, it would not have helped. The images are burnt into my brain forever but they are too painful to speak about to people who have not shared them. And without sharing, who can understand?

They came with bullets and killed the children.

Listen.

A house. At night, we lay awake. The adults murmuring, the flicker of firelight. The rumble of the sea; we feared the sea at night, never during the day. At night the flick, flick of the waves, the phosphorescence, conjured spirits, memories.

Poverty, yes. But warmth. A sense of belonging. A sense that we were one, in our place — not contented, *nee*, never that, but at least in our place.

Until the dogs. The guns. The noise, screaming and violent, driving us out.

Children crying.

I was also a child. I knew the sea, the sound of waves, the shape of clouds over the water, the space, the blueness rippling to the horizon.

The little house was home. But the water and the sky above it were our world.

Ja.

The guns drove us out. The dogs drove us out.

There were trucks. The men and their dogs. I remember the snarling teeth of both dogs and men as they herded us into the trucks, the grinding of gears, the stink of petrol fumes, the open, rutted space under a blank sky. No trees, no water, no sea. A voice saying, 'Here.'

I stood, looking about, seeing nothing familiar. No home, no people, no birds we knew, no sound of water breaking upon the dunes. *This? This is our place?*

One more thing. *Onkel* Sondag, Uncle Sunday we called him, descended from the old Xhosa heroes, shouting against the brilliant sky, hands clenched and raised, running at the men with guns, shouting: 'Here? You bury us here?'

Then the guns sounded, once, twice, and Uncle Sondag, face down in the dust, hands stretched out, clutching at the dust, once, twice, and still.

And two boys, children, *ja*, they saw *Onkel* down in the dust, fingers slack in the dust, a smear of dust on his cheek, his outraged eye, and they also charged the guns and the guns went pop pop and the two boys squirmed in the dust and were still. And I felt my eyes grow round and fearful and I stared at the boys lying in the dust and at Uncle Sunday lying in the dust and I did not move because I was frightened.

I did not move.

The men in their peaked caps, taut white faces, white, white, white, with their dogs on steel leashes, tongues red between white teeth, laughed.

Later there was the mission school; someone had decided I was bright. At eighteen I matriculated, the only pupil in all that barren plain to pass the school board examination.

Already I knew my place in the white man's world. Already I knew I did not intend to stay in it.

What was taken by the sword will be reclaimed by the sword. The cries of the people will be heard. The oppressors will be put down. Their dogs, their guns, will not avail them. The blood of *Onkel* Sondag, the murdered children, the thousands of the dead, will be appeased.

I, Adam Galeka Shongwe, say this.

Anna and Mark drove back to Cape Town. Neither of them spoke, but the weight of the futile meeting lay upon them both. Back in the cottage at last, Mark looked at her.

'And now?'

She didn't know. 'I've blown it, haven't I?' Yet was certain she had been right. Without mutual respect they would have learned nothing from each other. She wondered how Jack Goodie would take it when he heard that she'd met an ANC activist and had then walked out before he could tell her anything.

I'll make up a yarn, she thought. What he doesn't know can't hurt him. But was angry, all the same. 'Sanctions are supposed to help them. Why bother, if they're all like him?'

Yet she was not really thinking about sanctions. Strange how impressions of the man lingered. Normally, after meeting someone she didn't like, her mind discarded him so completely that she found it difficult to remember anything about him at all. Not this time. Shongwe's physical presence — his impressive size, the sense of power — was as vivid as though he were in the room with her still. Above all, she found herself remembering that extraordinary mixture of sorrow and anger that had revealed itself in his fierce eyes, even in the way he had dismissed her so peremptorily. Of no account, because she was a woman.

It made her angry again to think about it. It was primitive, barbaric. Yet perhaps it was the culture and not the man that was to blame. If he had been brought up to believe such nonsense of course he would dismiss her, his cause too important to waste time with people whom he believed did not matter.

Now she wished she had stayed in the face of his contempt, had somehow discovered a way to bludgeon him into acknowledging that she did indeed matter. By running away, she had justified his prejudices.

Not that it would make any difference now.

She thought: These Africans, white and black, are so different from us. Different attitudes, different backgrounds. No wonder a meeting of minds is so difficult. Yet with Pieter Wolmarans, I believe I have made at least a beginning.

Now *there* was a character. Roots so deep in the soil it was surprising he could move at all. Yet, seeing him, listening to him, she had caught an echo of how her great-grandmother had been; for the first time in her life had the faintest inkling of how Anneliese had come to do the terrible thing she had.

I shall never be like them, she thought. I would not wish to be, yet perhaps by meeting Pieter, talking with him, I've gained a measure of understanding that I didn't have before. As I had hoped to do with Adam Shongwe.

How easy all these things seemed, from a distance! Reason resolving problems ... But how two men as dissimilar as Pieter Wolmarans and Adam Shongwe would ever come to a settlement she had no idea. Thank God, she thought, that's not my problem.

She smiled at Mark, hand on his arm. 'Thank you for trying, anyway.'

That night Anna was passionate. Selfish, too, which normally she was not. She mounted and used him, riding and riding, hair a sweaty tangle, breath hoarse, moving her body a fraction this way, a fraction that, seeking the moist and compelling path to her own satisfaction. Back arched, head thrown back, she cried her release into the darkness — in which images flowed.

Oudekraal. Anneliese, bereft, hatred like a fiery brand blazing in her night. Adam Shongwe, his presence as well as his skin a darkness in the curtained room of the little house. All one. And herself, with them.

In the morning she drove back to the farm for what she suspected would be the last time. The sense of imminent departure made her more acutely aware than ever of the countryside through which she was driving. The vine terraces, the mountains, the trees clustered along the banks of rushing streams.

Oudekraal has become part of your life.

Perhaps it has, she thought. It is in my blood, after all.

It was a thought that she suspected she would never have had, had she never left Australia.

Pieter said, 'I would like to talk to you about what happened to send Anneliese Wolmarans away from this place to Australia.'

'Don't your grandfather's journals say anything about it?'

'Only the bare facts. What happened and how it was decided that she had to go. Of course, all the district knows the story. But how she felt about things ... No.'

He paused, thinking. 'I suppose it is too much to hope that she told you her side of it —'

'She told me everything.'

'I am surprised. I was sure she would have been too ashamed to do that.'

'She was not ashamed at all. Until the day she died she was proud of what she'd done — although she told me once there were times when she still heard screams.'

ELEVEN

Sydney, 1996.
Anna had planned to arrive at *Hugo's* for her lunch with Mark Forrest at twelve-thirty and did so, on the nail. Usually she made sure that she was the last person to arrive at a restaurant, having learned over the years how important it was to make an entrance, but today she had other ideas. She sat at the table by the window overlooking the harbour, nursing a mineral water and thinking over what she wanted to say to Mark when he arrived. The announcement of a marriage break-up could hardly rate as a triumph, however positive a spin she put on it, but at least it would give her the chance to get her version of events on the table before Mostyn got in on the act.

She had been there five minutes when Mark arrived.

He had returned to Sydney only three years before, after the enormous success of his book. Even so, it was amazing that, in such a close-knit community, they had managed to avoid each other so completely in that time. Now, catching her first glimpse of him, knowing every inch and particle of him at once, she felt a savage jolt of recognition, of memory.

Stop it, she told herself. That's not what you're here for.

He spoke to a waiter, who pointed to her table. She watched as he threaded his way between other tables, nodding and smiling to the people he knew. After so many years, she found herself watching the shadow of the lover she had known, the actuality of the stranger she had not met. For the first time she was nervous about their meeting.

He stopped by the table. She saw he was as unsure of himself as she was; to help things along, she stood and gave him a chaste peck on the cheek before they sat down together.

For a while they exchanged a trivial succession of words that emphasised rather than concealed the important silences that lay between them.

'Busy?'

He shook his head ruefully. 'Flat out. And you?'

'I began to wonder if I was going to get here at all. When I left the office, my secretary was bellyaching about the number of messages I had this morning. About a million people all wanting me to ring back. I'll have to get hold of them this afternoon, I suppose.'

Both of them had been too busy for too many years to waste much time on chit-chat; soon Anna was telling him why she had wanted to see him.

'I've broken up with Mostyn. I thought the *Reporter* might like to run a small item about it. Something on the lines that our views about a number of things have become basically incompatible and that we've decided it's best to separate. For the time being, anyway. We remain good friends. That sort of thing.'

Mark frowned dubiously. 'Will that be enough?'

'Why not? People who know us will read between the lines and the rest don't need to be told.'

'It's nice to know that one of you doesn't believe in washing dirty linen in public.'

Anna looked at him. 'What's that supposed to mean?'

'Are you telling me you haven't seen today's *Trumpet*?'

Stillness, like an animal scenting danger. 'Why should I read that rag?'

'Mostyn controls it, doesn't he? It ran an interview with him this morning.'

Anna was shocked to her boots; she knew it showed and for once didn't care.

'The bastard must have planned it —'

Mark shrugged. 'Mostyn's always been a planner.'

Until that moment, Anna had managed to convince herself that it had been a spur-of-the-moment job; it was a little hurtful to realise that it had been nothing of the kind.

'It's a highly sympathetic interview,' Mark warned her. 'Sympathetic to him, that is. I assumed that was why you wanted to see me.'

'What's he been saying?'

'Plenty. None of it particularly complimentary. I'm amazed no one told you about it.'

She thought of the unanswered calls and shook her head helplessly.

'I brought a copy of the article with me,' Mark told her. 'You ought to read it. If you don't mind being put off your lunch.'

'To hell with lunch.' Anger was a cold fist about her heart. 'What's he been saying?'

'I'll read you some of it.' Mark took a slip of paper out of his inside pocket and unfolded it.

'I'm quite capable of reading it myself.' She stretched out her hand. Banner headlines: the *Trumpet's* speciality.

HARCOURT SPEAKS. SHE LEFT ME NO CHOICE
TOP BUSINESSMAN TELLS OF HEARTBREAK
by CAROLE GITTINGS

Anna had met her once at a party. Voracious eyes; hard, brilliantly painted mouth. One of the *Trumpet's* top sleaze-merchants. She ran her eye swiftly down the printed column.

'It's the shareholders I worry about,' Mostyn Harcourt told me. 'They're the ones who lose out when a key director takes her eye off the ball.'

Queasiness was a thick clot in her throat.

'A genuine interest in the well-being of people less fortunate than oneself is praiseworthy,' he said. (Unctuous prick.) *'It's something that's always interested me greatly. And, of course, the production of wealth is beneficial to the whole community.'* (He's never given a stuff about the community.) *'But ambition can be a terrible thing. For thirteen years my wife and I have been as close as two people can be, so I think I can claim the privilege of giving her some advice. Pursuing your personal career is all very well, Anna, but you've got to remember you've a responsibility to other people, too. I'm not trying to do her dirt,'* he told me with evident sincerity, *'but I can't help thinking about the little investors who've entrusted her with their money. To leave them in the lurch for the sake of a place in the government of this state, if that's what she's planning to do ...'* He shrugged and smiled bravely. *'A bit too rich for my blood, I'm afraid.'*

At the end, like a dagger waiting in ambush, this:

Tomorrow: A woman's rise to power, Carole Gittings continues her exposé of the boardroom — and bedroom — politics of our nation.

Anger as hot as lava. 'Carole Gittings obviously hasn't forgotten who pays her wages.'

Mark slipped the cutting back into his pocket. Smiled cynically.

'You're surely not suggesting that would influence her?'

'He's her boss, for God's sake!'

'A journalist's only boss is her conscience.'

'In your dreams.' But she smiled too, a little ruefully. She found that even after all these years Mark still had the power to make her feel good, despite the circumstances. She had been right to phone him.

'The point is,' Mark said, 'most of the *Trumpet's* readers won't know Mostyn's her boss. They'll take what she writes at face value. What are you going to do about it?'

She hesitated, unsure of her ground. 'Publish a rebuttal?'

He shook his head. 'Nobody would read it. The *Trumpet's* readers don't care if the story's true or not. If they weren't hooked on sleaze, they wouldn't buy the paper in the first place. The people who matter don't buy the *Trumpet*, but will hear about it just the same. People like your co-directors. The last thing they'll want is blood all over the papers. You can't ignore it, all the same.'

'Tell me what to do,' Anna said.

Mark thought, You have to admire her nerve.

Tell me what to do ...

As though the years of silence had never happened. To say nothing of the incident that led up to it.

He had always told himself that the time would come when she would turn to him again. In the early days, the pain still fresh, he had promised himself that if it ever happened he'd send her away with his boot up her backside. Those feelings were long gone; now he was simply glad they were together again, if only for the time it took them to eat their lunch.

The truth was he had never got over her. He did not understand why but, sitting and watching her, knew it was so. I admire her, he thought, I suppose that's it. That business with Shongwe in Africa ... And what she's done with her life since. It took guts and he'd always been a sucker for guts.

Hardly justification for an obsession that had lasted fifteen years. Even to say it sounded ridiculous.

On the other hand, it might have been the making of him. Tennis had promised the world but in the end had never delivered. He remembered telling Anna how journalism, instead, would push him up the ladder to fame and fortune. So it had, he supposed, but wondered how far he'd have gone if Anna and he had never met — hadn't broken up, come to that.

From the first he'd had an eye for a story, for a picture, but the business was littered with the bodies of people just as good, technically speaking, as Mark Forrest. What you needed in this game was a blood-and-guts determination to get to the top. If he had got there, it was because Anna had ditched him, all those years ago. At the time it had seemed like the end of the world but he'd been furious, too, thank God, and that had saved him. He had been so determined to prove to her — and to himself — that he was good for something that he had been like a shark scenting blood in the water. Instant attack.

Now here they were again, facing each other across the lunch table, and it was even possible to believe they were still as they'd been fifteen years before when the phone had rung in his Cape Town office, and a voice had told him that Shongwe wanted to see her again, after all.

He didn't want her to go, certainly not alone, but the messenger was quite specific.

'By herself. No one else, or there's no deal.'

'I shall need to be there, too.'

Shongwe, it seemed, did not agree. Anna — alone — or nothing.

Madness. When she got back from *Oudekraal*, Mark told her so but Anna, it seemed, did not agree either.

'The whole point of my coming to Africa was to meet people like Shongwe.'

Mark had hoped there might have been other reasons but for the moment was willing to put that thought on hold.

'I don't think you understand what you're getting into.'

Her face was flushed, her eyes unfriendly. 'But I'm sure you're going to tell me.'

'Shongwe is an indicted criminal. It's an offence to have anything to do with him.'

'I seem to remember you introduced us.'

In reality it was not the authorities who worried Mark. The worst they could do was chuck Anna in jail or, more probably, out of the country. They certainly wouldn't *kill* her. Shongwe's mates were a different matter altogether: cut your throat as soon as look at you and not too fussy about the colour of it, either. Not the types to be chivalrous because they were dealing with a woman — quite the opposite, in fact.

He tried to tell her this, but she wasn't interested.

'Why should he want to kill me? He won't get anything out of that. Quite the opposite. And you said yourself that I needed an African point of view.'

Yes. But I never meant you to go in there by yourself.

Mark couldn't bring himself to say it, knowing how she would react.

I want protection, mate, I'll ask for it.

The fact was that, despite all her visits to *Oudekraal*, Anna still had something of the stereotyped vision she had brought with her from Australia: black was beautiful, white ugly. Mark had no patience with blinkered attitudes, in Anna or anyone else. Of all continents, Africa was no place for bleeding hearts. Of course, some blacks were beautiful, some whites ugly, but the reverse was equally true. He had seen what some blacks had done to their own kind: necklaced men, beaten and disembowelled women, the stench of blood in the African air. What had happened in Guguletu was still fresh in his mind, too. For the rest of his life, he would suffer nightmares of fleeing frantically through the streets and alleyways with those *tsotsis* after him, knowing what they would do to him if they caught up.

Anna had also been in Guguletu, but what she had seen there had only reinforced her prejudices. Now there was no stopping her.

'I'm going, and that's an end to it.'

And did so: alone, as ordered, while Mark gnawed his fingernails down to his armpits, waiting for her to come back.

An hour, she had told him. Maybe two.

That had been shortly after midday. The hour passed. The second hour. Three o'clock. Four o'clock.

Bloody hell.

He didn't know what to do. The police were out of the question. He rang his contacts. Nobody knew anything.

He waited.

Five o'clock. Six.

He decided he'd give her until dark. If she weren't back by then ... But what could he do? Bringing the cops into it would mean serious trouble all round. Worse, it would be certain to make things even more dangerous for Anna than they were already.

So in the end he did nothing, mooching round and round the cottage, watching the clock and imagining ...

Rape, torment, death.

She came back at nine o'clock, to his unspeakable relief and monumental fury.

'What the hell have you been doing?'

She was having none of that. 'Making up my mind about sanctions. What you wanted, isn't it?'

It had been what he wanted, but he hadn't expected her to take half the bloody night to do it.

'What took so long?'

'Talking. Seeing things.'

'What sort of things?'

He had been frightened for her, but there was more to his anger than that and she spotted it at once. It made her clam up. She still answered his questions but made sure she told him nothing.

Two children, slapping each other with words.

'Where did you go?'

'What took you so long?'

'Whom did you see?'

Nagging and nagging, unable to leave it alone.

And she, battle flags painted on her cheeks.

'I told you. All sorts of places.'

'You can't rush these things.'

'Adam's mates.' Her eyes dared him.

Adam. That was the crux of it. Both of them knew it.

She said, 'You don't own me, you know.'

'What about sanctions? Have you decided?'

Even that she would not tell him. 'Jack Goodie makes the decisions. All I do is give him the facts.'

Lying in bed, back turned ostentatiously to back, the darkness spiked with resentment.

Mark thought, She's done it to get back at me. Because of what happened after the riot. Then I left her standing; now it's her turn.

Yet he could not be sure whether he was right or not. Uncertainty fueled rage. There had been a time, shortly before their break-up, when he might have lifted his fists to Mary-Lou Aspinall and her smart mouth. Indifference had saved him; he hadn't cared enough to bother.

This time he cared.

Adam's mates.

The next day was no better. Then, suddenly, it was much worse.

A newsflash from the Ministry of the Interior. A series of raids in Guguletu. A number of suspected activists had been arrested. There followed a list of names. Mark ran his eye down it. Shongwe's name was not there but there were several that he recognised. One in particular. Abraham Qwele, the headmaster who had saved his life.

No tennis this week.

He had hardly finished reading the announcement when he heard the klaxon. He looked out of his office window in time to see the Landrover draw up outside the building. Painted yellow, like they all were, with the blue logo of the South African police. It was hard to think of anything more damaging to the country's image than to run in a member of the international press corps, but you could never underestimate the stupidity of the authorities in a police state. He was fully prepared to be carted off when the two cops — one of them his old mate Scholtz from Guguletu — came marching into his office. Then it turned out that they hadn't come to arrest him, after all. Just, as Scholtz put it, to have a chat.

They — or Anna — had led the police straight to the

black activists. Not deliberately, of course. After Mark's disappearing act during the riot and the business of the film, they'd staked out the cottage. All they'd had to do when Anna left was follow her and observe while she met Shongwe's messenger. After that, it had been easy.

'What was she doing in Guguletu?'

'You'll have to ask her.'

'We're asking you.'

'I don't know.'

'What is Miss Riordan doing in South Africa?'

'On holiday.'

'She works for a leading Australian politician.'

'So?'

They got nothing, would get nothing. Anna wasn't the only one who knew how to dodge questions.

She would have to be warned, all the same; Scholtz said as much.

'We don't care how well connected Miss Riordan is. We do not wish to cause her embarrassment but will not permit her to flout our laws with impunity. When is she planning to go back to Australia?'

'I don't know.'

'I would suggest sooner rather than later. As for you —'

'Yes?'

Scholtz wagged a finger under Mark's nose. 'Be very careful.'

'Sooner rather than later,' said Anna. 'What's that supposed to mean?'

'It means tomorrow.'

'No.'

'They'll deport you, if they have to.'

She looked at him, suddenly helpless. 'What do I do?'

From his closed face she saw that, for the moment at least, she had lost him.

'Shove off back to Canberra,' he told her. 'Why not? You've got what you came for.'

A response to rattle teeth; yet, even now, Anna was willing to make one more try. 'You know sanctions were only part of it . . .'

A forlorn offer, which he ignored.

'Abraham Qwele was one of the people they picked up. The schoolmaster. The bloke who saved my neck.'

'It wasn't my fault!' Furiously she spat the words at him.

'I never said it was.'

But his tone had said it, and both of them knew it.

It was terrible. What they'd had so briefly together had been beautiful and full of light, like a crystal vase. So precious. She had begun to believe — had even convinced herself that he, too, had believed — that it might be the real thing at last. No longer. Now the vase had fallen and lay in pieces about them.

Anna managed to book a flight for the following day. SAA to Johannesburg and Harare, QANTAS to Perth, Sydney and, at last, Canberra. A God-awful hike.

Mark ran her to the airport. It was a frosty time. She tried desperately to think of what she could say to put things right, knowing that if she couldn't come up with the right words before she left it would be too late. Distance and hurt and anger would bury them.

She could think of nothing. Instead could read Mark's mind so clearly, see what she knew he was seeing.

The black body humped, back tight with muscle. The heavy arms supporting. The tang of sweat. The vision all the more painful because the man was black and therefore alien. The difference in pigment meant the man himself was different, other than human. She saw herself in Mark's imagination. Flung carelessly, profligate limbs sprawled wide. Crying rapturously into the black and sweating face. His sweat mingling with her own. His semen ... She knew that Mark would not permit himself to think of the dark, potent semen. But his subconscious would have thought of it, oh yes.

What in fact had happened between Shongwe and herself was irrelevant. Mark had become a prisoner of his own imagination.

For her part ...

Sanctions were only part of it.

It was the best she could do. It was not enough, without further explanation they were doomed, yet she found she was incapable of saying more. She was not accountable to Mark Forrest for her actions but his pain was mirrored by her own. He no longer trusted her and, without trust, they were nothing.

They parted at the airport. Their expressionless faces were like twin blades, cutting each other. They were joined by their determination to be apart.

On the long flight eastwards, Anna sat back in her business-class seat. She thought, So now I, too, have been forced out of South Africa, one jump ahead of the police. In their book I am guilty of a crime, as Anneliese, seventy-nine years ago, was also guilty.

TWELVE

As the days passed some of the colour came back into Anneliese's face. Each night, before they slept, Elizabeth reported to Deneys on his sister's progress. How each day she seemed better. Still nothing much to say for herself but, with patience and time, she would recover. Elizabeth was sure of it.

'She's eating well,' she said. 'You see how her face is beginning to fill out again?'

'I was thinking the same thing.'

Meaningless words, spoken to comfort. Watching Anneliese, Deneys saw only the darkness, remembered still the chuckling laugh. Yet hoped Elizabeth was right, that miracles might prove to be possible after all.

'I was afraid she might blame me,' Elizabeth said, 'for having been born British.'

The thought had troubled him, too. He remembered how Dominic Riordan had accused him, the day he had spoken of Sarel Henning, but it seemed Anneliese had said nothing.

'Let us be thankful for that, at least.'

'You'll see,' she told him. 'Things will work out.'

It seemed too much to believe, yet that night Deneys slept with a lighter heart. Reason denied it but Elizabeth's words had re-awoken hope.

In Anneliese's mind, still entangled with the past, there was little room for hope.

Death trotting up the winding path from Lydenburg; the bay horse with tossing head, the grave face of the bearded man, the glitter of sunlight on the ammunition belts across his chest as he told her of her husband's dying.

The pulsing eagerness of flame, devouring her home, her life. The dead weight of what had been a child borne in her arms to the expectant earth.

No, she had no feelings to spare for the valley or anyone in it. At times she thought how easy it would be to hate them all with their smugness, their easy talk of forgiving. Bring them the fire, she thought. Bring the flies and open graves. Then let them talk, these strangers whom I used to know.

Every day when she awoke, her first awareness of daylight was overwhelmed at once by her sense of loss and disbelief. Of hatred, too, and an implacable anger. Yet time diminished even that. Little by little, she started to remember the things she had forgotten. The lanes joining the farms along which she had run so often as a child; the fields where they had played beneath willow trees that still trailed their green fingers in the river; the circle of mountains, peaks white with snow until well into spring, where occasionally Christiaan had taken them when he went hunting. She remembered her breath smoking in the cold air, the soapy smoothness of the saddle leather, the tumbled wildness of the *kloofs*, the narrow valleys where they hunted *duiker* and other antelope and — once — a leopard that had been preying on the flocks. The harshness of its pelt, the pattern of rosettes flattening beneath her hand. The long body stretched upon the stony ground, the dark lips snarling in death, the great incisors that could rip open an antelope. Or a man.

So many memories.

Each day she walked or drove alone through the valley. How much she wished she could return to those days of childhood, not to erase what had happened since but to regain the sense of belonging that she had known in those days, the knowledge that this was her place.

It was impossible. Nothing in the valley had changed; quite possibly nothing ever would, but that made no difference. The change was in herself. She no longer accepted what the people hereabouts held as an article of faith, that nothing beyond their ring of mountains mattered or even existed. Even Deneys, who had fought all through the war, had become infected by it. For him, the past was a book with its cover firmly closed. Anneliese's book remained open, its pages stained in blood.

All the same, there were one or two changes since she had left as a bride nine years before. Old Isaak Kok had died and his widow had sold the store. A man called Henning owned it now. A good man, she was told, with a wife and two children. Brave, too; she heard all about the dramatic rescue of Hendricks's wife and child from the flood.

There was another stranger, also, an Irishman from — of all places — Australia. Even Deneys, who had known him in the war, didn't know what he was doing in the valley. Would have wished him gone, she suspected, and with reason. He shamed them all, living at *Amsterdam* in a tumbledown cottage that even a coloured man would have refused, and sleeping, rumour said, with little Miriam Plaatjies. No doubt he was not the first, but that was not the point. His offence was to do openly what a lot of other men had done only in secret. Hypocritical, perhaps, but the conventions had to be observed.

Except that since the war Anneliese no longer had time for convention. On the contrary — how shocked Deneys would have been had he known it — she was fascinated by the idea of a man, a stranger at that, who not only broke the rules but got away with it. So one day, when she was out for a drive and saw a strange white man walking towards her, she reined in and spoke to him.

He was civil enough and soon they were chatting as though they'd known each other for years. For the first time she heard how he had visited *Uitkyk* with Deneys.

'There was a broken doll,' he said. 'I mind it well.'

'There is no one to miss it now.'

She spoke calmly, judiciously, as though the loss of a child or two were of little consequence and, if his words had once again ripped open her unhealed flesh, there was no one to know but herself. Yet somehow he must have read Anneliese's thoughts. He reached up to her in the little Cape cart and placed his hands over hers.

'I pray they will die in torment.'

No need to ask whom he meant.

'It will take more than prayer,' she told him.

'A great deal more.'

'And a target.'

They were speaking the secret language that only survivors of the war could have understood. It gave her a wonderful sense of release, that here was someone — at last — who had not forgotten, who understood that the war would never be over.

'I know where there's a target,' he said.

Anneliese felt her face go white. 'Where?'

He told her about Henning, how he had seen him at the hospital in the uniform of Cronje's Scouts.

'And you've done nothing about it?'

'I told your brother.'

She refused to believe. 'Deneys would have killed him long ago.'

Dominic Riordan shook his head. 'He knows.'

A blade pierced Anneliese's heart. To know and do nothing ... It put him on the side of the killers of her children.

'I shall ask him,' she threatened.

Riordan nodded as though he had expected nothing else. 'Do that. Then we'll be talking again.'

She returned to the house, her body shaking with fury.

Deneys saw her expression. 'What on earth's the matter?'

'I have been talking to your friend Riordan, that's what's the matter. He claims one of Cronje's Scouts is living in the valley. He says you know about it.'

She watched him closely, saw the flicker on his face.

'You do know!'

He would admit nothing. 'I know Riordan claims that Henning was a Scout. That doesn't make it true.'

'And you haven't tried to find out?'

'I have not.'

'I don't believe it! A *Scout*, for God's sake!'

'The war is over.'

'For some of us it will never be over.'

'What do you plan to do, then? Start fighting all over again?'

'Some of us remember how, even if you don't.'

Coward. She did not say it, but the word lay heavy on the air between them.

'I absolutely forbid it.'

As soon as the words were out, he knew he had made a mistake.

Rekindled hatred smiled within her smile. 'Forbid it as much as you like, brother.'

'Sarel Henning is a neighbour. A good man. A brave man.'

'A Scout. That's all I care about.'

'*May* have been a Scout. Now he's just a neighbour. With a wife and children of his own.' Which compounded the mistake. 'You can't be sure he was in the Scouts,' Deneys insisted. 'Dominic may be wrong.'

'I shall have to find out, shan't I?'

Two days later she came to him again, hatred triumphant in her face. 'Dominic was right,' she said.

He looked at her, heavy. 'How do you know?'

'I went to the shop and asked.'

'You spoke to Sarel Henning?'

'I spoke to his wife. I said there was talk her husband had been in the Scouts, and was it true?'

'And she said it was?'

'She said it was a lie.' Hate sparkled; he remembered how once her face had been open and laughing and filled with love. 'I saw how she looked in all the corners of the shop, as though she would have liked to run and hide.'

She smiled. In her eyes he saw the sulphur pits of hell, with the damned writhing in them. 'I told her how lucky she was that her children had survived the war.'

Dominic had heard that the Cape was beautiful and so it was, totally unscarred by the fighting that had taken place a thousand miles away. Too unscarred, if such a thing were possible. He had expected that the land would be undamaged but had never imagined that the people themselves would have remained so unmarked. Their kin had fought and died in the north yet he would never have known it. Everywhere he could sense a willingness to place their necks under the heels of the conqueror and it made him sick.

Given the choice he would have moved on but, with nowhere on God's earth to welcome him, he thought he'd better stay where he was. At least he had work. The foreman of the farm *Amsterdam* had left the valley in a hurry — something to do with a black woman, Dominic never heard the full story — and he was offered the job.

It wasn't a bad billet. The cottage wasn't much, but he'd lived in worse. There were other benefits, too. One of the hands had a daughter. Miriam was a pretty little thing, despite being several shades darker than any woman he'd known before. Fifteen years old, he guessed; high cheekbones and eyes that knew more about the world than they should have at that age. Of course, the native girls grew up much earlier than white women.

One day, coming back from the fields, Miriam gave Dominic the eye. No one ever needed to do that twice. He gave her a kiss, squeezed her tits and the next thing she'd moved in with him. Not permanently, of course; he wasn't going to have that, but she dropped in two or three times a week, and very pleasant it was. His rations were part of his pay; there was plenty of wine; from time to time, Miriam helped herself to some of her father's *mampoer*, a home-made brandy strong enough to kick a hole in your head. Comfortable enough, then, and to begin with he was happy with the way things had worked out. Then came the business of Sarel Henning, and his feelings changed.

The men who had ridden with Cronje were lower than vermin. In the Transvaal the Boers would speak neither to them nor their families; no store would serve them, even the churches would not admit them. They were cut off, totally and forever. Quite right, too. Dominic told himself that hell was full of people like Sarel Henning, hoping to find comfort in the thought.

He warned Deneys about him. Afterwards, told himself he should have known better; the Irish might like to keep their hatreds hot but Deneys was a different animal entirely. Not only would he do nothing — he warned Dominic off Henning in no uncertain terms.

'Leave him alone!'

One word to his boss could have seen Dominic out on his ear, so he bit his tongue and let things lie.

Once again he wondered why he bothered to stay. The comfort of Miriam's thighs and the brandy were part of it, of course, but neither was the real reason. He was waiting, with no idea what for.

Then Anneliese, and he knew.

'I am the way, the truth and the life.' Dominee de Wit's voice rang across the field above the sound of the breeze, the voices of the birds. 'No man cometh unto the Father but by me.'

Nagmaal. Wagons outspanned under the trees at the side of the field, the canvas canopies dappled with sunlight.

'Judge not, that you be not judged.'

The people stood with heads bowed, the smell of the fresh grass about them and the sunlight kindly on their necks.

'The devil is come into this valley. I have heard talk of vengeance. Vengeance is the Lord's. Christ himself prayed to the Father to forgive the men who had crucified him. Make yourself like Christ. Put the past behind you and go forward with forgiveness in your hearts and trust in God.' He raised supplicating hands to the bright sky. 'Oh Lord, grant us your brightness so that together we may fulfil your purpose in this place and in our lives. Amen and amen.'

After the service, the Wolmarans walked back to *Oudekraal* together.

'What was all that about?' Christiaan grumbled as they went up the steps and into the house.

'Deneys was sending me a message,' Anneliese said sweetly.

Christiaan hated riddles. 'What are you talking about?'

'Anneliese believes that Sarel Henning rode with Cronje's Scouts,' Deneys said. 'The dominee heard about it and preached a sermon about forgiveness. That's all I know.'

'Except that you told him what to say.'

'No one tells Dominee de Wit what to say.'

She smiled sceptically; she did not believe and was right.

Christiaan's blue eye measured his daughter coldly. 'The war is over. We want no settling of debts in this valley, just because a man fought on the other side.'

'The war is *not* over,' Anneliese said. 'And debts should be paid.'

In her room, the door closed securely behind her, she looked out through the window at the sunlit evening, the leaves of the great oak shimmering in the breeze.

Peace, she thought. How I hate it.

Guilt's red claws savaged her. Look at me. Well dressed, well fed. That is the true crime, to survive when my children are dead. Evil is not violent, she thought. It is still. It is deadly. It is forever.

This valley had been home once. No longer; home now was a broken building staring across a weed-filled valley cropped by goats. Not even that, she thought. It is the place where the dead lie.

Now the grave at Koffiekraal would be no more than a mound of earth returning slowly to grass, but she remembered how it had been, a gaping mouth in the red soil. She remembered everything: the white faces and staring eyes of the children, the women's apathy, the stench.

The memory of what was done to us, she thought. That is my home.

She could hear sounds from the *nagmaalvlakte*: voices, the creak of wheels, whips cracking like gunshots as the wagons headed home. Slowly the shadows lengthened. The sun disappeared behind the mountains and darkness settled upon the valley. She lay fully dressed upon the bed. In the darkness her open eyes observed images: the voiceless faces of the lost, the cleansing and triumphant fire.

She had spoken to Deneys. Flesh of her flesh, as the Bible said. He had rejected her. She had appealed to the rest of the family; they had rejected her, too. She was alone. Yet perhaps not quite. The Irishman from Australia would help her, she thought.

There was a time when she would not have chosen to have anything to do with him. He was disreputable, the subject of talk throughout the valley with his coloured woman and his fondness for liquor, but now none of that mattered.

She went back to him, as he had told her she would. She told him what she planned to do, watching his eyes for fear, revulsion.

'Good,' he said. 'Good.'

They made their plans.

It took time for Anna to accept that her relationship with Mark was dead. Even the jagged resentments that had caused their separation did not destroy them at once, but by slow and agonising inches.

They continued to write — brief letters, self-consciously matey. They saw each other whenever Mark was in Australia. They avoided speaking of what was better forgotten, but it didn't help. Their silences skirted the edges of what had or had not happened in Africa.

The act of love might have healed them. She wanted it so much and believed that Mark did, too. One gesture, one touch, would have been enough. She could not make it. Shongwe would have divided them, even there. Particularly there, perhaps.

Resentment rather than passion made her breasts ache.

Back in Canberra, Anna tried to re-assemble her life. Jack Goodie watched her, assessing what, if anything, had happened in Africa. She allowed him to read nothing in her expression, the movements of her body. It was not that he was interested in any physical sense. As far as Jack was concerned, Anna could do what she liked with whomever she liked and be damned. It was the potential for weakness that drew him, a prowling fox scenting carrion. That she would not show him.

It wasn't that difficult. Despite everything, she enjoyed being back in Canberra, owner of herself once more. She missed Mark, her flesh enclosing his, the hot throb and thud of another life within her. She hoped it might be no more than that, a hunger for sex.

It was a theory she tested by going out with Owen Cannon. She had known for months what he wanted. She persuaded herself she was eager; before leaving her unit even changed the sheets on her bed in readiness.

Within minutes she knew it was hopeless but Owen did not — or would not — accept it. He tried to wheedle his way into her apartment, into her bed, into her body. Was sulky at her refusal. She knew that in his head he was calling her cock-teaser.

His resentment wearied her; to win peace she even considered letting him have what he wanted, but could not. She, no one else, would decide what her body did and did not do. And with whom.

On his next visit to Australia, Mark phoned. Anna flew to Sydney. They had lunch together at the *Ristorante Venezia*. No one else, yet they were not alone. Two images sat beside them. Anna could not help remembering Owen Cannon's hot fingers, delving painfully, was certain that Mark was tormented by a parallel image, the imagined spectacle of Adam Shongwe breaching her sundered loins. She knew that both of them had hoped to restore what they had shared together; before the meal was over knew it was hopeless. The gulf of anger and bitterness that divided them could not be bridged. When they parted at the end of the meal, it was for good.

The following day Anna took some leave and went into the Blue Mountains. She must have stayed somewhere; certainly she ate and slept, but afterwards remembered nothing. A single memory remained, of sitting alone on a high point overlooking a densely-forested valley, the tree-covered slopes beyond. The forest was beautiful, silent. It had existed for centuries without her; God and bushfires permitting, would exist for as many centuries to come. The vicissitudes of her life, of everyone's life, had made no impact.

She was alone, without bitterness. No pain, even, after months of pain. She was conscious of no feeling whatsoever. Watching the self-sufficient trees, she wondered whether she was there at all. She had the oddest sensation that in isolation, even self-imposed, nothing of herself was real. It was ridiculous — as though her existence depended on anyone other than herself. She denied it vehemently, yet the sense of unreality remained.

She returned to what the world called civilisation. She got on with her life, although the flavour of that moment lingered.

She wondered whether it was how Anneliese had felt. When the time came finally for her to turn her back on everything and everyone she had held dear, had she, too, experienced this sense of emptiness, this inability to believe in her own existence?

'The children and their mother,' Dominic said. 'We've no quarrel with them. You're sure they'll be away?'

'To their cousins in Paarl,' Anneliese told him.

'You realise we may not be able to stay on in the valley afterwards?'

Anneliese's suspicions, razor-sharp, stirred at once. Those who should have loved her had turned their backs; why should she expect any better from this stranger?

'The idea frightens you, does it?'

He shrugged, turning her anger aside. 'It's your home.'

'I don't care about that.'

'Fine, then.'

The night when she had told him Henning's family would be away came at last. Now, before they did what must be done, there remained one further thing that Anneliese was determined to carry out: the consecration to bind them both.

As soon as it was dark, she slipped away from *Oudekraal* and walked along the lane to *Amsterdam*. Only the cicadas and the rows of vines climbing the darkened slopes saw her pass. Their voices spoke to her of her childhood. It was still not too late; if she turned back now, Dominic Riordan could say nothing. Everything would go on as before. The choice — her future in this place against the memory of her murdered children — was gloved in the familiar, once-dear darkness as her spirit, too, was gloved in darkness. Keep her face towards the future that she had chosen or that had chosen her, perhaps, and the days would be dark indeed. Was Deneys right? Should she somehow bludgeon herself into forgetting the past?

It was impossible. Too late for forgetfulness, for avoiding her lonely destiny. The open grave at Koffiekraal festered in her heart. What she was about to do would not cure her — nothing on earth could do that — but the blood of her children called to her own blood, and she could not remain deaf to it.

They had agreed that she would meet Dominic at ten; deliberately, she arrived two hours earlier. To do the one more thing that must be done before she could revenge herself upon those who thought, so foolishly, that they had brought her down.

What they were engaged upon was not so much the killing of a criminal as the celebration of a sacrament. They had to be as one in their performance of that duty; anything less would be sacrilege.

Candlelight shone through the cloth drawn across the window of the cottage in which Dominic lived. It was little more than a hen coop and, when Anneliese pushed open the door and walked inside, it was as though she had disturbed a hen coop, indeed.

Miriam, screeching, snatching at dribs and drabs of clothing to cover a nakedness that Anneliese cared nothing about.

'Be silent!' Dominic shouted. To her he said, 'You might have knocked ...'

There was a hint of laughter in his voice, and she liked him the better for it. She did not care what he had been doing with that foolish child, cared nothing for the colour of Miriam's skin, although some, no doubt, would have thought themselves offended. A man was a man, after all, and had a man's needs. If he *were* a man.

Which was what she was about to find out.

They got rid of Miriam without difficulty. No doubt she was glad enough to go. With the door closed behind her, they looked at each other. He had done nothing to cover himself. Why should he? He had not asked her here; she knew she must take him as she found him. Which she was more than ready to do. The candle flame glinted upon the hairs of his white chest; beneath the skin, the muscles flexed as he turned on one elbow to look at her.

'I thought we said ten o'clock?'

'As well I got here early,' she told him, 'or you'd have been wasting your strength on that child.'

He cared nothing for her words. 'So I would.'

But had not; there was no scent of spilled sex in the room.

Below his ribs his belly was ribbed with muscle.

'Have you come to say you've changed your mind?'

He knew well she had not changed her mind; knew, too, why she had come. He showed no surprise as she made ready, watching with grave eyes until she was as naked as he was.

She joined him on the bed. He questioned nothing, hand and mouth questing. She felt him planted deep within her, the heat, the slowly-awakening pulse. She looked up into his face.

'One and one make one,' she said.

He looked down at her, eyes questioning. 'Meaning?'

'What we are doing –'

He moved, a stealthy yet assertive thrust, and Anneliese closed her eyes for a moment. She willed herself to speak calmly while desire, her own quickening breath, frayed the edges of her words.

'— must be more than a killing. A sacrament ...'

A raised eyebrow again questioned her. 'Getting rid of a traitor. Where's the sacrament in that?'

Still he moved. Softly, deeply in. And out. Her will fought him, even as her body flowed.

'It must be. Or we are no better than he.'

'And that's why you're here? Because it's a sacrament?'

Gently he mocked her. She was losing her thoughts now, losing everything, but it was important that he understood.

'I am myself. One. Yourself one, also. Separate. But like this we are united. We have become one. That is how it must be.'

Was that indeed what she felt? Truly, in her heart and womb? That she should be one with this man?

His shoulders hunched. He drew her closer. She felt his scalding length. Probing. She knew he still did not understand but could speak no more, lost in heat. She was no longer sure of what she had been trying to say.

So the two became one, as she had said, and she believed herself content. And later became two again.

She thought that Dominic must think he had saddled himself with a mad woman, not because she had come here, he would know better than that, but because war did strange things; she had heard how some men, faced with the prospect of death, needed sex to prove to themselves that they had not turned their backs on life. The sexual act in itself did not mean much, probably had not even surprised him particularly, but she had seen from his expression how confused he had been when she had started talking about sacraments...

While all the time they were holding themselves tight, working to bring themselves to the boil together, feeling the nerves starting to skitter in their bellies.

One and one make one.

What a moment to choose.

It worked out right in the end. Anneliese felt her eyes roll back and the shudder begin, deep within her. Yet the truth of what she had been trying to explain to him remained; as soon as their breathing was back to normal she began to talk again, to herself as much as to him, impelled by her secret frenzy to go on and on about rites and sacraments and the healing hand of death, as though killing a man were ever more than simply that.

It made her wonder how she'd behave later, with all this nonsense bubbling away inside her.

The way it turned out, she needn't have worried.

There was no moon, the night velvet-black. Crouching side by side in the bushes, eyes fixed on Henning's store, Anneliese could hear the river's liquid voice as it flowed down the valley. The store itself was dark, but light showed through a heavily barred window at the rear of the building.

She could smell uneasiness like sweat on Dominic's skin, even before he put his mouth to her ear.

'Sure you want to go on with it?'

She stared at him. She could see the outline of his face, his eyes shining in the starlight. She laid the whole weight of her eyes upon him.

'What are you saying?'

'Maybe we should talk to him first, give him the chance to clear out. That's all we want, isn't it? Only that?'

She was willing to be furious. 'Lost your nerve, have you?'

'All I'm saying is we need to be sure.'

'We've already talked about it.'

'Talking and doing are two different things. Kill someone, it leaves a taste.'

'I have also tasted death,' Anneliese said. 'You think I can't take it again?'

The light in the window went out.

Now was the time for action, not for yapping about what was already agreed.

'Come on!'

The track glowed faintly in the starshine but nothing moved. Even the trees held their breath. Dominic picked up the can of coal oil they had brought with them. Side by side, they sprinted across the road together. In the shadow of the building they paused. The window of the store reflected darkness.

Dominic put the can on the ground and unscrewed the cap. The oil's pungent odour lanced the air. 'Ready ...'

Anneliese was carrying a steel bar. Around her neck hung a canvas bag containing kerosene, a wad of cotton material, matches.

'Now!'

She swung the bar with all her strength.

At once everything was fluid, movement and noise blending in a rush of frenzied action. The crash of glass. A shout of alarm from the rear of the shop. For a fraction of a second Dominic hesitated. Anneliese whirled towards him, screaming in frenzy.

'Do it!'

The shattered window gaped. He swung the can, spraying oil as far into the shop as it would reach. Anneliese was holding the cotton cloth soaked in kerosene.

Fingers fumbled as she struck a match, held the flame to the cloth. Its abrupt brilliance punched their eyes. Dominic flung the can through the window. Anneliese threw the blazing cotton after it. There was a dull thud as the fuel ignited. At once the interior of the store was lit by a cascade of violet and yellow flame.

They fled, pausing at the bend of the lane to look back. Shadows flared across the night. Flames roared, licking through the shattered glass, reaching for the roof.

A second thud. The air shuddered, heat slapping their faces, as somewhere in the chaos of flame a drum of fuel exploded. A column of sparks soared into the darkness. There was a scream, barely audible above the roar of the flames, then another. A chorus of screams.

Mouth open in shock, Dominic turned to Anneliese.

'You told me he was alone! You promised —'

She ignored him. Patterns of orange and black flared across the walls of the building as she raised exultant arms, shaking her clenched fists to the stars.

'See how you like that, you bastards!'

She ran, hearing Dominic following behind. The flare and crackle of the flames faded behind them.

They reached the communion field, silent beneath the stars. Beyond the trees the grey shape of *Oudekraal* loomed against the darkness. Briefly Anneliese remembered the wagons sleeping here beneath their hooped canvas covers, but at once the image vanished, erased by the evening's work, and she knew that henceforth her memories of the valley would no longer be of peace.

Behind them, beyond the stark shapes of trees, a red glow stained the sky.

'Henning's family ...' Dominic accused.

Her mind was still filled with the blood-red images of

distant flame. She looked at him, dazed, as though waking from a dream.

'What about them?'

'They were there all the time.'

Puzzlement faded. She smiled. 'Where else should they be?'

'You told me they were away. If I'd known —'

'As well you didn't, then.'

'So now we wage war on children, is that it?' Anguished tears shone on his face. 'I could strangle you for this! Making me responsible —'

'Why don't you, then?' She threw the challenge in his face, contemptuously.

At once he changed his tune, although anguish remained. 'Murdering children ...'

She denied nothing. A gust of wind shook the trees. Beyond their clutching branches, a fresh explosion of sparks flew like orange stars.

She said, 'We agreed what had to be done.'

'But children ...'

His fingers raked his face, as though trying to scrape away horror. Anneliese was cold, unmoving. 'Other children have died.'

There was nothing more to be said. She turned her back on him and walked with slow and measured steps towards the house.

Breath tight in his throat, heart pounding, Dominic walked on down the lane to his cottage. Nausea and disbelief walked with him. When he reached the cottage he found it empty; Miriam had not come back.

He was thankful, did not think he could have put up with her questions after all he'd been through that night.

He went to bed, slept intermittently, brief moments of oblivion islanded between recurrent images of horror. The fire snatching breath from the children's mouths. The screams. He had warned Anneliese that killing left a taste; now the taste was in his own mouth, while Anneliese had seemingly felt nothing. He remembered her expression, the fists raised in triumph, and dreaded the morning.

'Mary, Mother of God.' Again and again he repeated the incantation, as though somehow it would make everything right. 'Mary, Mother of God ...'

Daylight came. He dragged himself off the bed, stuffed food into his mouth with dirty hands, went to work as usual. He willed his face to show nothing. He laughed, talked, all the time believing that no one was answering him, that eyes watched knowingly wherever he went. Finally, mid-morning, Deneys arrived.

Deneys was barely out of bed when he heard the news; he knew at once that he would have to get the police in. It would be risky but worse by far if he did nothing. He knew people would suspect Anneliese of being involved with the murders; sit on his hands and they would be sure of it. In any case, silence would serve no purpose. The English had eyes and ears everywhere. They would be certain to hear about it; try to cover it up and they would think he had something to hide. They would descend on the valley and turn everything upside down in their determination to track down the killers of the man who had fought for them during the war. In the country, unseen eyes saw everything that happened; a word in the wrong place would bring ruin on them all.

Their only chance was to report the killings and hope the authorities would take it as a sign of innocence.

He told Anneliese so.

She laughed at his anxiety. 'Are you saying I had something to do with it?'

'There's bound to be talk —'

'Let them talk.'

'Everyone knows how you felt about Sarel Henning —'

'I wanted him out of the valley. That's no crime.' Her brazen smile mocked. 'Bring in the English police, by all means, if it makes you feel better. I've nothing to hide.'

Deneys knew something she did not, but did not want to confront her with it if he could avoid it.

'If it wasn't you it has to be Riordan.'

Storm clouds gathered in her eyes. 'Nonsense!'

'No one else had any reason to kill him.'

'You would never point your finger at Dominic Riordan —'

'Why not?'

'You rode with him in the war, for God's sake!'

Anneliese would always assess a man's worth by the side he had fought on, but Deneys could not afford such sentimentality; he had other responsibilities.

'Dominic Riordan hated Henning, just as you did. He recognised him, told me we had to do something about him.'

'And you would tell the police that?'

He watched her in silence.

'I can't believe you would do such a thing.'

'I shall do whatever is necessary to protect this family. Yourself included.'

'How many times do I have to tell you?' A hail of furious spit. 'I had nothing to do with it.'

It would have to be the truth, then.

'Elizabeth saw you leave the house. What she saw others may also have seen.'

She stared at him, expression defiant. 'All right. I did go out. It had nothing to do with Henning.'

Deneys was losing patience with her nonsense. 'Anneliese —'

'You want to know why?'

'You're talking rubbish —'

She smiled as a viper, if a viper could smile. 'I was going to see Dominic.'

Like an axe, striking him down. He pretended, to himself as well as to her, not to understand.

'Why should you do that?'

She laughed in his face. It was something he would always remember, how his sister paraded her shame with a laugh.

'So I could fuck him.'

The word brought blood to his face. Which was why she had used it, no doubt.

Again she laughed. 'That plain enough for you?'

He came so close to striking her, yet did not, knowing she would welcome it. There was only one thing he could do.

'I shall go and see him. You will stay in the house.'

Even now she mocked. 'What if I don't want to stay in the house?'

'Then I shall have you locked in your room.'

That wiped the smirk from her face. 'You wouldn't dare.'

But he would and she could see it. Pleading replaced mockery. 'You won't kill him?'

Deneys laughed bitterly. 'You think that would help?'

She made no attempt to follow when he rode over to *Amsterdam*. As well; had she forced him, he would have made good his threat.

He found Riordan in the workshop working on a wagon, a handful of labourers about him. Deneys gave the men a look, and they edged towards the door. Not fast enough to please him.

'Get rid of them.'

Dominic jerked his head and they took off. Deneys was alone with the man who, by Anneliese's own words, had dishonoured her. On his way to *Amsterdam* he had been thinking what to say; now his mind was as clear and hard as crystal.

'Tell me why I should not let them hang you,' he said.

Dominic stared, thinking that his last hour had come. Tried to put a bold face on it, all the same.

'What the hell are you talking about?'

Deneys clenched his big fists. 'Sarel Henning and his family were burnt to death in their store last night.'

'I heard about it. Terrible thing to happen. Terrible.' The words tumbled over each other in their hurry to get out of his mouth. 'I'd no time for him, as well you know. All the same, an accident like that —'

'Be silent.'

Dominic saw there was no point in lying; Deneys clearly knew the truth of what had happened. Besides, they had ridden together; they owed each other more respect than that.

'I didn't know about the kids,' he said.

'I don't care about the kids.'

Which was the last thing he'd expected to hear. He almost said so; managed to keep his mouth shut for once.

'I'm getting the police in,' Deneys said.

Dominic was shocked; where he came from they settled their own arguments, and it had not occurred to him that here things might be different.

'Why would you be doing that?'

'If they think I'm trying to cover things up —'

Deneys would be under suspicion, too. Of course; he should have thought of it.

'Who might have seen you?' Deneys asked.

'Miriam will have guessed, but she'll say nothing.'

'I'll speak to her.'

Dominic did not want Deneys Wolmarans scratching about in his affairs. 'I'll deal with her. It's my neck.'

Deneys turned on him savagely. 'Not only yours.'

They went to the cottage. Miriam wasn't there but Dominic knew where to find her. She made a fuss but he was in no mood for her nonsense and in the end she came quietly enough. He pushed her ahead of him into the house. When she saw Deneys she tried to bolt, but Dominic was holding her too tightly for that. She stood there, shaking and moaning, tears everywhere.

'Oh *baas*. Oh *baas* ...'

'Be silent,' he said.

The same words he had spoken to Dominic. They worked, too, as they had with him. 'Look at me,' he said.

She stared up at him, mesmerised, as at a snake.

'Are you listening?'

She nodded, terrified, eager to please.

'Be sure you are. I shall tell you once. The only way you can get out of this alive.'

Dominic watched as Deneys instructed the girl quietly, not seeking to panic her; when he had finished, he made her say it back to him so that he was sure she knew what had to be said.

'You spent the night here with the *baas*. He never went out and neither did you. You knew nothing of what had happened at the Henning place until someone told you this morning.'

He scowled, trying to frighten her into remembering what she had to say. 'Got it?'

'Oh yes, *baas*. I got it.'

'I think she has,' he said to Dominic, as he mounted

his horse to return to *Oudekraal*. 'The best we can do, in any case.'

'I'm grateful.'

Deneys stared coldly down at the Irishman. 'If you think I'm doing this for you, you're very much mistaken.'

And cantered off, leaving Dominic with the girl like a sodden rag at his side.

Keeping the police happy proved difficult. An inspector and three men were sent all the way from Cape Town, an ominous sign.

Inspector Hardcastle sat at his ease in *Oudekraal*, booted legs crossed, knee cocked insolently. His lips were full and red beneath a black moustache as smooth as paint. A plaited leather crop dangled from one hand. Everything about him oozed power and the awareness of power and the contempt that that awareness brings. Christiaan and Deneys faced him. Christiaan, master of *Oudekraal*, and Deneys, his heir, both of them the scions of a family that had held this place for more than a hundred and fifty years. Inspector Hardcastle, recently arrived from England, the smell and arrogance of England upon him, had them standing before him like children before a master, and it was as a master that he spoke to them.

'It is a question of loyalty,' he said.

Christiaan said, 'You have no reason to doubt the loyalty of anyone in this valley.'

'Don't we?' The red lips smiled, yet the black eyes remained as hard and expressionless as jet. Hardcastle was enjoying himself. 'There is not a single Englishman in this valley. Two members of this household,' — he did not honour Deneys with as much as a glance — 'took up arms against the Crown —'

'One,' Deneys said.

The black eyes sparked; Hardcastle was not a man to be interrupted. By defeated enemies, in particular.

'Your sister's husband —'

'Was never a member of this household.'

'He died in rebellion against his Queen.'

'Some would question that.'

'Some would question whether we have not been too tolerant of traitors.' Hardcastle pointed his crop at them in turn. 'My sources tell me there's another man in the valley. An Irishman. Or Australian. Who also fought. No doubt about his treason, at least.'

'The terms of the Peace,' Christiaan said, 'said there would be no talk of treason.'

'Not for those who still wage war.'

'No one in the valley is doing that.'

Hardcastle cracked his crop down on the surface of the table. 'Are you saying it was an accident? A man, his wife and two children all burned to death? We know how you Boers hate the National Scouts. If anyone in this valley killed the Hennings because of politics ... or for revenge ...' Casually he said, 'I was sorry to hear that Mrs van der Merwe's two children died at Koffiekraal.' He stood, tapping his crop against the side of his boot. 'I shall question her later. And the other members of your household. In the meantime, I shall pursue my enquiries in the valley.'

And was gone. Strutting.

'Not many years ago, I'd have seen him off at the end of my gun,' Christiaan said. 'If he thinks he's going to question your mother —'

'He will question whoever he likes.'

Christiaan looked his son up and down. 'That damned war did something to you.'

'They call it realism. We can't stop them. If we try, they'll send troops. And the Hennings are dead, after all.'

'I will not believe your sister had anything to do with that.'

'She did it all right. I've spoken to Riordan. They did it together.'

Christiaan shook his head, shaken into an appalled silence. His own daughter ... But practical considerations had to come first.

'This Riordan ... Will he keep his mouth shut?'

'He will. It's his neck, too. But I'm not sure about that woman of his.' He told his father how he had tried to frighten Miriam into holding her tongue.

'Hardcastle will frighten her, too,' Christiaan said.

'I know. And there's another thing ...'

Until he had met the Inspector, it had not occurred to him that the authorities wanted not a culprit but a victim. If it were expedient to blame Deneys or his sister or Dominic Riordan for the murders, they would do it. Hang them, if they felt like it, as a reminder of who was running the country. Proof was unimportant; proof could be fabricated.

He told Christiaan his fears.

'They would never do it.'

'A man like Hardcastle?'

Again Christiaan shook his head. In his world they had sorted out their own problems. The five convicts they had hanged because they would not waste bullets on murderers ... But those days were gone. He turned troubled eyes to his son.

'What do we do?'

'Hardcastle knows I had nothing to do with it. Anneliese and Riordan are a different story.'

'Who cares about Riordan? They can hang him, for all I care. We had no trouble until he came here.'

'And have him say it was all our idea?' Deneys shook his head. 'That won't do. We shall have to get them both away.'

THIRTEEN

To go and yet to stay. A mystery.

Everyone knew that Inspector Hardcastle and his men were sneaking about, poking their noses here, asking questions there. It was only a matter of time before they picked up some word or other, but Anneliese cared no longer.

By morning they would be gone. Yet only in part.

All along she had been telling herself how she hated the valley, felt only contempt for those who'd had things too easy in their lives. Yet, in truth, she knew she would never leave it.

Deneys would be coming for them soon, when it was dark. 'I can't promise I can get you away,' he had warned them.

He would; she could feel it. She didn't know how he had managed to arrange things so quickly but, somehow or other, it was done. Doors had been opened, eyes closed with money. To Cape Town first, then on board a steamer that would carry them to a place in Australia called, she had been told, Fremantle.

An English name. Even now she wondered whether she was right to go, to banish herself to this far country of which she had neither knowledge nor feeling. And

Dominic ... What was he to her? A lover from whom she made a battlefield. The battle was over; now that she had no need for him, she had discovered it was impossible to be rid of him.

Deneys had explained to her why he had to go, too; if he stayed, he might pin blame on the rest of the family.

Anneliese had been horrified. 'But that means I shall be stuck with him forever.'

Deneys's face had been grim. 'You should have thought of that.'

'Cut his throat, he won't say anything.' But knew that gentle Deneys would sacrifice her long before he would do such a thing.

'No choice,' he told her.

He was wrong. There was always a choice. Even now, she could go or she could stay. Stay and be hanged, admittedly, but still a choice. She watched through the window, seeing not the gathering darkness but the slow unfolding of the years.

Darkness like a cloak, the lamps in the house turning yellow, the air with a sting of ice. Steam rising from the men and horses gathered before the *stoep*. Her father reading from the Book. The sharp clatter of hooves as the men spur away. One thing out of so many.

Another: The slow, tender, stiff-boned courting of the farmer from far away. The wedding. The coming together of the flesh in apprehension, pain, finally in wonderment. The act of departure, eager for the future, yet sad for what would be left behind. The sadness showing itself, despite her efforts. Her mother saying, 'A woman's destiny ...' She, who had expected never to be alone again in her life, lonely and apprehensive because of it, wondering why.

The huge, dusty *veld* stretching like a golden shield beneath a sky of sapphire, the cold mountain streams where they *outspanned* their wagon. Besides which, for the first time, she thought she might come to love her husband after all.

Children's faces.

Death and more death, hatred providing a bitter focus to a life that had ceased to be a life at all.

Now this.

'We are going to Australia.' Anneliese said it aloud, tasting the words. They meant nothing. What had Australia to do with her? At first she had refused to consider it. It was Dominic who had talked her round.

'We shall be safe there. Australia's a good country. I've parents, a sister, Dana. You'll like her. We'll be able to make something of our lives. Something for us and for the future. Together we shall conquer the world, you'll see.'

'Under an English king?'

'Sure, and why not? If you come with me, if we stay together ...'

'Yes?'

'We'll raise our children to spit in the king of England's eye.'

Children in Australia. And she had thought Lydenburg far. Yet still he had not found the words to turn the key.

'Is that why you want us to go? To save our necks?'

'We'd be fools not to. But that's not the only reason. Put all this behind us, we'll be able to forget the fear and hatred. Get on with our lives together.'

'Is that what you want? For us to be together?'

'If you do.'

Did she?

This man whom she hardly knew, whom she seemed to have known forever. In him she saw everything she had lost in her own life. Things that only now, in the moment of losing them, she realised she had had.

The opportunity for freedom. Without fear, as Dominic had said. Without hatred. Could there be such a place on earth?

Dominic had made her realise that freedom was not only possible but desirable, if one could bear the responsibility and the pain of freedom.

She remembered hearing how an escaped prisoner had climbed high into the mountains until at last he had come to a precipice. The dogs were close behind him and he had launched himself into the air as though to fly to freedom. At the time she had thought how foolish he was. Now she understood that he had succeeded, that he had found freedom by doing it.

They would hurl themselves into the yielding air. In hope of freedom. Together.

So be it. The key turned. The lock creaked open.

Deneys came, with horses, after dark.

'There's no need for you to be bothering yourself on our account ...' Dominic blustering, putting muscles in his voice to show the world how much of a man he was.

Deneys wasted no time arguing. 'If I don't come with you, you'll never get away.'

And that was that.

There was no knowing whether Hardcastle and his men would be on the lookout, even at nine-thirty at night, so all three of them held their breath until they had followed the winding road up to the pass and the valley was lost behind them. Ahead lay the world and emptiness. Anneliese felt very small, very lonely, but had come to accept there was no other choice open to them. She would not have undone what she had done, would have done it again a hundred times over to assuage the ache of sorrow and anger that still weighed her down, far heavier than the loss of home, kin and the life she might have had.

The valley gone, they increased pace. The rhythm of the hooves beat its knuckles against the darkness. Deneys rode with his legs long in the stirrups. Dominic was no horseman but out of necessity became a jockey, riding hunch-shouldered in the saddle, lurching up and down, elegant as a bucket of rubbish in a dray, yet clinging on somehow, cursing in monotonous undertone until Deneys told him to shut it.

Dawn saw them out of the mountains and halfway across the flats. They rested for a while under an isolated exclamation of thorn trees. The sun came up and all of a sudden there were shadows, miles long, pointing their dark fingers in the direction they had to go.

They rode on in rising heat, the only living things in a vastness where the air shimmered and mirages, copper-tinted, stalked the middle distance. Behind them the sun climbed higher, overtook them and began its western slant. They reached the outskirts of the city at dusk. Lights pricked out of purple haze as they entered a long street set with buildings. Deneys led them to a house where they were admitted without argument or delay.

A young woman, silent, with eyes that avoided them, served a meal. Anneliese could not eat. Her heart was devastated, as though the fire that had devoured the Hennings had raged there too, leaving nothing but ashes and a terrible, brooding stillness. She was so tired she could have wept but sat silently, the food grown cold before her, her chin challenging the future. At her side, Dominic golloped everything that was put before him.

Eventually it was time. For the first time the woman spoke.

'Be careful,' she warned Deneys. 'They have patrols everywhere, particularly near the docks.'

They went out, muffled to the eyes against the nip wind, but her heavy cloak could not warm Anneliese against the cold of imminent departure. She saw the glint of water, silver-shod beneath a rising moon, and almost hoped they would be stopped while there was still time. To make an end of things beneath the shadow of the mountain, vast and silent against a rime of stars, representing all she had known and that now was fleeing from her forever. If they were captured it would be the end of them, no doubt, but at least it would be here, in her own land which at that moment was vastly preferable to the unknown country that awaited her beyond an infinity of salt miles.

She wondered how she would be able to bear the fact of going but rode on, caught in the inexorable rhythms of departure that now had taken over her life.

They reached the wharf without trouble. It lay, silent and deserted, before them. There were vessels tied up here and there, hawsers taut as bars in the faint lamplight. The shapes of warehouses were dark along the water's edge. She could hear the slop of waves against the piers.

The ship they wanted was a hundred yards away, its gangway down. *The Star of Erin*. No doubt Dominic would regard that as a good omen. Lanterns gleamed.

'We'll leave the horses here.'

'Thank God for that.' Dominic's voice breathed in the darkness.

Their footsteps echoed from the buildings as they walked along the quay. A hundred men could be hiding in the shadows and they would never see them. Anneliese could smell her own sweat, taste fear like copper in her throat.

Deneys stayed with them, walking tall at her side. At one time she had been willing to hate him, calling him traitor because he had been against what they had done, had been blind to her need for violence to still the clamour of her lost children. Yet he had proved himself a good man, despite all. He was getting rid of them to save his own neck, no doubt, but perhaps not for that reason alone.

They reached the gangway. The ship's engine rumbled softly amid a hint of steam and coal. A shadowy figure advanced from the shadow of the bridge, if bridge it were. Anneliese's heart bounced sickeningly.

'Mr Wolmarans?'

Deneys said, 'Yes?'

Both of them whispering, with good reason, while Anneliese and Dominic watched. Eventually the man turned to them. 'Go aboard, please.'

Dominic scurried up the gangway, wasting no time. Anneliese went to follow — the last time I shall feel Africa beneath my feet, she thought — when Deneys stopped her, his hand on her arm.

She looked at him, saw his anguished expression.

'For God's sake, why?' His words like bubbles burst painfully in the darkness. 'How could you do such a thing?'

'You know why! Because he was a Scout.'

'Not Henning. Riordan.'

What could she say? It had been an act of rebellion, a determination to strike out against her past. She had embraced her unknown future in the body of the Irishman. Whom she did not love, who was equally unknown to her.

It was too hard to explain. Kinder that Deneys should believe she had done it for love. That he might learn to forgive, in time. The other ... Never.

She said, 'Because I wanted to.'

Dominic and the seaman were waiting at the head of the gangway. She placed her hand on Deneys's arm. 'I must go ...'

He nodded. They embraced. These arms. This still-hard body. He stood back, relinquishing her to the unknown. The moment of parting had brought them close for the first time since her return to *Oudekraal*. He said no more but his silence said it all.

Head high, not looking back, Anneliese picked her way up the steep gangplank. As soon as she was on board, the seaman guided them along a narrow corridor redolent of smoke and fried food. He opened a door. 'Captain Evans' compliments and will you please remain in the cabin until we're at sea?'

The door closed behind them. They were in darkness. She sensed Dominic's presence beside her but made no attempt to speak, to touch him.

They waited as stiff as statues for what seemed hours, the hull vibrating softly beneath their feet. A sudden increase in engine noise. Voices. A clang and crash. The cabin swayed. She sensed the vessel drawing away from the quay. She took a deep breath.

Safe, at last.

FOURTEEN

Anna and Mark sat facing each other, separated not only by the spilled crumbs and stains of food but by the memories of the people they had once been and now were not.

Anna studied him surreptitiously. His eyes were still blue but beneath them the skin was shadowed, with tired creases. His irises, once as white as porcelain, a brilliant glare in his tanned face, were now tinged with yellow, a hint of red at the corners.

Age. She was vain enough to wonder what he saw when he looked at her. She, too, had aged. Thirteen years, after all. Thirteen action-packed years, as Mostyn's wretched *Trumpet* would no doubt say. It didn't seem like it.

They both had crazy schedules, did not have time to sit over a lunch that had already taken a sizeable chunk of the afternoon. Yet neither of them suggested leaving. Instead ordered more coffee, dawdling deliberately, exchanging desultory talk about this and that. No dewy eyes, no hearts going pit-a-pat; neither of them was of the age or temperament for such nonsense. Yet, undeniably, things had gone well between them. They had discovered that resentment, at last, had been eroded by the years. They might see each other again, they might not; for the moment, it didn't matter. What did matter was that today they had come to safe harbour together, a peaceful moment in lives that for the most part had neither. It was comforting and unexpected and, for the moment, enough.

Anna smiled at him across the table. His strong hand lay relaxed upon the cloth.

'Still play tennis?'

'When I get the time.'

Inconsequential talk, comforting because of it. Like old friends; a long-married couple, even.

She had believed in him so much, in them both.

He believed she had fucked that black man.

There. She had put it into words at last. She hated that bestial word, yet it was the right one. It was a bestial act that Mark imagined, with nothing of tenderness or goodness about it. He believed she had fucked the black man. In lust.

So resentment still lingered, after all. Yet she too had done inexcusable things in her life, remembered one such episode now.

As far back as she could remember, Tamsin Fitzgerald had wondered what it was about people's names that sent a signal, not only to the world but to themselves, of what they really were.

Three years before, in Year Seven, their form teacher — Mrs Rose Teakle, could you imagine it? — had spent a whole session explaining how important names were. Not only did they tell the world what to expect from the person who had the name; they could even change that person to suit the name they'd been given. Uriah Heep would have been a different person if his name had been Bob Smith. Totally weird, coming from someone they all called Treacle behind her back.

All the same, Tamsin thought, there might be something in it. She stood before the mirror, trying to see behind her reflection. The face behind the face.

Tamsin Fitzgerald. Different, you could say that. A bit of a ring to it. She rounded her lips, mouthing *Tamsin* ... Her mouth was so close to the glass that her breath bloomed upon it. *Tamsin Fitzgerald* ...

It was no use. She hated it, hated the signal it sent to the world of who she was. No, not hated — *despised*, rather. She despised herself for having such a name.

She thought of her father, Archer Fitzgerald, boozing in the back room he called his study, talking big as always when he had a load on. All the things he was going to do. One of these days. She wondered if he believed it himself. Certainly no one else did. She couldn't imagine how her mother put up with it, the boozing, the tears and rages, the rags and mouse droppings of his dreams.

One of these days ...

Sure, Dad. Sure.

An Irish name, he was always telling them, between hiccups. Fitzgerald. The family name of the dukes of Leinster. Whatever that was supposed to prove.

The name of a drunkard. Of a drunkard's wife, too feeble to stand up to her useless husband.

Couple more years, I'm out of here.

Tamsin Fitzgerald. She imagined someone asking her what it meant. Imagined her answer. Daughter of a piss-cat.

She pictured herself in a few years, tipping in the booze. Because of a name. Letting a useless husband treat her like dirt because of some duke back in Ireland.

She thought of her great-grandmother, dead a month earlier, her loss still razor-sharp. Nobody had messed with her, that was sure. Anneliese Riordan. Anneliese

Wolmarans, originally. A drum roll in Dutch. It was she who had opened Tamsin's eyes to what could be done.

'All things are possible,' Anneliese had said. 'All. Remember that.' What would Anneliese have been like if she'd been called Tamsin Fitzgerald?

She stood on tiptoe before the mirror, straining her body upwards, stretching, stretching, her hands cupped beneath her breasts. I am ... Anneliese Wolmarans. She shouted the name silently at her reflection. Pondered. No. The name was not hers to take. It would be like stealing her great-grandmother's soul from the grave.

What, then?

Scary, when you thought about it. Like turning yourself into someone else. What if you didn't like that person? Would it be too late to change back again?

She thought some more, facing her reflection. Ceremoniously she leant close. Her lips almost touched their reflection as they exchanged a secret only they could hear. Again her breath bloomed the glass.

'Anna Riordan.'

She smiled secretly. At the new person she had now become.

Three years later, in her final year, Tamsin wrote her exams. While she was studying she fenced herself away from everything: her collapsing house, her collapsing family. Most of all, from the emotion that over the years had consumed all others: a sense of horror and loss that this, *this*, was her life.

Somehow she must have succeeded. She stared at the results unbelievingly. Straight As.

'The door is open to you,' the careers teacher said. 'Medicine, law —'

'Finance,' Tamsin said.

Mrs Giles was not sure about finance. There seemed something ignoble about a career devoted only to the making of money. Yet, undeniably, that opportunity also existed.

'Finance,' she agreed doubtfully.

'I'm sick of being poor,' Tamsin told her.

For all her doubts, Mrs Giles, the product of another unhappy family, understood. The father had much to answer for, like many fathers.

It was easily arranged. The required door opened to her without difficulty. She would start at the School of Commerce when University re-opened.

She went away for a holiday, with a mate. They explored northwards along the coast, putting up at caravan parks. Nothing happened and everything happened. It was her first glimpse of another life, a reality she intended claiming as her own.

All things are possible.

It became an incantation, endlessly repeated. She returned to the house where nothing had changed or ever would. The disgraceful building and tousle-haired garden, the sense of decay that had achieved permanence. Parents as decayed as the rest. Mother, ineffectual, personality in tatters. Archer Fitzgerald, drunk, with ideas.

Tamsin compared what was here with what she had seen in the world. A coldness in her mind told her that the moment had come to do something about her life.

Her father said he wanted to talk to her. 'Seriously,' he said, the words loose between his teeth. 'Man to man.' Laughed. 'Or man to woman.'

The study was dark, curtains drawn to shut out reality. Her father spent most of his days here, the darkness illuminated by a kaleidoscope of dreams.

'Sit down.'

She did so, observing the visible rituals of obedience.

'You've done well,' Archer said. Even now liquor was not far from his hand. He lifted a glass. She heard it glug, going down. He wiped his wet mouth. 'I hear you're thinking of going into finance.'

'Yes.'

'Good choice. Just what I've wanted, someone else with a trained mind around the place. Always had faith in you, Tamsin. We'll do great things together, you and I.'

Winking, chortling, drinking. She watched, appalled, as he ranted. The things he would do, the ideas he had, the mountains they would climb together. Again he drank; again he laughed, the iciness in Tamsin's brain growing as she observed this apology for a man offering her a share in his madness.

The stench of alcohol like a pestilence.

'You'll see,' Archer said, holding the future like a gun to her head, 'you'll be proud of your name before I'm through. You'll boast of the fact that you're a Fitzgerald.'

Enough. So small a thing on top of the endless torrents of words, a lifetime's humiliation, yet enough to unleash the contempt that had corroded her for so long.

'I doubt that,' she said. 'I'm going to change it.'

His fuddled wits limped after her. 'Change?'

'My name. I'm not Tamsin Fitzgerald any more.'

Like walking off a cliff. She had the sense that she was saying the name for the last time; that if she ever used it again, she would be speaking of the dead.

'How can you change it? It's your *name*, for God's sake!'

'Not any more.'

'You're getting married,' he guessed.

'Of course I'm not getting married.'

'Then —'

'Anna Riordan. That's who I am.'

Realisation at last. With the realisation, rage.

'What the hell are you talking about? You're a Fitzgerald! It's in your blood! In your heart and mind! Fitzgerald! Till you die!'

Horror in his voice as well as rage. Discarding the name was like saying that neither it nor he existed; he could not, for his life, accept that.

'You can't just chuck it, like so much rubbish! It's your name!'

A bludgeoning hail of fury. Neither words nor anger touched her. She had passed beyond a barrier into a profound stillness where nothing her father said or did would ever touch her again.

'Anna Riordan,' she said. A seal upon her future. She turned and walked out of the room.

His final threat howled behind her. 'You won't wear my name, you don't stay in my house.'

She did not answer, closing the door on her father, on the name that had been hers, the life and person that had been hers. Trepidation mingled with triumph, but she would acknowledge neither. They had no place in the cold and incisive being she had become.

Coldly, incisively, she walked down the steps to the dilapidated garden. She held her head carefully, determined to spill nothing of the moment, the sense of newness and recommencement. Anna Riordan, walking proudly into her new life.

Anna sat in the train on her way to University in Adelaide. Life was a flower, opening up to her. Each of her senses was alert to what was going on about her: the zippety-zip of telegraph poles, the rhythmic throb of the iron wheels like a metronome in her head. One and two; one, two.

Time passed. The landscape blurred and swayed. Anna leant back. One and two; one, two. She dozed; opened her eyes to a sense of danger, a middle-aged man watching her from the opposite corner of the otherwise empty compartment. He must have come in while she slept.

Seeing her awake, he smiled. Her heart thumped. She sat in her corner, feeling her flesh draw inwards, keeping him out. So far he had said nothing, done nothing, only smiled. Which was enough.

'Good sleep?'

Perhaps he only wanted to be friendly. She hoped.

He edged a little closer. A thickset man in nondescript clothes, weather-beaten face, a farmer's broken hands. A half-smile, directed through the window. Yet at her, too, she feared.

'Not much to see.'

Again a little closer. Now he was opposite her; his tweed-clad knees threatened the space between them.

Beyond the glass the wires rose and fell. Zippety-zip. Tension a network of wires through her body. I should get up and leave, she thought, but did not. She did not want to make a fuss, and changing compartments would do that, if only in her head.

'I got a daughter about your age,' the man confided.

The rails had drawn a long bow through the bush so that now the sun shone straight into Anna's eyes. Being unable to see the man made her feel even more vulnerable, yet still she did not move. Like a rabbit pinned in headlights, she crouched.

A silence prolonged enough to suggest that all might yet be well.

'Not as beautiful as you, though. You're gorgeous. You know that?' The voice emerging from brightness, delved softly, stroking her breasts, parting her thighs.

She said nothing.

Quietly, with an air of terrifying inevitability, he leant forward and placed his big broken hands lightly on her legs. A feather touch, at once withdrawn; it might have been the unaware touching of friends in conversation. But was not.

I want you to leave me alone. That's all. No fuss. No screaming. Just go away.

Horrifyingly, Anna could not bring herself to say even that. Instead sat petrified, the memory of his touch flowing through her.

The compartment door slid back. The noise of the speeding train came in, and a man. Perhaps young. The farmer sat back.

'No harm,' he said, voice as casual as the feather-light hands.

The newcomer's arrival released her. She stood and blundered blindly out. In the corridor she clung to the rail, stomach churning, eyes staring blindly through the smeared glass.

Behind her the compartment door opened again. She flinched.

'You okay?'

A concerned voice. She risked a glance. The man who had come in a minute ago. Young, indeed; about her own age. She jerked her eyes away at once, saying nothing.

Leave me alone, she screamed silently. Go away.

When she looked again, he had gone.

How could I just sit there, doing nothing, letting him do what he did? I should have screamed, slapped his face, anything. As it is, he's got away with it. It means there will be another time, another woman. It will be my fault because I didn't have the guts to make a fuss. Maybe he's out of my life, but what about her? Or the woman after her? How could I? How *could* I?

I cannot leave it here. If I do, I shall feel guilty, always.

A month later, Anna followed one of the students when he left the campus. She did not know him; never knew why she had homed in on him in particular. A certain vulnerability of mouth and eye, perhaps, a hint of the tentative about the way he walked. She did not even know what she was going to do until she did it. Which was nothing very remarkable.

He caught a bus into the city. She did the same, watching the back of his unsuspecting head as the bus lurched and roared along. He got off, went into a bookshop. She, sauntering, guarded the entrance until he came out. He walked on. She followed. All that day. He met no one, talked to no one, went to roost at last in a huddle of backstreet units. A lonely boy. The next day the same. When first he noticed her, when doubt congealed into certainty, she did not know. Only that at one point, walking aimlessly, it seemed, beside the river, she could tell by the set of his shoulders, the furtive sidle of his walk, that he was on to her. What of it? Still he walked, self-consciously now, while Anna, connected to him by that invisible strand of shared knowledge, followed. A waiting game that by its nature she was bound to win. He left the footpath. Turned to face her. She walked at him, daring him. At the last moment he put out his hand. Imploringly.

'Why are you following me?'

'You're mad.' She ladled contempt into her voice.

'You *are* following me.'

She looked. As at a louse.

'Quit it, d'you hear?'

What she heard was uncertainty, the break of panic in his voice.

'I'd see a doctor, I was you.'

She walked on, Ms Nose-In-The-Air.

Glorious. It was not only men who could terrorise.

Several men — students, even one of the lecturers — made advances, or would have made them, had she permitted. She did not; after the episode of the train, her subsequent revenge stalking of the timid boy, she wanted nothing more to do with men. Crazy — it was a man's arrival that had saved her, after all.

Crazy or not, it was how she felt. Then she met Ben, who she supposed qualified as a man of sorts. She saw him, briefly, at a Student Union meeting. They exchanged a dozen words, no more. Afterwards she always seemed to be running into him, so regularly that she began to wonder if he was arranging it on purpose.

You're psycho, she thought. You're the one who haunts people; don't start imagining the rest of the world's as nutty as you are.

Ben was tied up with some green outfit. She agreed with them, in theory, but the way they were going about things was hopeless.

Told him so once, after she'd let him talk her into having a cup of coffee with him. 'Yelling only annoys people. You've got to get them on your side. Why don't you pass your exams first, get somewhere in industry or politics, somewhere people will listen to you?'

In some ways she thought he was an idiot, yet still respected him. At least he cared enough to try.

'The world needs more people like Ben Champion,' she told a friend, surprising herself.

He laughed. 'The guy's a nut.'

It was easier to laugh along. 'Isn't he, just?' She owed Ben nothing, had no reason to feel disloyal. Yet did.

Anna had never had what you would call a real boyfriend; had never felt the need for one. Like everyone, she supposed, she had thought about love, what it would be like to be burnt by that fire. There was a problem: love would involve a man.

'Not necessarily,' suggested a woman in whom Anna had confided. She caressed Anna's arm, smiling brilliantly into her eyes. 'There are other options.'

Anna had no wish to hurt; withdrew her arm, none the less. Several of her acquaintances were shacked up in girlie relationships, but she knew that path was not for her.

A man it would have to be. Or men. Those who claimed experience talked of safety in numbers. But Anna was talking of love, in which numbers would have no place.

The trouble was that she wanted freedom, too, had pledged herself to it. It was difficult to see how she could be free and at the same time in bondage to a man. Which she suspected was what love would mean.

She found herself looking at Ben with a fresh eye. She only had to snap her fingers, she knew that. Still she hesitated. On the surface he was nice enough, but how could you be sure? Her mother must have fancied her father, once.

The idea of Ben as a lover . . .

She couldn't imagine it. All that dog-like devotion. And he was ignorant, too, like all men; had never known what it was like to be alone in a railway carriage, to be terrorised simply for being a woman and helpless. Had never felt such an absence of power. Eventually, surprising herself, she told Ben about it.

'I thought there was something ...' He was pleased because he'd guessed right. It didn't occur to him that she might have feelings, too. His obtuseness angered her.

'I was terrified. Don't you understand?'

'Why? Nothing happened.'

'A total stranger sticks his hands all over you? You call that nothing?'

'You should have told him to piss off.'

True, and futile. She could not expect him to understand what she did not understand herself but was disappointed, none the less. She believed that love was sharing, a partnership. His reaction ruled out any possibility of that.

There was another option: lust. About which she had also thought. Experimentation might be safer if she didn't care so much. Ben owed her something, she decided. And was a man, after all. She could use him without danger of entanglement.

She thought, We all have to start somewhere. So did.

Afterwards wondered what all the fuss was about. She discovered that what Ben needed was not a lover but a mother. Which she had no inclination to provide.

They remained casual friends. She had feared he might be difficult but he was not. She realised with astonishment that he was scared of her. Was afraid she might have hurt him, too, but that couldn't be helped. She had found she needed more strength than Ben could offer. Odd, when you thought about it, for she despised the concept of male domination.

What Ben could not supply, she would. She would build her own strength, brick by brick, like a wall. She would use the wall to shut out weakness and desire.

In her last year at University, Anna was recruited by Ogilvie Schuster, one of the world's top accounting firms.

Ben, dogmatic as ever about the things that mattered to him, was horrified.

'I never thought you'd betray your principles like this.'

'Why do you always assume yours is the only way of doing things?' said Anna angrily.

'I don't. But to spend your whole life making money...'

What a waste, his voice implied. His impracticality exasperated her. 'You can't do much without it.'

He would not listen. 'Once you've got your feet in the trough, you'll end up like the rest of them.'

They parted, furious with each other. She marched along the path by the river, shouting her anger at the black and indifferent swans. 'Sanctimonious bastard!'

Passers-by gave her a look, but she ignored them.

She refused to waste her life in gestures. Sort out the economics and the rest would follow. She had to believe it; there was nothing else.

She joined Ogilvies and Ben, who had taken a job with Aboriginal Affairs, disappeared into the hot interior, sacrificing himself on the altar of insufficient funds. She heard nothing; did not forget him exactly but, with the pressures of her new life, he soon drifted from her mind.

Ogilvie Schuster stretched her to her limit. She responded eagerly, felt herself grow. Very soon everyone knew she was headed for partnership. She knew it, too, but with mixed feelings, wondering whether that was really what she wanted from life.

She kept up her political and welfare contacts; at a meeting of the local Labor group met Jack Goodie, down from Canberra to trawl for prospects.

Must have seen something in her that he liked. A week later, he phoned. It was the opportunity she had been looking for, the chance to prove that she, too, could be strong, as Anneliese had been strong.

FIFTEEN

Dominic and Anneliese reached the top of the pass and rested to catch their breath, staring at what lay ahead. From this point the track descended in a series of corkscrew bends until it disappeared into the trees far below. As far as they could see, the ragged landscape rose and fell like the waves of a strong sea, each crest and the valleys between submerged beneath a tide of trees with here and there a slash of water sparkling in the sunlight where a cascade plunged vertically into the depths.

'Getting somewhere at last,' Dominic exulted. 'We'll be home directly.'

Anneliese looked across the steeply folded hills. She could hear the wind blowing in the tops of the trees and see the waterfalls, but of human presence she could see nothing. The forest overwhelmed her. She and Dominic might have been the first humans to emerge out of the hand of God at the beginning of the world. The thought would have frightened her, had she permitted it.

'Getting somewhere?' she repeated. 'And where might that be?' She spoke defensively, on her guard against this new land, the new life that threatened so alarmingly.

'Not more than an hour now,' he told her. 'Most of that downhill.'

He unstrapped a water bottle from his waist and drank thirstily before passing it to her. She too drank. They had filled the bottle a mile back and the water was cool, with the strong peaty taste of the mountains. He pointed across the valley to a peak on the far side, its rocky head grey against the hard blue of the sky.

'The house is over there. Where we're going. You can't see it from here, but we'll get a better look when we're further along.'

'It looks a lot more than an hour to me.'

He winked. 'More or less.'

He strode on, whistling, and after a moment she followed him. Like a child, she thought, always saying what he wants to be true, rather than truth itself.

What am I doing here with this man? she wondered. This is not my place. Increasingly she feared that Dominic, hiding from reality behind a façade of easy lies, was not her man, either.

She would have to make them so. Africa was gone. This land of forest and emptiness was the only place that remained to her, as Dominic was the only man.

It is up to you what you make of them. As though the forest itself had spoken to her.

It was your choice to come here. Your ancestor Colin Walmer went to a new land and created something of value where before had been only wilderness. Now it is your turn.

The house was not as far as she'd feared, no more than three hours from the pass. The unpainted wooden buildings stood below a high ridge, beside a torrent that roared its way downhill between great rocks. Behind the house, a fenced yard contained horses, fewer than she would have expected for a man who was supposed to deal in horses. The patch of ground on which the house stood was the only level place she had seen since the pass. The house itself hung upon the edge of a precipice so high that from its unglazed windows you would be able to see nothing but air and the forested slopes far beneath.

'There are eagles,' a voice said behind her, 'if such things interest you.'

She turned, startled. She had heard no sound, but a big man now stood not more than two yards behind her. He wore stained breeches and riding boots, a rough jacket with an unmended tear on the pocket. A tall man with a strong neck. Big hands with broken, dirty nails. Black, assessing eyes. A beard, also black but threaded with silver, covered half his chest. His face was the colour of leather and heavily lined. He stood with massive chest thrown out, chin up; a man used to his own way and with no plans to change.

He stared unsmiling at Dominic. 'You're back, then. I always told your mother you would be, one of these days.'

Dominic gave a cry and flung himself forward into the other's arms.

'Da!' he said. 'Da.'

His father patted his back, while above Dominic's shoulder the hard eyes appraised the woman his son had brought home with him.

'And who might this be?'

She expected Dominic to break away, to introduce her, but he did not. He glanced back at her but his arm remained around his father's strong body.

'Anneliese, Da. She's from Africa.'

'Is she, now?' Firmly, the old man put his son away from him. 'Let's be havin' a look at her, then.'

He took his time, examining every inch. She guessed he was trying to make her nervous of him. Small chance of that — she had seen too much in her life to be embarrassed by such nonsense now. Unflinchingly, she stared back. They had not exchanged a word yet already she knew that this man would be all over her if he saw an opening and she had no intention of giving him one.

She saw a smile somewhere at the back of the dark eyes as their gazes clashed. A man who relished a challenge, then, even from a woman; a man confident he could handle her or anyone.

'You'll know me the next time you see me,' he said. 'From Africa, is it?'

'From the Cape.' She found she was proud to say it.

'I always thought the people of Africa were black.'

'Some are.'

'And what brings a white African to Jack Riordan's mountain?'

'We killed a man,' Dominic told him.

Anneliese saw that Dominic did not notice, or perhaps did not care, how his father looked at her.

'It's what happens in wars.' Jack spoke without taking his eyes from her. 'So you were in it, too?'

'She was, Da. Her children —'

Jack spoke through his son. 'I was asking her.'

'Yes,' she told him steadily, 'I was in the war.'

'In the actual fighting?'

'There are other ways of waging war.'

'No friend of the English, then?'

'Nor ever shall be. Some wars never end.'

She read approval in his eyes and knew she had said the right thing.

'Good,' he said. Suddenly his eyes challenged her no longer. He stuck out his hand as though she, too, were a man. 'Jack Riordan,' he said. 'Welcome.'

His hand was rough, hard, warm. A man's hand, signalling the strength not only of fingers, but of mind and will. She continued to feel his touch long after their hands had separated.

He turned to Dominic. 'Best get indoors and greet your mother. Let's hope the shock doesn't kill her.'

'Dana, too,' Dominic said. 'Unless she's married.'

Jack Riordan stared at him, an odd expression on his face. 'I was forgetting you wouldn't have heard.'

'She is married, then?'

Anneliese, standing a little to one side, saw that the idea did not please him. He had talked of her often, saying how pretty and full of life she was, how Anneliese would be certain to love her too. A girl like that was bound to be married, and sooner rather than later. It had been three years since Dominic had last seen her, after all.

Slowly Jack shook his head. 'Your sister is dead.'

Dominic gulped, trying without success to close his mouth. 'What happened?'

'She had a baby, a boy called Dermot. She died in the having of him.'

'She was married, then.'

'She was not.'

Dominic's hands lifted to his face. Whatever he had been expecting, it was not that.

The old man said, 'I know fine who the father was, not that it's any help. I chased him off once, took a shot at him to scare him. Thought we'd seen the last of him, but he was too smart for me.'

Fury as hot as fire in Dominic's voice. Through clenched teeth he asked, 'Where is he?'

Anneliese knew Dominic would kill him, was astounded that the man was not dead already.

'We'll not be setting eyes on him again. He knows fine what would happen to him if we did.'

'Who was it?'

Families, too, could be punished.

'No one any of us knew. A travelling man.'

A travelling man and Dominic's sister. And no one to kill because of it.

'When was it?'

'Three years since.'

Dominic turned on him, viper-swift. 'I see you're over it.'

He stopped in mid-syllable; would have wrenched out his tongue, no doubt, but it was too late for that. The two men stared at each other.

'I'll pretend I never heard that,' Jack said, 'seeing you're just back. But don't be putting me to the test another time, you hear?'

'Da ... I'm sorry.'

Forgiveness was not bought so cheaply.

'Get into your Ma.' Jack's voice sliced. 'We'll be joining you directly.'

Dominic had been away three years; now Jack scraped his son off his boot like so much dirt. Well, he deserved it.

After Dominic had gone indoors, Jack Riordan's eyes returned to Anneliese.

'I am sorry about your daughter,' she offered.

'We do not speak of her. She shamed us all.' He turned away. 'We'll give Dominic a few minutes with his mother. While we're waiting, you can have a look at these.'

He led her into the yard behind the house to see the horses. She followed him, wondering. A daughter dead, the wound of his loss ripped open; now he wanted to show her horses. As though the dead girl had never been, Anneliese thought, a girl betrayed by a man, by life itself.

She wondered what had happened to the baby. It would be a cold place for a motherless child, up here on the mountain top with a man of Jack Riordan's granite to rear him.

She tried to concentrate on the animals the man was showing her. They were good horses, rough-coated to handle the cold.

'I would have expected more,' she said.

He was standing so close she could sense the iron length of his body as he looked down at her. 'Why should there be more?'

'If you're a trader in horses, there must be more.'

He laughed; she saw he was pleased with her. 'There's level ground beyond the crest. It's good grazing away from the trees.' He eyed her keenly. 'Like horses, do you?'

'All Boers like horses.' She looked back at the house. 'Why build down here if the horses are over the ridge?'

'Out of the wind and snow. In winter the wind can cut you to pieces in these parts.' He smiled, winking. 'Out of the way of other things too. The police don't love us much, but down here they can't sneak up on us without our knowing.'

'They can check on your horses, though.'

'Check and welcome. We've nothing to hide up there. Everything as it should be.' Again he winked. 'Any strays we hide in the forest.'

Anneliese knew that he was paying her a great compliment by trusting her with such information while she was still a stranger.

She took a chance on his approval. 'What happened to the baby?'

He looked at her. She waited for him to say it was none of her business, which would have been the truth. He did not.

'In the house. He's sleeping now, but you'll be seeing him directly.'

'Who looks after him?'

'The missus does. A bit of a handful for her, but it can't be helped. Now you're here you'll be able to give her a hand. She should be over the shock of seeing her darling son by now,' he said, and Anneliese heard the slightest sting of derision in his voice. 'Best come and meet her for yourself.'

Following him back to the house, Anneliese thought again how hard this man was. Dominic had told her tales about him, yet she suspected that she had not heard the half of it. It made sense; you had to be hard to survive in a place like this, and Jack Riordan had made himself master of it and of all the people in it.

He needn't think he's going to master me, she thought. He's not going to treat me like one of his horses. Yet there was pleasure in having the protection of a strong man in this wild place.

Mrs Riordan was not interested in sharing the baby. She was not interested in welcoming Anneliese in any way at all. She was a small woman with grey hair scraped back and sharp and critical eyes. If she had wept because of her son's return Anneliese could see no sign of it; tears would not come easily to this woman. Jack Riordan might rule, but his wife was his deputy and not about to share herself or her life with anyone, least of all with a foreign woman as unwelcome as she was uninvited.

Carmel Riordan compressed her lips, looking Anneliese over. 'I suppose we must be thankful there's not a bone in your nose.'

'Bone?' Anneliese didn't understand.

'Africa,' Dominic explained.

She was indignant at such ignorance. 'We are civilised people,' she said. 'Not savages.'

'Are ye Catholic?'

Anneliese's chin challenged her. 'Not Catholic, either.'

'Not Catholic and not married. I'd say just as well, in the circumstances.'

But disapproved passionately, and Anneliese saw that nothing she could say or do would ever put things right between them.

Another burden, she thought, and the strangeness that was all about her did not help. There were statues of saints everywhere; a picture of a bleeding heart hung on one wall. Perhaps the saints spoke to Mrs Riordan in their pious, china voices, watching everything with their pious, china eyes, but to Anneliese they might have been fetishes in a *kraal*.

There was a hint of incense in the house, along with the saints. It might have been the stench of idolatry, the way the two women eyed each other. She told Dominic so that night. 'She doesn't like me.'

They lay on the mattress that had been chucked in the corner the old man had allocated them. There was no covering on walls or floor; the house was as rough as the mountains that surrounded it. The wind whistled between the gaps, and through the thin mattress Anneliese could feel the boards, coarsely hewn from green timber, on which they were lying. The night was full of sounds: the creaking of the house, the high thin crying of the wind, the bellow of the torrent beyond the wall.

The voices of loneliness.

'She's got to get used to the idea of you,' Dominic said.

'I'm not Irish and not Catholic. She'll never accept me.'

'Give her time.'

Anneliese knew that it was not a question of time; the gulf between them was too wide ever to be bridged.

Dominic said, 'My father took to you well enough.'

'He looked me over like he owned me. Or planned to.'

She had hesitated to say it, fearing to make Dominic jealous. Instead he laughed. 'Just his way. Take no notice.'

Not so easy with Jack's eyes assessing every inch of flesh beneath her dress, knowing that it was only a matter of time before his hands tried to follow. The fact that Dominic took it so casually made her feel more alone than ever.

This is their life, she thought, their country. I shall never fit in. I do not understand how I shall survive at all when I am so utterly alone. She could have wept, but would not. If he doesn't care, she told herself, why should you?

Yet did; was angry with Dominic for not caring. If he had been a man like his father ... She knew already that he was not and never would be.

'You don't need to be taking any notice of the old man,' Dominic reassured her. 'He's a devil, I know, but a devil who'll stand beside you in your time of need!'

Who would demand a price for it, too, she thought. And expect to be paid.

Already Jack was re-asserting control over his son. Dominic had not been in the house an hour before his accent had begun to pick up his father's brogue. If it had been only the accent she wouldn't have cared but it was not. There was something in Dominic's eyes that had never been there before, that looked at her and said, This is mine.

It was bad enough when Jack Riordan did it but at least in his case it was how the man was. Dominic was putting on an act, and she was not going to stand for that. If Dominic imagined he could start behaving like his father simply because he was back in the old man's shadow, he could think again.

Now he placed his hand on her breast. There was a possessiveness in his touch that displeased her. She was not, never would be, a thing. She moved restively.

'They will hear.'

'They're asleep.' His hand continuing to knead her flesh. 'If they're not, they'll be too busy playing their own games. They'll not be caring what we're up to.'

His words conjured a distasteful and incredible picture, of Dominic's parents lying in bed together, doing the things that people did together. She could imagine Jack very easily, but the mother, that dried up old hag ... She didn't want to think of it.

As for the sexual act beginning here, she did not want that either. That first time in the cottage at *Amsterdam* she had done what she had in order to prove to herself that she had succeeded in breaking the chains of her previous life. Since then the act had lost its significance, become no more than a nightly collision of the flesh. Yet she resented it, not because it did not matter but because it did. His touch aroused in her a passion that she seemed helpless to resist, obliterating the rational, separate person she wanted so much to be. She would be the creature of no man, particularly of this man she did not love, yet once his hands were on her she was lost. In the beginning, she had enticed him into joining with her in one great gesture of revenge; now it seemed she would be paying for that act for the rest of her life.

As always, she could do nothing to prevent him as Dominic's hand explored her, kindling heat. She was drowning, dissolving, and for the moment did not care. Once again, sensation consumed all. The groans of the house, the icy passion of the torrent beyond the wall, the whickering of the horses in the yard became part of the whole, filling her as Dominic himself was filling her with an awareness of life, rough and demanding and indescribably fecund. At the last, she stretched out her neck and bit down on his shoulder to keep herself from crying out.

Afterwards he objected, half-laughing, half-angry. 'Jesus and Mary, woman, you savaged me half to death!'

'Serves you right.'

Feeling her senses languid, drifting, awash in secret triumph. Because at last, for the first time, she had managed to avoid him. It had not been Dominic's face that had looked down at her out of the darkness.

They would have to go. Dominic would not want it but it was unavoidable. They were too many for this house. If they stayed, Jack — she herself, perhaps — would end by destroying them all.

For a month nothing, although daily Anneliese expected it. A routine grew up. Each day the men went off with the horses. The women, however they might feel about each other, also contrived to live together in a sort of harmony. And always there was the boy.

Already, at three years, he had a hint of his grandfather's eagle look, yet in him it was diluted, the bones of his face showing none of the old man's arrogance and strength. Anneliese had loved him from the first.

'My baby,' she cried, lifting him high and running, running, loving the crowing laugh, loving him.

She had expected his grandmother to resent her feelings but, after the first week or two, she had not. Because they were both intruders, Anneliese thought.

Over the years, the old woman had established a structure of hours and days that continued to govern all their lives. Out of bed at this hour, meals at these hours, this day for washing, this for cleaning — a framework of duties holding her life together. The baby, even after three years, disturbed the ritual. As did the non-Catholic, foreign woman who never, as long as Carmel Riordan lived, would be other than an intrusion and reproach. The scarlet woman who had trapped her son.

They lived together, cleaned the house together, used the wooden tongs to lift the steaming washing out of the tub together, breathed the same air together. Until Anneliese, unable to bear it any longer, fled from the house and walked. First to the yard with its horses, then further until, a month after their arrival, she was disappearing for hours into the forest. The vast emptiness, the silence, the lofty communion of trees consumed her, setting her free.

Later, when she was confident that the forest would not harm her, she took the boy.

She had been frightened at first, not of Dermot but of her feelings for him. She had known a son before this, had clutched him despairingly, willing his ragged breath not to cease. Had lost him, for all her efforts. Ever since, she had been devoured not only by his death but by the conviction that she had failed both him and herself in her inability to keep him alive. She was afraid that if she took Dermot into her heart she would re-awaken guilt.

It did not work out like that. There was a sense of healing in once again bestowing love upon a child. He was not hers, yet each day, more and more, became so. She gloried in it.

She apologised to his grandmother, fearing jealousy, but Carmel Riordan did not care.

'If it keeps the pair of you from under my feet,' she said.

So the walks became longer, she carrying the child when he was tired, and the trees, the rocky defiles and slopes littered with leaves, welcomed them.

One afternoon, wandering from their normal paths, they found the enclosure where Jack Riordan kept his stolen horses. That night she said nothing, but Dermot spoke for her, prattling about the horses they had seen in the forest.

She felt the weight of Jack's eyes. 'I'd have expected you'd mention it yourself.'

'You told me they were there. Remember?'

'I remember it well.' He watched her consideringly. 'Dangerous knowledge,' he said at last.

'You needn't think I'll talk,' she said. 'I told you: some wars never end.'

He turned again to his plate. 'Be sure you don't forget it.'

The next day, because Dermot wished it, they visited the horses again. There Jack Riordan found them.

'I was thinkin' you might turn up.'

'The boy likes to see them.'

He watched the child looking through the wire at the horses. 'Taken a dead set for you,' he said.

'I think so, yes.' She was pleased.

'Not the only one.'

'Oh?' Alarm flickered. 'Who else?'

The moist red lips smiled through the beard. 'Why, Dominic, of course.'

The message of his eyes and smile said nothing of Dominic. She felt as an antelope must, sensing the lion's presence, unsure when the attack will come.

'He thinks the moon and stars of you. He's always saying so.'

'I'm glad.' But was not and she suspected Jack knew it.

'I do, meself. I've a great admiration for a woman of spirit.'

The caress of his voice. He was so close; she could sense his closeness, her body's reaction to it.

He put out his hand and moulded her cheek.

She jerked her head away. 'Don't!'

'If it's Dominic worries you, I've sent him across the other side of the valley to have a look at some stock they've got there. He'll not be back for hours yet.'

'Why tell me that? Where you send him is none of my business.'

'Well now, maybe it's not your business and maybe it is. Maybe it's not, and maybe it is.' Again he touched her cheek. 'I've a powerful strong feeling for you, Anneliese.'

The way he stood over her, stealing the very air from her lungs.

'That's your problem, not mine.'

Again she jerked her head but this time his hand did not leave her but lingered, lingered. She felt sparks in her skin at his touch. He smiled slowly, all the time in the world at his back.

'And you feel the same.'

'I never —'

'Knew it the first day I set eyes on you.'

He dropped his hand so that, instead of her cheek, it caressed her breast. Once, briefly, and gone, yet she knew that his eagle's eye, watching her closely, must have observed the shock like a jolt of electricity that scoured her and left her heart hammering in her chest.

'Auntie . . .'

Dermot, whom both had forgotten, was still watching the horses. Anneliese, released, went swiftly to him.

'What is it?'

'That one has a baby.'

At her back Jack Riordan said, 'Come tomorrow. And leave the lad behind.'

For the rest of the day the words plagued her. Not only the words; the texture of his voice, the fleeting pressure of his hand on her breast stood between her and the evening's routine. Until at last, berthed on the mattress in the corner that had become theirs, Dominic turned to her, and she said no.

'I don't feel like it tonight.'

At that moment she wanted nothing to do with him, with any man. Yet she felt the need to excoriate feelings she was unable to control. A part of her even hoped that Dominic would insist, would impose himself upon her by force. She thought it might bring her back from the cliff edge upon which she was teetering, but he said nothing, turned on his side and was presently asleep. She lay awake, body flushed and restless, dreading the morning and what she would or would not do.

'Dermot ...'

Who came running.

'Are we going to see the horses, Auntie?'

'Not today.'

He started to object, but she would have none of it. A gust of anger, as violent as it was unexpected, shook her.

'Be quiet or I won't take you at all.'

'There's no call to be speaking to the boy so severely,' Carmel Riordan said.

'He must be taught obedience.'

'Screeching at him like a shrew ...'

Shrews don't screech. Somehow she managed not to say it.

She grabbed Dermot's arm, yanking him out of the house and down the slope so quickly that his feet barely touched the ground, and so into the green embrace of the trees.

'Want to see the horses,' Dermot whined.

'No!'

Then she thought, Why not? What can he do with the child there? It might even be better, give him a signal to keep away from me. If I don't go at all, I shall only be putting things off. I shall feel him behind me always.

They went; they watched the horses. Tension dried her mouth. They saw no one. Later that night, Jack said nothing, by word or gesture. The next day the same, and the one after that. The fourth day, he was there.

'I said to leave the lad behind.'

She had to stand firm or she would be lost, irretrievably. Permit him an inch, just once, and there would be no denying him.

'If I told Dominic —'

'Dominic?' The same rich vein of contempt in his voice. 'Dominic will do nothing.'

'Don't be so sure.'

'Lift his hand to his own Da? I'd flatten him, he tried anything like that, and well he knows it.'

She had to defend him. 'He's done worse things in his time.'

'Not with me he hasn't.'

Gently, confidently, his hand took her by the nape. *This is mine*.

Fight him! she ordered herself.

But could not. Stood shaking as his hand moulded her body. So gentle, but so sure. *This is mine*.

One more minute and it would be true.

Somehow she broke the spell. Breath shuddering, she stepped backwards from him. She expected him to come after her but he did not, stood watching with darkly smiling eyes.

'Tomorrow,' he said. 'Leave the child.'

She spoke again to Dominic. Again he dismissed her fears. 'It means nothing.'

A time for desperate speaking. 'The way he's behaving, he'll have me on my back the next time.'

He turned on her at once. 'You'd like that?'

Like a blow; to her pride, his own. So be it, she thought.

'You think it was easy for me to say it? Well, I've warned you. It is up to you what you do.'

Dominic tried; Anneliese, who heard it all, had to give him that. He went out, looking for the old man, with something like dread in his face. Found him in the barn, Anneliese following to loiter in the shadow cast by the open door.

'She's my woman,' Dominic said.

She heard Jack laugh. 'Question is, can you keep her?'

'With my gun, if I have to.'

'You could be right.' Jack's voice was amused. 'There's one or two in these parts I wouldn't trust with her or any woman.'

So he mocked.

'Don't imagine she's helpless,' Dominic warned him. 'She's a mind of her own.'

Again the riotous, lusting laugh. 'That's a bit of bad news. A woman with her own mind means trouble in the home. Or hadn't you heard?'

Anneliese standing in the door's shadow, the shadow of the man who was no more than a broken stick beside his father. *Fight him*, her mind cried. *Fight him*!

It was hopeless. With a sense of betrayal, she heard Dominic plead.

'Don't do it, Da. Please?'

'We need to be getting a parcel of animals together,' Jack said kindly. 'For the fair at Jim Jim.'

Anneliese at his side, Dominic had stood and watched the fire consume their enemies. Here, with this old man whom he hated as much as he loved, he was helpless.

They went out together for the horses. They passed close by her, unseeing, Dominic trotting in the big man's shadow.

That night Dominic said, 'I spoke to him. It'll be all right.'

Silence, then, hanging like the scales of justice between them, while Anneliese judged and found him wanting.

'On your own head be it,' she said.

She went to the horse paddock without the child, as Jack had known she would. She had just begun to believe he might not come, after all, when he arrived. As she had known he would.

She would have fought him but was so sick of fighting, of all the strange ways of this strange land. Whereas Jack Riordan, with his brutal hard body, his brutal hard mind, seemed never to tire. His strength was a tower, guarding her from the strangeness. A tower in whose shade she could rest.

Dominic's father. She thought, May God forgive me.

Afterwards, she looked at him. 'Never again.'

Words only and well he knew it. Yet he nodded.

'It was a fever, so it was. A fever in the pair of us. I'm not saying it's quenched.' His hand moved gently, caressing. Her eyes closed, her soul was open to his touch. 'I've a fancy you'd be a hard one to get out of a man's blood, but it wouldn't be right. No more, as you say.'

She had said it and meant it yet it was like a sentence of death to hear him say her own words back to her.

'We shall have to leave.'

No argument. To stay would be ruin.

'Where?'

'We'll find a place.'

'Take the boy with you.'

Like sunlight through cloud. She looked at him. 'What will Mrs Riordan say?'

He smiled lazily, sunlight striping the barrel chest. 'Be rid of him and thankful, that's what Mrs Riordan will say. What I'll *tell* her to say.'

He would, she knew, and the woman would obey, she knew. As, in her place, Anneliese would have obeyed. Still she hesitated, fearful of visiting yet more damnation upon herself.

'She'll be lonely without him.'

'Not for long.' He laughed. As he had a few minutes earlier, that great weapon of his pumping deep inside her. 'She's got me. I'm enough for any woman.'

The truth, God knew.

'This is no place for a lad. Two old people like us. He needs proper parents, a proper chance in life. I owe Dana that, at least, after letting that damn mongrel get to her.'

'What will I say to Dominic?'

'What you like. He'll go along, whatever you tell him. You know that already.'

So Dermot went with them. They trekked away and Anneliese did not look back. But that night, camped beneath the everlasting trees, she sucked Dominic in and in and again in, seeking to lay his seed on top of whatever other seed might lie within her. Seeking to obliterate all that had gone before.

They went north. Where there was work they stopped, for an hour or a day or a week. For a month they picked grapes along the banks of the great river. It was a good time, the best they'd had.

One evening after work, they wandered down to the river bank, sat in the shade and watched the water while Dermot played nearby.

Dominic tipped the bottle he had brought with him.

'It was grand, seeing the old people after all this time.' He wiped his mouth. 'You were right, though; we're better on our own.' His laugh brayed. 'Two women in one house? Impossible.'

When Anneliese had first told him they would be bringing Dermot along, he had not been so merry.

'Take Dana's kid?'

'Of course Dana's child. How many are there?'

'What are we going to do with him?'

'Raise him as our own.'

'Life's likely to be hard enough without that. We don't even know where we're going, for God's sake.'

'Wherever that may be, Dermot is coming, too. Make up your mind to that.'

Dominic had thrown a fit of the sulks. 'Bring him along, then, if it makes you happy. We can all die of starvation, for all I care. Why not? Just so long as we agree it's you's got the caring of him.'

Care for him Anneliese did. Like a tiger. There was a man along the river, ran one of the little boats to ferry people across. He stood Dominic a drink, offered a few shillings to take the boy off their hands. Said he'd raise him to learn a trade on the water. The way he explained things, it seemed like a good opportunity — good for the boy, good for themselves. You didn't raise a child like that for nothing, after all.

Well. You'd think the man had offered to strangle him, the way Anneliese performed. Screeching about kidnap and child slavery. Nearly threw him in the river. They had to move on quickly after that, with Anneliese still breathing fire and slaughter along the way.

'You ever dare do anything like that again —'

'All I did was talk —'

'Just try it, that's all.'

She'd shaken him, although he would never let her see it. He wouldn't have put it past her to murder him, the way she looked that night. After that, Dominic left well alone. She wanted the kid along, so be it.

Anneliese, walking alone amid the vines. The sight and smell of the grapes was almost like coming home. Not quite; like viewing the past through a lens that distorted everything yet left the fundamentals unchanged. Grapes and sun. Harvest and growth. Anneliese, too, had growth inside her.

It is Dominic's. Silently she screamed the affirmation at the dun-coloured water. *Dominic's*!

God help me. God help us all.

SIXTEEN

A thin girl in a white apron held the edge of the door as though guarding the interior of the house from an army. She stared suspiciously through tiny, close-set eyes that took in everything about the visitors. The dusty, stained clothes. The tired boy. The broken shoes. The belly.

'No,' she said.

The door was closing.

Anneliese repeated her request. 'I need to see your mistress.'

On top of everything else, an accent. A foreigner, no doubt with the diseases of foreigners.

'No.'

The door scythed shut. The maid turned away, dusting her hands, delighted with herself for carrying out her guard duties so successfully.

'Who was it, Polly?'

Gertrude Fairclough, fair hair damp with heat, had a complexion that already, at thirty, had fallen victim to the climate, turning from the peaches and cream that had been so admired in Melbourne to its present (and future, alas!) uninspiring yellow.

'A beggar woman, mum. With a child.'

'Did you give her anything?'

The maid's narrow shoulders were affronted by the idea that she should have given anything to anyone.

'No, mum.'

Mrs Fairclough, a regular softie, looked distressed at the idea of a woman on the road alone. In this heat.

'Perhaps we should have let her have something —'

Polly moved at once to quell the foolish impulse. 'She never asked for nothing, mum.'

Mrs Fairclough was perplexed by the idea of a beggar woman who did not beg.

'What did she want then?' Sharply, suspecting Polly of keeping things from her. As she was sure she often did. Marooned in this big house in the far north, in this life that had turned out so differently from the tropical idyll she had envisaged ten years earlier when Ambrose had besought her so romantically to marry him, Mrs Fairclough was well acquainted with loneliness.

If only I had a friend, she confided in letters to her sister, whom she trusted. Only one.

There was no one; it made her life difficult.

Polly wriggled resentfully, sensing criticism. 'To speak to you, mum.'

'And you sent her away? Without asking me first?'

'I di'n think you'd want to be bothered.'

'Go after her,' Mrs Fairclough instructed, delighted at the chance to assert herself. 'Bring her back.'

Which Polly, cross as two sticks, did. Left them just inside the closed front door. Let the old bitch get on with it, then.

Mrs Fairclough, seeing Anneliese's belly, wondered what she had let herself in for. And the boy ... She eyed him nervously, uncertain of boys, having no children of her own.

'Would you like a cool drink?' she offered.

The boy scowled.

'He would. If it's not too much trouble.'

Mrs Fairclough was pleased. There was a bell on a side table. She rang it imperiously.

When Polly came, she said, 'A tray of cool drinks, Polly. If you please. For three.' How pleasurable it was to play the mistress, if only briefly! 'Please come through,' she said to the strangers. 'We can sit inside.'

Which they did, waiting for drinks that took a long time coming. Until they did, Mrs Fairclough, obeying some obscure protocol, would not discuss the purpose of the visit. Instead made small talk, which she missed so much.

'Do you come from these parts?'

'No.'

'Do I detect a hint of an accent?' Roguishly, willing to make friends, if only for a minute, with this strange woman.

'I am from South Africa,' Anneliese said. Even at this point, she was unwilling to conceal her heritage. 'I am a Boer.'

With whom the Empire had so recently been at war.

Mrs Fairclough seemed to think nothing of it. 'How interesting! And what brings you to this part of the world, Mrs —?'

'Riordan.'

It was easier than van der Merwe. Might avoid the need for later explanations, too, perhaps.

'My husband is Australian. After the war, I came here with him.'

Mrs Fairclough knew nothing of this woman with her proud face and heavy accent, yet her heart was touched.

'It must have been hard for you.'

Anneliese sensed an opening, decided to see if she could prise a way into this rich woman's heart. 'My first husband was killed in the fighting. My two children —'

Mrs Fairclough lifted horrified fingers to her lips. 'Surely they were not killed, too?'

'They died, yes.'

'So precious,' Mrs Fairclough mourned. 'I wonder you could bear it.'

'We bear what we must,' Anneliese said.

The drinks came. Mrs Fairclough, flustered, concerned for the dead children, served them herself.

'Forgive me, my dear,' she said to Anneliese, 'you wanted to see me. How can I help you?'

'I am looking for work.'

'They do not employ women in the fields.'

'Not in the fields. In the house.'

Out of the question, of course; there was little enough to do as it was. Ambrose would never permit the extra expense. Yet she would have liked to help this woman, who was also a stranger in this place.

'Where is your husband?'

'He is looking for work, too. As a cutter.'

'That should be no problem. My husband tells me he has a need for more labour.'

'It is not easy,' Anneliese said. 'The plantations want no women around the place.' She smiled, one woman sharing confidences with another. 'Especially in my condition.'

Mrs Fairclough tiptoed fastidiously around the idea of the coming baby.

'When?'

'The end of next month.'

'But what will you do?'

Anneliese had sensed the woman's rejection but would not acknowledge it.

'I had hoped to have it here. Or somewhere. Under a roof, at least.'

Mrs Fairclough was swayed painfully. To send a woman away in this condition ... Barbarous. Well-spoken, too, despite the accent.

'Have you worked in a house before?'

Anneliese knew better than to say her family owned a large farm in Africa, with servants of their own.

'All my life.'

Mrs Fairclough dithered. It was impossible. Yet the woman offered the prospect of companionship, for which she yearned so much. Impulsively she snatched her decision out of the hot and lonely air.

'If your husband is taken on, you may stay.'

'To do what?'

'We can discuss the nature of your duties later.'

In the meantime, they did not even know each other's names.

Anneliese introduced herself and Dermot.

The woman bent and solemnly shook the little boy's hand. Who snatched it away ferociously.

'And I,' she said, straightening, 'am Mrs Fairclough. Mrs Gertrude Fairclough.'

One of the regular cutters had fallen sick, so they were in. From the first, Dominic had a harder time of it than Anneliese. He had worked hard in his time — some of those grape-growers would work you fair to death, given half a chance — but had known nothing to match this.

Twelve hours on, twelve off, cutting cane stalks as hard as steel. Cruel work, especially when you weren't used to it. By the time he was finished for the day, Dominic could barely stand; in the morning was so sore he had a real problem getting out of his bunk and for the first ten minutes staggered about as stiff-limbed as an old man.

He got no sympathy from Bull Bullen, the gang boss.

'Bit too lady-like for us, are you? Not up to doing a day's work?'

The Bull stayed on Dominic's back all day, breathing fire down his neck if he slackened off for as much as a minute.

'C'mon on, Lady Godiva. Raise a sweat, why doncha?'

Dominic went to see Anneliese, eyes reproachful in his haggard face.

'I'll not be taking much more of this, girl ...'

Anneliese took no notice. They were lucky to have found a place at all. Mrs Fairclough was kind, if foolish, and Anneliese had no intention of going anywhere until after the baby was born. Not then, either, given any choice.

In the meanwhile, her work in the house was negligible: sort the linen, help Polly who, however, would not let herself be helped. Polly resented the newcomer, sensing possible competition. She stood at the kitchen sink, clattering cutlery ferociously. Another back as stiff as steel. At first she tried to put on airs, to remind this beggar off the road of her place, but Anneliese ignored her. Then she tried to get her to lift weights — a spare bed, a chest full of china — that were beyond safety or her strength, but Anneliese was having none of that.

'Thinks she's so *slim*,' she told Dominic. 'So sly. Sly as a fox, give her half a chance.'

Which she had no intention of giving. Anneliese, gashed by a hundred cuts from life's dagger, was too much for Polly. Who sulked.

Yet, after a few weeks, things improved. Dominic's body began to get the hang of what was required. Now he was young again, cheeky with it, although Anneliese was too far gone for him to be able to work off his energies on her. For her part, Anneliese felt she was lugging the world's weight around.

Not much longer, she told herself, but the baby seemed in no hurry. Perhaps today, she hoped each morning, only to be disappointed. Day by day. Now it was her turn to have a problem getting out of bed. Then, in the middle of a hot and sultry night, the waiting was over.

She had forgotten what it was like; or perhaps it was something you always had to learn anew, however many times you experienced it. The mounting pressure as the Thing took over, you its prisoner, helpless and shaking, within your own body. *The Thing*; because that was what it was. No personality yet; no feeling of love or tenderness. The mind even denied it individual life. Because the Thing, too, was helpless, the prey of a natural will greater than itself, greater than you, impelling it downwards, inch by agonising inch, forcing and raping the body that contained it, wrenching and opening a passage where surely there was too little space for it to go. Inch by inch. Hour by hour. An infinity of pain, eyes staring at blood-red darkness, tortured limbs spread, every muscle engaged in the expulsion of the Thing that tormented her.

Surely it hadn't been as bad as this before?

Mrs Fairclough helped. Needed for once in her life, Gertrude was surprisingly competent, hands sure, voice a consolation even as Anneliese was savaged by the fiery teeth of pain.

'Do something!' Sweat in her voice to mirror the sweat pouring from her body. 'Anything!'

Nothing anyone could do. Then, in the fiery furnace,

something creaked within her, creaked again, broke loose. It moved and Anneliese knew, even before Gertrude's excited exclamation, that it was coming at last.

Tenderness, then, a drowning lassitude as the pain slipped away, its teeth blunted.

'Is it all right?'

The little creature, live now, real now, a person now, lay against her breast but, for the moment, she was too exhausted to turn her head to look down at it.

Gertrude's voice echoed in a deep well of weariness. 'He's fine. He's gorgeous.'

A boy, then, and entire. For the moment, nothing else mattered.

Sleep engulfed her.

'Look at the hair he's got on him! Black as night!' Dominic's face beamed though he cradled the baby nervously. 'Jack. That's what we'll be calling him. After the old man.'

'No!' Had spat out the word before she could control it.

He eyed her. 'What's wrong with that?'

'It's just ... I'd thought a more Irish name?'

'I wouldn't wish Dominic on me worst enemy.'

'Give me some others.'

'Hell, I dunno. Donal, Patrick, Sean —'

'That's a good name. We shall call him Sean.'

He stared doubtfully at the baby to see if the name fitted. 'If that's what you want.'

He returned Sean to his mother, pleased to be rid of him. 'I gotta get back to work. That Bullen'll kill me, else.' And, went, glad to be gone from this room of babies and birth and women.

Anneliese looked up at Gertrude Fairclough, who was as proud as though she had given birth herself. 'Thank you for everything you have done for us.'

Gratitude brought back all Mrs Fairclough's jitters, eyes and hands jumping like cats. 'Nothing. It was nothing.'

'Do you know where Dermot is?'

The Englishwoman leapt as though ordered. 'You want me to fetch him?'

'To introduce him to his brother.' She smiled at the light flooding through the window. At life. 'What day is it?'

'Saturday. February tenth.'

'Saturday, February tenth,' Anneliese repeated.

There was a wonder in it, in everything. The white-painted room, the blue sky rimmed with cloud that she could see through the window, the fine down on Mrs Fairclough's upper lip. Even the heat. Life, wonderful and complete.

'A good day for a new child.'

And she hugged baby Sean to her heart. Fulfilment flooded her. New beginnings, when nothing would go wrong ever again.

Strange that Dominic should have wanted to call the baby Jack.

Dominic had known from the first that there was bound to be trouble. He was an outsider, had taken the place of a bloke who'd been a member of the gang for four seasons. All right, that wasn't his fault, but it stood to reason they were hardly likely to welcome him with open arms. The fact that he'd never handled a blade before didn't help.

The last thing he wanted was a barney, so he did the best he could. Tried to joke along, his usual trick. It had worked with the horses and the grapes, he'd managed to get the occasional smile even out of the solemn-eyed Boers, stolid as cattle, but somehow, this time round, he never got it right.

He knew it yet seemed unable to do anything about it, the impulse that kept his mouth flapping day and night too much for his sense or even his instinct for survival. Everyone, Dominic included, knew it was only a matter of time before he fell foul of Bull Bullen, the boss ganger.

There was no one in the business could cut cane like Bull when he'd got a head of steam up, but he was a mean bastard when he wanted to be. He was another one full of mouth but in his case he'd got the muscles to back it up. He could out-talk you without raising a sweat and punch his weight better than any man in Queensland. Didn't matter if you were cutting cane or drinking in the pub, he told you what to do and you did it, or he belted you and you did it. All one to the Bull.

He was what you'd call a natural leader, meaning he felt the need to lord it over the rest of humanity. Any new bloke was a natural target. Most cottoned on pretty fast but Dominic had been places and seen things that the others didn't know about, and it made him slow to learn. Wouldn't have mattered if he'd kept it to himself, but he went on and on about it. Enough to drive a bloke dilly. Got right up the Bull's nose. If there was anything he hated, it was a new bloke too big for his britches.

Saturday night most of the blokes had a few grogs at the pub down the road, fuel them up for the next week. End of the shift, they were washing up when Bull spoke to Dominic.

'Comin' in? Wet the baby's head?'

They'd all heard about the kid, of course, but that wasn't why Bull had asked. Lesson time coming; Dominic could hear it in his voice. Shit, no, he thought, but it was no use. There was nothing he could do about it, at all.

'Why not? I'll have a jar with you, gladly.'

Knew at once that he'd said the wrong thing. Another bloke would've said, Thank you, Bull. *I'll have a jar with you, gladly*: like he was doing them a favour. Asking for it.

Down the pub they had a beer or two, then some of the blokes switched to rum. Bull was swilling it down like water. If Dominic had needed any confirmation, that was it. He'd seen Bullen in the pub before, knew that when the Bull got full he was a bad bastard and no error.

Everyone else knew what was coming, too. He wouldn't have minded betting they were already taking money on the result. Not one of them would expect him to last more than a minute. He didn't expect it himself but wasn't going to run away from it. Nowhere to run, in any case.

After an hour, the Bull strolled across to Dominic, taking his time. Dominic was leaning on the bar with a pot of rum in his hand.

Bull gave him a grin, teeth like gravestones. 'This Africa caper ...'

'What about it?'

'Lies.'

Dominic tipped his drink down, watching Bull over the rim.

'Is that so, now?'

'Course it is. You're as full of shit as a Christmas turkey.'

So it had come. Bull, big round head and yellow eyes, muscles in his back pumped up and ready, was daring him to take a swing. Seemed a pity to disappoint him. Dominic had the empty pot tight in his fist. He swung it sideways so fast it was a blur. A thud like an axe biting wood and the next thing Bull was staggering back, blood streaming down the side of his face, with Dominic all over him, gouging, punching, kneeing.

He knew he had to end it fast if he were to have any chance at all. For a moment it looked as though the Bull might go down, which would have given Dominic an opening to get to work with his boots, but somehow he didn't and Dominic had missed his chance. From then on, it was like a butcher hacking up a steer while it was still alive.

Bull worked slow. One step, flat-footed, and hit. One step and hit. Each time the fist went in to the wrist and you could've heard the sound out in the paddock.

One step, hit.

Blood all over.

One of Dominic's eyes was gone, bruised and swollen up and dripping blood. Bull pulled back, set his feet and swung. His fist took Dominic on the side of the head and he bent under it, a shiver running through him like a tree when the axe hits it.

He didn't go down and, when Bull came in close to polish him off, he let him have one right on the nose. There was a creak you could hear above the men yelling and suddenly there was blood all over Bull's chest.

Made no odds; hitting Bull was like hitting a wall.

The muscles behind his shoulder stood out big as a rock and he belted Dominic again. There was an explosion of light and pain and now the other eye was gone. Couldn't see a dicky. Dominic knew he'd had it yet even now wouldn't give up. He threw a roundhouse punch into the darkness. Felt the Bull's teeth under his knuckles but, again, it was like he'd hit a wall.

Now Bull was hitting him at will. Both eyes, nose, mouth, digging those great fists under his ribs again and again, like he was picking his spot.

He could feel blood and pain, not much else. His eyes were tight shut, his nose a mash. He was still holding out his fists but there was no strength in them and his knees were giving up under him.

And still he wouldn't go down.

Then Bull slung his left to set him up and slammed in the right so that Dominic's feet left the floor and he fell forward on his face. And lay there.

For a minute he must have been out of it entirely, then slowly the world came back. Voices.

'Thought Bull had killed him, for Christ's sake.'

A sudden jab of pain as the Bull shoved him with his boot.

'Giddup,' he said.

No way Dominic could move.

Again the tip of the boot jabbed.

'Giddup.'

Another voice said, 'Take it easy ...'

'Keep out of it,' the Bull said, his voice coming and going through a blur of pain.

'No, I won't. He needed a lesson, fair enough, but I ain't going to put up with this.'

Dominic tried to open his eyes but couldn't. And still the voices came, booming and dying away, like noises in a cave.

'Lanky Smiles,' the Bull said. 'Wipe your boots on him, Lanky.'

Lanky was one of the cutters, a good bloke, a few years older than the rest, normally happy to do what the Bull wanted. Not this time.

'Not me, mate,' Lanky said. 'I gonna see how he is.'

'Touch him, I'll settle for you, too.'

'Do what you gotta do. But I'm going to see to this bloke.'

Dominic felt him kneel at his side. The Bull did nothing to stop him. Dominic hear him say, 'God, what a mess...'

There was a slosh of water as someone brought a bucket. Dominic groaned as Lanky turned him. Every inch of him was agony and he sensed it would get a lot worse before it was better, but he was still too far away for the thought to worry him. They were dabbing away at him with a cloth while he lay there, the pain worrying him with steel teeth.

Slowly the world came back.

'Let's get him up...'

Somehow, swaying, he was on his feet, blokes holding him on either side. They were leading him, pulling him with gentle hands. His feet were dragging; in his broken nose the air seethed like molten lead; somewhere beyond the pain, cane frogs were croaking in the darkness.

Eventually they came to a standstill. He could hear someone fumbling with a door. They guided him inside, helped him onto his bunk. Left him there. He heard the diminishing murmur of low voices. Silence at last.

Ambrose Fairclough was working in his office when he heard from his field supervisor that two of his cutters had been involved in a fight the previous evening.

'Who were they?'

'Bullen and Riordan. The new bloke.' In case the boss had forgotten.

'What started it?'

Bill Dodd had been with Fairclough for eight years; all the same, was not about to dob in another worker. Not even Bull Bullen, who was no mate of his.

'Dunno.'

'How badly is Riordan hurt?'

'Pretty crook. He'll be right, though, give 'im a day or two.'

Ambrose had not wanted this Riordan in the first place. An extra pair of hands was always useful, but the way Gertrude had engaged the wife, without even asking permission ... He wasn't going to put up with that. At the same time, he did not intend giving her the chance to accuse him of harshness.

'Fighting gives all of us a bad name. Let him have a week to get over it, then get rid of him.'

'What about Bullen?'

Fairclough flashed a glance at Bill Dodd's stubborn face. From which he knew better than to expect confidences. 'Tell him I wouldn't want to lose him.'

'No!' Mrs Fairclough said. Her voice, normally as dead as the stagnant air, was shrill. 'I shall not permit it!'

'The man picked a fight with the gang boss —'

'I do not care about the man.'

He did not bother to hide his exasperation. 'What are you talking about, then?'

'Mrs Riordan, of course. And her baby. The child is two days old. I shall not permit you to turn them out onto the road.'

For his part, Fairclough would permit no insubordination from his wife or anyone. Yet felt a twinge of uneasiness at talk of babies.

'The Irish are always fighting, you know that.' He repeated what he had said to Bill Dodd. 'Brawling in pubs gives all of us a bad name.'

His wife stared at him with an unfamiliar boldness. 'Tell him to behave himself, then. Because his wife is staying.'

Her defiance infuriated him, flying in the face of what he considered the proper order of domestic life. Yet there was a hint of desperation in her voice, of hysteria, almost. It certainly had nothing to do with the baby or indeed anything outside herself. About to slap her down, Ambrose hesitated.

'What will she do if she does stay?' he wondered cautiously.

'She will assist me. About the house. In the garden.'

'That's Polly's job.'

'Polly . . .'

Who would have been mortified had she heard the tone in which her mistress disposed of her.

Ambrose sighed. In the sugar business one had to deal with all sorts — kanaka and white; even, occasionally, people of one's own class — and he had not built a flourishing plantation without an instinct for handling others. He had seen his wife become increasingly neurotic in recent months — the tropics did that to some people — and wished her to be cured, if it could be done. She seemed to have taken a fancy to the strange woman. Perhaps, if he humoured her, things between themselves might improve. There was a need: their relationship had developed such jagged edges that it was no longer possible for them to get close to each other. And a man, in the tropics as elsewhere, became resentful when denied the comforts that marriage was supposed to bring.

'I couldn't put Riordan back in Bullen's gang,' he said. 'We'd have to find him something else to do.'

Sensing victory, Mrs Fairclough was wise enough to take no advantage.

'Mrs Riordan was saying her husband is good with horses. Let him look after them. If you think that would be best.'

Carefully she deferred to her husband's greater wisdom, of which Ambrose, at least, had no doubt.

Looking after the horses had always been a problem; yet for the sake of domestic discipline he could not be expected to accede too readily.

'Horses,' he repeated. 'I'll think about it.'

That evening, after giving Dominic a few hours to get over his battering, Anneliese went to see how he was.

'*Ag man ...*'

She stared at him, appalled. His face was reworked so comprehensively that she doubted he would ever look the same again.

'What was it about?'

'Nothing.'

He spoke with difficulty through torn lips.

She had no patience with such nonsense. 'That is impossible —'

'Soon's I'm on my feet, we're out of here,' he said.

'No.'

'Whaddya mean?' Glaring at her.

'Mr Fairclough was going to discharge you because of what happened. Mrs Fairclough talked him out of it.'

He was resentful of any woman intruding upon male territory. Even the boss's wife — particularly her, perhaps.

'Tell her to keep her beak out of it.'

'She did not do it for you! She did it for the baby. For Sean.'

She had discovered how helpless men were when confronted by the threat of a child.

'We owe it to Sean to stay. For the time being, anyway.'

He attempted ferocity, for his pride's sake. 'I get back to that gang, there'll be murder done.'

'They need someone to look after the horses.'

The battered lips twisted scornfully. 'And have everyone say I'm afraid to face him? That'll be the day!'

Anneliese stared at him. She had learned to understand

him well. Bullen had beaten him almost to death; now, to restore his idiot pride, he would run headfirst into a brick wall rather than accept help from anyone. She had no patience with such nonsense. They were destitute; now, out of the blue, they had been offered a measure of security after months on the road. She would not let Dominic walk away from it simply because some oaf had blackened his eyes for him.

'I have told her you'll do it.'

Rage, no less potent for his body's weakness. 'And I'm telling you I won't!'

'You walk out of here, you go alone.'

To emphasise her words, she slammed the door behind her as she left. Yet in truth was not much concerned. Dominic would be off his feet for a day or two. By then she thought he would understand she meant what she said. He had better; she would abandon him, if it came to it. Baby Sean, now, was her priority.

And remained so.

They stayed, as Anneliese had been determined they would. Dominic tended the horses, as arranged. He had always had a way with them and now spent hours in the stables, seeking the company that was no longer available elsewhere. He had been spoiled; until Sean's birth Anneliese had been there for him always. Even after the row over Dermot and the ferryman, he had still had priority in her life and had come to expect it. No longer. Sean was the first thing she had owned since the death of the children in Africa and she focused all her attention on him.

She took the baby everywhere, did everything for him. Gertrude Fairclough and Polly (won over by the baby as never by the mother) would have helped, had Anneliese permitted, but she did not. She would allow no one to come between her and the child. It was unreasonable; she knew it and did not care. She was fulfilled as never since *Oudekraal*. For hours she chattered to Sean in Dutch, entertained fantasies of raising him to speak the language so they could converse secretly together. Even Dermot had to take second place to her son.

Her obsession made Dominic uneasy. 'You'll be ruining the boy.'

She took no notice, knowing that he, too, was jealous in his way.

One day Dominic said, 'I'll not be having Dermot brought up in a houseful of women.' And bore him off to the horses, where he was spending more and more of his time.

He taught the boy to ride, frightening him half to death. In his own childhood Jack had taught him by chucking him on top of a horse; when he fell off, he had clambered back on, again and again, until at last, miraculously, his body had learned what it had to do. He was never a natural horseman but had learned enough to fall off only occasionally. He hadn't minded; when at last he managed it, had laughed with his father, each as triumphant as the other.

Dermot was different. When he fell, he was not interested in renewing the challenge; when Dominic forced him back into the saddle, he fell off again at once. And again; until man and horse and child were dizzy, desperate with frustration.

'I'll swear he does it deliberately,' Dominic said. But persevered until Dermot could ride, after a fashion, then lost interest. Instead took to going down the road to the pub. Never on Saturdays, because then the cutters would be there. He went during the week, slipping away from the stables when his work was done, to down a pot or two in the solitude of the bar.

A pot or two or three or four. Until the moon swung overhead as full and boastful as himself, and it was all he could do not to go looking for the Bull with a cane-cutter's blade in his hand.

Must have retained some vestige of sanity because he never did. Never went to the room that Anneliese shared with the children at the back of the house, either. Instead, he returned to the stables. Whence he emerged, red-eyed and frowsty, stinking of liquor, in the morning. Yet did his work properly, despite all. Which saved him and them.

Ambrose Fairclough did not care how much his employee drank, provided he caused no trouble and did his work. It was a small price to pay for the transformation that his wife had undergone since the coming of the woman. He didn't know or care what she did to earn her keep. As far as Ambrose was concerned, she was worth every penny he paid her, simply by being there.

In fact Anneliese had become Mrs Fairclough's companion. Her employer forgave her even the baby, and wanted her with her always, questioning her unceasingly. About Africa. About herself. About how she thought and felt. About the seconds and minutes and hours of her life.

Until, after tea, Anneliese had to escape to the mosquito-singing darkness, the stagnant air of the canefields, and walk and walk. She could have screamed at having to reveal so much of herself to this woman. Who meant well, she knew, yet who took it for granted that Anneliese was her property, to be used as she wished, to talk, to reveal, to provide the dimension of living that Mrs Fairclough had never known. It was what she was paid for, after all.

Blerry English, Anneliese thought, they leave nothing and no one in the world alone.

Looking for a fight, she went to the stables, where she found Dominic asleep and snoring in the straw. She woke him without pity for his fuddled senses, the red eyes that stared with little comprehension. With Mrs Fairclough she was compelled to bite her tongue, had no intention of doing so with this boozed-up oaf whose conduct endangered the future of them all.

'Carry on like this, Mr Fairclough will put us out on the road.'

Dominic indignant. 'I do my work and well you know it. 'Tis all he cares about. No harm in a little drink.'

'*A* little drink?' She scorned him, no longer prepared to tolerate his version of the truth. 'More than one, I think.'

He glared belligerently, raking his whiskers with dirty fingernails. 'Payin' my way, aren't I?'

'Are you? When you drink all your wages?'

'The season's nearly over,' he told her. 'Week or two, they'll be off south for the lay-off. Then things'll be right, you'll see.'

'I hope so.' For the hundredth time she willed herself to show patience, to smile. 'You'll try? Yes?'

'Course I will.' He licked dry lips, favouring her with his stinking breath. 'Come to keep me company?' he asked, attempting roguishness.

She evaded him.

'Sean's crying. I must get back.'

Perhaps he's right, she hoped. When Bullen had gone, perhaps things would improve.

The men went south, the stripped paddocks lay empty. Fallow ground was ploughed, the black soil readied for planting. As for Dominic's drinking, nothing changed.

Anneliese was at her wits' end. For his own wife's sake Fairclough might continue to tolerate the situation so long as Dominic made no serious mistakes but, drinking the way he was, something was bound to go wrong eventually. It would mean the ruin of them all; Fairclough was not a forgiving man where work was concerned. Gertrude had talked her husband into keeping Dominic once; she would never manage it a second time.

'Why do you do it? Why?'

He would not tell her why, could not put into words the resentment he felt at life for granting him a job only through the intervention of a woman. Of being a man who had disgraced himself by failing to stand up for himself in a fight.

Instead lifted her skirt, winking. She could not bear it, pushed him away.

His response appalled her. Weeping and raving, he threw himself down amid the clop and clatter of uneasy hooves, shouting about Bullen and fire and dead children, the man his father was and he never would be.

Frightened, she scolded him. '*Nee man*. You're talking rubbish.'

He turned. Stared with hatred as she bent over him.

'You know what I'm sayin'. You mind well what kinda man my Da is. Who better?' He raked spittle into his mouth and spat full in her face. 'You think I didn't know?'

'You can't,' Mrs Fairclough said, eyes panicking. 'I won't let you.'

Anneliese's expression remained frozen, as though her employer had not spoken. Desperately Mrs Fairclough's voice beat at that icy façade, determined somehow to reach her, to demonstrate her pain.

'It's because of your husband's drinking, isn't it? My husband has spoken. But you needn't be ashamed. Really. It's not your fault. There are men — some men — who are like that. It is not our fault. Don't you see?'

The jumble of words forced its way into the light. Her eyes implored amid the tangled sounds.

Anneliese's expression did not change.

'You are my friend.' Now Mrs Fairclough was reduced to pleading. 'My salvation, even. I shall not permit you to leave me.'

Desperation had forced her to speak; now she found she could not stop. Stammering, close to incoherence, she said, 'Even if my husband is forced to dismiss him. It doesn't mean you. You can stay. Let him go. It'll be better that way. He's no good for you. Think of yourself. Think of your children.' Hysteria stained the hot air amid the spray of jumbled, pleading words. 'Where will you go? If you leave here — what will you do?'

All the time you, *you*; what will *you* do? how will *you* survive? — when Anneliese knew that she was really saying something different:

What about me? How shall I manage, alone for the remainder of my life, exposed to the scorn of my husband, of Polly, myself? How shall I survive? Haven't we been friends? Haven't I taken care of you? I took you in off the road. I helped you when you needed help. Have you forgotten?

Mrs Fairclough's face was wet and blubbering, soft as marshmallow. As always when terror overwhelmed her, her skin was flushed, her eyes flushed, tears leaking. Despicable. Weak. Unworthy of love.

Cravenly she begged pity. At last she succeeded in penetrating the icy stillness that Anneliese had erected to protect herself from her employer's ignominy.

Like a dark flame within her, Anneliese felt fury and distaste ignite. 'You know nothing! Nothing!' she cried. 'We are going together, as we came. You English think you own the world. Did you really imagine I would abandon him after everything we have been through together? We have fought the English all our lives. We shall go on fighting them. We shall go, now.'

The blade of her scorn pierced Mrs Fairclough's heart. She wiped her streaming face with her hand, drawing the tattered cloak of her dignity about her as she rescued what she could of self-respect.

'You are cruel. Unkind. I thought you were my friend. Go, then.'

Go they did. Anneliese's back was straight, her face like stone. She felt Mrs Fairclough's reproachful eyes watching from behind the net curtain as she walked down the driveway. Beside her Dominic shambled, grumbling, stinking of booze. She ignored him, shepherding the two boys. She had had the chance of friendship, of a place, but pride had its price. After the words that Dominic had hurled, so hatefully, she could not stay, fearful of what might come out. With strangers she would not care but Mrs Fairclough, for all her foolishness, had come too close to be still a stranger.

She reached the drive and turned, heading northwards. She did not look back.

Six months here, a year there. Dominic picked up rags and tatters of work, enough to keep them alive. Droving, mostly; he never went back to the cane.

They headed inland. The land swallowed them. They lived like shadows, drifting across an empty landscape guarded by the blood-red fortresses of termite mounds. The ramparts of low hills barely broke a horizon that ringed them like a hoop of iron, confining them, ever-moving, to a single spot, a single instant, as though the landscape were moving with them, pinning them always to the same place.

The boys would have grown up savage had Anneliese not made it her business to civilise them. The first town they came to after leaving the Faircloughs, she bought a Bible. Each night, wherever they were, she read it to them, as her own people had read to their children in their journeying through the savage wastes of Africa. Would have read to Dominic, too, had he been willing, but always, when she fetched the Book, he would walk away and sit a little apart, his back against a rock, his face turned always to the emptiness that lay ahead of them. She could see his silhouette against the stars as she read, while the cattle bellowed mournfully in the darkness and the fire formed a lake of rosy light into which she and the children dipped their feet.

They had no liquor with them. Dominic, whom liquor had enslaved, was fine away from the towns but whenever they came near one, and he with money in his pocket, he would be gone. Sometimes for an hour, sometimes for a day, a night. Anneliese never knew when he would come back, but when his money ran out he always did. He was tethered as securely to her as she to him, their shared lives binding them closer than any priest.

There were times when she was lonely, waiting through the long nights while he drank away the little they had. What of it? she thought. All of us are alone.

That is why men, who are weaker than we, drink or fly upon the wings of impossible dreams, trying to escape what is, in their eternal pursuit of what might be. While we, stronger than they, learn again to do what we have always known best: to endure.

SEVENTEEN

Adrift.
Not only emotionally; Africa, Anna thought, had put a jinx on her. Everything in her life seemed to have gone wrong. Even faith in her own political future had failed her.

Jack Goodie was not a gentle man yet put it to her as gently as he could. 'Nothing I can do about it, Anna. I didn't make the system. You know what they say: I never promised you a rose garden.' And laughed.

Anna was not laughing. 'You knew, though. You knew what I wanted.'

'I can fix you up with a seat.' Jack rubbed his chin dubiously, not too keen on even that idea. 'Maybe. Want me to have a try?'

A member of parliament had no power. A ministry was what she had wanted. These things didn't happen overnight; she understood she would have to serve her time. But to dive in without a promise or even an understanding...

'Be straight with me, Jack. You know I've got what it takes. What are my chances?'

'You want me to tell you how many pollies out there are asking the same question? Blokes in the unions? Blokes we owe favours?'

Blokes.

'I've no chance, have I?'

'Your time's coming. Not yet though. Public opinion isn't ready. Neither's the Party.' He tried a joke. 'You know how it is with progressive organisations. Always years behind the rest.'

'I'm not going to waste my life on the off chance something may crop up.'

'I tell you what you should do.' He'd put in a word for her with a bloke he knew, the top gun of a big company. 'Get a few years in commerce under your belt. Who knows? Maybe you can come back to politics later.'

'I shall still be a woman, wherever I am.'

'Be thankful.'

'Why?'

He grinned. 'You make the world beautiful.'

She would have hit him if she'd thought he meant it. She made up her mind. 'Okay, then. Set it up for me.'

Two days later she flew to Sydney to meet Jack's friend. The discussion went well; the job was hers if she wanted it. Afterwards she went for a walk and bumped into Nicki, an old student acquaintance she hadn't seen since university.

Nicki was all bubbles: an airhead, but fun. After the mutual exclamations, the hugs, the dancing around on the pavement, they went to a cafe Nicki knew. They tucked into sinful cakes glossy with chocolate and cappuccino steaming in mugs a whale could have swum in. They exchanged confidences.

Well, sort of.

Nicki had always been like a public address system, so Anna was deliberately vague about both her past life and her plans for the future. Which, in any case, were still uncertain.

Nicki was less reticent. So far as Anna could make out, her life was a non-stop party: booze and fun and plenty of men. It all sounded very tiring.

'You could be the answer to my prayers.' Nicki grinned conspiratorially. 'Are you free tonight?'

Anna remembered that with Nicki it always paid to be cautious. 'I might be. Why?'

'Come and have a drink with me. There's someone I'd like you to meet.'

Anna watched her thoughtfully across the table. The allegedly high life had not dimmed the sparkle in her innocent blue eyes but Anna knew her from old.

'Who is it?'

A butter-wouldn't-melt smile. 'A feller. Ever so good-looking.'

She had assumed it wouldn't be Dracula but the mystery remained. Nicki wasn't into sharing where fellers were concerned. Who was?

'Why me?'

Nicki had always been one for innuendos, spurts of breathless confidences. Hard facts were something else; for those you needed a crowbar, but Anna was good with crowbars and eventually managed to prise the truth out of her. Or something close to the truth.

'Mostyn Harcourt,' she whispered, leaning across the table in her spy-of-the-month manner. 'A merchant banker.'

Anna had never heard of him but permitted herself to be suitably impressed. 'And he's a friend of yours?'

An old friend, it seemed.

'We go back a long way. To our early days in the bush, can you believe?' Nicki laughed, up and off the scale; she had always been exuberant. 'We've had a wonderful relationship. Marvellous.' Nudge, nudge.

'And you're seeing him tonight?'

'Well, that's the plan.'

'So the question remains. Why me?'

Had to get the crowbar to work again before she got the answer to that one, although she had half guessed, anyway. Nicki had met someone else.

'Tom Neal ...' As though Anna were bound to know who he was. 'Pots of money,' she said, blue eyes wide. 'And keen.'

'Keen?'

'I think he wants to marry me.'

'I can see that Mostyn doesn't fit into that scenario,' Anna said. 'Why on earth did you agree to see him tonight?'

'I don't like shutting the door in his face. I'm not married yet.'

And Nicki wanted to keep Mostyn on ice in case she needed him again later.

'But not tonight. It wouldn't do, would it?'

Obviously not.

Anna was amused. 'So you want me to be a substitute. What makes you think he'll go along with it?'

Nicki, airhead or not, had plans to cover that.

'We meet at the hotel. The three of us. Then I sort of slide away.'

'Leaving me holding the fort.'

But could see no harm in it. It was not as though she had anything else to do for the evening. 'So long as he understands I'm not as old a friend as you are.'

Righteous shock in eyes that were strangers to both shock and righteousness. 'Nothing like that!' But you couldn't keep Nicki down for long. The bubbles resurfaced as she winked. 'Unless you want to, of course.'

Which Anna thought was as unlikely a prospect as she could imagine.

She knew he was a bastard as soon as she set eyes on him. That was all right. She had this new job under her belt but was still smarting from what she thought of as her failure in Canberra; a bastard might be just what she needed. Someone whose strength could restore her own strength. She was thirsty for someone with strength and Mostyn, undeniably, was strong. He was confident, hard, knew exactly what he was and where he was going. A man of possibilities.

'One more drink,' Nicki said, 'then I must fly.'

And did, leaving them to get on with it. They talked sense, they talked nonsense, they laughed. They watched each other speculatively.

Eventually Anna said she must get home.

By the way he'd been looking her over, she wondered whether he might offer her a lift, even suggest going on somewhere. She hoped not; it was too soon for that. Was grateful to him when he did not. They parted casually and she walked away, jostled by scurrying commuters. Stopped suddenly as an overwhelming desire for the man she had just left hit her in mid-stride. She no longer had any idea where her feet were taking her. Mostyn Harcourt ... The strong compact body, the keen, assessing eyes. She stood quite still on the crowded pavement, drawing air deeply into her lungs.

This I don't need, she thought. To find a man attractive was one thing, but this ...

When she'd got her breath back, she walked on, more slowly. Nothing to it, of course. He wasn't the first man she'd fancied nor would he be the last. Strange, though: the sudden loss of breath, the feeling that she had walked into a wall.

Back at the hotel she laid her clothes on the bed, walked naked into the bathroom and turned on the taps.

While the bath filled, she fetched a bottle from her suitcase, poured herself a gargantuan Scotch. Took a swallow, felt it shudder down. Good.

She took the glass with her into the bathroom. Leant back in the bath, eyes closed, yielding to the water's stinging heat.

The phone rang.

Damn.

She picked up the extension. 'Hullo?'

'What did you think of him?' Nicki, conspiratorial, eager to probe.

Anna closed her eyes, feeling her heart thump with relief. Wondered, all the same, how she would have felt had it been his voice on the line.

She smiled, body as soft as cream in the hot water. 'He was okay.'

She took the job, left Canberra with surprisingly few regrets. In Sydney found herself flung into a whirlpool of activity both stimulating and alarming. She felt herself respond to the challenge. She relished it, began to grow.

She saw Nicki occasionally, was invited by her to a party to meet her new fiancé. Mostyn Harcourt might be there, she hoped, but was not. She heard the odd snippet about him though. At work she allowed his name to trail casually into her conversations and heard more. He was a comer, one of the rising stars at Heinrich Griffiths. People said he was a ruthless, highly competent son-of-a-bitch. Already he had a nickname, a measure of his status. Hatchet Harcourt. A man destined for power.

Perhaps it was the power she found so attractive.

One evening he phoned and asked her to have dinner with him.

She took a long time getting ready, making up her face with particular care. She wanted to stand out, but not to the point where she frightened him. She judged him to be conventional in such things; most men were. Of course Mostyn was not like most men. In the end she compromised: conservative, yet not too much. Wondered whether she'd overdone it, all the same.

What the hell. He doesn't want to go out with a company executive, let's hope.

He picked her up punctually. He was informally dressed, the sort of clothes that look casual and cost a thousand bucks. He did not comment on her appearance but his eyes did and she knew she'd got it right. Felt, too, the same hot gush of passion that she had experienced after their first meeting.

They went to a restaurant: starched tablecloths and harbour views. He held her hand, watching the lights of the city shining upon the black water. She thought that later he might try to hold more than her hand, wondered what she would do if he did. He did not. He took her home, refused her offer of a drink. Did not even kiss her cheek. She thought she must have blown it, was all the more delighted when he phoned the next day to suggest they do the same thing again.

So it went, one thing leading to another, yet for reasons she did not understand she still held him off. He tried, the decorum of that first evening long gone now, but still she would not let him do more than kiss her.

I want him, she thought, so why am I being so stiff and starchy about it? Knew that was the point. She wanted him too much, was afraid of getting in too deep. She scolded herself for being ridiculous. She would lose him if she wasn't careful; this was the nineteen-eighties, not the eighteen-eighties.

If I let him touch my breast he will perhaps be satisfied, she thought, knowing that such half-measures would satisfy neither of them. Yet still she held him off. The nightly, abbreviated embrace became their ritual of courtship, her senses reeling under the impact of his tantalising fingers, her own burgeoning yet unfulfilled warmth.

Memory broke the impasse. Her body's reactions brought back images of days she had thought banished from her mind forever.

The dust of Africa, the rhythmic stamp and shuffle of Africa, the baying anger of Africa. Above all, the aftermath of that first meeting with Shongwe, herself riding Mark in frenzy, striving unsuccessfully to exorcise feelings that even she had not understood.

Mostyn, feeling her shudder, believed he was the cause. He pressed ardour more closely so that, at last, she yielded. He imagined wrongly that it was to himself, knowing nothing of the rhythms and memories that had, in truth, solved his problem for him.

Yet the culmination was like a fire consuming them both. Afterwards they held each other, knowing that whatever barrier had existed was there no longer, that something fundamental had been resolved between them.

The drums of Africa echoed in her blood. Never since that time had Anna known the golden surge and nerve-flutter of delight. It made her tender, although whether to this lover or to memories of the past she could not have said. Nor did it matter. He had restored gentleness and joy to her.

Mostyn Harcourt, ruthless, thrusting, indifferent to the tenderness of others, was an unlikely bearer of such gifts, but she was convinced their relationship was something apart, that different rules applied to them than to the rest of humanity. The past had united them; now she was grateful to him for enabling her to forget it.

With Mostyn I shall conquer the world and myself, she thought exultantly. She could not wait for the days to pass so that she could get him back to her apartment and make love to him again.

His hand moves quietly, with purpose. Anna, waiting. Her thighs slant in offering. She feels his palm and fingers enclose her, gentle yet firm.

I am here.

The tremor begins. Deep within her the pulse. Ah. His other hand, feather-light, touching. A finger, parting. The pulse throbs. Moisture. Her mouth sucks air. Nerves cry yearningly. Yes. The word thrown silently from behind closed eyelids into a blaze of light. Yes.

Anna had thought in terms of a relationship, an infusion of confidence to set her feet once again securely on the path. Instead, she discovered a commitment to another being that she had never expected to feel again. Had reservations, nonetheless. She had thought that Mostyn would set her free; instead, he had enchained her. He made her feel — God! — *grateful* for proving that she was capable of what in moments of self-mockery she called finer feelings. Yet she knew she would not have missed the experience for the world.

Late one night, she went for a walk through the city's stone streets. Her heels rang; she remembered another time when the hooves of horses had aroused similar echoes. The water of the harbour gleamed, lolling in fragmented glimpses between the stern shapes of buildings.

'I am complete, at last.' She exhaled the realisation into the city's stained air, the hint of salt about Darling Harbour. 'Complete!'

Only a foraging cat seemed to care, pausing momentarily in its headlong flight into shadow. She resumed her walk. Completeness was conditional; the future, like the cat, vanished into darkness. It also offered freedom, of a sort, yet what was the use of that if it brought subjection? In a man's world, there was a sexual price for everything.

Most men didn't even realise it, took for granted a servitude that to them was part of the proper order of things. Mostyn was not one of them, admittedly, but had been born with an instinct for seizing any advantage that would give him the edge in whatever battle he was fighting.

Battle? she thought. Is that what it is?

It was exactly what it was, a battle for dominance. Mostyn was a winner, and to win you had to fight.

Which made it all the more astonishing when, a month later, he asked her to marry him.

Her heart lurched. She said yes and discovered she had been waiting for his proposal since that first meeting. Their future might well prove a battlefield, but she found she relished the challenge, the promise of fulfilment.

Mostyn thought so, too. 'What a team we'll make!' he said exultantly.

Anna wondered if that was why he had proposed, to forge a strike force for the battles that lay ahead. It no longer mattered. She was head-over-heels in love with him, in that state of euphoria where she could examine with clear-eyed awareness the character of the man she was marrying and not care.

They got married, Hatchet Harcourt and the woman who thought she was going to tame him. It was a great occasion. Money flowed like champagne. The snowy marquees, the caviar, the smoked salmon and wedding cake. The sunlit air gleamed like a cascade of bubbles. Half the big names of the city were there, pirouetting figures on the carousel of a jewelled and magnificent clock.

After guests and media had departed, Mr and Mrs Harcourt retired via stretch limo to the suite that had been accorded the honour of witnessing their post-nuptial consummations. Which they might have celebrated at once — the much-admired dress crushed and discarded on the floor, the peeled white wand of Anna's body emerging like a Botticelli Venus from a foam of lingerie and troubling memories — had it not been for a final engagement which they had both agreed must be honoured.

Dinner in a private room where their future was toasted by a dozen hand-picked and influential guests. Chairman of this. With wife. Managing director of that. With, but discreetly, someone else's wife. Those who inhabited the upmost pinnacles of the mountain to which both bride and groom so ardently aspired.

'Planning on starting a dynasty?'

Laughter climbing on the back of champagne, but decorously. No one in this company was likely to put a foot wrong.

Moderate backslapping, cheek-kissing; it was over. Or just begun. Afterwards, lovemaking almost put out the lamps of memory.

The alien rhythms, the dust rising, the almond eyes shining in the closed and guarded room. The subsequent goading of flesh and spirit, the frenzied night ride into sunrise.

Almost.

'There's a vineyard in my life, too,' she had told him, early in their acquaintance. At once Mostyn, obsessed with vineyards, had been interested. She told him about *Oudekraal*, the place it had come to have in her life.

'You sound as though you're half in love with it,' he had said, amused by feminine frailty.

Instinct put her on guard, denying what she suspected was the truth. 'I wouldn't say that ...'

When they had decided to marry, she had suggested honeymooning in South Africa, where she could show him the farm, introduce him to *Oudekraal*'s owner.

'Not South Africa.' Mostyn, ever conscious of the importance of political correctness, shook his head regretfully. 'Anywhere else ...'

The citadel of apartheid was a no-no. Instead they flew first class to France, where Mostyn had interests in a number of vineyards.

They spent a week doing Paris — the Louvre, the Bois de Boulogne, Notre Dame, the palace of this, the chateau of that. To please Anna, they wandered along the quays of the Seine, watching the reflections in the water flowing beneath the old stone bridges. They inspected the work of artists, climbed the slopes of Montmartre, ate at pavement cafes. They braved the homicidal rush of traffic.

The second week they travelled to Bordeaux and then to Burgundy, visiting the vineyards that were Mostyn's obsession. It seemed foolish to miss the opportunity, while they were in Europe, to examine the prospects for future investment.

He would have gone to Germany, had Anna permitted, had suggested he fly over on a quick trip, leaving her to go shopping in Paris. Indignantly, she rejected the idea. He considered she was being foolish but, for the sake of harmony, went along, thinking well of himself for doing so.

Shopping, indeed, thought Anna crossly. Lots of bedroom ceilings — that was what she intended to see. It was what honeymoons were for, wasn't it? Germany could wait.

Still, she couldn't complain; she saw several ceilings. In between, they inspected vineyards. It was September and the grapes were ready. They, too, were being harvested. Anna wondered if they felt as she did, ripe and bursting with desire under the late-summer sun. Machines trundled between rows of vines that oppressed the earth with their geometric regularity. Here and there, knots of hand-pickers in blue shirts, arms sienna-brown, deftly cut the heavy bunches and placed them in the wicker containers they drew on iron wheels behind them. One of the oldest of rituals, the whole world caught up in a slow and timeless celebration of the fecundity of the earth, with themselves as spectators.

'Stop the car,' she commanded.

Startled, Mostyn did so. Anna got out and walked off the ribbon of burning bitumen into the vines. The leaves, a green forest with here and there a hint of lemon and russet, surrounded her. This section had not been harvested; the grapes hung, the bloom still on them. She lifted a bunch gently on its stalk. It weighed heavy in her palm.

Like my own breasts, she thought, when I inspect them before the mirror.

A strip of grass ran down the middle of the row and suddenly, urgently, she wanted her husband. Here, on the grass between the endless rows of vines bearing their offerings of grapes. She turned to where he stood by the open door of the car. He looked perplexed, not too well pleased. She had found already that he resented anything he did not understand or approve — in his wife, most of all. She suspected he would not approve of this, but did not care. The slowly moving pickers were far away on the other side of the valley.

'Come here ...'

He came. He thought she had found something; in a sense, perhaps she had.

'What is it?'

She took hold of him. 'This.'

He was startled. That she could understand. Upset, too, which was harder to forgive.

'What are you doing?' Whispering, as though they were surrounded by ears, by eyes.

'What do you think?' Hand moving.

'Here?'

'Yes.'

'We can't.'

'Yes, we can.'

And she was determined to prove it, *had* to prove it, although why she could not have said. He did nothing, so she did. Her fingers worked his zipper. He sprang out. She had him. She went to kneel on the ground before him, the weight of the sun on her back, the weight of the unharvested grapes within her flesh, her bursting loins. He stepped back, hands batting frantically at Anna's hands.

'No!' He turned, scurrying back to the car, hands hauling his trousers tight.

She watched, angry and humiliated. Worse than that: bereft.

They flew back to Sydney. In her mind and heart Anna still carried the scar of what had not happened.

Had it been so much to ask?

I would like to celebrate my hundredth year lying with my husband amid the rows of vines, she thought. She smiled at the incongruous vision, prepared to believe they might both be past it by then.

How would we have felt if we had gone to Africa? she wondered. Making love out in the open, under the sky of Africa; the idea made her shiver.

How many times had Anneliese done it? she wondered. *Outspanned* upon the banks of rushing streams, the water ice-cold, the mountains towering overhead, with beyond them the galaxies, diamond-bright ... Upon the open *veld*, amid the scents and emptiness of Africa, the campfire to keep away hyena ...

It was hardly something you could ask your great-grandmother, so she never had. It didn't matter; Anna was convinced she knew. Hundreds and hundreds of times. And in Australia, too, on that long meandering journey northwards through the continent's emptiness, with the two children and Dominic beside her. Anneliese had told her so much about it, although not that, of course. Never mind. She knew the answer; what she wanted to be the answer. Hundreds and hundreds of times.

EIGHTEEN

For years they trekked across the empty land. The outside world meant nothing to them. Rumours of strikes, of fires and floods, passed them by. Even the death of the king Anneliese had loathed so passionately meant nothing now. If they continued to preach hatred to the boys, it was from habit and because it had become its own justification. Hatred and the children — without them their lives would have meant nothing. Without Anneliese's son Sean, in particular. Sean was tough, always filthy, quick as sunlight. From the first, after he started running about, he had the knowing look of someone much older. Anneliese found it hard to remember that he had ever been a baby who relied on her for everything; Sean and helplessness were worlds apart.

He was as direct as a blade. When he wanted something he went straight for it, like a thrust for the jugular. He wanted so many things. Things he could carry off, hide like a dog burying a bone. He shared nothing.

Anneliese continued to love him with the passionate, unreasoning love that she had felt from the moment of his birth, the love that had first overwhelmed and then excluded all else, but there were times when his black, monkey's eyes, hard as glass, troubled her too. One day, when Sean was four, they arrived at a river. It was mostly dry, but with pools here and there reflecting the brilliant sky like mirrors of emerald.

Water in this arid land was usually too precious for washing but here, in the emerald pools, there was enough to wash them all.

'Get your clothes off,' Anneliese told Sean. 'You're filthy.'

He was, dust in every nook and cranny of his body. She dragged off his clothes, despite his squawks. Rivulets of mud had hardened on his skin, yet his body had the sweetness of a young animal.

She washed him in the algae-thick water, scrubbing with a cloth while he squirmed indignantly, fish-slippery between her hands. The slender stalk of neck. The head poised and alert, arrogant even now. She scrubbed under his arms, despite his protests. She ran the cloth over the velvet skin of his body, along the line of ribs like the fingers of a bony hand. She scrubbed between his legs, the taut buttocks and jutting, small-boy's pod, the sturdy legs and dirt-encrusted toes. Each time she did this she felt as though she were shaping him again from the clay of her own flesh, a rebirth filling her with awe that she had been the agent in the creation of so perfect a being.

She would have liked so much to play with him, but that he would not permit. He tolerated what she was doing, barely, but as soon as she had finished, his skin scarlet from the cloth, he was off up the bank to stand naked and unashamed in the hard sunlight. He stood looking down at her, chest thrown out, head back, and she saw Jack Riordan in him, the bones of the eagle head already plain, the stance that challenged the world. Then he turned and ran off, secure and entire as only a young male, conscious of strength to come, could be.

That was the day Anneliese and Dominic first fell out over him. Afterwards she could not remember what Sean had done; given cheek, most probably — he was always one for that.

'Time I took my strap to him,' Dominic said.

'No.'

'Or he will grow up wild.'

Let him, Anneliese thought, if wildness is his destiny. No one is going to tame him while I have breath.

Aloud she said, 'Don't you dare.'

Stares, then. 'Are you threatening me, woman?'

Her fury erupted. 'I've stayed with you every step of the way. Always. Even when we were settled at the Faircloughs I left with you rather than have us divided. Sean is your child' — she would go to the rack before she admitted the possibility of anything else — 'but if you take your belt to him, I swear we shall all leave you at the next town.'

Face hot with rage, he raised his hand. She thought he was going to hit her. She stared, challenging him, and at length his hand fell. He turned away, and Anneliese knew that she had beaten him. She watched as he stamped off through the bush, booted feet kicking dust. He was gone a long time but, like herself, had nowhere else to go. He would be back.

Yet, in truth, that was the day when part of him stayed away forever. Dominic saw, finally, that Anneliese had turned her face from him and the shutters came down over his heart. For a long time, he said as little to her as he could. As for Sean ... it was as though he did not exist.

Instead he tried to make up to Dermot, unsuccessfully. Dermot evaded him, as he did the rest of them. He was a gentle boy; Anneliese had always been convinced he was too fine for the life they led. Through his eyes, she watched the changing colours of the bush, the panoply of stars above their nightly camps. A dozen times she sat with him, trying to make contact, but it was no use. They had nothing to say to each other.

From the first, Dermot had known that the most important things in the world were the ones you couldn't see. Dreams. The watching faces of the forest. Sometimes he thought life was lived at two levels, the dreams incomparably more important than the people and things about him.

He had always wanted attention. He could no longer remember his earliest days, yet they had marked him forever. There had been no time for stories, then. No inclination, either; neither Carmel Riordan nor Jack had been the sort to sit down with a baby and tell him the fantasies he craved.

'I'm too busy.'

'Don't be bothering me now, Dermot.'

The first seeds of deprivation. Yet there had been other seeds, also planted before memory. The flare of his imagination had illuminated the forest, the sky, the horses tossing their manes in the yard behind the house. Spirit horses had peopled his sleep, so that he was aware before he was aware of anything of the dimensions of the invisible.

The woman who had appeared one day seemed to share his dreams. With her he saw the spirit horses, the black wings of the forest spread wide to enfold him. He went with her and the man; the world changed. He learned to give them names: Ma and Dominic.

Even the texture of the light was different, no longer the green air of the woods, but the harsh brightness of an endless space.

A river somewhere. A vastness of light, the smell of wet, the fingers of things poking emerald out of mud. The woman and man screaming at each other. Fury's spiked shadows haunting sleep.

Afterwards, the woman had less time for dreams. There was another child, upon whom she focused all her attention. Dermot was aware of an emptiness, the aching vacuum of non-love. He looked for her but could no longer find her, came to understand that she was wholly taken up with the baby.

It did not occur to him to hate the newcomer but perhaps a part of him hated. Increasingly, he wandered through the forest of his imaginings. The other world — of touch and smell and sound — was there still but increasingly unimportant, as though the branches of his secret forest conspired with him against the light.

There it was that Dominic found him.

They'd had little to do with each other before but now, as though he too had fallen out of the sunshine of the woman's love, Dominic joined the child in the half-darkness. Did more than join him; he peopled the enchanted wood with tales of splendour, of songs and triumphs and glories, of Taliesin the harpist and Cuchulainn the giant, of wrongs done, of lives spilled again and again over the centuries, of vengeance crying from the blood-stained earth.

It troubled Dermot that such cruelties should exist.
'But who did these things?'
'The English.'
'Why?'
'Because of the evil that is in them.'
'When I am older I shall fight them. Fight for Ireland.'
'Good boy.'

The baby who was a baby no longer became an intrusion, moving into spaces Dermot had taken for granted were his own. It snatched away the things it wanted, as it had earlier snatched away the woman's love. Sean's will was diamond-edged; Dermot sensed already that he would never be able to stand against it. Sean took what he wanted, always; got away with it, always. Increasingly, Dermot came to accept that he was second-best in all things.

His dream forest remained his sanctuary, his salvation. Dominic still joined him there, but less frequently. He too had changed, become morose, his voice often thick and tangled, raving incomprehensibly. Then Ma would come and drive him away. The muddled ravings would sag first into incoherence, then headlong into sleep, snores shaking the walls of whatever shelter they were in.

A muddle of years. Of which one episode remained, star-bright.

Sean, his own hat lost or merely mislaid, snatching at Dermot's, screeching, I want it, I want it.

Dermot, four years older, twelve against eight, held him off, at first good-naturedly despite the scarlet rage painting Sean's face, the lashing fists and feet.

You can't have it, Sean.

Who fought still, silent, ferocious, focused.

Such unnatural intensity alarmed Dermot. Awareness of his own feelings infuriated him. He shoved Sean away, violent in his turn, so that Sean fell. He rebounded and bore in, screaming. As though nothing but death would stop him.

Anneliese's arm and urgent face, separating them.

Dermot, be patient with your brother.

He's not my brother. His own rage, spurting. He's not, he's not!

Dermot! A slap, ear echoing. Be silent!

Suddenly it was too much. He seized the hat from his own head and flung it down. Take it, then.

At once Sean, no longer screeching, snatched it and bore it off: not in triumph but silently, resentfully, as though he were the one affronted.

The woman's eyes like fire. Don't you take that tone with me, young man.

Later, he heard the two grown-ups talking.

I don't understand what got into him.

Sean got into him, that's what. A good punch in the head, that's what Sean's needing. If he doesn't watch out, he'll be getting it, too, before he's much older.

Dermot had better not try.

Not from Dermot. Me.

Dominic, incoherent or not, became his friend.

Anneliese watched as aggravation deepened between the two boys. It was not a case of the younger standing up to the elder; in all things, Sean was the aggressor, yet could no more help himself than could the fire that swept before the wind, devouring all in its path.

For the moment Dermot was safe, the four years between them wide enough for breathing space but, as they grew older, the gap would narrow, and Anneliese feared for Dermot and his place in their little world.

She said as much to Dominic, who dismissed it.

'Dermot'll lick him one-handed for years yet, if he's the mind to.'

If he's the mind to — exactly. Dermot did *not* have the mind, whereas Sean had been a fighter from the first. Anneliese watched with pride as her tough little boy set about bruising the world's face with fists amazingly strong for his years, yet muscle had little to do with how he was. Sean's greatest strength lay in his head and will. There was no way on God's earth that Dermot would ever be able to stand up to him. Sean was born to govern and govern he would, like another man who travelled with them always.

Watching the boy as he grew, Anneliese often found herself wondering what had happened to Jack. It was most unlikely she would ever know, yet something of the man, unprincipled bully though he had been, remained with her. Defiant of logic, she told herself that one day she would find out, knew that until she did so that chapter of her life would remain incomplete.

Towards the end of 1914, they met Scott Macdonald in the town of Waroola, way up at the top end of the continent. Scott was another man built like a tower, blue eyes as hard as glass and so pale they were almost colourless, a skin burned to leather by the sun. He told them he owned a cattle station three hours out of town. He boasted of it quietly, proud of the place and what he had done to establish it, and Anneliese respected him for it.

War had broken out in Europe; his son Gavin had enlisted with the AIF and was even then on his way to Europe. Scott Macdonald was desperate for someone to help him on the station. They were a godsend to each other; Dominic would never admit it but Anneliese was convinced that he was as sick of the vagrant life as she was. Godsend or not, Macdonald was a cautious man who liked to know what he was getting for his money, so the three of them talked for a long time in the hotel, sizing each other up.

'Just me and my daughter,' Macdonald cautioned them. 'It's a rough and ready place, ma'am. You know how things are in the bush. It may not suit you at all.'

'Your wife —'

'Dead five years ago, I'm sorry to say.'

Anneliese saw an opening. 'Perhaps it needs a woman's hand. What is your daughter's name?'

'Sylvia, ma'am. She's eleven.'

Anneliese smiled. 'In which case she may need a woman's company even more than the house does.'

'As you say, ma'am. As you say.'

They parted, Macdonald promising to return at six with his decision. Dominic was convinced things had not worked out. It was all she could do to stop him drowning his sorrows there and then. Afterwards, she always remembered the struggle she had to keep him out of the bar. If she had failed all would have been lost, for Dominic would have been roaring drunk by the time Macdonald came back, but desperation gave her strength. At six o'clock that evening Dominic was still sober and Macdonald told them that the job was theirs.

So at last, after years on the road, their vagrant days were done. Hottentots no longer, Dominic Riordan and Anneliese van der Merwe, with the two boys, came to Paradise Downs, to the Macdonalds and the new life and division and death that is the destiny of every human soul.

NINETEEN

Anna saw now that the business in the vineyards had been a mistake. It was not in Mostyn to do such a thing. He knew how to break out but only in what he would have called a civilised way. A break-out with constraints. A country club style of roughing it, strolling around razor-cut golf courses, dunking in swimming pools that shone like sapphires. Unscheduled, glamorous weekends, with breakfast on a terrace over newspapers and coffee, the glint of a safe and civilised sea in the distance. In that setting Mostyn was attentive, considerate, even passionate. He was an inventive lover; surely no one who was totally selfish could be that? They made love regularly, as often as four times a week, yet she always believed that it was on one of those weekends that she fell pregnant.

Something else that was unscheduled, but welcome, too, at least as far as Anna was concerned. Mostyn was more aware of the disadvantages.

'It won't help your career . . .'

Anna had never seen why she should be only a baby machine, why she couldn't combine a career and motherhood. They could afford it; help was available. She had always imagined she would hate the discomfort, the intimate examinations, the probing and prodding of her distended flesh. She found that she welcomed all of it. Not that it mattered. Two months into the pregnancy, Anna went down with German measles. Against which she had not thought to be inoculated.

After the termination life was still, as though something intrinsic to her being had ceased. So still.

Six months later, when Anna received the offer from United Minerals, she was at first astounded, then cautious.

'It's so much ...'

Mostyn laughed. 'Plenty more where that came from.'

'But how?'

He winked. 'I've known Harry Dann for years. I heard they were looking for someone. I made enquiries, thought it would be a good opening for you. I had a word, got him to agree. Simple, really.'

It was the way things worked. Took a bit of getting used to, all the same.

'One thing,' Mostyn said.

'What?'

'I had to say we weren't planning a family, anything like that.'

She had said it herself a hundred times. No other child would be aborted through her stupidity. It hurt, though, having it formally acknowledged.

She smiled brightly. 'No problem.'

Walking into the boardroom was like entering ambush country. The long glossy table, leather-upholstered chairs, the gilt-framed portraits of past chairmen of the board. Above the table hung a crystal chandelier. At the far end of the room, a large window framed with pale blue drapes surveyed the harbour. The eyes around the table, watching.

'Good morning,' she said.

The murmured response. All men, of course.

The enemy.

Which was how they would think of her, no doubt. Yet the innocent would have detected nothing but courtesy.

'Ms Riordan,' Harry Dann introduced her. She had retained the name for business. 'Good to have you on board.'

That was it; then down to work. Anna was not deceived. They would all be watching, alert for incompetence, for unwarranted aggression. Error would be judged harshly here. She was here by merit, she reminded herself. Connections might have got her the job, but merit would earn her place.

She must have done something right. Within a year, she had been invited to join the boards of two other companies. Anna accepted both, went out with Mostyn to celebrate. Was a bit taken aback when he ordered a bottle of Dom Perignon.

He laughed at her expression. 'My treat. You've arrived, girl, and don't you forget it.'

Not only her; Mostyn's own career was heading into orbit. He, too, had branched out, was picking up directorships like peas out of a pot.

They decided they could afford a more prestigious address. Found a place on the north shore of the harbour that had been owned by Ruth Ballard, the famous author. Whose work Anna, although not Mostyn, had read much and admired enormously.

Anna stood on the verandah and looked across the water at the city. 'How could she bear to leave it?'

Mostyn neither knew nor cared. It was the right place for them; the past didn't matter.

The new address brought them luck. By the time summer came round again, Anna was serving on the boards of six listed companies, one public utility, and had long felt comfortable in her new environment. All the offers had come because of her growing reputation, with Mostyn having nothing to do with any of them.

No Dom Perignon now. He was put out by the way she was stepping out from his shadow. A wife who was a credit to him was one thing; one determined to make an independent name for herself was something else entirely. Another thing he didn't like: the way she was getting her views, and herself, reported in the media. Particularly when some of her opinions were, to put it mildly, controversial. She seemed hell-bent on using her newly acquired position to promote causes that were dear to her heart. Women's rights, for instance.

'The way we've been treated over the years — are still treated — is nothing short of disgraceful.'

'You're doing all right, aren't you?'

'That's got nothing to do with it.'

'If you're good enough you get to the top, man or woman.'

It was rubbish, and she said so.

Mostyn had always been a belligerent man. In the past she had known that side of him only by repute; now he flourished aggression like a sabre. 'Think what you like. But keep it to yourself. Okay?'

'No. It's not okay!'

'It won't do your reputation any good.'

'I'll worry about that.'

'Maybe you'd better.'

The infuriating thing was that Mostyn was right.

Harry Dann had a quiet word with her. 'The board's uneasy. Nobody's denying you the right to your own opinions ...' It was exactly what they were denying but at least Harry said it to her face. There would be others saying the same thing behind her back.

'None of you care what I think,' she told Mostyn. 'It's being a woman that's the problem.'

'That's crap. I was the one got you on the bandwagon in the first place.'

'Because I'm your wife.'

'You got a problem with that?'

'I want to be judged by who I am, not by who I married.'

'The world doesn't work like that.'

'It's time it did.'

It was a sniper's war, each taking pot shots at the other. At last, having fought, and fought again, and again having fought, Anna grew sick of it. She decided to change her tactics. She would give in to him, agree with everything he said, everything he did. Her acquiescence would drive him mad.

She was delighted with the subtlety of her idea, convinced it would work. It didn't. At heart Mostyn was a bully. The more she yielded the more aggressive he became. He bludgeoned her unceasingly, voice and mind and will, until she felt as though he had brought a club to her. At times wondered whether he might do that, too.

She saw that she had made a mistake, that to survive she would have to stand up to him. It would be hard; she would have to fight to win back the ground she'd lost, but it couldn't be helped.

The Saturday morning after she'd made her decision, with Mostyn in the office looking over some papers he would need on Monday, she packed a bag and took off into the Blue Mountains. She left no message, no contact number. She stayed at a place a friend had recommended, a small hotel where, for a price, she was treated like the royalty that, at least for a day or two, she had such need to become.

She sat for hours on a terrace overlooking a wide valley. She watched an infinity of trees, the grey and green crags of mountains, remembering the time after her break-up with Mark when she had also watched the trees. With every minute, she gathered courage, breathing it in with the cool mountain air, honing herself for the confrontation that had to come.

It would have to be on her own terms.

Sunday morning she phoned him, fingers crossed that he would be at home. He was.

'Anna? What the hell's going on?'

She did not answer, told him where she was. 'Join me for lunch, why don't you?'

Waited, imagining the rage, the smoking tyres burning rubber on every bend.

He arrived. She received him on the terrace. Graciously. Offered him a drink.

He bared his teeth at her. 'What is this bloody nonsense?'

She smiled. 'Later ...'

By his expression he could have hit her but would never provoke a scene here, where neither of them knew whose eyes might be watching, whose tongue might talk.

He devoured a beer — ferociously. She smiled at him — sweetly.

'Don't you dare do such a thing again —'

'I shan't.'

It sounded like submission, but Mostyn knew her too well. He eyed her uncertainly.

'Because, unless we sort out a few things, I'm not coming back.'

She had him hog-tied and both of them knew it. He glowered, saying nothing as she spelt things out.

Freedom. Equality. Dignity.

Words. He had never taken them seriously. Still did not. 'You're my wife —'

'And hope to remain so.'

He tried to turn her attack, to mock. 'You sound like a French revolutionary.'

She would neither lose her temper nor yield. She spelt out what she meant by the words.

'Partners...'

The concept was alien to him. The world was submissive; he had made it so. He expected her to submit, too. He was lost, confused by these new expectations. She saw that she must help him.

'You remember what you said when I agreed to marry you? You said what a team we would make.'

Which confused him more than ever. To Mostyn a team was people who did what they were told.

'Not us. We work together. We discuss. We are *partners*.'

Lightly she stressed the word. 'Equals.'

It took time to persuade him, but she didn't mind. Hatchet Harcourt was a long way from St Paul; she would never have trusted a sudden conversion.

At last, dubiously, he agreed. 'I suppose we can give it a go.'

The idea of sharing was so foreign to him. Yet he had driven up here, had not walked out as soon as she put her ideas to him. All might not be lost.

They ate lunch, shared a bottle of chardonnay.

'Did you bring a suitcase?'

'No.'

'Never mind.' She went to reception. 'My husband is staying ...'

Bore him off to the room that she would graciously permit him to share. She knew by his expression that their fight had made him as randy as a goat. She was the same; could have eaten him where he stood.

She closed the door, turning to him. 'Can you think of a better way to spend Sunday afternoon?'

They devoured each other. If Mostyn knew he was a trophy of war, he gave no sign.

Our new life, she thought. Hope sang in her veins. Now all things would be possible.

TWENTY

Settling to their new life at Paradise Downs created problems.

Anneliese had persuaded herself that Dominic and Dermot, fourteen by now, wanted to settle down as much as she did. She was wrong; the tinker's life suited them both down to the ground. Left to themselves, they would have gone on wandering forever. Dermot told her as much.

'No need for you and Sean to come with us, if you don't want.'

Spikes in Anneliese's eyes. 'So you go your way and we go ours, is that what you're saying?'

'Why not?'

Never in a blue fit would she agree to that. She was totally opposed to anything that might divide the family. 'We're staying together, no matter what. Your wandering days are over, *my seuntjie*, let's be clear about that.'

'And Dominic?'

'Your father will just have to make the best of it, won't he?'

That first day, Dermot wouldn't have pissed on Paradise Downs. Rotten house, never seen a lick of paint in its life; a million miles of nothing; a moon-faced kid called Sylvia.

He got off on the wrong foot there. Called her Sylvie. She soon put him right.

'Sylvi-er,' she said. 'With an a.'

Stuck-up git.

Fact was she could have done handstands in the nude and Dermot wouldn't have wanted a bar of her. Neither of her nor Paradise Downs.

It was true that until now his life had been nothing special. With Anneliese and Sean so close and Dominic the way he was — at least he'd tried to be friends with him, Dermot had to give him that — he'd been pretty much on his own for years. Yet that first day after their arrival he looked back on their previous life and saw only freedom. By contrast, Paradise Downs gave every sign of being little better than a jail.

Dermot had never liked being told what to do, yet it was this, ironically, that made things come good for him. He found he was expected to work like a man but was treated like a man, too, which made up for a lot. Hard, dirty work it was; for days on end he was hardly out of the saddle. He would never make a great horseman — nothing like Sean, who might have been born on a horse's back — but he managed.

Sean had things a lot better. All his life he'd known how to get away with murder; now they were at Paradise Downs nothing had changed. Dermot expected nothing else — Sean was four years younger, after all — but there were days out in the bush, covered in dust and half-dead with thirst, when he had this picture of Sean fooling around in the creek behind the homestead. It made him feel real crook.

Anneliese had always said Dermot was jealous of Sean but it wasn't that, or not entirely. Far more important was the fact that Dermot never knew where he was with him.

Sean never let on what he was thinking. That business of the hat ...

Another time, when they were both still kids, Sean had found a pebble Dermot wanted for his collection. It was no use to Sean, but giving was not in his nature. He wanted Dermot to pay for it.

'Tuppence,' he said.

Dermot stared. 'You know I ain't got no tuppence.'

'Your problem.'

Dermot tried to snatch it off him but Sean chucked it away to stop him getting it. Dermot searched and searched but never found it.

Dermot had discovered that he couldn't trust him, either. The minute he couldn't get his own way Sean was off, bawling and telling tales.

'You're his big brother,' Ma scolded him. 'Can't you be more patient with him?'

Or:

'Dermot, why aren't you ever happy with Sean?'

Being patient meant always letting him get his own way and, no, Dermot wasn't happy about that. Made no difference.

'I'm ashamed of you, being so jealous,' Anneliese told him. 'I wish you'd get over it.'

It was hopeless fighting the pair of them. Dermot had learned long ago to steer clear of him. Arriving at Paradise Downs brought them together, though, if only for a time. Mainly it was because of Sylvia.

Sylvia was something new in their lives. Until now, they'd had nothing to do with girls. She was round-faced but pretty enough, Dermot supposed, although she didn't have much to say for herself. To begin with, he reckoned there was nothing to her at all, that prettiness was all she'd got, but in time learned there was more to her than he'd thought.

Anneliese told him she was shy but it wasn't that. She was secretive, just as Sean was. She never even let on about the waterhole; they had to find that for themselves.

It was Sean who found it; he was always prowling about, asking questions, taking things to pieces to see how they worked. As soon as they arrived at the homestead, Dermot noticed a line of trees half a mile away, the grass greener than anywhere else, but it was Sean who went to take a look. When he came back he was jumping.

'A deep waterhole,' he said. 'We can go swimming.'

The two boys went together. Sure enough, the pool was deep, twenty yards long and ten wide, shaded by trees.

Dermot started to pull his shirt over his head, then paused. The water was thick with algae; no way of knowing what might be under the surface. There might by anything. Snakes; crocodiles, even.

'Reckon it's safe?'

Sean was already out of his clothes.

'Soon find out.'

And leapt in, knees to his chest. There was an explosion of water, the pock of splashes cool on Dermot's skin. Ripples surged across the surface and lapped against the exposed roots of the trees along the other bank.

Dermot watched. Sean was in the middle of the pool, blowing and snorting. He seemed all right. He slung off the rest of his gear and went in after him.

Next day Macdonald got him working. Dermot never had much time for swimming after that but, whenever he could get away from station chores, he was up there. Sean always went, too, and they fooled about in the water, ducking and splashing each other. Those evenings were the first time they had ever been close.

They never invited Sylvia but it wasn't long before she was there, too. At first Dermot didn't fancy the idea of her sitting on the bank watching them fool around with nothing on, but he soon got used to it.

One evening Sean decided to talk her into getting into the water with them.

'I can't.'

'What's stopping you?'

'My dad would beat the daylights out of me.'

'What for?'

'You're boys.'

'So what? You've been looking at us for weeks. Now it's our turn.'

Still she would not.

'I'm coming to get you,' he warned.

He made to scramble up the bank. At once she took off but after ten yards stopped, looking back uncertainly.

Sean stood facing her, his pale skin gleaming in the gathering dusk. Dermot couldn't see his face but knew he was grinning at her, daring her to join them. Knew, too, that he was showing himself to her.

'Come and help me, Dermot,' he called, without turning his head.

Dermot stayed where he was. He was fourteen and the idea that she might take off her clothes had aroused him. No way was he getting out of the water and letting them see the state he was in.

Sean pranced a few sharp-toed steps towards her and she took off again, this time without stopping. He waited until she was gone, then strolled back casually to the waterhole.

'Tomorrow,' he said.

Dermot never believed it would happen, but Sean was right. Next evening, she was there again. This time she'd brought a towel. Dermot couldn't take his eyes off her as she peeled off her dress and shoes. Kept her drawers on, though. She clambered down into the water and stood at the edge, thin arms crossed over her chest.

'You want to swim with us you got to take everything off,' Sean told her.

To begin with she wouldn't so they ignored her, fooling around in the middle of the pool as though she weren't there at all. She gave up in the end, fidgeted around under the water for minute, then chucked her wet drawers up on the bank.

She glared at them defiantly. 'Satisfied?'

'No hiding when you get out,' Sean warned her. 'All of us got to be exactly the same.'

Dermot began to wonder if he would have the same problem as the previous day but now she was in the water it didn't seem to bother him any more. They started to muck around and soon he never gave the matter a thought.

After that she came every day. If Macdonald knew he never said anything. The waterhole became their place. No one else came there; the world with its bellowing cattle and dust lay beyond the fringe of leaves that separated them from other people.

It never occurred to Dermot that things might change but, a year later, they did. One day Sylvia didn't turn up, nor the day after. It was three days before she was back, and then she only sat on the bank and didn't get into the water with them.

'Got shy all of sudden?' Sean jeered.

'Don't feel like it today.'

He winked at Dermot. 'Maybe we should chuck her in.'

The threat did not bother her as it would have once. She didn't join them but, when Sean got out of the water, she didn't run away, either.

'Come on!'

She looked calmly up at him. 'No.'

He made a lunge at her but she took no notice, so he did it again. It was a game, no more than that; then Sean lost his temper and grabbed her. Before Dermot could move, he'd dragged her to the edge of the water and pushed her in. She stood there, drenched dress clinging to her body, and for the first time Dermot saw that her breasts had started to grow. Nothing much, no more than a bit of a bump where before there'd been nothing. It was odd; when she'd had nothing on he hadn't spotted it yet now, with the wet dress clinging to her, he could not see how he had missed it.

She did nothing, only stood there.

Dermot reckoned Sean might have been a bit scared by what he'd done but, being Sean, was not going to admit it. Instead, he jumped in after her and tried to duck her.

'Leave her alone,' Dermot warned him.

Sean took no notice so he grabbed him and held his head under the water. Sean tried to kick but Dermot was too strong and wouldn't let him go.

'You want to get out, now's your chance,' he told Sylvia.

She gave him a look as though she'd never seen him before and scrambled up the bank. When she was safe, Dermot let Sean go. He came up, gasping and red-faced, punching furiously.

For a moment it seemed that Sylvia was going to say something but, in the end, she didn't. Instead she turned, a small, sodden figure, and walked away into the darkness.

'Keep away from here in future,' Sean yelled after her, then turned on Dermot. 'What's the matter with you? Gone soft on her, have you?'

He was still mad, so again Dermot held his head under. Only when he started to lunge to and fro as though he were drowning did Dermot let him go. Sean never said a word but was still mad at Dermot for taking Sylvia's side. It wasn't much but it turned him. They were never so close again.

The next day, after work, Dermot went looking for her. 'Get into trouble?'

She shook her head. 'I told Dad I'd fallen in.'

'Did he believe you?'

'Why not? It was true, wasn't it?'

'I'm sorry about it.'

'Doesn't matter.'

But it did. It changed the relationship between them. Dermot, the oldest, had always been a little apart from the others. Things they found funny had often seemed downright stupid to him. Now everything was different.

Growing up was no fun. Everything in Dermot's life was changing, not only around him but inside himself as well, and because it was happening to Sylvia as well it brought them together. Now it was Sean who was on his own. He didn't like it but they didn't care. They started to talk to each other instead of just swimming although, in truth, Sylvia never said much. Dermot made up for it, telling her about all the things that interested him, what he'd seen on the track, what it was like to chase a mob of cattle through the bush — stuff like that.

He never knew if she was interested or even listened but told her, anyway.

Sylvia's dad had good eyes in his head; he started to come up with all sorts of extra jobs he wanted done, so that Dermot had even less time than before. He still managed to see her occasionally, though.

The trouble between Macdonald and Dermot was one of temperament. Sylvia's Dad was a tough, hard-driving sort of bloke and Dermot wasn't. He liked to stand and look at things, to feel the world about him, and Macdonald was not like that at all.

'Let's get on, Dermot. No time for dreaming. We've got a station to run.'

There was certainly plenty to do. Mustering, branding and cutting, moving the herds from one section to another, putting out feed for them in the dry, rescuing them in the wet ... No end to it, but it also meant that Dermot spent a fair bit of time with Dominic, and that was good.

Dominic was better than he'd been for years. There was no liquor for him to lay his hands on, so he had no choice but stay sober. He broke out once or twice a year when they took cattle to the railhead. Then it was all fury and what he'd do to the king of England if he ever got him in a dark alley. Rubbish talk. Yet his feelings had to come from somewhere and, when he was sober and they were working together, Dermot pestered him to tell him the history of Ireland and why the Irish hated the English so much.

'Ireland must be free.' Again and again Dominic told him. 'Ask your mother what happened to her in Africa.'

For the first time Dermot heard about the children, the husband who'd died, the farm burnt to the ground. These same English had done it all.

'Like devils ...' He found it hard to believe anyone could do the things these people had done.

'Never forget it,' she said. 'In Africa they had ten times our numbers. They were bound to win, yet still they killed the children. Afraid what would happen if they let them grow up, I suppose.'

Hatred was a new thing for Dermot, but he learned it, sure enough. Put it with a romantic notion of the world, and it was like making a bomb. How he was going to prove himself he didn't know, only that he was destined for something tremendous.

Two years after they arrived at Paradise Downs, they got news of the Uprising in Dublin, how the brave patriots had fought the English. Heard, too, of the reprisals the English took, the numbers who died.

'Heroes all,' Dominic said.

It was the only time Dermot ever saw him weep when he was sober.

He had still not learnt the distance between saying and doing, and repeated what he had said when he was a kid on the track. 'When I'm old enough, I'll go to Ireland to fight,' he told Dominic, looking to please.

Remote as they were, they still heard the news regularly. There was carnage in Europe as the war wove its bloody horrors over the lives of millions. In their corner of the world it would not have meant much but, with Macdonald's son in the thick of the fighting, the arrival of the post was always a ritual fraught with terror.

Paradise Downs was only three hours out of the town, so the mail was dropped off at the gate pretty regularly. Macdonald, never one to let others do his dirty work, rode out to pick it up himself. They used to watch his face when he got back to see if he were smiling or not. So far Gavin's luck had held, although there was no saying when that might change.

Other echoes reached them. The rejection of conscription; names they'd never heard before — Lone Pine, Mouquet Farm, Pozieres, the Somme — became household words; in Canberra, Billy Hughes was chucked out and somehow got back in again; there was rumour of a mouse plague in the Mallee and strikes in Sydney; Russia got rid of the Tsar and was out of the war; the first rail link was opened between Melbourne and Fremantle. Still the war went on. It was a strange business; as a family the Riordans hated the English, yet both Irish and South Africans were fighting with them against the Germans. It was hard to know what to believe.

Finally, between one day and the next, it was over. It had been dreadful, yet its absence left a gap. Even for people like them, it had become so much a part of their lives that it didn't seem right for it to have stopped so suddenly. Made them wonder what they'd have to talk about now the boys were coming home. Macdonald was laughing, though. Gavin had come through without a scratch. Soon he'd be back.

Dominic said, 'Maybe we'll have to hit the road again.'

He sounded hopeful. For a moment Dermot was hopeful, too, then remembered Sylvia and decided he didn't want to go anywhere, any more.

Sylvia had told Dermot during one of their talks that when she was a kid she'd wondered what she'd do if there were crocodiles in the creek. There never were, of course. Only the arrival of the Riordans, four years earlier, had been a threat.

'When Dad told me a new family was coming to the station I was scared stiff,' she said.

Dermot was intrigued by the idea that anyone could have been frightened of him.

'I was afraid of newness,' she explained. 'I didn't know what to expect.'

'Are there any children?' the eleven-year-old Sylvia had asked her father. 'Any girls?'

If there were girls, it might be all right. Because it was a friend she wanted, above all things. Someone with whom she might exchange confidences.

'There are children,' her father told her. 'Only boys, though. No girls.'

Sylvia knew nothing about boys. Nothing about girls, come to that, but assumed girls would have been easier. A boy could not be a friend.

Her father had said nothing about their ages. For some reason she had assumed they would be younger and smaller than she was. She would be able to pet them, perhaps. To discover that one was almost a man, the other rough and pushy, not in the least like a pet, was a disappointment.

They had extraordinary names, foreign-sounding. 'Dermot and Sean?'

They were Irish, her father explained.

Which might explain it. Yet their mother did not sound Irish, her accent like a thickness in the throat.

Sylvia watched, saying nothing. It was safer not to become involved. Not necessary, either; she had already learned that life always came to you, if you waited long enough. Although she had hoped for a friend, being alone had never bothered her. Just as well; Gavin, her brother, might have been a tree for all the friendship he'd ever shown her. When he went off to the war she had hardly noticed the difference.

Her father was little better. Not his fault; what did he know about eleven-year-old girls? He saw her from the outside, her height and colouring, the sound of her voice, her look. But to feel what was really her, to see the world through her eyes, that he could not do. Not surprising; she could barely do it herself.

Her mother would have understood; she was sure of little, but that she knew. She remembered her smell and touch. The fact of her. Her mother had shielded her from the world. She had died before Sylvia could ask the questions she now would ask. About her own childhood, the life and knowledge and feelings that had been hers. Too late. Now no one could tell her, and Sylvia knew herself diminished because of it.

She could not put her feelings into words. It was like groping after shadows she could neither understand nor describe. Yet she knew they existed, as dreams exist. Now, with the arrival of the Riordans, there was Anneliese.

Anneliese looked at her and saw her heart. That Sylvia did not want. The idea of anyone truly seeing her was terrible. Only one woman could have helped. Without a mother to turn to, she was determined to keep everything that was herself to herself. Do that and she would remain Sylvia, intact behind her skin, the boundaries of Paradise Downs, the vastness of the land that protected her with its emptiness and heat. She would be safe.

She never even went to Waroola, if she could help it. She wanted nothing to do with a world whose echoes menaced her stillness. Now, with these Riordans, the outside world had come to her. A girl might have been acceptable. One younger than herself, controllable, one in whom she might safely confide. Or not, as she preferred.

The Riordans boys were *not* controllable. She used silence to fence them out.

Yet watched. When they found the creek, she knew. It had been her place; now, violated by their pale and violent bodies, their noise, it was hers no longer.

But could perhaps be reclaimed.

She walked to the waterhole; sat watching, even in time submitted to their demand that she join them. She thought that safety might lie in showing the world the face it wanted her to have, so with Sean she was defiant, with Dermot dreamy, pretending interest in the things that mattered to him, the images that peopled his mind. He was so much older than she, almost a man, yet seemed sometimes no more than a child. The notion might have stirred her but did not. He had no business to be so vulnerable. He brought her pebbles, grasses, a corella's feather. She inspected them gravely, feeling nothing. She held herself in secret behind her eyes. She was safe.

Her own body betrayed her. The flow of blood, the developing breasts. The prospects of being adult threatened her, cracking the shell that surrounded her. She was afraid that the world might enter, now that the child was gone.

It was something she had to live with. She put it to the test and found, as she had feared, that it was no longer safe to reveal even her body to a world determined to bruise her.

Sean's hands, violating her peace.

The fact that Dermot moved so quickly to protect her gave no comfort; even concern was a violation.

When she got back to the homestead her father took in the drenched clothes, bedraggled hair.

'What happened?'

'I fell in. I'm fine.'

So she was, in the sense he had meant. The truth was different but there was nothing either of them could do about that. She knew she could not keep herself apart forever. Very well, she would choose the next best thing. Control was what mattered. Not of her body; that wasn't important. Not even of her life. Of her peace: *that* was everything.

She let Dermot see he interested her. They found moments. He was gentle. If safety were possible with anyone, she might be safe with him.

She decided they should marry. Not here; Paradise Downs was full of people who knew her too well. Her father; Sean, with his arrogant chin; the woman from Africa, who saw into her and, Sylvia believed, despised what she saw. All watching. Stay here, and she would be too much exposed.

She knew already that Dermot would never break through the screen she had built around herself; he would imagine that by penetrating her body he had captured her. She would take care never to let him suspect anything else. She would be safe.

First, of course, she had to put the thought into his mind. The war was over, Gavin had left Europe, would soon be back. Sylvia made up her mind it would be best to arrange things before he got home.

Her sixteenth birthday fell in January. There was a celebration of sorts. A few drinks, a song or two, beef turning on a spit. Her eyes met Dermot's beyond the fire. She drifted towards the waterhole, knowing he would observe and follow.

It was hot and humid, the darkness a dense cloth weighing upon her. Clouds covered the stars.

He came, as she had known he would. She kissed him, made no attempt to stop him when he placed his hands on her breasts. They were developed now, the nipples tender yet strangely tough to the touch. She permitted him to run his hands over her, fended him off without difficulty when he tried to lift her skirt.

'Plenty of time for that later.'

She spoke confidently, but was not. She was discovering things about her own body she had never known. Instinct guided her uncertainly, parting her lips, letting him see her tongue.

'Where shall we go?'

'Go?'

'When we leave Paradise Downs.' She saw that the idea of leaving had not occurred to him and was pleased. She would not wish him to be ahead of her in this, in anything.

'We won't hang around here, surely? Not after Gavin's back? It's going to be his place, eventually. No room for anyone else.'

They heard the sound of hooves, voices. They turned but could see only the fire burning brightly in the distance. The screen of leaves divided them from the world, as it always had.

Her dress was open. His hands stroked her breasts. She felt her body's response, the ache, the moist softening. Her body would satisfy him, she thought. Herself would remain.

He said, 'I'll speak to your father ...'

She stared. 'What for?'

'To get his permission.'

Which he would never give.

'What if he says no?'

'We'll have to wait, I suppose.'

'No!'

'We're under age.'

She didn't care about that. She had brought him to this point; delay and he might change his mind. 'I won't be twenty-one for five years. I'm not going to wait that long.'

He remained troubled. 'I must speak to him. We just run off, he'll come after us.' With a gun. But did not wish to mention guns.

Sylvia thought. He was right. 'Speak to him, then. He says okay, we'll get married, then make up our mind where we're going. But if he says no, I want us out of here.'

He didn't like it but would do it.

'Talk to him now,' she urged, 'while he's in a good mood.'

Whey they got back to the fire they knew at once that something had happened. The crackle of flame; the faces staring silently. One belonged to Jim Sykes, the postie from Waroola.

Sylvia went swiftly to her father. 'What's happened?'

He turned to her, groping, as though unable to see her or anything.

'Your brother,' he managed. 'Gavin is dead.'

The influenza had killed him, as it was to kill thousands more.

Gavin Macdonald, Scott's only son, the heir to Paradise Downs, had fought through the whole war. He had been at Mouquet Farm and Menin Road, had survived the hand-to-hand frenzy of Polygon Wood, where men had smashed at each other with guns and bayonets and bare hands, had seen men die of gas and drown in the mud of Brookseinde. All this without a scratch. And now he was dead on the transport bringing him back from Europe to Australia.

The impact on his father was devastating. Anneliese had never been close to Scott Macdonald, had held herself in reserve with him as with all the men who passed through from time to time on their lonely way to who knew where. She knew they called her starchy; cared nothing for their opinion. Now she went to Scott Macdonald where he sat on the verandah of the big house, his eyes brooding upon memories, on dreams that were no more.

She said nothing, only sat. Macdonald gave no sign he knew she was there. After twenty minutes, she rose and went silently away. The next day did the same. And the next. For a month she sat with him in this way. Never in all that time did they exchange a word. Finally she began to talk. Of Koffiekraal. Of Stoffel and Amalie and all the others who had died. Of the mass grave as red as blood in the raw earth.

She talked without expression and without pause, the words spilling ceaselessly, a stream of images upon the hot and silent air.

At last Scott moved in his chair, restlessly. 'I had no idea.'

Anneliese looked at him, saw tears shining in the furrows of his hard face. The big man who had seemed cast from iron was weeping for his lost son, his lost hopes, even perhaps for the world of suffering of which they both were part.

Anneliese would have taken him in her arms but knew better. Instead she rose, as she had done so often before, and walked soundlessly into the house. There she paused, secretly watching the bereft figure in its cane chair. She nodded once, satisfied, then went on with her work.

Scott sat without moving until it was dark, then rose and went to his room. Early the next morning, the boards of the house echoed to the sound of boot heels as he strode swiftly to the steps and down into the yard. Anneliese watched as he crossed to the stables. Within minutes, mounted on his favourite gelding, wide-brimmed hat on his head, he clattered out of the yard and rode away up the slope between the scattered gum trees until he reached the crest and disappeared.

Anneliese turned away. Neither she nor Scott would ever refer to what had happened yet the knowledge filled her with warmth, knowing she had helped him find healing.

Sean had come through from the rear of the house and now stood at her shoulder, staring up the slope after the vanished rider.

'About time,' he said.

'He has been in hell,' Anneliese told him. 'Now he is back.'

'Where's he gone, anyway?'

'Just riding.'

But knew there was more to it than that. Released from hell, Scott Macdonald was re-establishing contact with life. Which, to him, was Paradise Downs.

'Don' get it,' Sean said.

Anneliese, to whom love of land needed no explanation, longed to explain to him the importance of loving something beyond oneself but knew there was no point. Sean wouldn't have known what she was talking about.

Sean had been the dearest thing in her life for so long, but now there were times when she felt she did not like him at all. As he had grown, he had drawn more and more into himself. There were other things: the way he stared about him, chest out-thrust, chin pointing pugnaciously, as though he owned the world or intended to, yet kept a veil over his thoughts. She no longer knew him but believed he had the potential to be dangerous. It troubled her.

She said as much to Dominic. Who did not care.

'Good thing. Means he'll be able to stand on his own feet.'

The heat of the north had dried Dominic out. Now he was thin and laconic; scrawny neck, adam's apple like a walnut, blue eyes washed almost white by time and distance. He spent days away from the homestead, working in distant parts of the station. It suited them both. Time had separated them, even as it had drawn them together. Their lives were inextricably entwined, yet nothing physical remained between them. Nothing of love, either, unless love meant being at peace with each other, communicating without speaking. She had always known she did not love him although perhaps habit could turn to love, in time. She thought sometimes it was as much as they could hope for; more than they deserved, perhaps.

When she thought about it, she could still recall the cauldron of fire and vengeance from which their shared lives had emerged, yet the memory, once as vital as the leaping flames themselves, had grown dim long ago. The sixteen years when they had wandered like the Israelites in the wilderness stood between Anneliese and everything that had gone before. The passions of the past were now no more than echoes, even the enigma of Sean's parentage no longer an issue.

The drink had eased its hold on Dominic at last; or perhaps it was simply the lack of opportunity that had blunted its claws. The previous year his wages had gone up to fifty-three shillings, with the promise of a further twenty if, as was increasingly likely, Macdonald put him in charge.

Safe harbour, then, for them both. Even the fear that Gavin's return might have seen them once more on the road had been removed.

'Horse-breaking tomorrow,' Sean said. 'I wonder if Macdonald will turn up?'

He did. Iron mouth and watchful eyes; he might never have been away at all.

In the mustering yard the air was razor-sharp. Tension and dust, the whirligigs of mounted men, the rocketing frantic thrust of horses attempting to break free, to not submit. One brumby stallion in particular. Eye glaring white, red-rimmed nostrils, the whole body trembling.

Dominic eyed it dubiously. 'Goin' to be a handful, that one.'

'Let me,' Sean said, lust thick as phlegm in his throat.

The years and dust had pared the Irish from Dominic's voice yet still it showed through on occasion. As now. 'Break your back soon as look at you, so he would.'

Sean watched, raging, as one of the black hands, arms and legs like wire cables, mounted. Exulted secretly as he was flung unceremoniously off. Again he mounted. Again flew cartwheeling. Another man tried. Same result.

'Dermot?' Dominic's voice was doubtful.

Dermot shook his head. 'Not me.' No shame in saying no; there were easier ways of getting killed.

Scott Macdonald said, 'Someone had better do it. I'm damned if I'll cut him.'

Again Sean pleaded. 'Da —'

'No.'

'Let him.'

Something in the way Macdonald said it. Dominic glanced at his boss, knowing the words had been more than a suggestion. Yet he still resisted, if only for the sake of resistance. 'It would be madness.'

'No it wouldn't. Let him have a go.'

Dominic shrugged. 'Up you get, then. And for God's sake don't be killing yourself,' he told Sean ferociously, 'or your mother will murder me.'

And he walked away, his turned back demonstrating clearer than words what he thought.

'Your chance, Sean,' Macdonald told him. 'Show us what you're made of.'

Sean swung up into the saddle. His heartbeat filled his ears; his mouth was dry as sand. He wound the reins tight around his wrist and whacked his knees high into the brumby's ribs. He could feel the power trembling beneath him. Like a bomb, he thought. Tension and terror clawed him. He looked down at the men holding the stallion.

'Let him go!'

The world exploded. Eyelids crushed shut, his only concern was to stay on. Somehow he survived the first moment's frenzy, the bucking lunacy of the gallop around the yard when he thought his backbone was going to break into a hundred pieces and come smashing up through his brain. He thrust in with his legs until his muscles screamed and his knees felt as though they would meet in the middle of the animal's body. Around and around, bucking and rearing. Somehow he stayed on.

The stallion made for the gate and he was powerless to stop him. Just in time someone flung it wide and they were gone in a wild gallop, more flying than running. Up the slope, avoiding the trees by a miracle, a succession of miracles, and they were in open country. Ears back, neck outstretched, the stallion ran. Tears streamed down Sean's face. Still he held on.

Suddenly the animal stopped. It was all Sean could do not to be flung ten yards over his head into the neckbreaking dust. Then away they went again, round and round, bucking and jumping, Sean still clinging to its back. He felt as though he had been pounded into a sackful of broken pieces, blood and bone and muscle pulverised into jelly, yet would not give in, knowing for the first time that he would hold on, if necessary, until both of them were dead.

'You are mine. Mine!'

He screamed the words in the horse's ear, hating him, loving him, fighting and fighting him. Until death, if need be. Beyond death. If need be.

Back in a frenzied circle, heading for the creek. Down the crumbling bank the stallion plunged and into the water.

Sean thought, He's going to roll, try to drown me. For the minutest fraction of a second, his will sagged. The animal was indefatigable. No way he or anyone could ever tame him. But doubt passed as quickly as it had appeared.

Let him drown me, then. I'll hang on until he drowns the pair of us.

They plunged deeper in an explosion of green foam. And stopped. Sean clung precariously, barely daring to breathe. Between his legs, beneath his hands, he felt the wire-taut muscles relax. The great body was wracked by tremors that built to a climax and died slowly away. Cautiously he leaned forward and patted the great neck.

'There you go, mate. There you go.'

He sat up straighter in the saddle. He used the reins to turn the animal, to clamber back up out of the water. When they were on top of the bank he slipped from the saddle, still holding the reins, and grabbed a handful of grass to rub the stallion down.

'There, then. There.'

Gently, over and over again, letting him hear his voice.

When he was finished, he wanted nothing more than to lie in the dust and sleep. Instead he climbed wearily into the saddle and rode back to the homestead.

'I'll be damned,' Macdonald said. 'I thought we'd find you with your neck broken.'

Sean was unable to answer. He slid from the saddle, staggered and almost fell. He took the reins and offered them to the owner of Paradise Downs.

'Your horse.'

Macdonald considered him thoughtfully. He ignored the proffered reins. 'Put him in the stable. He's had enough excitement for one day.'

The next day Macdonald came looking for him. It was a rest day, as far as such things existed at Paradise Downs, and Sean was where Macdonald had known he would be, by the horse yard. They leant side by side on the fence rail, staring at the great stallion as it circled the yard. Sunlight gleamed on its coat, its movements were as fluid as water.

'Good animal, that,' Macdonald said. 'Get a fair price for it, I reckon.'

The words were like a hand tightening on Sean's heart. Sell him? After all that? Protest rose in his throat but he fought it down. It was Macdonald's horse, Macdonald's decision. What had happened did not matter. Possession — ownership — was all.

'Right,' he said casually.

The news of Gavin's death had derailed Dermot's plans to speak to Macdonald about Sylvia and himself. Afterwards she got at him about it. 'You promised.'

'I couldn't. Not when he'd just heard about Gavin.'

She pouted. 'What's Gavin got to do with it?'

'I will speak to him. I will.'

'When?'

He did not know when. Before he'd summoned up his courage, Macdonald spoke to him instead. 'I hear you've been getting matey with my daughter...'

Dermot couldn't imagine how he'd found out. 'I was going to speak to you about that, Mr Macdonald —' Spluttering nervously.

Macdonald put an axe through his apologies. 'Sylvia's just sixteen. Far too young to be thinking of marriage.' His eye, uncompromising as a gun muzzle, focused on Dermot. 'That is what you had in mind?'

Oh yes, he assured him quickly. Exactly what he had in mind.

'Whoever marries my daughter will inherit Paradise Downs, one of these days. You sure you're up to it?'

'I'll do my very best, Mr Macdonald.' Eagerly, displaying a confidence he did not feel.

Macdonald grunted sceptically. His bleak expression seemed to share Dermot's secret doubts.

'Sylvia won't be twenty-one for another five years,' he said. 'Too much to ask of any man. Show me you've got what it takes, you can have her in three.'

Dermot felt his face light up.

'Thank you, Mr Macdonald. Thank you.'

'Just between the two of us, mind. Nothing official. Make sure it stays that way.' Gently, threateningly, his massive fist took Dermot by his shirt front. 'And no monkey business. Hear me?'

Dermot thought Sylvia would be pleased; discovered, once again in his life, that he was wrong.

'I'm not waiting three years!'

'What else can we do? You're under age.'

'Who's going to know the difference, once we're away from here?'

'And have your dad come after us with his gun?'

'Get to Waroola, hop on a train, he'll never find us.'

Dermot wasn't game for anything like that. Besides, there was the prospect of Paradise Downs that Macdonald had dangled under his nose, so temptingly. He tried to get Sylvia to see that three years wasn't that long, but she wouldn't listen.

'If you cared for me, you'd want to take me away.'

She sulked, unavailingly. Dermot had made up his mind to ignore her; it would be crazy to chuck away their future for the sake of three years.

He confided in Dominic, who was not so sure. 'You think Macdonald's given you a good deal?'

'Of course.' Dermot's confidence bled a little. 'Why? Don't you think so?'

'What I think is you're getting a three-year jail sentence with no guarantees at the end of it.'

Dermot wouldn't have a bar of that but Dominic hadn't finished. 'You always said you wanted to fight for Ireland. Whatever happened to that idea?'

Of course they both knew Dermot had never meant a word of it.

'Ireland's been waiting eight hundred years.' Dermot said airily. 'I daresay it can hang on for another three.'

Dominic had no patience with such nonsense. 'So as soon as you're married you'll pack up and go to Ireland, is that it? And what happens to Paradise Downs in the meanwhile?'

'One step at a time,' Dermot told him. 'Time enough when we're married to decide what we want to do.'

'You talk as though it's already settled.'

'Macdonald promised —'

'Promises ...' Dominic dismissed the notion, contemptuously. 'He doesn't want to lose a good worker, that's all his promises mean. A kangaroo's got as much chance of running Paradise Downs as you have.'

Knew before he'd said it that he might as well have saved his breath. Sylvia — the breasts and bones and blood that were Sylvia — blinded Dermot to all else. All the same, it pained him to see the boy building such dreams out of nothing. For one last time he tried to make him see sense. 'If you really believe Macdonald means what he says, you'd best be doing something to stop him changing his mind. I wouldn't be taking too long about it, either, if I was you.'

'Doing what?'

You'd think the boy was an imbecile. 'Put her in the family way, what else?'

Fury and embarrassment. 'Why don't you keep your beak out of my business?'

'Paradise Downs is up for grabs now Gavin is dead. Do you think Sean's the sort to turn his back on a chance like that?'

'Sean?' Indulgently, as though Sean would be the last person to do such a thing. 'He's not interested, Dad.'

'You don't think so?'

'Of course not. Besides, he knows how I feel about Sylvia.'

'You've lived with him all these years and you think that'll stop him?'

'He might have tried once but we're a lot closer than we were. He'd never do it now.'

'Someone tipped Macdonald off. It wasn't me. It wasn't you. Who did it?'

Dermot could be as deaf as deaf, when it suited him. 'Maybe Sylvia said something . . .'

'So be it.' Dominic, sighing and defeated, remained determined to grab the final word. 'I've heard it said, somewhere.'

'Heard what?' To the last Dermot would lead with his chin.

'Against stupidity even the gods labour in vain.'

TWENTY-ONE

Sean waited until he knew Dermot was a day's ride away on the far side of Paradise Downs.

'Coming for a swim?'

Sylvia shook her head. 'No.'

'Walk, then?'

'What for?'

'Got something I want to talk to you about.'

'Talk here.'

He wouldn't. Later he wandered up to the creek, making sure Sylvia saw him go.

She came, eventually. Dusk sifted through the branches of the trees. Sean was standing at the edge of the water chucking stones. Plop. Ripples spread like echoes. Plop.

'What did you want to tell me?'

'Nothing.'

The rhythmic swing of the arm. The stone flying into the dark. Plop.

'You said —'

'I know what I said.'

She stood beside him, at a loss. 'I'll go back, then.' But did not. 'That horse you broke. My father says he's going to sell it.'

'I know.'

'It's not fair. It ought to be yours.'

'It's not. It's his. He's got the right to sell it if he wants.'

'Don't you care?'

'No.'

Surely he must? Yet could not be sure; she had never been able to read him.

'Your Dad going to marry again?' he asked.

The question shocked her. 'Course not.'

'Men do.'

Flinging a stone. 'Not him.'

'Gavin's dead. He needs a son.'

She supposed he was right, but did not like to think about it. Another woman. Another child. She stared at the water. She thought how Dermot had never spoken to her father, for all his promises. He doesn't want me, she thought. He never wanted me.

'If your Dad doesn't have a son, who gets Paradise Downs?' Sean asked.

'I will.'

'You can't run it by yourself.'

'My husband will help me.'

He laughed. He had given up on the stones, now stood close beside her in the cicada-singing darkness. 'Got one lined up, have you?'

'Might have.'

'Long as it's not me.'

She tossed her head. 'Fat chance.'

'Or Dermot.'

'Why not Dermot?'

So he had been right.

'He's not game enough. Not for you or Paradise Downs.'

'You don't know anything about it.'

'I know him.' He put his hand on her arm. She flinched

but did not move away. 'You saw what he was like with that horse. Wouldn't get up on him, even. Scared to have a go.' His voice was very close. 'You don't want to chuck yourself away on him.'

His fingers were warm against her inner arm. She sensed that things might get away from her very quickly if she let them. Resolved to put a stop to it at once.

'Dermot and I are getting married.'

If she'd thought the news would scare him off she'd made a mistake.

He laughed. 'Your old man will never allow that.'

She wrenched her arm free; could have spat at him.

'He has agreed.'

'When's the wedding, then?'

Her face fell. 'In three years.'

Again he laughed, mercilessly. 'He really expects you to wait that long? What about Dermot? Didn't he have anything to say about it?'

His hand was back on her arm. How she wished she could flourish Dermot's defiance in Sean's face, but the truth was stronger. 'He told him we'd wait.'

The burden of the admission was terrible. She wanted to move away from him, to break the contact between Sean's cruel strength and herself, but could not. Her will was fluttering like a moth trapped in a web. She knew already she was helpless.

'You'll never marry Dermot.'

His voice as close as his body in the singing dark.

'Of course I shall.'

'If it had been me, I'd have told him right out. Taken you away altogether, if he'd said no.'

'Would you?'

She looked at him uncertainly. Words were easy, but she sensed this boy, who was already so much a man, would do whatever was necessary to take what he wanted from life. Including herself, perhaps.

His hand moved. Her will was dying, dying. Slowly, deliberately, he placed his hand over her breast. He covered her lips with his own.

She stood motionless, doing nothing to stop him. For the first time she understood that it might be easier to yield to a strong man than manipulate a weak one.

Stop it, Dermot. No more, Dermot. *Speak* to him, Dermot. Tell him what we're going to do.

With Sean there would be none of that. Whatever had to be done he would do. Perhaps she would be able to hide herself inside her own surrender. Be safe, after all.

For the first time in her life she did nothing as a man's hand lifted the hem of her dress.

Later he smiled down at her. 'I've put my brand on you.'

It had not been in the least as she had imagined it. In truth she had felt nothing much at all, only his weight grinding her body into the dust, her will into the dust. Yet she was convinced she had been right to let him do it.

By taking me he has made me safe. He will possess only what he wants: the body, the land. Things. He will never have me, because I don't interest him. In his mind I don't exist, even. I am safe.

There would be no more talk of Dermot.

Macdonald, whose eyes missed nothing, saw what might have happened.

'I'm going to hang on to that stallion, after all,' he told Sean.

Sean eased his jeans over his narrow hips. 'Up to you. It's your horse.'

'Darn right he's mine. You can ride him yourself, though, if you want to.'

Sean gave no sign whether he would want to or not.

'Breaking horses,' Macdonald said. 'You're good at that. Stick to it, I was you. Stick to stallions. Leave the mares alone.'

Sean threw him an eyebrow. 'What about the fillies?'

'Them, most of all.'

There was no tension between them. They both understood that there were times when certain steps were necessary. The land demanded strength. Dermot and Paradise Downs — impossible. And Dermot, after all, had been shut out.

'Three years, I told him. She'll be nineteen by then.' Macdonald, eyes contemplating distance, seemed to address the air. 'Reckon that should be about right.'

Anneliese, too, saw what was happening, but did not interfere. Sean was fifteen, so young it seemed barely credible he could be playing such games. Yet, in head as well as body, he was as old as anyone she had ever known. Had been born old, it seemed. Already Sean knew what he wanted from life, would take it, use fist and gun to hang on to it when he had made it his. Whereas Dermot ...

Dermot, always, would be the prisoner of dreams.

TWENTY-TWO

After several years as a professional company director, Anna discovered that her executive responsibilities were taking over her life to the point where hardly anything of herself remained. Meetings and more meetings consumed her days, formal dinners and only marginally less formal cocktail parties her nights. When she wasn't at her desk or in a boardroom, she was in a plane. When she wasn't in a plane she was in a city, one of dozens. Perth, Melbourne, Darwin. Singapore, Paris, London, New York. All of them had been strange to her once, even exotic; now she knew them as well as the reflection of her face in her hand mirror, but — as with the reflection — only in part. She was familiar with Wall Street and Lombard Street, with Kettners, The Ivy, the *Tour d'Argent*, with the arcaded courtyard of Raffles Hotel, with the Ashoka and Claridge's. She knew nothing at all of the real cities or of the people who inhabited them.

One evening at a dinner in Singapore to honour the Premier of South Australia, she found herself talking to Craig Warren, a young and good-looking man who told her he was a journalist.

She thought his job might bring him closer to the real people. She asked him if this were true, only to discover that he was Adelaide-based, was there only to cover the Premier's visit. Even the beautiful young woman at his side, whom she had thought to be Singaporean, turned out to be Japanese, Yukiko Fukuda from Osaka, an executive in a finance corporation.

No help there.

Why should I know the people of the countries I visit? she thought, when she had a moment to think. I don't even know myself.

Or her husband, whose life was as busy as her own. Once they had found time for passion, for moments of sharing, the mutual pleasures of each other's company. Now they passed like birds in flight, like the strangers they were in fact becoming.

From time to time, she received offers, as no doubt Mostyn did. The half-wink, the sideways glance, even outright solicitation became standard features of her life, but her hectic pace burned away too much energy for beds — even the one at home — to be anything but places to sleep. If from time to time she heard rumours that her husband's life was less chaste than her own, what of it? Discretion was essential, but for the rest ... Fidelity was for lovers, which they had long since ceased to be.

Occasionally, in the intervals between meetings, or staring from her hotel balcony at the grey dawn of yet another day in yet another city, she wondered at the gulf that had developed between the life she had originally planned and the way it had turned out.

What had happened to idealism? To the idea that wealth was a weapon to be used in the service of humanity? That power created its own obligations?

She remembered what she had told Ben Champion, at uni. *Why don't you get somewhere in industry or politics, somewhere people will listen to you?*

And his response? *Once you've got your feet in the trough, you'll end up like the rest of them.*

At the time she had not believed him. Now she looked at her life and knew he had been right.

It troubled her increasingly. She tried to talk to Mostyn about it. Perplexed, almost offended, he stared at her before laughing away such romantic nonsense. The accumulation of things — and the power that things provided — absorbed him utterly, as it did everyone he knew. Life was simple: to grab and grab. There was no room for ulterior motives.

'What's your problem? You're doing all right, aren't you?'

It was exactly what he had said to her years ago, when they had first disagreed over women's rights. As before, it was an answer that answered nothing, but Mostyn had neither the time nor the patience to argue further. Ears alert to the growing growl of the Asian tigers, he flew out to Jakarta and Bangkok.

Anna, at home in a blessed interval between engagements, walked in her garden, examined beds of flowers planted by hands other than her own, looked out at the harbour's blue blaze, sunlight gleaming upon the windows of the distant city that was no longer a place of glory, and wondered how she could have let herself be made captive by a life so devoid of meaning or fulfilment.

Was Mostyn right? Were her feelings no more than sentimental rubbish? Social considerations were the responsibility of government. She — and the companies she commanded — paid such taxes as they could not avoid, observed the law, more or less. Her function was to generate wealth, not spend it on worthy causes.

And yet.

Around and around the garden, unresting, until the first blue light of evening came stealing and Mrs Casey called her in to a supper of salmon pie — one of her specialities — and salad.

Anna swallowed her questions with the fish but later, unlike the fish, they returned. Mrs Casey had gone home. Without any notion of what she was about to do, Anna went into the bedroom. She switched off the lights, leaving only a shadowy gleam from the city across the water. Standing by the open window, she took off her clothes, piece by piece: the handmade Italian shoes, the Armani suit, the lingerie from the *Rue de la Paix*. Naked except for a plain gold necklace and wedding ring, she went out of the room, down the stairs, across the terrace. Bare feet silent upon cool grass, Anna Riordan walked amid the night air, the errant scent of flowers, the breath of the sea from the water. It was a gesture without risk — no one could see her in the dark — yet remained meaningful, an action both of affirmation and defiance.

Mostyn was not right. The generation of wealth could be good, certainly, because of the opportunities to do good that it created, but the accumulation of wealth for its own sake was greed.

She could see it so clearly; heard Mostyn's response, too, as though he had been standing beside her.

'Idealistic crap . . .'

She answered him, throwing her words into the patient night. 'Idealism, yes. Crap, never. Because without idealism and the people with courage to apply it, regardless of what it may cost them, humanity has no future.'

It was as well he was not there in the flesh; she could not have borne such devastating proof of their utter incompatibility.

I have to discard so much of my life, she thought. I have to return to what I know is truth.

She lay on her back upon the grass. Above her flared the silent stars. Peace came to anoint her mind, her skin puckered by the breeze. She ran her palms down the pale length of her body, re-identifying herself beneath the cool garment of flesh. Afterwards, chilly now, mind empty, she went indoors to lie in the bath surrounded by scented steam. There was a stillness, precious and infinitely fragile.

She towelled herself dry, brushed her teeth, went to bed like one drugged, conscious of the serenity of life regained.

She slept. Woke at peace, amid the soft stirrings of a tranquil dawn.

Life resumed, but at a slight remove. Through the morning's disciplined frenzy, the meetings and phone calls, the faxes, the deferential bullying of assistants, the stillness that had come to her the previous night remained. The day's tensions beat upon it but could not break through to her inner peace.

Yet still she had doubts.

The world's practical problems — poverty, injustice — could be addressed only through wealth. Once again she remembered the conversation she had held all those years ago with Ben Champion, her student friend and first lover, how she had dismissed the impracticality of his pure idealism. First generate the wealth, then use it. It had been Mostyn's argument, precisely. Except that the people with the wealth did not use it, while those who would do so had nothing to use. It seemed impossible to balance the equation, yet Anna knew what she had forgotten for so long, that fulfilment depended upon her finding a way.

The question continued to nag her, but intermittently, the whirligig of day-to-day decisions claiming priority, as it always did. Then, within a single week, two things happened to bring matters more sharply into focus.

First came an interview. With half an eye she was watching a current affairs programme on television, a pile of board minutes in her lap, when suddenly it reached out to snatch her absolute attention.

Mark Forrest. The face, so well-remembered. The familiar athlete's body. The hand gestures. The past, returning with the force of a blow.

Mark, it seemed, had written a book. *Cry from a Dark Continent* was about South Africa, about what he was claiming was the real South Africa. Anna watched the movement of his lips on camera, the mouth that even now could awaken memories.

'We have to get away from the idea that the situation there is simply a political problem,' he said. 'It's much more serious than that. Meaningful change will need change not only of policies but of hearts. On both sides.'

The interviewer, known for his political slant, was dismissive of the notion that fault could lie with other than South Africa's whites; world opinion had defined the conflict years before. '*Both* sides? That's hardly the informed view, would you say?'

Mark said, 'It's the truth.'

The interviewer chuckled, indulgently. 'That sounds dangerously like an expression of principle.' As though principles were something deserving shame.

The next day, driving into the city, Anna stopped at a book shop and bought Mark's book. Over the next week — between meetings, in airport lounges, in the bath — she read it in great gulps.

TWENTY-THREE

Back in Africa after his final break-up with Anna, Mark Forrest filled the gap with nonsense.

Always parties; always girls. In time his pain became so familiar that he almost ceased to be aware of it. When that happened, the party-going petered out, too. One girl remained. Krystyna de Koch, an Afrikaner and member of the security police, no less. At first it amused him to sit down, later lie down, with the enemy. Then he forgot all that nonsense and she became simply a woman, breasts and thighs and a fall of lustrous dark hair that in moments of passion she drew gently across her mouth, a scented tent in which he could hide his face and tell himself he was cured of Anna Riordan and all her works.

They drove to the high emptiness of the Drakensberg, the saw-toothed mountains sublimely beautiful against a sky the colour of gentians. They walked for hours among the peaks, saw antelope: eland and duiker and wildebeest. Lonely and wild and beautiful like so much of Africa; with its sudden precipices and yawning descents dangerous, too, like so much of Africa. They camped under peaks that still, in October, contained the icy breath of snow. Firelight flickered on their faces and, later, their ardent bodies. They listened to the mysterious silences of the night. The air crackled with frost, the stars were an icy furnace, and Mark thought he would stay in Africa forever.

He was sure Krystyna would marry him, if he asked. Africa was still news and likely to remain so; he would never be out of a job. He thought that the grandeur, ugliness and colour of Africa, the unceasing exclamation points of African existence, the calamities and triumphs and savagery so much more vivid than elsewhere, might be the refuge and salvation that he had been seeking all his life.

Cruelty and hatred, he thought. Glory, too. If I did not hate it so much, I could not love it as I do.

Half-drunk on sex and whisky, he took another swig from the bottle and smiled down at Krystyna lying beside him in the double-sized sleeping bag. His mind focused on a future that seemed not only desirable but right.

In the dying firelight her eyes were a gleam of white against the russet and gold of her face. He opened his mouth to ask her to marry him. Before he could speak, she reached up and placed her fingers across his mouth.

She said, 'No ...'

He cocked an eyebrow, humouring her. 'You don't know what I was going to say.'

'Perhaps.' She sat up and looked past him at the mountains, no more than a ghostly rumour in the darkness. 'You do not understand Africa.'

It touched his professional pride. 'I wouldn't say that.'

'Neither Africa nor the Afrikaner.'

He smiled, hoping to lighten her mood. 'Who could ever hope to understand them?'

'We have very long memories.'

Many Afrikaner rituals were tied up with the distant past, but Mark knew she was not talking of that.

'The authorities think of you as the enemy because of what you write. To them you will always be the enemy.'

'I'm a journalist. I report what I see.'

'You damage us in the eyes of the world.'

He would not accept blame. 'Your government damages you.' Yet Mark knew that his reports were of necessity slanted to suit Sydney's requirements; total objectivity was impossible.

She shook her head. 'No one who is not African will ever understand us.'

Her words struck an elegiac note. It troubled him; he did not want to lose this woman, too.

'So teach me and I'll learn.'

'You should leave Africa,' she said.

'If I did, would you come with me?'

A coal clicked in the dying fire.

'No,' Krystyna said.

Anger. 'Has your boss put you up to this?'

Inside the sleeping bag, her hand caressed his thigh. 'My boss doesn't get into bed with me.' She smiled, coaxing him, but Mark was in no mood to be coaxed.

'I'd say he's here right now.'

It was deliberately hurtful, yet her smile did not flicker. With sudden desolation, he knew that he had indeed lost her.

'We are a backwater here. No place for a journalist of your talent.'

That was nonsense. 'The action never stops.'

'Things will quieten down again, you'll see. People will forget us.'

'You think the blacks will forget?'

'We shall make our own peace with the blacks. Afrikaner, Zulu, Shangaan ... We are all African. We do not need outsiders to show us the way. We have been living with each other for centuries.'

Her hand continued to move on him. He turned to her, yielding to the increasing intimacy of her touch.

'You think that, why are you here with me now?'

'I am an Afrikaner,' she said, 'but a woman, also. It is the woman who is here with you.'

At the last, he managed to salvage something with a joke. 'Thank God for that,' he said.

Mark did not leave Africa. He did not even leave Krystyna, or not entirely. They still spent occasional nights together, but the urgency was gone. He remained unsure whether the break-up had been her idea or whether her boss had indeed warned her off. It did not matter; either way, it came to the same thing.

He told himself that a foreign correspondent had no business with a wife. At least there was one consolation; in sharp contrast with his feelings after his break-up with Anna, he did not ache. In his heart he knew that Krystyna had been right. He would never be truly African, would not wish to be, perhaps. They would not have been right for each other, their differences far greater than the attraction that had drawn them together. He was grateful to her; thanks to the clarity of her perception, he had escaped unscathed from what would almost certainly have been another catastrophe.

She had been right about something else, as well. The tide of protest was ebbing. Every day there was less to report. Even the police no longer hassled him. Perhaps, as she had said, it was time to move on.

Certainly Australia thought so. Mark was one of the favourite sons of the Sydney mafia; when they approached him about a possible move to London, they asked him nicely. It meant nothing; if they had made up their minds they needed him there, they'd have packed him off, never mind what he thought about it. They hadn't but, in truth, he had no reason to refuse. It would be a great career move; the most ardent republican could hardly call London a backwater.

Yet he hesitated, intuition urging him to stay.

To prove him right there came a sequence of killings: one black, several white, then more black, deaths by the dozen — and everything changed.

A contact in the African township of Atteridgeville tipped Mark off that a child — a choirboy on his way to practice — had been killed by the police. He checked and found there was something in the story. He flew up from Cape Town to interview the police officer in charge. Who, at least to begin with, was a pleasant surprise.

Mark had taken it for granted that the cops would give him a hard time — they always did — but Colonel Niewouldt, grey-haired and fatherly, seemed to be the exception. Not that he was about to accept blame for anything the police might have done.

'The Enquiry uncovered no evidence against the constable,' he told Mark. 'The only witness was the madam of a brothel. We interrogated her, but she could not even identify the officer she claimed was involved.'

Mark was sceptical; he had been lied to so often. 'The version I heard, she claimed he wasn't in the line-up.'

'It's what she would say, isn't it? Listen,' the Colonel said, 'Children, old people, are attacked every day in the townships. The *tsotsis*, ruffians, are everywhere. It saddens me to say it, but this kind of business is commonplace.'

'The boy's father blames the police. Mrs Kumalo, the brothel keeper, blames the police.'

Niewouldt slapped an exasperated hand on the surface of his desk. 'Then let them bring evidence. Do that and we shall prosecute. You think we enjoy it? A child dead and the police blamed? These people ... If the sky fell on their heads they would blame the police.' He breathed deeply for a moment, nostrils flared, lips indignant. 'We took statements from everyone,' he said. 'If you want to see them you are welcome.'

This was co-operation, indeed. Mark began to wonder if his contact might have been mistaken, after all.

'I would like that. Thank you.'

The Colonel lifted his telephone, spoke briefly. A uniformed officer brought a bulging file and led Mark to a vacant office with a desk and a chair. He placed the file upon the desk and pointed to a bell push in the wall.

'The Colonel instructs that you should be locked in. For security reasons, you understand. When you have finished, please ring the bell and we shall come and let you out.'

He left the room; Mark heard the key turn in the lock. The idea of being locked up by the police would have disconcerted him, had he let it. He sat at the desk, opened the file and began to read the statements of the witnesses in the case of Moses Majozi, the thirteen-year-old choirboy who had been beaten to death on his way to church.

The first statement was from Bishop Amos Phalimanze, leader of the church to which Moses had belonged:

I, Amos Phalimanze, by the Grace of Jesus the Nazarene, bishop of the three million members of the Zion Christian Church of Africa, say this.

Our members are not of this world. All things other than work and prayer are forbidden. We do not visit beer halls. We do not attend football matches. We do not smoke tobacco or other drugs. We do not involve ourselves in politics or protest.

Simon Majozi, his wife and children are members of our church. Simon is a good man, strong in the Lord, the foreman of a construction company in Pretoria. Friday night Simon and his family returned home from church. His youngest son, Moses, thirteen years old, had something to eat, then set out to return to the church for choir practice. The rest of the family went to bed.

One hour later, his daughter awakened Simon. She told him that a messenger had come to say that his son had been badly beaten by the police. Simon and his wife got dressed at once and ran to the spot with the messenger. They found Moses lying unconscious in the roadway. Mrs Kumalo, one of the crowd, told them what had happened. She is not a member of our church, and they knew her by sight only. They put the boy into a car and took him to the hospital at Kalafong.

Thoughtfully Mark put the paper down and turned to the next one, the statement of the Mrs Miriam Kumalo whom the bishop had mentioned in his testimony and who, according to Colonel Niewouldt, ran a brothel in the area where the incident had taken place.

Name?
 Miriam Kumalo.
 You run a shebeen in Sibeni Street?
 Shebeen? I do not know that word.
 It is a very common word among people of your profession. As you are well aware, it means you sell liquor without a licence. You are a shebeen queen and

brothel keeper. Do you wish me to explain what the word 'brothel' means?

I have friends who take cool drinks in hot weather. Meet other friends. Some of the Colonel's friends also come.

Do not be insolent. What did you hear that night? While you were selling cool drinks to your friends?

One woman say, come quick, there is big trouble. So I go and see this white cop in the alley with a boy.

A black boy?

Of course black! You think we have white boys here? The boy is lying on the ground. The cop has his gun out. He is kicking him.

What did you do?

I run up to him. I ask what he doing. He take no notice, but kick the boy again. His boot marks are all over the boy's shirt. I say to him, I know that boy. He not one of the Comrades, those men who are always rioting. He go to church. All the time in church. I push the cop away. I tell him, how you do this thing? You like me to kick your kid brother like this?

What did the policeman do?

Church? he say. What he doing on the street, then? I say, he going to church. He choirboy. His eyes go round. Choirboy? Fokking hell! Then he run back to his car, drive off. I take his number. He see me. He reverse so fast I have to jump out the way. He say, what you doing? I say I report him to Pretoria. He point his gun at me. He say, you sure you don't want the front number, too? Then he drive off.

And the boy?

He still lying there. I send a man for his father. When he come, he drive him to the hospital at Kalafong. That all I know.

Once again Mark turned the page.

My name is Pauline Tshabalala. I am a nurse at the Kalafong hospital. Friday night at the hospital like rush-hour in the city. How! So many people. Stab wounds, bullet wounds. So many. All night rush, rush. This boy brought in, left on a stretcher. After maybe one hour, I get to look at him. I see at once he very bad. He cannot speak. There is blood on his head and in his ears. And his body, when I look, all bruises. Blood all over. His parents are there. I tell them not to worry, we fix up their son real good. When we take him into X-ray, we see his skull is all broken and there is blood on the brain. Nothing we can do. Presently he die. I go to tell the parents. They sitting there holding each other's hands. I tell them their boy is dead.

Finally there was a statement from Colonel Niewouldt himself.

I am a Colonel in the South African Police. As officer commanding the Atteridgeville Unit, I confirm to the Enquiry that the police carried out all procedures correctly and in accordance with standing orders.

I visited the location of the incident personally and took statements from all witnesses.

The witness Miriam Kumalo is a woman of poor character who runs a shebeen and brothel in Sibeni Street, Atteridgeville. During interrogation, Miriam Kumalo alleged that she had seen Konstabel Venter kicking the deceased, Moses Majozi.

Konstabel Venter states that he was on patrol in Atteridgeville at the time of the assault on the said Majozi. He surprised two men attacking a third who was lying on the ground. He drove up to give assistance, whereupon the assailants fled. Konstabel Venter pursued the pair on foot, but was unfortunately unable to detain them. He returned to the scene of the incident, where he was assaulted by the complainant Miriam Kumalo.

He denies categorically that he was kicking the deceased. He denies categorically that he was in any way responsible for the injuries suffered by the deceased. He left the scene only when it became apparent that his own life was in danger.

At a subsequent identification parade, Miriam Kumalo was unable to identify Konstabel Venter.

After full enquiry, I am of the opinion that no blame attaches to Konstabel Venter, who is in fact to be commended for his attempts to save the boy Moses Majozi, despite considerable danger to himself.

I so advise.

Mark closed the file and rang the bell. The same officer took the file and checked it carefully before escorting him back to Colonel Niewouldt's office.

'I understand the Enquiry followed your advice and exonerated the officer?'

'Of course. There was no evidence against him at all.'

'Except for Mrs Kumalo.'

'Mrs Kumalo ...' The colonel dismissed the Kumalos of the world. 'A woman of bad character who could not even identify the officer concerned. She was just trying to make trouble.'

'Yet she saw him. According to your own testimony, she even assaulted him. Why couldn't she identify him after that?'

Niewouldt's eyes regarded him frostily. 'Listen to me,' he said. 'We have our own way of doing things in this country. They may seem strange to you, a foreigner, but they work. We know how to keep our house in order, believe me.' He smiled, jovially, the father figure who had delivered a rebuke but was willing to forgive. 'Now, tell me. Have you seen everything you need?'

It was pointless to talk to this man any more.

'Thank you.'

Niewouldt smiled and smiled. 'You're quite sure?'

'Thank you.' Through clenched teeth.

Niewouldt, avuncular, walked Mark to the door. 'You journalists are always complaining about the police. Our lack of co-operation. Well, our shoulders are broad enough to put up with it. But I hope, on this occasion at least, you have no complaints on that score?'

They had been discussing nothing less than the crucifixion of the truth, yet his voice contained no hint of mockery.

'You have been really co-operative,' Mark said.

Why say anything else, when all was lies? Back in Pretoria, Mark phoned his contact. 'I want to meet Miriam Kumalo. And the father.'

Miriam Kumalo said, 'Of course I could not identify him. The bastard was not there.'

Simon Majozi said, 'I am black, he is white. I have no power. My son is dead. I can only say hallelujah, it is over. The vessel is shattered. The water has drained away.'

Mark filed his report. Sydney loved it. Someone, predictably, came up with the headline:

SLAUGHTER OF THE INNOCENTS

A Moses Majozi Commemoration Fund was formed, proceeds to go to apartheid's victims.

A campaign was launched to send letters of protest to the South African embassy. Outside which a few banner-carrying demonstrators marched and yelled for the cameras.

'Great copy!' Tyler on the Sydney desk exulted. 'Gone over great with our readers.'

'You still say I don't understand Africa?' Mark asked Krystyna.

'You understand nothing.'

'Enough to know whose side I'm on.'

Yet was troubled. As though he had sold Moses and his family to a gloating world to win a skirmish in a war concerned more with politics and power than with humanity and suffering.

Then came the affair of the Pangaman, so-called after the heavy blade he used to dismember his victims.

The Pangaman was Zulu. He murdered white people, breaking into houses at night and hacking the inhabitants to pieces. A lunatic — that was the most comfortable explanation.

Mark had a feeling there was more to it than that. He dug deep, came up with a story of another of apartheid's victims. An orphan, hounded unmercifully, deprived of work or a place to live, a man jailed for stealing food who, on his release, still without work, waged his own bloody war against the whites who had pilloried him.

A fine story with plenty of blood and the requisite anti-apartheid twist. Tyler would love it. And yet...

Something was missing. Mark couldn't put his finger on it, but was sure it was there.

He went to Krystyna for help. The Security Police were not concerned with ordinary crime, but she had contacts.

A policeman, another Zulu, filled in the background and Mark found he had no story after all — or none that Australian readers would understand.

The Pangaman had been an outcast not merely from white society but from his own. The cause lay seventy years earlier when his grandfather had first seduced, then run away with, his own cousin.

'Only a dog would have done such a thing,' the policeman said. 'The *AmaDhlozi* were enraged.'

'Who are they? The tribal elders?'

'The spirits of the dead.'

'But surely you don't believe ...?'

'All Zulu believe. All the time those spirits live in our houses. They are as real to us as our own shadows.'

'But what happened seventy years ago has nothing to do with him. It wasn't so terrible, in any case.'

'To a Zulu it is very terrible. To sleep with a woman of the same clan ... The *AmaDhlozi* turn their wrath not only on the man and the woman, but on their descendants, too. All are cursed and driven out. Forever.'

'And that's what happened to the Pangaman?'

'Oh yes.'

The policeman clearly accepted the proposition that the Pangaman should be cursed because of what his grandfather had done seventy years earlier. 'He is doomed. In the old days, he would never have known life at all. His father would have been strangled at birth. He knows this. The pain of knowing is what makes him kill.'

'But he claims to be Christian,' Mark protested.

'Makes no difference. If you anger the shades, better you die.'

As the Pangaman died, hanged in the Pretoria jail.

'Good riddance,' the Zulu policeman said.

'You say you are a Christian, too. You think he has gone to hell for what he did?'

'Hell can be no worse than what he knew in this life.'

Enough to know whose side I'm on.

Mark had told Krystyna that and believed it. Yet it was not always so easy. The story of the Pangaman had been bad enough; now, after yet another outburst of violence in Guguletu — the African township where he had gone with Anna and had so nearly been caught by the *tsotsis* — he interviewed an old lady whose family had suffered in the riots:

My name is Fana Viyuseli. I am sixty-nine years old. I have borne five children. We are Zulu, from the country, although we have lived in the town for many years. In my time here I have seen many things. A year ago the boys in this place played football together. Now ...

My own granddaughters. I warn them. Stay away from this politics. It too dangerous. They not listen. Like all the kids in this street, they support Black Consciousness, hate supporters of the United Front.

Last week Front men caught the younger one. They burned her alive. There, in the street.

Listen, I do not like these people. Always they kill. They blow up a house in the next street. They break into homes, shoot people. Hundreds of people. Babies and grandmothers. Kill me, too, maybe, one of these days. They throw fire into houses, watch while all the people inside burn up.

My other granddaughter frightened, run away. Cannot come home ever again. She only fifteen but if she come the police will put her in jail or the Front fighters will kill her. Whatever she do, she dead. These people, they kill everyone.

'You call them Front fighters. But the leaders cannot know,' Mark said.

Fana, a Zulu who hated the Xhosa leaders of the Front, shook her head scornfully. 'Who cares what they know? Their fighters killed my granddaughter!'

Mark did not believe there was any question of the Front leadership being involved. No way; he did not even bother to report the story to Sydney. There would have been no point; Tyler would never have had a bar of it.

The remains of thirty-two African women were recovered. They had been thrown alive into pits of flame. People were saying it was the biggest mass killing in South Africa's history.

Journalists, foreign correspondents in particular, were supposed to be hardened to horror. They could not hope to survive the constant trauma if they permitted themselves to feel too much. Mark subscribed to the view, had thought that after all he had seen he was proof against anything, but now images tormented him. Writhing, screaming bodies. Stench and smoke. The murderers, watching. Over seventy youths were arrested, all Front supporters. It could have been another frame-up by the police, of course. Mark hoped it was, but his contacts in the townships were strangely noncommittal. He remembered again what he had been told by the old woman Fana Viyuseli.

If what she had told him were true, if reports of this latest massacre were also true, did it mean that the angels, too, were steeped in blood? Never. He refused, absolutely, to believe that the leadership could be in any way involved. It was unthinkable. Yet Krystyna was right. He did not understand this country. He would never understand.

He phoned her. She had heard the news already.

'Alive. They burned them alive ...'

He was choking, close to tears. He had believed he had known everything, now knew nothing. There were no certainties left.

Krystyna was merciful. She came to him silently. Mark hoped she understood a little of what he felt. She held him. They grew still together.

'Who can hope to understand this strange place?'

Over and over he said it.

'Hush, now. Hush.'

He was not consoled. Even here, with her. A friend? A spy?

'Hush, now. Hush.'

He filed his report on the killings.

Tyler said, 'You say blacks did it?'

'Yes.'

A moment's silence. Then, 'Not the image we're trying to project.'

'It's what happened.'

'Can't we say it was set up by the government?'

'No!'

'They've done it before. They're still doing it.'

'Not this time.' Mark took a deep breath. 'Phil, are you going to run it or not?'

Tyler sounded surprised. 'Of course.'

And did. The bare facts, no more.

'I'm taking some leave.'

'Now? The whole place is liable to explode any day.'

'I don't think so. If it does, I'll come back.'

'Well ...' Doubtfully. 'You were right last time, I suppose.'

He went to the Natal coast, north of the tiny settlement called Chaka's Rock. He went alone, stayed at a small hotel on the beach. Krystyna would probably have come, had he asked her, but he needed solitude like oxygen. Solitude to think, to feel, to be.

He walked the beaches of yellow sand, so different from the white sands of the Cape. He watched the surf run landwards between the jutting teeth of headlands. He looked for fish in the weed-clad pools, ate shellfish at a restaurant he had discovered. Went to bed. In the morning, walked again.

I have been at fault all this time, he thought. We have all been at fault. We have been choosing sides, the good against the bad, yet in truth there are no sides. There is only one people, one universality. Not only in South Africa; in the world. There is human aspiration and human suffering, no more.

No more? He walked on, his feet in the sea's sudsy fringe. Surely to God there was enough there to keep a writer busy all his life.

The following morning he got up early and went to the bedroom window. For a long time he looked out at the sea, brilliant with early sunlight. He breathed the salt-rich air. He turned his back on it, went to the desk and began to write.

TWENTY-FOUR

Cry from a Dark Continent summarised the South African situation more clearly and dispassionately than any account Anna had previously read. Mark had avoided the oversimplifications of those who, wedded to political correctness, attributed blame by race. He did not attribute blame at all, merely recorded facts. Appalling facts they were, indeed, yet his book was much more than a grim recital of murder and deprivation. Through each tale of brutality shone the humanity of the narrator, his passionate care for Africa and the human condition. For truth, also. Mark's book brought horror, certainly, but also hope, the affirmation of his belief in humanity's indestructible potential for goodness. From every page his voice rang out, awakening memories that were unbearably poignant. It moved Anna more deeply than she would have believed possible. She knew she had read a great book.

Though she wept, she was also envious. Mark had found his path, the path that had so far eluded her. Perhaps, she thought, his book will help me there, too. It was certainly possible; after reading it, she saw, more clearly than ever, the direction in which she should go, yet the gulf between intention and performance remained.

She had thought about it so much at one time, yet had somehow lost the path. Recently she had found it again, yet still had done nothing. It was not good enough. She had talents, too. She must use them, not simply to generate wealth but to employ that wealth as a power for good. Perhaps, with faith and persistence, she would be able to prove both to herself and others that Mark was not the only one who knew how to serve.

A week later she attended a board meeting of United Minerals. United had put in an offer for Saturn Consolidated. Ever optimistic in the face of what their chairman called corporate rape, Saturn's directors were trying to fight them off. Lawyers' letters were flying to and fro; it was shaping up to a real bloodbath. Anna, competitive instincts honed by years of conflict, was as eager for battle as the rest of them.

It was an all-day meeting, planning strategies, sharpening corporate knives. There was endless bickering, as always in such situations.

Suddenly it happened. Anna's mind was overwhelmed by the memory of Africa, the smell and drumbeat of Africa. By other images, too; she looked covertly at her colleagues, their jackal teeth shining, and wondered what they would think if they could see what her memory now recalled: herself, two weeks earlier, lying newborn naked on the grass under the Sydney stars.

The feelings awakened by Mark's book returned, flooding. Before she knew it, she had shoved back her chair and stood up, gasping for air. Harris Donnelly, the financial director, had been droning about extra funding; Anna's movement dried the tongue in his mouth.

Everyone looked at her.

Somehow she managed a smile. 'Excuse me a moment.'

She walked out, steady on her high executive heels. In the Ladies Room, she leant on her hands and stared at her reflection in the mirror. She breathed deeply, waiting for the erratic thud of her heart to ease.

Furiously she thought, I cannot permit this. There are things I have to do in my life, but it is the future, not the past, that matters. I will not be influenced by what is gone.

Except that the past was not gone; it was her memories of it that had caused her to flee so precipitously from the meeting. She thought again of the woman whom Mark had mentioned, the Afrikaner who claimed that she was African, a white African, like all the Afrikaner people. If she were right it meant that, at least in part, Anna herself was African.

Certainly Anneliese would have said so. Standing before the mirror, staring at her reflection, Anna remembered herself at fifteen, Anneliese summoning her to that hot room redolent of approaching death to lecture her yet again on how her farm in Africa must be reclaimed, how without it her spirit would never rest. How it was up to Anna to do something about it.

She thought of the extraordinary story in Mark's book, the Pangaman cursed forever by events that had taken place years before his birth. The *AmaDhlozi*, as real at the end of the twentieth century as in the days of Chaka the king, their vengeance accepted as fact by a modern policeman. It was a way of thinking so alien that to read about it was to enter a world where people flew, trees talked and the spirits destroyed living men. By the reckoning of both Anneliese and Mark's friend, Afrikaners both, Anna was of that world, too.

The Pangaman's heritage had been death. Her own was less onerous, but real, nonetheless.

Anneliese's voice. *My spirit will not rest ...*

Dear God, Anna thought. What a burden the past places upon us.

Again she stared at her reflection. A white African. In that light, the concerns of the boardroom were both bizarre and irrelevant. She had no place there. Yet, if not, where was her place? The boardrooms of the city, of all the other cities, had become her world. Despite her recent doubts, a major part of her still wanted nothing else.

'Damn Mark Forrest!'

Horrified, she realised she had spoken aloud.

Enough. She splashed water on her face, touched up her make-up and returned to the boardroom with smiling apologies.

In Anna's world, even momentary weakness was dangerous. For the rest of the meeting, she was stiletto-sharp, pouncing on every flaw in the revised proposals they were planning to place before the Saturn shareholders. At one point Harris Donnelly tried to argue a point. It was obvious he was wrong; she should have let his proposal fail by default. She could not do it. Ruthlessly, she dismembered the argument, and the man.

It was a way to make enemies but at that moment Anna did not care. She had to demonstrate that she was still in control. Only afterwards did it occur to her that she had been proving her point, not merely to the men around the table but to herself.

A white African, indeed.

Her walkabout caused talk.

'You okay?' Mostyn asked.

'Of course. Why not?'

'I hear you had a turn the other morning.'

'Caught short.' She smiled. 'Happens to the best of us.'

It had happened to Mostyn once; he had told her about it, making a joke out of what he would not have found funny at the time. He didn't find it funny now. 'As long as you're not pregnant.'

'Hardly likely, is it?'

Any criticism, however oblique, raised his hackles. 'What's that supposed to mean?'

'It takes two, you know. We haven't been that matey in recent months, have we? Unless you think I've found a toy.'

As rumour said he had, more than once. It was sad that she cared so little.

Underneath his laughter, he was embarrassed. 'What a way to talk.'

Indeed. She remembered staring at her reflection in the Ladies, her mind filled with memories not only of Mark but of everything that had happened in Africa. Memories that once had fuelled her response to Mostyn himself.

She had not thought of Adam for years. Anneliese Wolmarans and Adam Shongwe. How they would have fought had they ever met — the fighting evidence of their shared heritage. Mark somewhere between, both onlooker and chronicler; not African, yet with the talent and insight to capture the truth of Africa.

With her mind full of such notions, who was Anna to complain of Mostyn's piffling infidelities? She remembered her friend Monica Talbot going on and on about the humiliation of catching her first husband with his hand up the wrong skirt, thought how humiliation seemed to mean different things to different people.

Monica had taken him to the cleaners, the settlement making headlines in all the papers that published that sort of garbage. She had told Anna how, for weeks afterwards, her phone had never stopped ringing, hopefuls trying their luck with the latest, suddenly rich, ex. The story had delighted her, yet Anna would have found that humiliating, to trade her self-respect for cash.

It was easier for her, of course; it was years since she had cared about Mostyn's bimbos. The time she had run away to the Blue Mountains had been her last contribution to saving their marriage. When Mostyn had followed she had thought she'd won but in truth things had never come right between them. At bottom, they were incompatible, staying together out of habit and convenience. It worked as well as most marriages and if, from time to time, Anna felt she was missing something, what of it? She had her health, her work. She was good at what she did, was excited by the potential of what might be possible in the future. What she had to do was find a way to marry her present way of life to her instinct for social justice. In that, perhaps, she would find salvation.

For the second time in as many weeks the past returned, this time in the form of a notice announcing a meeting organised by Australians Against Apartheid, a group of which she had been a member for years.

The meeting would receive a report-back from the organising committee. It would also be addressed by a distinguished guest speaker, a member of the central committee of the African National Congress.

Adam Shongwe was in Australia.

Anna cancelled two appointments to be there. Deliberately, she sat near the back of the hall, planning to see rather than be seen. It was a forlorn hope, both hall and audience too small for anonymity.

Across the half-dozen yards that separated them, the force of Adam's personality reached out to seize her. At once the intervening years were gone. She saw him as she had on that first occasion in the tiny Guguletu house, heard the note in his voice, angry and contemptuous, as he dismissed her.

They send a woman to talk to me?

She remembered, too, the later meeting and what had followed from it, the quarrel with Mark, their eventual separation, the remaking of both their lives.

All brought about by this man.

The chairman was droning on about funds, about boycotts of South African products, about ...

Anna shut out his voice, concentrating only on Adam Shongwe's eyes. They were as yellow and almond-shaped as she remembered; like their owner they seemed not to have changed at all. They were everywhere, staring at each member of the audience in turn. She watched them move closer to her, fought down a ludicrous impulse to lower her face, avoid his challenging gaze. Instead, she sat deliberately erect, chin up. Waiting.

The eyes reached her. Slid past. Returned. Not by a flicker did either acknowledge the other, but both knew. Oh yes.

The time came for him to address the meeting. He stood, his personality filling the hall as easily as it had the tiny Guguletu room. He spoke fluently, but with an uncompromising harshness.

'Within the last day or two, there has been criticism in the Australian press of the bombing campaign conducted in South African cities by the ANC. I wish to answer that criticism now.'

He spoke of struggle, of death, of outrage, of the South African government's own terror tactics, of its refusal to talk. Yes, bombs had been placed in bus shelters and post offices, black people and white had been killed or maimed in the ensuing explosions.

'I make no apologies.' So he challenged them, making plain his contempt for their white, middle-class assumptions of victory easily won, their distaste for blood and pain. 'We are fighting a war and in a war, always, there are casualties. It is the price that must be paid.'

The bombing campaign out of the way, he slipped easily into what was obviously a ritual speech, smooth and non-confrontational, in which he praised all supporters of the armed struggle, white as well as black, calling them brothers and sisters.

Anna listened, face impassive, eyes fixed upon him, but he did not look at her again.

He ended with a warning of more vengeance, more blood.

'Recently there has been much talk of a book by an Australian called Mark Forrest. I have read it myself. *Cry from a Dark Continent* serves a purpose. It focuses world criticism upon the regime, weakening those who for so long have kept us beneath their iron heel. But I have to say this. It claims that both sides, white and black, need to change their ideas about each other. It is not his place to tell us what we should think. He is not an African, he has not suffered as we have. In any case, the book is irrelevant. The apartheid citadel is already tottering. With or without the Forrests of the world, it will fall. When it is gone will come the reckoning. We shall purge the land.' He stared around at the audience, controlling them, taking his time about it. The room was subservient, silent, breath caught in throats waiting to cheer. 'There is a place where the *impis* of the Zulu king Dingaan destroyed the women and children of the Boers. To this day they call it Weenen, the Place of Weeping.' He raised his clenched fists above his head as his voice, harsh, ominous, triumphant, rolled over them all. 'Soon — I give you my solemn promise — for all those who have worshipped at apartheid's bloody shrine, the days of weeping will return.'

The audience was on its feet, applause like a riot in the hall. Anna slipped out of the door and was gone.

The next day her secretary buzzed her. 'There's some man on the phone. I didn't catch the name.'

It could have been anybody but Anna knew, at once. She took a steadying breath, conscious of the thunder of her heart. 'Put him through.'

'Anna Riordan?'

It *was* Adam, the warm African inflexion unmistakable.

'Good morning.'

She did not ask who he was; there was no need for games.

'I hoped to see you after the meeting.'

'I had to leave.'

'Had, or chose?'

He had always been direct but she believed she could match him in that, as in most things. 'Chose, perhaps.'

'Why?'

'I like you better when you're honest.'

'You mean my speech.' A hint of laughter. 'The first part was from the heart, I promise you, but some of our supporters are easily frightened.'

'So why are you calling?'

'To meet with you. To discuss investment in the new South Africa.'

'Which does not exist.'

'But which will.'

It was very different from the previous occasion: a suite in an up-market hotel in the middle of the city, aides in charcoal suits, Adam Shongwe himself sitting at his ease on a brocade settee. Which did not mean she could simply walk in. On the contrary, she was checked very carefully indeed by a young man with watchful eyes and a body honed to the edge of violence. To which, she judged, he was no stranger.

Some things were not so different, after all.

Adam, when at last she reached him, wasted no time on chatter or reminiscence. 'You are a person of influence in the Australian business world.'

She thought it might be prudent to discount such a notion. 'Some influence, perhaps. Not a lot.'

'Australian Businesswoman of the Year?'

That damn trophy, she thought. 'It doesn't mean much.'

'We are looking for investment. For expressions of interest. I thought you might be the person to speak to.'

'For the new South Africa which does not yet exist.'

'But which will.'

'So you say. I think my co-directors will prefer to wait until that is definite, not something that may or may not happen at some unspecified time in the future.'

'I shall be talking to other industrialists,' Adam said. 'Both in Australia and overseas. The organisations at the head of the queue will be the ones who will have the greatest influence.'

He smiled at her, very sure of himself in his London-made suit, but Anna was unmoved by threats, however smilingly presented. 'Judging from previous African experience, aid gives no influence at all.'

'No one has mentioned aid,' he said softly. 'We are talking investment. With remittable, hard-currency profits.'

'After tax.'

'Tax holidays could perhaps be negotiated.' Which certainly put a different complexion on things.

'You should send a fact-finding team,' he suggested. 'Come yourself, perhaps.'

'We might. Violence is likely to be a problem,' Anna told him. 'We hear of what is happening in the townships. Some people think the whole country is set to explode. If that happens, there won't be any profits to remit.'

'We shall make sure it doesn't.'

'Those same people doubt you can stop it.'

The amber eyes narrowed. He frowned, but did not speak. Smoothly Anna changed the subject, satisfied that she had made her point. 'When can we expect this change of power to take place?'

'It will happen,' Adam said. 'Nothing is more definite than that. But the date is not yet settled.'

'Perhaps we should talk again when it is.'

Again the frown, the assessing stare but, for the moment, he said nothing. Instead flicked a finger. An aide brought coffee, with biscuits, on an elegant tray. The china was the best. Whatever else, Adam Shongwe had learned to live well.

'Your friend Mark Forrest...' Calculated small talk to ease the tension that had entered the conversation. 'You have read his book, I assume. Did you like it?'

'More than you did, judging from what you said last night.'

'Some things have to be said for public consumption,' he said. 'It is the nature of politics.'

'Are you saying you did like it?'

'I found it interesting. *Cry from a Dark Continent* ...' The dark voice reflected upon the words. 'By admitting the confusion in his own mind, he has shown he may eventually come to understanding, after all. I told him once he would never be more than an observer. He didn't like it, but I was right. What I did not realise was how influential an observer can be.' He finished his coffee, returned the cup to the tray. He contemplated her soberly. 'I had great hopes for you, in those days.'

Anna managed a laugh. 'For me? Why?'

'I believed you had more potential than he did.' He smiled, but she saw lingering regret in the amber eyes. 'Perhaps I was foolish.'

His smile had diminished her. She would not accept it. 'Why should you think that?'

He ignored the question. 'Until I met you I had thought all white women fell into one of two categories. Those with jagged, autocratic voices, the majority. I hated them, but despised the rest — they were always so subservient, trying to convince themselves they would be black if they could. I remember one like that, all teeth and ardour, stringy hair scragged back. I saw her in a street demonstration, a would-be black among a sea of blacks. She mimicked our cries, shrilly, she flung her arms about, trying to imitate our fluid gestures of rage; she even joined in the *toya-toya*, the protest dance that is the property of none but ourselves.' Another smile, reflective and dark, and again Anna felt the power of the man, raw and forceful in the so-smart room. 'I remember telling myself that when the revolution came she would die with the rest.'

'I hope you don't think like that any more,' she told him. 'Not if you want investment.'

His thoughts, and perhaps her response, seemed to awaken anger. 'I asked you to come here today to give you the chance to share with us in rebuilding our country. And what has interested you most?' One by one, his voice tolled the bell of their discussion. 'Profits. Tax. Violence. The questions that every capitalist asks. I believed you were different, that you would have made a good comrade. Now I ask myself if I was wrong.'

TWENTY-FIVE

For once in their lives, Anna and Mostyn, both of them in Sydney, both without appointments, spent the evening together. Mostyn had suggested they should go out somewhere — to celebrate, as he put it — but Anna had said no.

'When we've the chance to stay home together? There's no point in having the house at all, if we're going to do that.'

So they had stayed. It was just the two of them. Anna had given Mrs Casey the evening off and, for the first time in ages, she did a stint in the kitchen.

Mostyn couldn't see the point. 'Have something sent in. A whole lot easier, surely?'

And probably a lot more palatable. At least he didn't say that, but the thought was no doubt in his mind, as it was in hers.

You are a perfectly competent cook, Anna instructed herself, ferreting around in the deep freeze. All the same, with the amount of practice she'd had in recent years, it made sense to keep things simple.

It wasn't too hard; Mostyn had always been a steak man and that was what she gave him, a fillet steak that she had ordered especially, collecting it on the way home from the office. For herself, she had stuck with salmon; she could hardly go wrong with that. Besides, it was her favourite, although she steered clear of anything as elaborate as Mrs Casey's pie.

It had given her an odd feeling, shopping for their evening meal, odder still to think that it was something that most married women did every day of their lives. Not that she was about to get dewy-eyed about that; she'd never been into the pastry-making kick at school and had no plans to change now. Changes in her lifestyle might be on the agenda, but becoming little wifey in the kitchen was, most emphatically, not one of them.

She did croquette potatoes, something she had been good at long ago, peas and broccoli from the freezer, baby carrots from the shopping mall down the road. For herself, a bottle of chardonnay, nicely chilled; another of shiraz, chosen with due ceremony by the man himself, to go with Mostyn's steak. To round things off, a lemon cheesecake, very grand, from a cake shop in the same mall. A splot or two of King Island cream, and they were in business.

Might as well pig out while we're about it, she thought, feeling not in the least guilty about it. What the hell, all the good old-fashioned books claimed that the way to a man's heart was through his stomach, and she had no aversion to thinking how the evening might end. Had even planned for it: no bra and sexy panties so brief they were hardly there at all. She had admired them as she stepped into them after her bath. They were gorgeous. So they should be; the price she'd paid, they cost more per square centimetre than the most expensive real estate on earth.

Never mind; she'd bought them for an occasion, after all, and if dining alone with her husband for the first time in months was not an occasion, what was?

It was warm, a night without wind, and Anna decided they should eat on the terrace. She brought out a linen cloth, the best cutlery, the Georgian silver candlesticks. The candle flames stood tall, with barely a flutter.

Lights, she thought, how I love them. Candlelight on the table, the underwater lights of the swimming pool, the clustered brilliance of the city across the harbour, the sails of the Opera House glowing distantly against the sky. The right kind of light, made for romance, made to order.

There were no kitchen disasters; everything went very well.

Mostyn polished off the last of his steak. 'Very nice,' he said approvingly. 'Delicious.'

It was nice to hear, although she knew he would have said the same thing, with exactly the same degree of enthusiasm, to the chef in any swank restaurant.

She brought coffee in the Queen Anne pot; she fetched a glass of port for her husband; she was little wifey to the core, if only for the night. They sat in silence together, contented and — for once in their lives — at peace.

Except that the way to Mostyn's heart had never been through his stomach but through balance sheets.

He savoured his port, took a sip, put down his glass. 'South Africa,' he said.

'What about it?'

'Big changes coming.'

They both knew that; one of the advantages of the financial world was that the intelligence was red-hot. Nothing took place anywhere on earth without their both being aware of it, almost before it happened.

'That cousin of yours ... Does he ever say anything about it?'

'Not a word.'

Anna had made it her business to keep in touch with Pieter Wolmarans over the years. Having discovered her roots she did not intend to let them go again and, with Mostyn — and the business world generally — so opposed to links with South Africa, it was the only way she could do it.

The trouble was that Pieter Wolmarans — like most men, Anna had decided — was no correspondent. At first she had heard from him only once a year, at Christmas. Then he had asked when her birthday was. After she had told him, he had written then as well, with never a miss. Two letters a year; it wasn't a lot, but she had learned to accept that it was all she was going to get.

They were short letters, retailing news about the weather, the prospects for the vintage, the perennial problem of alcohol abuse among the labourers. Once, proudly, he mentioned how *Oudekraal* had won gold medals at the Stellenbosch Wine Show for pinot noir, merlot and chardonnay. It reminded her of the time he had driven her around the farm, explaining how the chardonnay was suited to the altitude.

From the intelligence point of view, the letters were a waste of time. On several occasions she had tried to coax him into telling her about the political changes that were taking place in his country but he never had. Either he didn't want to talk about such things or, more probably, didn't care enough about them to be bothered.

Once she had shown one of his letters to Mostyn. His fascination with vineyards and wine had if anything grown stronger with the years, but it had always been a bottom-line interest, the industry's potential for profit. He had glanced swiftly through the letter and thrown it back on the table.

'I don't know why you bother ...'

But Anna had continued to write, to read Pieter's biannual replies. Certainly they contained nothing to excite the financial markets of the world, but they brought with them the taste and sounds of the wine farm that formed so much a part of Anna's heritage, and she read them eagerly.

Now Mostyn sipped his port again. 'Think he might be interested in selling?'

She stared. '*Oudekraal*? Never.'

'I wonder. He's not getting any younger —'

'*Oudekraal*'s been in the family over two hundred years. It's impossible. He'd never even think about it.'

Mostyn had spent the greater portion of his business career in pulling off impossible deals. 'He'll have to leave it, sometime. What's he going to do with it when he dies? He's got no family . . .'

'He mentioned a neighbour, once. A friend. Perhaps he'll leave it to him.'

'No chance of leaving it to you, I suppose?'

She would have thought he was joking, but about money Mostyn never joked. 'Why on earth should he do that? He's not set eyes on me for years.'

'You keep in touch, though. I thought that must be why you did it. And you are family, after all.'

She was displeased that he should imagine that was why she had kept writing. 'There's not the slightest chance of it.'

'I suppose not . . .' Would have preferred not to believe, but accepted, reluctantly, that she was probably right. 'All the more reason for putting in an offer.'

'You'd be wasting your time.'

'I'm not so sure. We'd let him stay there for his lifetime, of course. Put it in the agreement, if it makes him happy. That way he'll have the use of the money without having to change his lifestyle at all. None of his neighbours need know anything about it. From his point of view, I'd have said it was a pretty good deal.'

'I thought you didn't want anything to do with South Africa.'

'You told me what that black bloke had to say, the meeting you went to. He was right; things are changing over there. Soon they'll be crying out for investment. My bet is prices will sky-rocket, and sooner rather than later. Now's the time to get in, before the rush.' He drained the last ruby drops of port from his glass. 'We're looking at one or two mining prospects. I may go over there. If I do, it might be a chance to meet this cousin of yours.'

'You want me to write and tell him?'

'Let's rather take him by surprise.'

Mostyn's suggestion troubled her. She knew his ways too well; buy cheap, sell on as soon as he could see a profit. It was not what she wanted for *Oudekraal*. 'I don't want you playing ducks and drakes with it. It's my heritage, too, don't forget.'

He was unmoved. 'You said yourself there's no chance he'll leave it to you. In any case, you've not seen the place for years.'

'It was my great-grandmother's home —'

'She never went back, though, did she? Not once, in over sixty years. I know she used to rabbit on to you about it but, honestly, Anna, what could it have meant to her, after all that time? What can it mean to you?'

'It means a lot.' In saying it, found it was true. 'Perhaps I should come with you. We could explore it together —'

The idea attracted her enormously. She had hoped to honeymoon there; now, perhaps, it could become the place for a renewal of their married life. Which needed it so badly.

Mostyn smiled easily. 'The last thing I'll need. Me trying to tie up a deal with your cousin and you coming all sentimental on me.'

Anna sighed. 'Come and walk round the garden with me, instead, then.'

Perhaps, she thought, if we walk together, talk of other things, we may be able to restore the romantic feeling that Mostyn's talk has dispelled so effectively.

They strolled side by side but it was no good; the atmosphere was gone. Anna told herself not to be stupid. Mostyn had said nothing that was not perfectly reasonable; why should Pieter care what happened after his death? From his point of view, the proposal would have one big advantage, too; it would mean that *Oudekraal* would stay in what remained of his family. That should appeal to him. It made sense from her point of view, as well. *Oudekraal* would be reclaimed, as Anneliese had always wanted.

Yet, no matter how she tried to persuade herself, doubt persisted. If Mostyn bought *Oudekraal*, it would be neither for Pieter Wolmarans's benefit nor her own. It would be a straightforward business deal, entered into with an eye to profit. What Mostyn bought he could sell and, if he was right about the trend of prices in South Africa, that was precisely what he would do. If that happened, *Oudekraal* would be lost far more irretrievably than if Pieter had done what she suspected he intended, and left it to his neighbour and long-time friend.

A wind came from across the water; Anna shivered in her thin dress.

'Let's go in.'

And did so, but in a different frame of mind entirely from what she had hoped, all her thoughts of romance blown away by Mostyn's plans, as chill and unwelcoming as the wind that even now was strengthening from the sea.

Mostyn had finished his business in Johannesburg. Delighted with the deal, he spent a fun evening — success the biggest aphrodisiac he knew — and next morning flew on to Cape Town. He asked for directions when he picked up his hire car at DF Malan Airport. As instructed, he turned left when he reached the highway and headed towards Somerset West. A quarter of an hour after setting out, he took the left turn to Stellenbosch.

He'd booked a room at the Lanzerac Hotel, just outside the town. There were vineyards on both sides of the road, mountains rising high and rugged beyond them, but Mostyn had not come here for the scenery. He ordered coffee in his room, had a shower and change of clothes and settled down to study once again the material on the South African wine industry that he had begun to read during the flight from Johannesburg. *Oudekraal*, he read, was the biggest wine farm in the district. It had a high reputation as a top-flight winemaker, with a string of gold and silver medals to its credit at the Stellenbosch and other wine shows.

By the time he had finished, it was midday. He had a light lunch, took a stroll to clear his head and went back to his room to phone Pieter Wolmarans.

Whom he found at home.

'I'm your cousin's husband,' he explained. 'From Australia. I'm in South Africa on business and wondered if I might pay you a visit, if it's convenient.' His voice ladled charm. 'Anna's told me so much about you —'

'Is she with you?' The Afrikaans accent as thick as rope.

'Unfortunately not,' Mostyn soothed. 'Other commitments; you know how it is —'

'Where are you calling from?'

'I'm in Stellenbosch.'

'So close? Why don't you drive out, then? I suppose it's what you've come for.'

Wolmarans was clearly less susceptible to charm than some. Still, at least Mostyn had his invitation. 'I'll be with you in an hour.'

He drove out, following the route Anna had taken seven years earlier, seeing not the updated images of Anneliese's childhood but the fact that the vineyards were well tended, the buildings freshly painted and in good order, the general air of prosperity that pervaded the valley. Sanctions or not, political turmoil notwithstanding, it was obvious that in this part of the country at least things were going very well, indeed.

Oudekraal, like the rest, looked well maintained and prosperous. He got out of the car, feeling comfortable and relaxed, looking forward to meeting the man whose heritage, as Anna had called it, he had come to buy.

Of course it would not be for sale but, in Mostyn's experience, money always talked in the end and he had more than enough to shout the house down, if necessary.

A man in late middle age came out through the front door of the house and stood with his hands upon the green-painted railing of the verandah that ran the length of the building. He stared down at him and Mostyn knew he was face to face with Anna's cousin, at last.

'Good day,' he called, voice cheerful yet deferential, carefully tuned to what he judged would be Pieter Wolmarans's wavelength. 'Good day to you, sir.'

Hand extended, he walked across the gravel drive and up the flight of steps to the house. Above him, Pieter Wolmarans looked. And looked.

They shook hands, Pieter Wolmarans's hand as hard as horn within his own. There was a table with a chair at the end of the verandah, looking out across the valley, but Pieter did not lead him there, nor into the main part of the house itself, but in the opposite direction, along the length of the verandah and around the corner to the little office in one of the stone outbuildings.

Mostyn's mouth kept working, compliments spraying like water from a hose, but his eyes missed nothing. All the buildings were in immaculate order, even the ground around the house so clean of weeds it might have been tended by hand, the rows of vines running up the breast of the hill as pretty as an advertisement.

'Everything in tiptop shape,' he declared approvingly. 'That's what I like to see.'

Pieter Wolmarans said nothing.

The office itself, housed in a building that must have been a hundred years old at least, was tidy and well organised, with modern, grey-sprayed furniture, files neatly arranged and work stations where two women in their thirties were busy before computer screens.

At the back of the office was a smaller room behind a glass partition, and here Pieter led him. He closed the door and sat behind the desk, gesturing to the chair that faced him.

'Sit,' he said.

Mostyn did so, crossing his legs.

Pieter leant forward across the desk, his face expressionless. 'And what brings you to *Oudekraal*, Mr Harcourt?'

'I explained. I am Anna's husband —'

'And you flew all the way from Johannesburg just to see me?' A mirthless smile that did nothing to gild the heavy Afrikaans accent. 'That is honour, indeed.'

'I had business —'

'Let me tell you something about country towns, Mr Harcourt. There is something called the bush telegraph. It means that everyone knows everybody else's business. I daresay it is the same in Australia. You are an important man. Your name is known even outside your own country. You have extensive interests in the wine industry, worldwide.' A wintry smile creased his mouth. 'You see? We know all about you. I can assure you that if you'd had other business in these parts, I would have heard about it.'

Mostyn was not used to being put on the defensive and didn't like it. For the moment was bull-headed enough to stick to his story.

'Anna has told me so much about *Oudekraal* —'

'Of course. It is a part of her history, too. But that is not why you are here.'

The conversation was getting nowhere. For a moment longer they sat staring at each other across the surface of the desk but Pieter Wolmarans had apparently said his piece, had made it plain that he was interested neither in compliments nor small talk. Mostyn remembered what he had read about the legendary stubbornness of these old South African farmers and decided to come to the point.

'I have a proposition I would like to put in front of you.'

Not by a flicker did Wolmarans reveal the satisfaction he must have felt at pushing his visitor into such an admission.

'So talk.'

Mostyn did so. Instinct warned him that with this man he should waste neither time nor effort in hyperbole; he kept strictly to the facts, presenting them in as straightforward a manner as he could. When he had finished, he sat and waited.

Pieter Wolmarans stone-still behind the desk. 'So you are telling me you wish to buy *Oudekraal*?'

The banker in Hatchet Harcourt would not accept so direct a statement. 'Subject to proper examination, of course —'

'No.' As effortlessly as a knife pruning a vine, the single word cut off the flow. 'I thank you for taking the trouble to fly down to make me the offer, but the answer is no.'

Mostyn was untroubled by the refusal; at the start of negotiations, everyone always said no.

'From your point of view, it offers advantages that perhaps I have not adequately explained.' He raised his fingers one by one, enumerating each point. 'You would have immediate access to the capital. You would be guaranteed tenure for life. Most important of all, *Oudekraal* would remain in the Wolmarans family. The proud tradition of over two hundred years would be maintained —'

'No,' Wolmarans said again. 'Thank you once more for your interest, but the answer is still no.'

His stubbornness rising like yeast to match that of the man facing him, Mostyn persevered.

'As you said, I have interests in vineyards all around the world. These days, any estate wanting to compete in world markets has to invest increasingly large amounts of capital.' He sighed with false regret. 'It's the way of the world, unfortunately. Already the smaller, private estates are finding they can't compete. South Africa has been off the world scene for years, but that's all changing. Where are you going to get the capital you need, if not from people like me?'

Pieter Wolmarans's voice was firm and deliberate. 'I do not know what more I can say to you. Everything you tell me is true. But in no circumstances at all shall I ever consider selling *Oudekraal*. I would burn it to the ground before I did that.'

Mostyn began to understand that Wolmarans's objections were not part of a negotiation process, as he had assumed, but meant exactly what they said: refusal, cold, definite, absolute. Now, in place of stubbornness, he felt anger.

'I have made you a fair offer —'

For the first time, Pieter Wolmarans's face showed emotion. 'Can't you understand plain English, man? The answer is no. No and no and no. Finish.'

Mostyn was on his feet. 'I hope you do not live to regret it.'

Wolmarans was also standing. 'One question. If I may. Does your wife know of your visit here?'

Once again Mostyn's anger spoke before his head. 'Of course she knows! I discussed it with her before I left Sydney.'

'And did she approve?'

'Why shouldn't she? It makes sense, for God's sake. The whole proposal was designed to help you.'

'I do not recall saying that I need help.'

'You may not have said it, but that doesn't mean you don't need it.' Mostyn dusted his hands, dismissing *Oudekraal* and its owner from his life. 'My mistake. I obviously underestimated your resistance to new ideas.'

Wolmarans stood behind his desk, making no move to escort his visitor off the property. His eyes were still, dangerous, with sparks of anger in their depths.

'No fool like an old fool. Is that what you are saying?'

In the doorway Mostyn turned. 'You said it, Mr Wolmarans, not I. But you won't find me arguing with you.'

And was gone, in a whiff of sulphur.

Left to himself, Pieter sat.

Liefde God. Dear God.

Presently, unable to bear the confusion of emotions that his visitor had aroused in him, he got to his feet, fetched his hat, and walked. Between the long terraces of vines. Up the steep slope of the mountain, the muscles cramping in his legs until, an hour after leaving the house, he arrived at the summit. His body felt the climb, but he was used to walking in the mountains and was not at all out of breath.

He stopped and looked down at the chequerboard spread of the valley, the range of hills beyond with, in the hazy distance, the glint of the silver sea.

It was the place where he had brought Anna when she had visited, all those years ago. Could she really have known that her husband was coming here? Was it possible that she could approve of the idea that he should sell — *sell*! — his heritage in such a way?

If it were true, it would mean that he had misjudged her most seriously. He had all her letters in a drawer of his desk back at the house; not in the office, where instinct had directed him to take his recent visitor, but in the house itself, along with all the rest of his personal papers. He would have to read them again, to see whether they contained any hint of such an attitude. If, with the knowledge he now had, he detected any such thing, it would change a number of ideas. He did not want to believe it, was determined that until he had read them he would not believe.

The steep climb had driven away some of the toxins of Mostyn Harcourt's visit. Now he drew from his hip pocket his grandfather's silver flask, took a swig of the brandy it contained — *Oudekraal*'s best, he had sat by the still himself — wiped his mouth and sat down in his usual place, his back to the tree that might have been tailored to fit it. He had been brought here first by his grandfather, who had told him how *his* grandfather had brought him to the same place, seventy years before. Such little things. Yet not so little, perhaps, all part of the enduring fabric that had been *Oudekraal* for almost two hundred and fifty years.

He liked to think how, even before his grandfather's grandfather, the members of his family had come to this place in turn, generation by generation, to seek consolation and fulfilment from their land. He settled himself deeper into the earth, making himself comfortable. As always, his mind turned to the past, the landmarks of what had been his family's history.

Back in 1886 phylloxera had nearly destroyed the Cape wine industry. Christiaan Wolmarans had rescued them, the first farmer in the valley to use the grafted vines that could withstand the disease. At the time many had said he was a lunatic; there had been high talk about the criminal irresponsibility of those who brought such material into the country, but Christiaan had stuck it out, as he always did, and in the end it was those who had objected most vociferously who had fallen on their faces.

In 1904 began the catastrophe of over-production, and it was his grandfather's turn. Deneys, not long back from the Anglo-Boer War, helped to establish the Wine Growers Co-operative that saved the industry by controlling production and, eventually, the price of the wine itself.

Without their efforts, the Wolmarans would have been driven off the land years before, like so many others. As it was, *Oudekraal* had been in continuous ownership longer than any other wine farm in the Cape. Two hundred and forty-two years. A proud record.

It was a great thing to be wedded as securely to your work as his grandfather had been. Not that he had ever neglected his family. Wedded to wife, wedded to work, he used to boast. It made for a well-rounded life. He had been a contented man although he spoke often, with regret, of the sister who had fled South Africa after the Anglo-Boer war. Right up to the present day, there was talk how Anneliese van der Merwe and the man with her had destroyed the traitors by fire.

Deneys Wolmarans would never discuss it, Pieter thought, and neither shall I allow my mind to dwell on it. It happened so long ago; it is not for me or anyone living to judge, and the lady herself has been dead these many years. All the more shame, therefore, that when Anna had phoned him all those years ago, his first thought had been of scandal, of Anneliese's crime returning to confront the present as, eighty years before, it had the past.

I should have been ashamed of myself, he thought, as he had thought so often before. God will resolve all things, as the preachers are always saying, although how they can claim to know so much more about these matters than the rest of us has always been a puzzle to me.

The Wolmarans family had been first in everything: the first to plant grafted vines, the first to see the advantages of central marketing. In 1905 his grandfather had become the first in something else as well. He went to Cape Town alone and came back behind the wheel of a six-cylinder De Dion motor car. All red paint and gold tracery, two brass oil lamps in front, the spoked wheels a canary yellow. It must have looked very splendid, indeed, and Deneys had no doubt been determined that all his neighbours should see it and eat up their hearts with envy of the man who owned the first motor car ever to enter the valley.

He had told Pieter himself that he had driven it from one end of the valley to the other, very slowly, with his hand on the horn, while all the coloured folk — and some white ones, too — had come out to gape at him.

Pieter had always liked that tale; it seemed to him to demonstrate so clearly his grandfather's lust for life.

Deneys Wolmarans had always said he would live to be a hundred, but that he didn't manage. One day in 1950, when he was seventy-three, he went for a stroll and didn't come back.

They found him between the vines. Killed by a heart attack, the doctors said, with his face in the dirt that had been his passion all his life. Elizabeth, his wife of fifty-two years, died two days later, quietly, in her room at *Oudekraal*.

Wedded in death as in life; a good way to live out your days, Pieter thought.

His own father had been a bookish man, more interested in study than in vines and, when he died, *Oudekraal* was much as it had been when he had inherited it.

Again Pieter ferreted out Deneys's flask and had another mouthful of brandy. It seemed a shame to have so few memories of the man who had been his father, but the fact was that he had made little impression on the world while he lived or, indeed, after he had gone out of it. He had been a good man, though, well liked, and not all could claim as much.

Pieter's mother had died of typhoid when he was very small, and he remembered nothing of her.

Now, sitting with his back against the tree, feeling its sturdy presence behind him, he thought how, finally, he had come in his turn to hold the land that had been in his family for over two hundred years. Unlike those before him, he had not married and now supposed he never would. Sometimes he worried about what would happen after he had joined his predecessors in the graveyard behind the house. He knew there were some who would say he was a fool to care what happened after he was dead, but he could not help it. Whatever the law might say, the land had never been his. It was in his care for a few years only. He had to do what would be right for it after he was gone.

As to what that should be ...

He had always intended to leave it to Johannes Verster, his friend and neighbour. He was not of Wolmarans stock, but a good man who would care for the land properly. Then Anna Riordan had come from Australia and, for the first time, he had discovered that a descendant of the Wolmarans still lived. He had liked her, still liked her, but she was not of the country nor of the land. At first she had shown little more than polite interest in *Oudekraal* or the family history. This had changed; she had come to see him often, almost every day, he remembered, and he had begun to entertain hopes of her. Yet in the end she had gone away, as foreigners always do, and had never come back. In the circumstances it would not be right to will *Oudekraal* to her. So Johannes Verster it would have to be, although — good friend though he was — the idea did not sit quietly within Pieter's mind.

Wolmarans land, Wolmarans blood ...

And now this man, with his offer to buy what would never, as long as he had breath, be for sale. For how could one sell one's past? How could he sell the foresight and vision of Colin Stephen Walmer, the work and joy and heartache of himself and his descendants? How could he sell his grandfather's memories of Christiaan and Sara, invite bids for Deneys and Elizabeth, whose marriage had caused such excitement in the valley? For Anneliese herself, that lost soul who had lived in the house for a much shorter time than any of the others, yet whose spirit seemed to him to haunt it still?

Only one thing troubled him, his discourtesy in not offering his visitor a glass of wine. He will think I am as boorish as he is, he thought, but there had been no help for it. The wine, a bottle of the 1982 pinotage, the best of the recent vintages, had been ready for the corkscrew but as soon as Harcourt had opened his mouth he had known that it would be completely out of the question to drink with him.

He would never sell, never. Let the future fall as it would.

TWENTY-SIX

In 1921, while they were out in the cattle yards, Dominic and Sean had a bad row that almost came to blows and changed everything in their lives. It began over something Sean was supposed to have done and had not, but that was not where it ended. For a long time, Dominic had been itching to speak to him about the way Sylvia Macdonald was playing the boys off against each other. Now he dragged her into the argument and Sean, almost seventeen years old and never one to tolerate interference in his affairs, told him to go to hell.

It was terrible. Accusations flew like hail. At the end Sean raised his big fists; would have used them had Dominic not backed off, but Dominic was too old for fighting, and both of them knew it.

'Better be careful, old man,' Sean warned him, 'or one of these days, after I've married Sylvia, I might just chuck you off the place altogether.'

The idea of leaving would not have troubled Dominic but being chucked off, without any choice in the matter, was a different business entirely. He went into Anneliese with a look on his face as though a sword had stricken him. It took her a while to uncover what had been said, but she managed it in the end.

'Marry Sylvia?' she repeated. 'Dermot may have something to say about that, I suppose.'

'Dermot will never stand up to Sean,' Dominic said. 'You know that as well as I do.'

'It's not for Sean to say what happens. Scott Macdonald will never put us out on the road.'

'Maybe he won't. But Sean will get Sylvia, and Paradise Downs, which is what he's been after from the first. With that under his belt, he'll do what he likes.'

'And Dermot?'

'Dermot will end up with the hind tit, like he always does.'

He paced about the room, up and back, up and back, his swooping shadow keeping pace with him along the walls.

'I'll not give Sean the chance to put me down,' he said eventually. 'A man's got his pride or he's got nothing. We'll not be staying.'

After Gavin's death, Dominic's restlessness had returned like a plague to curse them all. Anneliese had known for a long time that he would like to move on; now Sean had given him his excuse. She saw a future in which the pair of them once again wandered across an infinite landscape, going nowhere. She could not bear it.

'I'd sooner be dead than go through all that again.'

He turned, snake-quick, a scowl like a black storm across his face. 'Take your pick. Stay here, if you'd rather, or come along with me. Either way, it'll not kill you.'

It was a form of boasting, no more than that. *Do what you like; I don't need you.* It would have made her life seem even more futile, had it been true, but it was not. Dominic was right in one thing, though; it was not Anneliese who died.

The following morning, Dominic had to take a party of men to round up cattle on the far side of the station and

Anneliese, frightened what he might get up to after the traumas of the previous night, decided to go with him.

It was so beautiful; that she always remembered. Open country patched with forest, towering limestone ridges, the river fringed with water lilies flowing deep and silent beside them.

She had hoped that Dominic would have forgotten what he had said about moving on, but he had not.

'Last time we'll be doing this,' he said. And laughed, as though the prospect delighted him.

Towards evening they made camp at the head of a valley opening upon the plain. Sun-flecked bush surrounded them; beyond, the open country was an azure haze. Bird song, the lowing of cattle, golden ladders of light falling from the summits of the trees. Everything at peace.

After the sun had gone, they wrapped themselves in their blankets and lay down to sleep, saddles beneath their heads. Anneliese stayed awake, watching the dying embers of the fire, remembering Dominic's words and contemplating the door to ruin that had once again opened before them. *Last time we'll be doing this ...*

In the darkness she spoke aloud. 'I shall not permit it.'

The shifting of coals in the dying fire was her only answer. She could have wept; she knew Dominic's infernal pride too well to think he might go back on his word now that he had wound himself up to the point of saying it.

She was lying apart from the rest, as always. She could see the huddled shapes of the men scattered here and there, the dwindling firelight casting its orange shadows over them. She could not distinguish Dominic from the others, but knew he was on the far side of the clearing beneath the great tree whose ghostly outline she could just make out against the darkness.

'I shall not permit you to do this to me,' she told him.

Then she felt it. From the first, she had heard the voices of this land more clearly than most of those who had been born here. There was no rumble of thunder, no breath of air to stir the leaves, yet she knew that a storm, still below the horizon but unmistakable, was on its way.

She watched the darkness, waiting until she felt the first gusts through the trees, brightening the fire's embers. That old tree was rotten; she had seen the cracks in its trunk herself. She knew she should go to Dominic, warn him to move into the open before the storm came. She did not. Something said, let him be. If God wills, he will survive.

Instead, she told herself she could be mistaken. She knew she was not, but did nothing.

So God stayed my hand and the storm came as I had known it would. It took the tree and brought it crashing down, crushing Dominic Riordan to death beneath its great trunk. As I had known it would.

So we are parted, after all.

The bushfires in this country are a terror to see, mile upon mile of country ablaze. You can hear the trees screaming as the fire takes them. It was a fall of timber that killed him, yet fire would have been more appropriate; I shall always believe it was the fire we lit in Henning's store that started him on his road to ruin.

Deneys, who had gone through the whole war with him, told me that Dominic had always laughed at fear yet, as we boarded the steamer in Cape Town, the stench of his fear was like a nine-day corpse in summer.

I have always believed that it was his memory of the fire that opened the door to drink; and drink, now, has brought him sober to his death. Jack, his father, may have been the cause of our first going out on the land, but it was drink that kept us there. Drink blighted our lives with futility, creating in Dominic the restlessness that would once again have destroyed us, had fate permitted.

I have to believe that, or I shall be unable to live with myself. Because I heard the gathering storm and did nothing.

I am free. Free of having to wander the empty tracks again. Free of memory, of the gulf between what is and what might have been. Free to forget what I no longer wish to remember.

I tell myself that none of the past matters. It will be hard to forget but by the power of my will, God permitting, I shall do it. For the rest ... I am alone, forever. Let that be my judgement.

May God forgive me.

After the funeral, the scrape of shovels in the thin soil, the meaningless words, Anneliese sat with the images that would remain forever seared upon her mind.

An explosion of dust and leaves, the wind bellowing in the darkness; the great tree bending, the crack and groan of the toppling trunk, so slow and then so fast, rushing earthwards. The crash and bounce of the fallen timber upon the ground. A hail of twigs and leaves, settling slowly. A diminishing roar as the storm raced away through the hills.

The stillness.

She had sworn to banish the past; now, for the last time, she chose to recall the good things.

The day she had first met him. The Cape cart, the peach trees heavy with blossom, the freshness of the vines, Dominic Riordan walking towards her down the green lanes of her youth. How they had talked, his face aflame with his passion for revenge. She never loved him but, even at that first meeting, he set her blood racing.

Before the raid on Henning's store she had gone to him deliberately, determined to create a sacrament from what she knew now had been no more than a lust for vengeance. He had thought she was mad — how clearly she had read him — but had not kicked her out. Oh no.

That naked girl skittering, breasts bouncing, mouth startled. After Dominic got rid of her, they fell upon each other. How much had been sacrament, how much simple lust, she neither knew nor cared. She remembered still how her body had responded to his touch.

His words, too, had enchanted her. *Together we shall conquer the world.*

He had told her that. She had permitted herself to believe him; knew now, with bitter resignation, that every syllable had been a lie. What in God's name had they achieved? They had outfoxed the great English Empire, that much was true, but what was that to show for two lives?

Raise our kids to stick their fingers in the King of England's eye.

He had said that, too. Well.

Wandering, drinking, held together despite all by a shared dream of vengeance and triumph. That had been their life. Instead of love, she had known only the stale memory of a dead and objectless hatred. Her entire existence had been built upon such things; now she could hardly credit the futility of it all.

The business with Dominic's father should have wrecked them but had only heightened her determination to keep them together, as though success in that would justify all else. They would stay as one, even if they came to hate each other in the process. They had to; the past was all there was.

And so the drink hollowed him out, dissolving the fire and pride, leaving nothing.

Those years of drift. That time with the Faircloughs; a dozen other occasions when the family would have fallen apart but had not, because she had not permitted it to happen. Despite Dominic's constant irresponsibility and drunkenness, his refusal to face life, she had held on.

And now? she thought. She had to put the past away, as she had told herself she would. *Put it away.*

Whether that would be possible was another question.

When he heard the news, Dermot felt as though his world had fallen part with the falling tree. He lived in a daze, doing what had to be done without thinking too much about anything.

'You are the man of the family now,' Anneliese told him.

Man of the family. His mind rejected it, instinctively. He was conscious only of emptiness where before had been warmth, a sense of sharing.

Once again he was alone.

Dominic had never really done much for him, yet in the years before they came to Paradise Downs, he had been the only one who had seemed to understand how he felt. The stories he had told had always been so much more than just stories; they had been a picture of what life should be like. It was Dominic's stories that had impelled him to say what he had about going to Ireland to help kick the English out.

Romantic nonsense yet, at the time, he had liked to believe he meant it.

Too late now; from what the papers were saying, it wouldn't be long before Ireland was free, anyway. At last; it should have thrilled him, but did not. All he could think was how he'd had the chance to hitch a ride in glory's chariot and had once again missed out. All he could do now was watch from afar as the golden wheels bore it away into history.

Dominic had known how he had felt. That was an article of faith; they had never talked about it, but he had known. With Dominic dead, it was more important than ever that he should believe that. There was nothing he could do about it now, in any case; his life was here, in this land so far from everywhere.

All his life Dermot had longed for glory. He had always known it was stupid — glory was not for people like him, who had never had the knack of bossing even his own small world about — yet the longing had remained.

There were still things he could do; perhaps now would be the time.

'Now Dominic's gone, I've changed my mind,' he told Sylvia. 'I don't feel like sticking around any longer. You want to take off, I'm game.'

She eyed him. 'You promised my dad you'd stay. Three years, you said. That still leaves a year to go.'

'There's no point. Face it, Sylvie, I'll never be able to run Paradise Downs the way your Dad wants.'

It seemed so, certainly; only a week earlier, Scott Macdonald had given him a blasting that had left him quaking in his socks.

'You're hopeless,' he had said. 'Absolutely hopeless.' And had stamped away, dusting his hands as though to rid himself of Dermot altogether.

Sylvia said, 'He'll need you more than ever now your dad's been killed.'

'He'll find someone.'

She looked at him as though he were dirt on the ground. 'So you'll just chuck it? That it?'

He hadn't expected her to turn on him like this. 'I thought you'd jump at it.'

'Two years ago I told you I wanted us to clear out. You gave me your word and then went back on it. Didn't even discuss it with me first. Now your Dad's dead, and all of a sudden you change your tune. It's not good enough.'

He could see he would have to sweet-talk her.

'We'll head south,' he said. 'Go to one of the cities, if that's what you want. All the bright lights ...' As though he knew any more about cities and bright lights than she did. 'You'll like that,' he told her. He'd no idea whether she would or wouldn't; would have promised anything to get her to say yes.

She wouldn't. He kept on and on, but could get her to promise nothing. She didn't have much to say about anything at all.

That night, after dark, Sean found Macdonald in his office. In the lamplight their eyes squared up to each other.

Macdonald spoke first. 'Yes?'

'Reckon I'll be moving on.'

'You're choosing a damned awkward time, you know that?'

Yet he did not seem too bothered. Sean thought, He knows what I'm telling him. All this is just going through the motions.

The thought encouraged him. 'Got to think of my future, don't I?'

'You've got a future here.'

A shrug. 'So you say.'

Again they watched each other under the hissing kerosene lantern. In the darkness the bugs pinged against the screens.

'What'll it take to make you change your mind?'
'You already know that.'

The next evening Scott Macdonald called them together in the homestead's shabby living room; Scott himself, with Sylvia beside him, Sean and Anneliese and Dermot.

There was a table with drinks, bottles and glasses. Macdonald gave them each a glass. Stood and beamed, while Dermot wondered what was going on.

'When Gavin died I thought my life had come to an end,' Scott told them. 'Now it's only a few days since Dominic was killed, too. I mourn him as a friend. We all do. But we can't go on living in the past. We have to look to the future.'

Dermot thought, He's asked Ma to marry him. He glanced at her but her face was too cool and white for it to be that.

'Anneliese,' Macdonald said, 'I'm only sorry Dominic isn't with us tonight.'

She nodded, the barest movement, and Dermot realised that she, at least, knew what this was all about.

Macdonald raised his glass. 'Sylvia has told me she and Sean are to be married. I am very pleased to give my approval.'

Dermot could not believe it. Mouth working, he stumbled forward. 'But —'

Anneliese grabbed his hand, pulling him back. 'Be quiet, Dermot.'

Rage but terror, too, feeling himself intimidated by the eyes watching him. Like I'm still a kid, he thought.

'No! Sylvie and I —'

Macdonald did not even have to raise his voice to silence him.

'Shut up, Dermot! This is nothing to do with you.'

Dermot stared at Sylvia in horror. *Say something*, his eyes implored her. *Tell them we're going away.*

Dermot had never spoken to her father, despite his promise, but that was him all over. Yet it was still not too late. Even now she waited for him to speak. She thought, They're fighting over me. It gave her a pleasurable feeling, quite exciting.

Only there was no fight. Dermot squawked once, then his mother yanked at his hand again and he collapsed. Like a kid. She watched him. It was hopeless. She would have to mother him all her life, make all the decisions. How could she ever hope to keep herself safe, doing that?

No, there was more security in the strong man than the weak. She looked hard at Dermot for what seemed a long time, then made her choice.

She moved to Sean's side and took his hand in hers.

It was as though the tree had fallen a second time.

Dermot knew that staying was out of the question. Later that night, he sought Anneliese out. 'Reckon I'll try my luck further south,' he said, taking care not to look at her.

She had learned years ago to face reality. 'It might be best. For a while. You can come back later, if you want. There will always be room for you here.'

Dermot had expected her to try to talk him out of it, had stiffened himself to resist her entreaties. Now this. She doesn't care, he thought. Nobody cares.

He could not bring himself to speak to Sylvia. Would not have spoken to Sean, either, but it was impossible to avoid him.

'I shan't be under your feet for long.'

'Please yourself.'

His indifference was like a lash about Dermot's shoulders. He wanted to let Sean know how he felt about the way he'd been treated. He tried, spluttering and stammering, but it was hopeless.

Sean cut him off before the protests were halfway out of his mouth. 'This is a tough country, Dermot. You're not cut out for it.'

Dermot hated him for putting the truth into words but said nothing; Sean was right. He turned and blundered away.

Later, brooding in his room, humiliation a mountain crushing him into the dirt, he thought that maybe he should kill Sylvia or Sean or himself. Perhaps I should kill the lot of us, he thought. Make a proper job of it.

Certainly it would be something to remember him by. They wouldn't think he was of no account, then. He imagined Sean's face, his voice pleading frantically for mercy. Sylvia's tears ...

Rubbish, of course.

Now she was to lose him, Anneliese's love for Dermot had returned in full measure. No, she thought, that is wrong. I always loved him, but somehow lost the way of showing it to him, or myself.

She had neglected him so much. There was no excuse. She could pretend she had always had too much to do, trying and trying to make sense out of the shipwreck of their lives, and it would be true, as far as it went, yet not the real truth. From the first day she had been there for Sean, but for neither Dominic nor Dermot had she found a place.

Sean, whom she no longer even liked, the strong and ruthless man who, seeing his chance, had knifed his brother as casually as he would have butchered a calf.

Sean, who had taken her love and hidden it, as he had hidden everything he had seized in his life, giving nothing back. There was nothing she could do. From his earliest days, whenever Sean saw something he wanted, when he stood with chest thrown out, chin raised in challenge, he would take it, exactly as Jack Riordan would have taken it. Land, horse, woman — all one. There had been no gainsaying either of them. They had both been too much for her, too much for anyone.

She had done everything she could to keep the family together; now it was broken, for all her efforts. It seemed sometimes that her whole life had been one of sacrifice. The surrender of her life in Africa had been the price she had paid for what at the time she had called justice; her denial of the passion that Jack Riordan had kindled so effortlessly had been as much for Dominic as herself; to preserve the family, she had wasted the precious days of her existence trekking from town to town across the dusty vastness of this alien land.

To what end? Dominic was gone; Dermot was going. And Sean ... Anneliese saw now that Sean had never been a part of them at all.

She no longer knew why she had given her life to avert what she had always known was inevitable. She was alone, and would be. Scott Macdonald had grown used to her, was comfortable in her presence. She could say without vanity that she still had the power of a woman over a man. Neither of them had forgotten their silent, healing communion at the time of Gavin's death. She thought that one day soon he would come to her. Not yet; it was too soon after Dominic's death; unlike Sean, Scott observed the proprieties in such things — which was why, when the time came, Sean would devour him, too. Already she could feel the weight of his eyes upon her.

It would bring them companionship, of a sort, a measure of peace to both body and spirit. As for commitment ... Never. She had done with commitments in her life.

Dermot had not wanted her to come to the train but Anneliese had insisted. For eighteen years she'd been making the decisions and saw no reason to change now.

She realised that Dermot, whom she had called the man of the family after Dominic's death, was dearer to her than her own son, however late she had been discovering it. After she saw him off on the train, she would in all probability never see him again but she took care to hide her feelings, from herself and the world. Instead bossed him, believing it was the last chance she would get.

'If you're planning to catch that train, you'd better get a move on.'

She managed not to pat him, not to straighten his shirt. She wanted so much to touch, for the last time. To let her love show. For the last time. She knew that such a display of affection would embarrass him but it was not easy to stand by, to do — and show — nothing. Separation ahead of parting — how she hated it.

It couldn't be helped, Anneliese told herself briskly. Bossing would have to serve. 'Dermot, come *on* ...'

First they had to undergo the ritual of farewells. Scott Macdonald, grim-faced, silent. Sylvia, who had knowingly acted as a catalyst in the enmity between Dermot and Sean, smiled and smiled, hiding herself as always behind her simpering eyes. Sean was there, too, despite all. Watchful eyes, dark hair, dark heart. His farewell was no more than a perfunctory handshake but it was better than nothing. Just.

As well Dermot's going, Anneliese thought. There would have been blood spilt, otherwise.

Anneliese and Dermot climbed into the buggy for the three hours' drive to town. Dermot took the reins — another last — and away they went, the wheels spilling a curtain of dust that cut them off at once from the group standing in front of the homestead, from everything that had made up their lives until that moment.

They spoke little on the journey. Dermot was dearer to her than anyone living yet now she could read him less clearly than ever. The penalty for all those years of neglect, she thought, but in her heart knew that blaming herself was an indulgence. Even as a child, Dermot had inhabited his own secret world.

'Sean's right, Ma,' he had told her. 'I haven't got what it takes to run Paradise Downs. I have to get away, find my own place in the world.'

Perhaps when he's stretched his wings he'll be back, she told herself, but without conviction; the need to make his own way had become a symbol in Dermot's life, and symbols were not given up so easily.

All the same, she dreaded his going. He does not have Sean's strength, she thought. Life could destroy him so easily.

I shall not weep.

She watched the countryside; the dust, the dry bush rattling by. So many journeys, she thought. The first when I was barely more than a child, travelling with my new husband across the *veld* to the farm that was to become my home and happiness and despair. Our way lay through the mountains. I remember how many streams there were. We saw *duiker* and once, with the dragon teeth of the hills all about us, there were *klipspringer*, the shaggy little antelope of the high places. So beautiful.

Years later, husband dead, home burnt before her eyes, those same mountains had mocked from afar as the train had carried them all to the camp at Koffiekraal. That had been her second big journey. The first and last time with Stoffel and Amalie. Flesh of her flesh, as the Bible said. Their deaths had cast an indelible shadow over her, yet she had not thought of them for a long time. For a moment it panicked her, as though she had laid down a section of her life in a corner and could no longer find it. Life went on, daily problems took over one's thoughts and there had to be an end to grieving. Yet to the emptiness there would be no end.

Now, driving through the sunburnt bush, she grieved for them again. For husband and children, for the farm and life they had shared. For herself, also, another stranger who had died long ago.

So many compartments in one's life, she thought. Dermot never knew Dirk or the children yet they are here, at my side, as much as he is. All of them part of this woman I have become, this forty-six-year-old creature of grief and happiness, regrets and hopes, of memories and love. Love linking all; of the land that was mine, of those who peopled it. All of them woven together with Dominic and his parents, with Dermot and Sean, into a pattern so tight that none of us can ever be separated from the rest.

Dirk, Stoffel and Amalie; Christiaan and Sara; Deneys and Elizabeth; Dominic and Dermot and Sean. Even Sarel Henning and his family. All part of the bag and baggage of her life. Others, too, travelled in the buggy with them. The children of Deneys and Dermot and Sean, the unknowable children of the future, formed a line stretching into the years ahead. Perhaps they will achieve what we have failed to do, she thought. There, at least, was hope.

They reached Waroola at last. Dust was everywhere; staining the fronts of the buildings, lying like brown flour against the walls, flavouring the air. In a month's time all would be mud, the tracks impassable.

'Lucky you're leaving before The Wet,' Anneliese said. 'Another month and we'd never have got through.'

The Wet and The Dry had become part of her life. If I went home they would not know me, she thought. Even to speak the language would be hard. For a moment she felt a pang at the thought of all that should have been her life and was not. I would give my life to see *Oudekraal* again, she thought, knowing it was impossible.

The bush, The Dry and The Wet, the laconic people who would always be strangers; these were her destiny now, forever.

'Time for a cup of coffee,' she suggested.

'*N lekker koppie koffie*, her memory mocked her. A nice little cup of coffee.

She could have done without the nonsense. It would be hard enough to say goodbye without echoes of the past making things a hundred times worse.

They went to the pub, ordered coffee, sat with their cups at a table in a corner. At this time of the morning the room was empty of everything but the smell of beer, the shadowy presence of all the men who had propped up the bar over the years.

'Have a beer, you'd rather,' Anneliese suggested, knowing he would not. Neither of the boys were boozers; Dominic's example had soured the taste of drink in their mouths.

They sat, not alone.

'Going off to make your own way. Your Dad would have been proud of you,' she said, acknowledging the presence of one of the ghosts. Dominic would always be Dad, as she herself was Ma, his proxy mother.

'He'd probably say I was a fool, turning my back on a safe job.' But was pleased, she saw.

She smiled grimly. 'He'd be right.'

'I had no choice, Ma.'

'I know that.'

Which exhausted all they had to say to each other. They waited in awkward silence while the gritty coffee grew cold; they gulped it down. Behind the bar a clock ticked ponderously. Finally, she could bear it no longer.

'Let us go, then.'

They crossed the road to the station, walked beside the train wreathed in steam. People stood about; at the far end of the platform men were loading what looked like mailbags.

Anneliese spoke to a porter.

'Five minutes,' he said.

Dermot turned, bag slung over his shoulder, took her work-broken hands in his. You could trace my life in my hands, Anneliese thought.

'I have to go,' he said. 'You understand that, don't you?'

She would not be able to bear it if he became emotional now.

'You'll let us know how you are?'

'Of course.'

He hovered helplessly, trapped between past and future. She took pity on him. 'We'll say goodbye, then.'

Briefly they clung together. So many years reduced to this.

He climbed into the train. She waited alone on the platform. They looked at each other through the window. He gave her a rueful half-grin; she tried to return it but could not. A whistle blew. The locomotive heaved its shoulders. Dermot raised one hand, silently. The train jolted into motion.

Others were waving, crying, calling, running along the platform. Anneliese would not. She stood unmoving as the train rolled away. The steadily receding carriages threatened to remain in her sight forever. She watched while they grew steadily smaller, became indistinct behind a ripple of haze. The rear of the train dwindled to a speck. To less than a speck. Was ...

Gone.

She walked back down the platform and into the hot glare. The emptiness of parting filled her, a space where formerly had been warmth. The street, the passers-by, were the same, yet everything had changed.

She walked to the buggy, climbed into the driver's place. She clicked her tongue; they moved forward in a light rumble of wheels. To the shop, first of all; not even saying goodbye to your son absolved you from the duty of stocking up during your visit to town.

At last the buggy was full. With the emptiness of past and future beside her, Anneliese started her long and dusty journey back to Paradise Downs.

TWENTY-SEVEN

The 1987 crash that destroyed Bond, Skase and a thousand smaller operators only strengthened Mostyn Harcourt. He had seen what was coming, moved from real estate into cash and bonds, sat back to wait out the storm. There had been wonderful pickings afterwards, the financial beaches littered with the wrecks of foundered dreams. He took a sizable stake in the *Trumpet*, the Sydney tabloid, moved into a whole range of strategic industries. He invested offshore; a tool manufacturer in Germany, a Silicon Valley investment in the States. For the first time he moved into Asia.

Three years later, on a visit to Indonesia, he was introduced, not entirely by chance, to men close to President Suharto. Mostyn always swore that he never interfered in editorial matters but the *Trumpet's* editor, always one to know which side his bread was buttered, had made no objection to publishing an article on the morning of Mostyn's departure from Australia.

MERCHANT BANKER HOLDS KEY TO
INVESTMENT IN PACIFIC RIM

The article had played up Mostyn's role as adviser to unnamed but highly placed clients throughout the region. A phone call from a friend at the Embassy to a contact at the palace, the transfer of a relatively modest sum to a bank account in Brunei had ensured that the right eyes saw the article.

Within months Mostyn had become heavily involved with members of Suharto's family in investments throughout Indonesia; real estate in Jakarta and Sourabaya, a holiday complex in Bali, a rice-milling enterprise in Central Java.

In 1994, on his fiftieth birthday, the board of Heinrich Griffiths presented him with a golden replica of a woodcutter's axe, mounted against a backcloth of purple velvet. He loved it, as he loved the nickname that had given rise to the gift, and ever since it had hung on the wall behind his desk.

Now, two years later, Mostyn occupied the managing director's office, complete with inlaid desk and Gill prints, upon which he had first set his sights years earlier. The board had approved a seven-figure package, salary plus equity tied to performance, that gave him not a majority holding but at least *de facto* control of the operations of the company.

Five years before, at the beginning of the nineties, he had suffered one of his few reverses when he had failed to pick up *Oudekraal*. The memory still rankled. He still thought of it — and a reckoning with the stubborn bastard who owned it — as unfinished business, yet in almost every other respect he had scarcely put a foot wrong.

He had everything: wealth, fame, power, a beautiful and stylish wife who in her way — although not always with his approval — was more of a public figure than he was.

He had nothing; as long as there remained fresh fields to conquer, Mostyn Harcourt would always be hungry. More money, more power; the lust for more drove him through his eighteen-hour days, made him the most dangerous predator in the Sydney jungle. Not only in matters of business.

One evening in October, he stood at the window of his office, staring out at the city that had become his empire. Twenty-four floors below, the diamond lights seemed to him more beautiful than any galaxy. Even Mostyn knew better than to make a takeover bid for the heavens but would have done so without hesitation, had he thought there was the slightest chance of success. Would have made a profit out of it, too.

He picked up his private phone, tapped out a number that he knew by heart. At the other end, the receiver lifted.

'Free this evening?'

A light laugh, breathless over the wire. 'You're a naughty boy, you know that?'

'That's what you like about me.'

Again the laugh. 'Among other things. When are you coming round?'

He checked his watch. 'An hour?'

It would give him time to look over the Belair contract. 'I'll be here.'

He replaced the phone. I'll bet you will, he thought. He opened the file, picked up his Mont Blanc pen, began to scan swiftly through the report that had come up that evening from the legal department. Forty minutes later he closed the file, locked it away in his desk and took the express lift to the parking garage in the basement.

All work and no play ... He was a great believer in old adages when they suited him, had no intention of becoming a dull boy. Not while he had Nicki, the friend from way back who had introduced him to his wife and who had been recently — and profitably — divorced for the second time. She would keep him up to the mark.

Anna had been on the periphery of the Women's Rights movement for years. She disagreed with much that they said, but it was a field where much work was still needed. By degrees she had become more and more involved.

A year earlier she had gone to Canberra to lobby Jack Goodie. He'd got the job of Foreign Minister by then and was making a fair fist of it, far better than the incompetent bag of venom and spite who had preceded him.

Foreign Minister or not, Jack was still the larrikin he had always been. 'My God,' he said when Anna walked into his office, 'The lady from hell.'

There was talk of sexism in some of the country's embassies and she wanted him to do something about it.

He groaned. 'You want me to change the Diplomatic? Might as well tell me to kick over Ayer's Rock.'

No Uluru for Jack, not when the cameras weren't turning.

'No need for me to get involved,' he said. 'The legislation's on the statute books.'

'Laws are one thing,' she told him, 'practice something else.' The sure way to Jack's heart was through the ballot box. 'Don't forget: an election's coming. More women voting than ever before.'

He looked thoughtful. 'I'll see what I can do.'

And did. It was only cosmetic but the principle of equality, in practice as well as in law, had been acknowledged. She went away pleased.

She must have rung a bell with Jack, too; two months later, David Gould phoned her. She had known the New

South Wales Premier for years. When it suited him he made derogatory noises about the big end of town but it never meant much, the worlds of business and politics a lot closer than some people liked to admit.

'There's a position on a Board of Enquiry,' he told her. 'If you're interested.'

He knew damn well she'd be interested. There was no money in it but as a way back into politics it couldn't be beaten. Anna had no definite plans, but keeping one's options open never hurt anybody.

The enquiry dragged on — boring, painstaking, useful — but things must have gone okay because a few months later she was invited to serve on another one.

Mostyn didn't like it. 'Playing footsie with the pollies. Bad for your image.'

It was his image, not hers, that worried him. Afterwards Anna supposed she should have taken more note of his concerns but in truth they hardly saw each other. Mostyn was out of the country a lot, chasing one deal or another. He had climbed into bed with Suharto and spent weeks at a time in Indonesia. The way that gang was pillaging the country it seemed obvious there had to be trouble coming but, when Anna tried to say so, Mostyn told her to keep her nose out of it.

Then David Gould made her his offer of a ministry. A month later, Anna came home to find her husband had walked out.

She was surprised how hurt she was; was hopping mad, too. More at herself than him; she should have been the one to walk. Indifference or perhaps an old-fashioned notion that marriages were supposed to last — how sentimental could you get? — had stayed her, and now it was too late.

She had to pick up the pieces of her life, her career. Because that too would be affected. Not many people liked Mostyn but plenty were scared of him; not for nothing was he called Hatchet Harcourt. The Harris Donnellys of the world might think she was wounded badly enough to risk trying to knife her. That thought didn't trouble her; she could eat Harris Donnelly for breakfast any day of the week, but she would have to guard her back. A nuisance.

She had lunch with Mark.

'At least you've still got plenty of supporters,' he told her. He was right. That night, after she had returned to her empty house, David Gould phoned her.

'Is it true?'

'Yep.'

'Dickhead.'

She laughed; brave try, girl. 'Me or him?'

'You don't qualify.'

'How would you know?'

There were plenty who said Anna Riordan had more balls than a man. 'Is that an invitation to find out?'

He'd been happily married for years. Faithful, too. Which made it all right.

'If I said yes, you'd run a mile.'

'Moira would murder me.' His voice changed. 'That ministry's still available, if you're interested.'

She was grateful; a gesture of support was just what she needed. As for the offer itself ... She had imagined she would jump at it.

'It's a kind thought.'

He heard the refusal in her voice. 'Why?'

'I'm tired, David. I need to think before I get into anything else.'

'Okay.' A busy man; no time to waste. 'If I can ever do anything...'

And was gone. Taking one of her potential futures with him.

She walked slowly through the house and into the garden. The fresh scent of the bedding plants came to her. She remembered how she had lain naked under the stars, facing the hopes and desires of what she had been determined would be a new life. Now she stood by the wall and looked across the harbour at the sun-bright city. The setting of so many battles, only a few of which had been creative.

What was the point of it all?

Mark Forrest had made a career, and a name, out of commitment. Someone else had done it, too: Ben, her old friend from uni, who had believed so passionately in the cause to which he had sworn to devote his life. He was still doing it; only recently she had seen his name in the papers about some conservation issue or other.

Her friends had laughed, calling him a fool, and she had laughed with them. He didn't seem such a fool, now.

Even Mostyn believed in what he was doing. Only Anna was the odd one out. She was in the business of making money, yet the accumulation of money for its own sake had never seemed a worthwhile objective.

She had told David the truth. She was too tired to climb back into the arena. That, like everything else in her life, would have to wait.

She saw now that what she had told herself would be no decision had in fact been a decision of the greatest importance. She had decided to do nothing, to wait; that, in a life that until now had been sacrificed endlessly upon an altar of frenetic movement, was a decision of momentous proportions indeed.

She had no doubt that she was right. Somewhere beneath all the nonsense in her life there had to be a sustaining passion. The trick was to find it. Do that and she would find herself, too, perhaps. She would be whole.

That did not mean remaining passive, accepting everything that Mostyn chose to chuck at her. She thought of Anneliese dying in her bed at ninety-five, the passion that had sustained her until the end. Anneliese had gone from riches to poverty; some would say she had achieved nothing in her life, yet she had lived with an intensity that even now, twenty-six years later, made Anna catch her breath in both admiration and envy.

Would Anneliese have sat back, meekly accepting what had been done to her? Never on your life. Perhaps Anna needed to learn a lesson from her.

Having lunch with Mark had been fun. More than fun; it had re-opened vistas that she had thought closed forever but, as far as her fight with Mostyn was concerned, it had achieved nothing. She accepted his judgement that she should not wage war through the press. Very well, but that did not mean she should do nothing.

She thought some more, then picked up the phone. 'Get me Maurice Steyn...'

Time for the lawyers.

Mostyn could not believe what he was reading. He threw the letter down on his desk and grabbed the phone.

'Get me Anderson!'

When his lawyer came on the line, he said, 'I've a letter from Anna's solicitor.' He shouted through the other man's protests. 'I don't care what appointments you've got. Just get here. Okay?'

Anderson took his time reading the letter.

Mostyn eyed him with increasing impatience. 'Well?'

Anderson read it again, carefully, put it back down on the desk. 'She's got you by the shorts,' he said.

Mostyn was having none of that. 'I made that bitch! Everything she has is due to me!'

'The courts won't see it that way.'

'It's your job to make them see it that way!'

'Most of her directorships went to her direct. You had nothing to do with them, any more than you had with those Boards of Enquiry.'

'I set the ball rolling —'

'She was the one who ran with it.'

Mostyn set his teeth. 'You saying I have to settle with her? On her terms?'

'You walked out on her,' Anderson pointed out. He wished that some of his rich clients might one day stop to consider before rushing headlong into matrimonial disasters of this kind. Although, as disasters went, this was reasonably mild.

'You could have done a lot worse. If the *Trumpet* hadn't published those articles —'

Mostyn brushed that aside. Whether he could have done worse was not the point; he resented having to settle at all, on any terms.

'It puts me in the wrong,' he complained.

'You *are* in the wrong.'

Mostyn Harcourt had never been wrong in his life. 'I'll fight her.'

'I strongly advise against it. All she wants is the house and contents, plus half your share portfolio —'

'*All*!'

'— in companies where you are not a director. Your general portfolio, in fact.'

'She's not getting any of my vineyards —'

'We can discuss that. Perhaps we can get her to agree.'

'What about my house?'

Mostyn had never been interested in the house. A roof over his head in a fashionable address was all he had ever wanted; in some ways a penthouse on the south side of the harbour would have suited him better, but now the house had become the most desirable thing on earth. Because Anna wanted it.

Anderson looked doubtful. 'The matrimonial home —'

'It's as much mine as hers,' Mostyn shouted.

'But you walked out.'

Mostyn changed tack. 'You any idea what my portfolio is worth?'

'Quite a lot, no doubt.' Anderson hesitated. 'Reconciliation is really the answer.'

Mostyn slapped an outraged hand on the letter. 'After that? I'll see her in hell, first.'

For the letter and another reason. He had walked out in rage after discovering that the bloody Premier had offered her a ministry in the next government. That, on top of the directorships that had not come from his patronage, the well-publicised and politically correct causes that he was convinced she supported only because they were fashionable. More and more he had felt himself becoming the junior member of their partnership and was not prepared to put up with it. He had cleared out in order to teach her a lesson, remind her how much she depended on his support. He had wanted her to come crawling. He should have known better. Anna was one of the very few he had never been able to push around. He remembered how she had forced him to chase after her into the Blue Mountains. That was another memory that still rankled.

'I've got mates in this town,' he threatened. 'Time I've finished with her, she won't get a job as dog-catcher.'

Anderson was alarmed. 'I advise most strongly —'

Mostyn had done with listening, if he had ever started. 'Write and tell her I'll see her in hell before I agree.'

Which, more diplomatically, Anderson did.

'What do we do now?' Anna asked.

Maurice Steyn placed Anderson's letter on the table and steepled his fingers.

'What other matrimonial assets are there?'

'The cottage in the mountains. The boat. A condominium in Delos. A couple of cars. I'm not interested in any of them,' Anna said. 'I just want to make an end to it. Leave us both with a bit of dignity.'

'Perhaps I should give Anderson a ring. But I have to warn you, if your husband wishes to maintain his adversarial stance —'

'Do what you must,' Anna said, defeated by her distaste for the whole situation. 'But I want the house.'

'And if he won't agree?'

'Then we'll take the bastard to the cleaners.'

'You'll give me a free hand?'

She hesitated. 'Yes.'

'You'll have to settle,' Anderson told him. 'She's willing to concede over the vineyards, but only if you accept everything else.'

'And that is?'

'As before. Plus the condominium on Delos.'

A hornet sting; Mostyn leapt. 'You telling me she's upped the stakes?'

'Steyn said if you don't settle, she'll go for fifty percent of the lot. You're getting off cheap. Let her have the house,' Anderson urged him. 'You never wanted it, anyway.'

Wanting it or not had never been the point. 'You're saying I have no choice?'

'None.'

'Very well.' Mostyn stared fiercely down at the city as though holding it responsible for the mess. 'Prepare the necessary papers. But she needn't think she's heard the last of it. I'll pay her back, you see if I don't.'

'Be careful. Slander is a serious business —'

'Better than slander.' Hatchet Harcourt smiled savagely. 'I'll make her sorry she ever tangled with me.'

TWENTY-EIGHT

Anna was astounded when Tracy rang from reception to say that Ben Champion was waiting in the foyer to see her. She had been thinking of him only the other day, as from time to time she did, with nostalgic fondness. She had never really expected to see him again.

'Send him up.'

She hadn't set eyes on Ben for years; now, waiting for him to be shown into her office, she felt like a girl on her first date. He'd been her first man, after all; if he had been more grown up both their lives might have been different.

A tap on the door.

Anna straightened her blouse, checked her hair in the hand mirror she kept in her desk.

'Come ...'

One glance and she saw this was no longer the youth she remembered. Ben's face was lean, a spider's web of sun-lines white about the corners of his eyes. His mouth was firm; he had the look of someone who had found himself, knew where he was going and why.

Maturity. She wondered if she could say as much for herself.

She took his hands in hers. 'What a lovely surprise!'

The Ben she remembered would have been awkward; now he smiled, accepting her pleasure at seeing him. It was a measure of how much he had changed, this man who had once been so close to her. Several times over the years she had seen him on television in connection with conservation issues; once or twice he'd been in trouble with the police; there had been rumours that he might nominate for the Senate on a Green ticket, but knowing these things and seeing the changes in his flesh were different matters entirely.

She had a meeting in twenty minutes, had been planning to run through the reports that would be tabled. Now she decided that for once in her life she would give preparation a miss.

'Coffee?'

It came at once; in Anna's office, things did.

'Tell me how you've been,' she said.

He smiled. 'Still beating the drum.'

'Planet Earth's most loyal supporter.'

He shrugged it off. 'Someone's got to do it.'

'Not married?'

'No one would have me.'

She doubted that, particularly as he was now, but did not pursue the subject. Too close to home, perhaps. 'Is this a social visit?'

'Not entirely. You're on the main board of Ryan's, aren't you?'

'Correct.'

'One of the Ryan companies is into forest management.'

'Gippsland Forestry. What about it?'

'Woodchips,' he said. 'You know how much forest has been destroyed in this country in the past ten years?'

'Gippsland has a policy of sustainable felling.'

'What does that mean?'

'What it says. We plant many more trees than we fell.'

He smiled cynically; for the first time she sensed his anger. 'Fell the hardwood and replace it with pine.'

'Timber is a resource. Like it or not —'

'No!' Violently. 'That's what all you people say. All trees are not the same. A pine plantation is sterile; indigenous forests sustain life. You're cutting them faster than they can regenerate. When they're gone —'

Anna had heard the arguments so often. 'I am sick of being told I'm an ecological vandal —'

'Don't behave like one, then.'

'We don't make a move without getting impact studies —'

'Not what I've heard.'

'It's true.' She looked at her watch. 'I have a meeting. I'll have to break this off.'

His face closed. 'I suppose I should thank you for seeing me at all.'

'Don't be silly.' She didn't want them to part like this. 'Why don't we have dinner later in the week? We'll have more time to talk then.'

They went to the Rocks, a restaurant she knew. As they ate, they talked of all that had happened in their lives. Anna's time in Africa, the prison term Ben had served once, how over the years both of them had become increasingly involved in the preoccupations that had shaped their lives.

'Business and conservation,' Anna said. 'We'd be unstoppable if only we'd learn to work together.'

'Is that talk? Or do you really care?'

She stared at him. 'Of course I care.'

'Then use your influence to get Gippsland out of woodchipping. That would be a start.'

She shook her head ruefully. 'No one has that sort of influence. Believe me.'

Ben scowled. 'Someone had better have it soon, or it'll be too late.'

She hadn't invited him to dinner to be told how she was failing the universe. 'You talk as though people don't count, that the only things that matter are trees.'

'It's because people matter that trees matter, as well. You can't have one without the other.'

Still too serious, she thought. He has never learned to smile. A pity; if he could get people to laugh, he could change the world.

'You have to make people feel good about the things you want. Keep telling them how guilty they are, they won't do anything.'

'They are guilty.'

'Makes no sense to tell them so.'

She made herself merry, laughing at his sombre expression. 'You should be pleased, seeing me again after so long.'

It worked. Eventually he smiled, too, light coming to a face that had known too much darkness.

After dinner they walked past the open-air restaurants, their canvas canopies spread like sails against the darkness. Still she laughed, determined to be happy.

They stood at the end of the jetty, hearing the water slopping against the piles and looking across the water to the lights necklacing the northern shore.

'The earth would be such a great place,' Ben said, 'if only people would leave it alone.'

He sounded pained by the immensity of the gulf between what might be and what was.

Anna was moved to comfort him. She put her arm around him, holding him tight.

'You told me once I should build a power base in business or politics,' he said. 'I never learned to do that. When I want something, I go for it straight.'

He spoke apologetically, as though his lack of subtlety had failed a vision they had shared. Anna remembered it differently; they had shared nothing but a fleeting and perverse attraction. I slept with him, she thought, but in retrospect remembered it as no more than an act of kindness, like patting a small boy on the head.

Neither of us was old, exactly, yet even then he made me feel more like his mother than his lover.

'You should help us,' Ben said.

'You told me once that if I got my feet in the trough I'd never take them out,' she reminded him, arm still about him.

'You saying I was wrong?' But laughed without malice.

'The jury is still out,' she said.

They parted. She had intended going back to her office but now she changed her mind. Instead she walked to the terminal and took a ferry across the harbour.

The breeze lifting her hair, she watched the darkness, the occasional blink of foam. The hull vibrated beneath her feet and the lights of the city receded steadily behind her. She thought about the evening, Ben's solemnity and how she had tried to make him laugh. We don't laugh enough, she thought. Life is such a sober business. What happened to fun?

She had a feeling of life slipping past her. I want to stretch out and grab it before it's too late. I want to live. Solemnity or not, she envied Ben. He had something he believed worthy of sacrifice. He had even been to jail. The cock-eyed way she was thinking tonight made that seem a gesture of extraordinary value. What have I got, she asked herself, to compare with that?

She shook her head irritably, suspecting self-pity. If you don't like what you've made of your life, why don't you do something about it?

Like what? Resign my directorships? Chain myself to trees? Stop shaving my legs?

You handle failure badly, she thought, that's your trouble. When Canberra fell apart, you hated yourself for weeks. Now you've broken with Mostyn and you're blaming yourself all over again. Post-marital depression doesn't suit you. Your husband's a shit. You're well rid of him.

The ferry reached the terminus; she went ashore and began to walk the mile that separated her from the house. Her shoes were not meant for hiking yet she strode along vigorously, as though by punishing her body she could dispel the desolation that threatened her.

Do something. Like what? Start an affair? With Ben? The idea was not as preposterous as it would have seemed twenty-four hours ago. She was dubious, all the same.

Do you really want another man in your life? Why should you assume he's interested, anyway? The only reason he came to see you was because he wanted something.

Stop Woodchipping; the slogan was like a banner draped across her brain. It was impossible. Thousands of jobs depended on it. Switch off the economy and everyone would be out of work. What good would that do?

Trouble with you, she mocked herself, you admire idealism even when you don't agree with its objective. You don't need a man; you need a cause. Although a sincere man with a cause, someone who thought more of others than himself, would be nice. Would certainly be a change.

She reached the house, went through the side gate into the garden, strolled pensively.

Her life was coming full circle. In the last month she had caught up with Mark, who three days ago had left on a return visit to South Africa, and now Ben. She had seen neither of them for years; each, in his different way, had been good for her. She had loved Mark; it was safe, now, to admit that to herself. She had enjoyed being with him again, finding that the old resentments had died at last. It would not be impossible to start over with Mark, she thought, if that was what they wanted.

With Ben there had never been so much, but he was a stronger man now, a committed man. Given the right degree of provocation, she thought, perhaps even a formidable man.

A cause he believed in...

Perhaps she really did need a cause, she thought. Something to make her life worthwhile. You're forty-one, she told herself, exasperated. A bit early to be quite so menopausal.

He had unsettled her nonetheless. When, two days later, he phoned to ask her out, she agreed.

It was not a light-hearted evening; Ben brought his obsessions, and his intensity, with him. To the point where Anna began to wonder whether he had asked her out simply to recruit her to the conservation movement.

'Years ago you told me I needed big business to help in my quest to save the earth.'

As before, she tried to tease him into a more relaxed frame of mind.

'Quest? How melodramatic!' Sadly, he seemed unable to respond.

'I make no apologies for what is no more than the truth. Exploitation is ruining the Murray River. Within ten or twenty years the South Australian wheat industry could be wiped out, yet nobody does anything about it. If we don't change our ways, we're facing disaster.'

He stared at her accusingly, as though it were her fault, but there was a limit to how much intensity Anna could take. She tried to change the subject, but Ben would have none of it.

'You're like the rest of the business community. Young people understand, but business and politicians don't want to know. Talk about the economy and they listen, but mention conservation and they couldn't care less. Yet conservation is economics, the management of resources. Without a healthy earth, we won't have any resources to manage.'

Anna thought she could not take much more of it yet liked him, despite all, for himself and the strength of his convictions. She did something she had told herself she would never do: invited him back to the house where, for half the night, they sat side by side on the settee, and watched the televised images of athletes swimming like otters.

From time to time she poured drinks; Ben's enthusiasm for conservation did not extend to alcohol, thank God, but as for sport ... He battled to show enthusiasm for something in which he had no interest but Anna was without mercy. She wanted to see it; he would just have to put up with it. She told herself it would do him good.

He is too fanatical, she thought. Yet defence of the environment was such a worthwhile cause. She felt guilty that she could not match his intensity; had already convinced herself, with only a little encouragement from Ben, that he was a much finer person than she was.

Perhaps it was her sense of inadequacy and guilt that conditioned her response when he took leave of her in the small hours. He stood outside the front door, invited her to go away with him the following weekend, and she said yes.

The door was barely shut before she was asking herself, very seriously, whether she had taken leave of her senses. It was one thing to respect Ben for his sense of vocation, understandable that his dedication, however trying it might sometimes be, should have awoken in her such a sense of inadequacy. It was something else entirely to have let him talk her into a weekend that was presumably intended to end in bed.

She went back into the living room. She stared at the familiar, comfortable furniture, the pools of light cast by the lamps. My sanctuary, she thought. A place of refuge that I have deliberately permitted to be violated by a man whom I like and respect, but most certainly do not love.

She could not go away with him. A bit late in the day to be changing her mind, but there it was. Cancelling wouldn't be easy; he had asked, she had accepted, they had both known exactly what they were talking about. How, without causing enormous offence, would she be able to get out of it now?

'You are a fool,' she told herself crossly.

Which didn't help. Somehow a way would have to be found. The alternative was out of the question.

She found the Glenfiddich and gave herself the biggest drink she had ever poured in her life. Gulped it down. Good malt whisky. What a waste. For the moment, she didn't care. She had a second drink, only marginally smaller than the first. The whisky, coming on top of everything else she had drunk during the evening, hit her like an axe.

Go on, make a real job of it, she told herself. Start by being sorry for yourself, then hit the booze. What comes next? Suicide?

Doing a real hatchet job on myself. A self-inflicted hatchet job on Hatchet Harcourt's wife. Good evening, sir or madam. Allow me to introduce. Hatchet's on the rampage, lawyers getting fat, please put a dollar in the old woman's hat.

You'll be drunk, directly. You're drunk now.

She did not care about that, either; for the moment, it seemed quite a good idea. She leant back, closed her eyes. The darkness spun and went out.

She woke with a mouth and a head. She struggled out of the chair, fetched a glass of water and tipped it down with a couple of disprins.

She stared at her reflection. Lady Macbeth after a night on the town. Let's get to bed.

She went back into the lounge to turn the lights out and saw the post where Mrs Casey had left it on the side table. She picked up the handful of letters, remembering the one that had been waiting to ambush her the day Mostyn had walked out.

No danger of that, this time. All their sharing and achievements, hurts and disagreements, had come down to the ultimate aridity, a succession of communications between solicitors. She looked around at the empty house. They had shared this, too, once.

She glanced through the letters mechanically, saw a stamp she didn't recognise. She paused, squinting at it under the light. An antelope of some kind, with scimitar-like horns.

South Africa.

A last-minute meeting had come up, unexpectedly. Anna phoned Ben and arranged to meet him at the Blue Mountains hotel that he had picked for their weekend.

In the end she had done nothing about cancelling, had told herself it was not cowardice, or at least not cowardice alone. Perhaps, if she let the arrangement go ahead, she would find once they were together that things would work out, after all.

It had to be the most forlorn of hopes and, within minutes of her arrival, facing Ben in the room he had taken, she knew it was not going to happen. Which left only one possible course of action.

After she had told him, there was an appalling silence. Ben stared at her, incredulous, white-lipped.

She waited. She was never normally lacking in courage, but was so completely to blame for the situation, for the humiliation that she had brought so unwittingly upon him, that now she was frightened out of her wits. Far worse, she was ashamed, wretched. She stood, submissively, awaiting his fury. The unbearable silence drew out and, with every second, Anna felt herself die a little.

Eventually Ben spoke, his voice controlled but as cold as the Antarctic. 'Let me get this straight. You agreed to come away for the weekend and now you're saying you've changed your mind?'

He made no attempt to conceal outrage. As for Anna ... It was strange to discover that she was still capable of tears.

'I'm beginning to think you don't know what you want.'

Her hands reached, clutching. 'I like you very much. Admire you, too. In your own way, you're the strongest man I know ...'

No word of love.

'You just don't want to go to bed with me.'

She wilted. 'Let's go to bed, then. Let's hold each other.'

Ben stared. '*Hold* you?'

'If we do, maybe I'll feel different.'

Perhaps she hoped that physical contact would overcome doubt. It wasn't that simple.

'And afterwards?'

A lopsided smile, closer to tears than laughter. 'We'll find out, won't we?'

Ben was having none of it. 'Sounds too much like masturbation for me.'

Her face went white. 'I've blown it, haven't I?'

Mercy eluded him. 'I reckon.'

In the circumstances it was a good thing they'd driven there separately. They shared a painfully silent meal, a night spiky with resentment. Both lay awake, taking enormous care not to touch. Eventually, thank God, it was over. First thing the next morning, Ben was out of there. To the very last they were polite. It was terrible.

Anna sat alone in the hotel's beamed dining room. A waitress brought her food. She ate, having not the slightest idea what it was. She drank coffee, felt tranquillity trickle back. She had hurt Ben and grieved for it; had probably lost his friendship and grieved for that, too. Yet could not deny relief. At the last minute, scruples and the letter that Mark had sent from South Africa had saved her. It would never have worked for either of them.

TWENTY-NINE

Shadows of the past filled Anna's mind. Mark, Anneliese, her cousin Pieter Wolmarans, whom she had not seen since she had visited South Africa fifteen years before. Most of all, perhaps, the farm *Oudekraal* itself, with its great house.

She flew South African Airways from Sydney to Johannesburg. The first class cabin attendant was black; something that she suspected would not have happened in the old days. She wondered what other changes she would find in the country that, after so long and so unexpectedly, had drawn her back.

For the hundredth time, she took Mark's letter from her bag and read it. *Cry from a Dark Continent* had become official reading at the University of the Western Cape, outside Cape Town, and he had been invited there to give an address. She had not expected to hear from him but was pleased to have done so. Was considerably less pleased by what he had to say:

I paid a visit to Oudekraal. Your cousin was very defensive, almost hostile. I think something has happened to upset him. In fact that is understating it; he gave the impression of being at his wits' end with worry, but what it was all about I don't know. I mentioned your name, but it didn't help. Quite the opposite, in fact. He couldn't wait to chuck me out.

She found it incredible that a person's roots could have such power. She had visited the country only once, fifteen years before. While there she had known happiness and sorrow, trauma and excitement, fear and a crippling sense of loss. She had seen the pristine gable of *Oudekraal* white as sugar against the grey-green bulk of the mountain, in imagination had driven in her great-grandmother's buggy along the dusty, vine-bordered lanes of long ago. All that, yet none of it had anything to do with her real life. Or so she had thought.

She had always told herself that one day she would return but had made no plans, had never dreamt that nostalgia would seize control of her in such a way. Revisiting her roots: a far-fetched explanation, if she had ever heard one. Yet what other reason could there be?

She had read Mark's letter, alarm bells had rung. She had tried, unsuccessfully, to telephone her cousin; when that hadn't worked, she had cancelled all her appointments and taken the first flight she could get.

She was known in every boardroom in Sydney for the coolness and objectivity of her judgements, yet that was what she had done. It was ludicrous.

It could have nothing to do with Pieter Wolmarans's troubles, real or imagined. They were not her concern, as he would no doubt be quick to tell her if she tried to interfere. The fact that she had not heard meant nothing; his next letter was not due until Christmas.

She had been restless for months; that could have something to do with it, but could hardly be the full explanation.

She would not even be in time to see Mark, who would be back in Sydney by now. Perhaps, if she really were hitting the nostalgia track, that was as well.

Your life is always so organised, she told herself crossly. Now look at you.

At Johannesburg's Jan Smuts Airport, she changed to a local flight, reached Cape Town by lunchtime. She rented a car, drove into the city and booked into a hotel standing beneath the mountain called Lion's Head. She sat on the terrace and looked at the sea. Now she was here, she realised how apprehensive she was of taking the next step. Mark had said Pieter Wolmarans had been hostile; she wondered how he would greet her. Not that she was planning to call on him straightaway; she had other priorities.

She wandered around the city, re-visiting the past. She jostled with the shoppers in the Golden Acre, took the train from Adderley Street to Simonstown. The waters of False Bay lapped almost to the carriage wheels. In the distance, lower slopes hidden in haze, she saw the dreaming summits of the Hottentots Holland mountains.

Fifteen years before, she had taken this journey with Mark, his hand in her lap, its heat warming thighs warm enough already without extra help.

I listen to the chug-a-lug of the wheels, watch the beach huts at St James form cubes of brilliant colour against the tawny sand. On the other side of the compartment, a coloured child is eating a banana. I watch him and experience an extraordinary sensation, of watching my own life emerging like the banana from its skin. I am sensitive to everything about me — the rumbling wheels, the swaying train, Mark's hand warm in my lap — and for the first time understand that one person can in fact be several people, each with a different potential for good and evil, sorrow and happiness. I have the power to become more than the individual I have known all my life.

'The road to Damascus —'

'What?'

Mark hears my murmur but not the words.

I smile at him, feel brilliance in my face as I press his hand ardently against me. 'Nothing ...'

They had taken that journey the day before the riot and the meeting with Adam Shongwe that had changed so much.

Now once again Anna sat in the train and looked at the water, the distant mountains, the textures of what her life had been. For an instant, fifteen years earlier, she had glimpsed another choice, had lost it again so quickly that now she did not even know what she had seen, only that it differed vastly from what her life had in fact become.

She stirred restlessly. There was no point in such thoughts, yet there was nothing imaginary about the sense of bereavement and regret that overwhelmed her.

When the train reached Simonstown, she ate at a restaurant overlooking the bay; a fish called *kingklip,* a half-bottle of bone-dry wine. She remembered how, fifteen years before, the whites-only beach had been deserted; now it was crammed with brown bodies. She clambered across rounded boulders to a tiny cove, she paddled in the warm water, she returned to the station in time to catch the city-bound train.

Back at the hotel she discovered that something had happened to her during her pilgrimage into the past; she was in a fever of impatience as she went to her room, made her few arrangements.

She had intended to phone Pieter Wolmarans when she was ready, ask when it would be convenient to call on him. Now she had other plans.

Early the next morning, she drove into the country. The mountains grew close about her. She needed no map to put her on the road to *Oudekraal*.

Watching the vines on either side of the narrow road, Anna remembered the vineyards of France, her catastrophic attempt to seduce her husband under the Burgundy sun; at least there would be no such problem now. Beyond the vines, the mountains were blue and moss-green against a brilliant sky. The first glimpse Anna had of the house was what she had seen on her first visit, the carved pediment framed by the giant oak tree that Pieter Wolmarans had told her had been planted over two hundred years before. So long a time, she thought. Generation upon generation of Wolmarans, moulding and changing the land, even as the land, inexorably, had moulded and changed them. My ancestors.

She parked before the house. For a moment she sat there, immersing herself once again in the history of this place. She got out into the stammering flare of torches, the angry cries of the crowd forming a tight circle around the bound and terrified prisoners.

She stared at the old house drowsing in the summer heat, and a man came and stood on the terrace, his hands on the railing. She looked up at him, as she had the first time she had come here. For a moment she felt shock; since she had last seen him, Pieter Wolmarans had grown old. Of course he had, she told herself. He had hardly been young fifteen years ago; now he must be in his late seventies.

He did not move as she walked across the driveway to the house. At the bottom of the steps she paused. 'Good morning.'

She had thought he would show surprise, perhaps even pleasure. He did neither but nodded silently, face expressionless.

Unsure of her welcome, mindful of what Mark had told her in his letter, she hesitated. 'May I come up?'

Again the nod. She climbed the steps to the terrace, while her cousin's eyes impaled her, coldly. He was as upright as she remembered, the massive body still hard, but a melting of his features showed clearly the years that had passed since their last meeting.

'So the ratpack is here again,' he said.

She blinked at the contempt in his voice. 'I have come to see you,' she said. 'Since I am in the district. Since we are related.'

'I was waiting for someone to remind me of that,' Pieter said.

'If you can tell me how I have offended you —'

'And of course you know nothing about the man who was here only yesterday.'

'Pieter, I haven't the slightest idea what you're talking about —'

'You expect me to believe that?' Eyes like blue flame. 'You don't have enough in Australia that you have to badger me here?'

She would get nowhere by being submissive.

'It might help if I knew what you were talking about.' She stalked past him, plonked herself down in the chair that still stood beside the small table at the end of the terrace. 'If you want to tell me what the problem is, perhaps we can sort it out.'

His nostrils flared; for a moment she thought she had gone too far.

'How many times do I have to tell you people?' he demanded, lips white. '*Oudekraal* is not for sale.'

Anna stared out at the open ground before the house. She said, 'Two minutes ago I was imagining the scene my great-grandmother Anneliese described to me the day her father — your great-grandfather — led the commando after the convicts. It was like being there myself. I could see the men on their horses, feel the wind ...' She looked at him. 'Of course you can't sell this place. I remember telling you that the last time I was here. How can anyone sell their past?'

His face had changed, suspicion turning to puzzlement, but she had not won him yet.

'Then why are you here?'

'I had a letter from a friend. Mark Forrest. He said he'd been to see you. That you seemed ... troubled. I tried to phone you, but I couldn't get through —'

'The phones are a joke,' he said. 'Like so much else in the new South Africa.'

'I was concerned. So I came.'

'From Australia?' His sarcasm was caustic. 'All that way just to see me?'

For a moment, she stared at him. 'Yes,' she said simply. 'To see you.' She saw that he was inclined to believe her. Yet he still had doubts.

'Do you know a man called Danie Myburgh?'

'No.'

'A land broker from Stellenbosch. He has been here three times in the past month, badgering me to sell *Oudekraal*. Each time I tell him it is not for sale, but he does not wish to listen. He was from Swellendam originally,' he said, as though that explained much. 'No local man would behave in such a way.'

'Who is he acting for?'

'An overseas buyer; that is all he will tell me. When I saw you drive up, I thought it must be you.'

Anna shook her head. 'It certainly is not. I don't want to buy *Oudekraal* at all but, if I did, I would approach you direct, not through a land broker.'

Suspicion did not die so easily. Eyes shrewd in the seamed face, he said, 'Yet you are here. Who is Danie Myburgh acting for, if not for you?'

She thought, *An overseas buyer*. 'I can't be sure ...'

'You know your husband came here?'

'He told me, yes. But only afterwards.'

'He was another one who wanted to buy. I told him no. Again and again I told him, but he wouldn't listen. In the end, I sent him away with my boot in his arse.' The grimmest of smiles. 'I suspect he did not love me for it.'

'I bet he didn't.'

'Did you approve of his coming here?'

'I did not.'

'Yet he is your husband.'

'Only just. We are getting divorced.'

'Not because of *Oudekraal*?'

'For *Oudekraal* and a hundred other things.'

'Even so ...' His voice was stern, as his face was stern. 'Those whom God has joined together ...'

'It takes two.'

'Perhaps. In my day, divorce was unthinkable; now it happens all the time. Sometimes I think I have lived too long, that I am out of step with the modern ways. It is none of my business, of course.' He sighed. 'As for our mystery buyer ... I have thought of little else since Myburgh first turned up on my doorstep. It is like being stalked by a lion. Or a hyena.' He stared at her assessingly. 'Do you think it could be your husband?'

'It's certainly possible.'

He shook his head, exasperated. 'The man must be stone-deaf. I told him no a dozen times.'

Anna wondered how to explain to this bachelor that Mostyn might want *Oudekraal* simply because Anna would not wish him to have it. That a once-loving relationship could become so degraded that its sole purpose was to hurt. Anything so vindictive would surely seem incredible to a man who had never known the traumas of a marriage break-up.

'You are saying Myburgh may be acting for your husband?'

She was sure — it had the stink of Mostyn all over it — but remained cautious.

'I have no proof.' But proof, perhaps, could be obtained. 'If I can borrow your phone,' she said, 'I may be able to find out.'

She dialled Myburgh's number, asked to be put through to him.

'This is Mr Harcourt's office. He has asked me to enquire whether there have been any developments.'

She listened, put down the phone.

'No further developments, he said. That settles it. He's acting for my husband.'

'He doesn't give up, does he? In some circumstances that might be admirable, I suppose.'

'There is nothing admirable about this, I assure you.' He looked his question; she smiled ruefully. 'A long story...'

'In which case let us be comfortable.'

He went into the house, returned with another chair, two glasses and an unlabelled bottle of wine wet from the refrigerator. He placed the chair beside the table, drew the cork from the bottle and, with a flourish, filled both glasses.

Anna inspected the honey-coloured wine. 'What is it?'

'*Oudekraal*'s best chardonnay,' he told her.

'I am honoured.'

'To welcome home the last of the Wolmarans. And to apologise for doubting you.'

She was embarrassed. 'It doesn't matter.'

'To me it matters a great deal,' he told her. 'If you had been a stranger it would perhaps have been excusable, but I have known you fifteen years. I should have known better.'

She saw that he meant what he said. Welcome to the family. Welcome to renewed trust. The wine was a double honour, then.

She raised her glass. 'To *Oudekraal*.'

'And to the Wolmarans.'

They drank ceremoniously.

'Tell me about this husband of yours.'

She did, as simply as she knew how. By the time she had finished, the bottle was nearly empty.

'Perhaps he is doing it because he has an interest in wine farms,' Pieter said. 'Perhaps it is only that he wants to buy a South African property?'

Anna saw he would be more comfortable with that explanation than with the idea that Mostyn was doing it out of spite, but she did not believe it. 'Perhaps ...'

'You do not think so?'

'I think he wants it, yes. For two reasons. Because he knows I wouldn't wish him to have it and because he thinks he'll be able to sell it at a profit.'

'So he would not keep it for himself?'

'I doubt it.'

'I see.' He thought about that for a while. 'If I will not sell, he cannot buy.'

'I wouldn't be too sure about that. Do you have any outstanding loans?'

'Of course. Every farm has debt. Equipment is expensive and operations must be financed until the crush.'

'Where do you get the money? From the banks?'

'At one time, yes. But with all the political changes the banks are less co-operative than they used to be.'

'Is that the only reason?'

She watched him making up his mind whether to confide in this woman whom, Wolmarans blood or not, he barely knew.

'There have been threats,' he said eventually. 'We have all had them. The land belongs to the people — that sort of thing. There have been deaths. Nothing like the Free State, where one white farmer is murdered every day, but one or two.'

'And the banks?' she prompted him.

'Are nervous.'

'Enough to call in their loans?'

'They have no wish to lend more, at any rate. And capital costs are rising all the time.'

'So where do you go for finance?'

'There are institutions that provide what they call off-market funding. Quite a number have sprung up in recent years. They are expensive, of course, but —'

'Is there any way Myburgh could know about your arrangements?'

'It's common knowledge. We all do it.'

'Then you may have a problem,' Anna said.

'How?'

'My husband's a banker. Contacts all over the world. If he wants to buy up your loans, he will certainly find a way of doing so.'

'Why should he?'

'To get hold of *Oudekraal*. Pay up or get out.'

'He would do that just to punish you?'

'His nickname is Hatchet. Hatchet Harcourt. He would do it, never doubt it. Especially if he sees the chance of a profit.'

Pieter leant back in his chair, whistling gently beneath his breath. 'There is nothing anyone can do about it.'

'I'm not so sure about that.' She smiled brilliantly at him. 'Do you think it would be possible to take me over the estate again, like you did last time?'

They went everywhere, as before; through the beds of streams, the water white as it gnashed its way past the stony fords, around rocky outcrops, past terrace upon terrace of grapes ripening towards the crush. Pieter drove the open jeep more like a rally driver than a man in his seventies, and Anna felt the land that was *Oudekraal* lay its hand once more upon her heart.

He must have sensed something of her thoughts. Back at the house, they sat once again at the terrace table and he smiled at her.

'Well?'

'I told you before. This time it's the same. I was thinking how impressed your great-grandfather would be if he could see the estate now.'

He was pleased. 'There is always much to be done.' He laughed a little. 'The work never stops.'

'Or the need for capital.'

Which wiped the laugh from his lips.

'I am not trying to interfere,' Anna said. 'What

happens here is none of my business. Except that, in a way, my husband has made it my business.'

'How has he done that?'

'If he gains control of the estate, do you really think he will allow you to stay?'

Silence as Pieter Wolmarans pondered the idea of being forced to leave the only home he had known.

'How do we stop him?'

Anna told him.

Anderson phoned to tell Mostyn that Anna was not available to sign the papers. It made him spit.

'Months of her bloody nonsense, and now she's not even here!'

'Steyn says she's out of the country. On holiday. That's all he was willing to tell me.'

Something must have come up. Given Mostyn's plans, he wondered whether it was anything he should know. He made a few phone calls, within the hour had found out what he wanted.

'What's she doing in South Africa?'

On holiday ... He didn't believe a word of it; the timing was too neat.

He looked at his watch. Three o'clock in the morning over there. Tough. Time Myburgh started earning his keep.

He dialled the number. He had told Anderson he would get even with Anna. He had issued the necessary instructions but had not followed them through. Time to put that right.

The phone lifted.

'Yes?' Myburgh's voice was blurred with sleep and exasperation; not a man who appreciated being woken in the middle of the night.

'Mostyn Harcourt. What have you done about that business I asked you to arrange for me?'

The voice quacked.

Mostyn's hand tightened on the receiver. 'What do you mean, you told me already? I haven't contacted you for days.'

Again he listened; when Myburgh had finished, he slammed down the phone. Stared at Anderson furiously.

'It's got to be Anna. That bloody bitch is up to something.'

THIRTY

'Let light perpetual shine upon this house, oh Lord. Bless the brothers and sisters who live within it and those who pass by upon the road to life or damnation.'

Two of them. The man who called himself Preacher Moffatt, fine unctuous voice, moist eyes watching around invisible corners; the hanger-on with him.

Anneliese never knew where they came from but one day, four months after the end of the Second World War, there they were, trudging up to the homestead, battered hats and dusty clothes, smiles smeared like jam across their lips.

She had always known trouble when she saw it.

Sylvia asked them to stay; it was normal bush courtesy, and they had walked far. Sean and Scott Macdonald were away on the far side of the run, so there were only the three women to greet them: Sylvia, mistress of the house, Anneliese and Sylvia's daughter. Sylvia had named her Margaret but to Anneliese she would always be Rëen, after the drought-breaking rain that had been falling at the time of her birth.

Rëen was nineteen, plum-ripe, eager like the rest of them to meet the strangers who had come to them from the big world. Anneliese watched as Preacher Moffatt sprayed wet words from a mouth as red as cherries, saw Rëen's eyes stray repeatedly to the young man she had privately named the hanger-on.

Archer Fitzgerald was a good-looking man, if you forgave the treacherous and discontented mouth. Very loud in his amens; Anneliese never trusted him and was right.

As weak as a reed, vain as a cockerel and, like so many of his breed, knew how to charm the geckos off the walls. He certainly charmed Rëen, who had little experience of men and none at all of good-looking ones.

They hung around for a week, then Sean came home and chased them off. South of Paradise Downs was an emptiness without water; too far for a man to walk to the next station, so the Preacher set out to return to Waroola.

He went alone. That had not been the plan but, at the last, Archer Fitzgerald fell as he came down the verandah steps. When he got up, he was hopping around on one foot, cursing and telling the world how he had broken his ankle into a hundred pieces.

Anneliese had as many doubts about that ankle as about its owner. Scott inspected it and said afterwards there had been nothing wrong, not even a swelling, but Archer swore to heaven it tortured him to put his weight on the ground. He made such a commotion that in the end it was easier to let him stay than chuck him out. Preacher Moffatt went alone, seemingly unconcerned at leaving his mate behind.

No complaints from Rëen, you may be sure. Very solicitous she was about poor Archer's ankle, always running to him with cups of tea and the like, while he sat at his ease on the verandah, looking out at the countryside like Lord Muck and happy to be waited upon.

It took an extraordinary time for that ankle to come right. In the end, Sean told him that if he couldn't work he would have to learn not to eat, and the next day he struggled out of his chair. Many protestations and winces, agony to curdle the milk, but only Rëen took notice.

Sean might as well have left him where he was; the work he did was always half-done and badly, at that. It was obvious to them all that Archer couldn't last.

One night Rëen came to Anneliese's room and said he was leaving in the morning, that she was going with him.

Anneliese loved her grand-daughter but in a kindly way, as one might love a kitten. She was as pretty as a kitten but without pride; Sean allowed none about him to have that, and Rëen had been weak from the first. Anneliese felt love but little respect; had no faith at all in her ability to survive someone as inherently useless as Archer Fitzgerald.

Anneliese wanted her to see she was heading for disaster but, for the first time in her life, found she no longer had stomach for the battle. She was seventy years old. She had never given her age a thought but now, suddenly, it seemed too hard to go on trying to protect later generations from their folly. If Rëen wanted him she must have him, and the consequences.

One question remained. 'What have your parents to say about it?'

'I haven't told them.'

'You must.'

She looked dubious, but Anneliese insisted. 'Or I shall tell them myself.'

Reproachful eyes gleamed in the half-light. 'I never thought you'd cause me trouble, Gran.'

'Trouble? You try to slink away, your father will come after you with a gun, and you will know more trouble than either of you can handle.'

So tell them she did. Sean warned that if she went he would wash his hands of her and Sylvia, determined until the day she died to protect herself from all things, said nothing.

Rëen came back to Anneliese, very quiet, yet with an air of determination her grandmother had not seen before. 'I'm out of here, Gran.'

Anneliese saw that she could say nothing to change the child's mind. 'With my blessing,' she told her.

'Won't you come with us?'

She laughed. 'Archer would love that, an old lady trotting along behind you.'

'I want you to come.' She meant it.

'Why, child? Young people must make their own lives. Old ones have no place.'

Yet in Africa it had been normal for old and young to live with each other in one large family.

'I would be afraid by myself,' she said simply. 'I know I am not good at a lot of the things that have to be done. I need help.'

'No one can live your life for you,' Anneliese cautioned her.

She came and sat by her, placing supplicant hands in her lap.

'I know what he is, Gran. I know he is not ... strong.'

'Do you love him?'

'I need to get away from here. He is my chance,' Rëen said passionately. 'Can't you see that?'

She could indeed. There was nothing here for her, nor would be. Her father, contemptuous of all the world, would grant the girl — and her foolish man — no space. Archer, broken creature that he was, presented what was probably the only chance she would ever have to make a life for herself. Otherwise she would sit here and rot, as

Anneliese, for twenty years now, had done. She and Scott Macdonald had found a place for each other once, but that had been long ago.

If she needed her grandmother to help her find the strength she would need, with Archer of all people, who was Anneliese to deny her that chance? It might mean salvation for her, also.

'If Archer himself asks, I shall come.'

Rëen hugged and kissed her and ran outside. Within minutes Archer was in the room, beseeching her to join them. He spoke lightly, as though the request had no weight in either his life or hers. She knew there would be trouble on the road ahead but said, Very well, if that was what they wanted, she would come.

Later the usual tropical storm broke about the house. Anneliese stood at the window and looked out at the rain gleaming like silver rods in the darkness. Rëen, she thought. She had said she needed him, but need was not love. Would it be enough? And would Sean agree?

Sean didn't give a damn — one less mouth to feed — but Anneliese herself made one stipulation before she agreed to go.

There were two unfinished stories in her life.

She had never heard from Dermot, after all the years. It had hurt her and still did, an aching sorrow that never went away. There were times when she believed she would sooner know that he had been ten years in his grave than endure this constant void of not-knowing, the doubts that gnawed and gnawed, giving no peace.

The second story concerned Jack Riordan, the one man in her life whose brutal strengths had not so much dominated as ignored her will, treating it, and herself, as of no account. A man wedded to his own gross appetites, whose existence had made so permanent an impact upon her life.

He would be long dead by now. She herself was seventy, which meant that Jack Riordan, if he were still alive, would be getting on for ninety. It was out of the question that so lusty a man would have made such old bones, yet Anneliese had a desire to return to that wilderness of trees and precipices and icy winds where she had first tasted passion.

Again and again in their wandering years Anneliese had talked to Dermot about the rough wooden house like an eagle's eyrie, perched high in the Victorian ranges. She had told him of the grandparents who had raised him to childhood, the mother who had died giving him birth. She had believed it was his right to be acquainted with his own beginnings, despite or perhaps because they were beyond his recall. It was her duty to tell him as much as she could about his life. Without that knowledge he would be incomplete, as Anneliese herself would have been incomplete without knowledge of her own childhood in Africa.

So Dermot had grown up knowing at least something about his family and the land from which he came. Those cold ranges were the only place outside Paradise Downs he could call his own; was it not conceivable that he might have gone there when he turned his back upon the north?

It was beyond hope that either Jack or Dermot would be there now, but perhaps, in that place peopled by memories, she might find a trace of what had happened to them both.

'There is somewhere in the south I have to go ...'

They agreed, Rëen because she would have been willing to agree to almost anything to have Anneliese's company, Archer because he did not give a damn either way.

So to the southern ranges, the land of vertiginous heights and howling air, of cascades white as bone and forests green and silent, Anneliese returned at last.

The house, empty now of eagles, was a wreck. No one lived there, or had for many years. Yet the area was not deserted. Some distance from the house, Jack had built a shed where he had stored his horses' winter feed. Here there remained human life, of a sort.

A witless woman, about forty years old, who stared and gobbled and tried to flee for refuge into the woods. Anneliese, for all her seventy years, was too quick for her.

The woman was submissive when caught, allowed herself to be led back to the fire that Rëen had built, while Archer, useful as a cockatoo, whistled about the place, poking his nose and what passed for his mind into corners weed-choked and mossed with damp.

It took a while to get the woman to speak although, once she got used to the idea, she managed well enough. She was slow to comprehend, certainly — not absolutely witless but timid beyond belief, unused to people. She flinched from the least of human sounds; the noise of speech batted against eyes as well as ears. You could see the impact of the sound upon her eyes.

It would have been merciful to leave her to her solitude but, after so many miles and years, Anneliese had not come back to this place to be merciful.

'Have you lived here long?'

Forever, it seemed.

'Alone?'

Yes. Alone. After the old woman died.

'Old woman?'

The woman led Anneliese by the hand to a clearing in the forest, fifty yards from the house. Stood, pointing.

Two patches of ground, side by side, each perhaps ten feet by five, from which the grass had been cleared. Graves, under the trees and talking leaves.

'Who's buried here?'

The woman. And, before her, the man.

So. Two graves. For the man and the woman. She had found Jack Riordan at last.

She stared silently at the patch of cleared ground but Jack was not there. The earth could not hold him; rather was he in the leaves, the impact of the cold and swooping air.

After many false turns, Anneliese found her way to the place where Jack had coralled his stolen horses. Saplings had grown amid rank grass; all that now remained was the remnant of fence posts, worm-rotten, tilting drunkenly towards the consuming earth.

Here she found him. Jack's presence remained, claimed by the forest, the memory of horses, as never by the grave that held only his bones. He had been a terrible man, harsh and brutal, yet he walked at Anneliese's side now as she made her way back to the house.

Archer wanted to move on straightaway, but Anneliese would not. Her instinct told her that in the woman's wandering soul, at least one of her stories might be resolved. It would take time to glean the truth; very well, time she would give.

First, the woman's name.

It took two days while the hunted eyes fled frantically from side to side, folded arms clutching her secrets to herself.

'Agnes...'

The whisper signified surrender; after that, it was easier.

It seemed that Agnes had not been here forever, after all, but had come.

'Where from?'

A sweep of the hand, embracing the forest, the world beyond.

'You came alone?'

No, not alone. Once not alone. But later ... Her eyes widened fearfully.

'Fire,' Agnes whispered, fingers clutching Anneliese's arm.

She could make no sense of it but persevered, prising open the lock of Agnes's tangled memory, her tangled speech. Discovered at last, after a week of questions, the answer, not to one of her unfinished stories, but to both.

The words remained fractured, incomplete, based upon Agnes' memories and what she had heard from others, but from them Anneliese was able to construct an edifice that might, at least in part, be the truth.

When the train pulled out of Waroola, Dermot had thought he was on his way to a new life. By the time it reached its destination, he knew he'd been kidding himself; there were no new lives to be had. What he was doing, what he had always been doing, was running from himself. Fat chance.

He stopped first in Brisbane, mooched about the streets, ended up bumming a job on a freighter. One trip was enough. Not a man for the sea, he discovered. He skipped ship in Melbourne, made his way east by easy stages. On foot, mostly; job here, job there. He met Agnes on the road. She was not much more than a child, wide-eyed, fey, perhaps a little mad. Her dad had died, her mother gone; Agnes as alone in the world as he was. They decided to join their lonelinesses together, found it worked.

They wandered on.

Back on the road, Dermot thought. Where I was always meant to be. He had thought he would be troubled by memories of the places and people of the north, but was not. He never wrote. Life contracted to the day, the hour, the minute. The world was what they could see, nothing else.

They came to the forested ranges. He could remember nothing, yet somewhere beyond memory, a subterranean recollection awoke stealthily to life.

They found a track, went up and up. At the top was a house, high above a swooning valley of trees and air and plunging cliffs. There was a man — old, but still a man, dominant over all, visitors included. A woman, a few years younger, with watchful eyes, a closed and suspicious face.

It was a week before he discovered who they were.

There was no place for them here, with these old people. The gap between them was unbridgeable; his grandparents had expunged him from their lives years before.

Dermot and Agnes left early one morning, wandered on, going nowhere. Or everywhere. Days later, they fetched up at Noojee.

Dermot got labourer's work at the new power plant. It was a far cry from mustering cattle in the northern bush, but enough to put bread on the table. Later he changed his job, got back in the saddle for a forest grazier named Ellis.

Mid-February. A hot day with a blustery wind from the north. A stink of fire.

'You take care,' Agnes told him. Crossly, as though blaming him for the heat.

'Sure.'

He paid no heed. This time of year, there was always fire about. Bound to be; more and more the forest was being invaded by weekend block owners who burned off scrub and briars to clear their land. Tourists, too, who left billy fires to burn out untended.

Always a smudge of smoke in the air.

'I'll be right,' he told her.

A nasty, uncomfortable day, all the same. By ten o'clock, the mercury was up around the hundred, the wind had strengthened, there was a steady rain of ashes from fires somewhere over the northern horizon. There'd been a flare-up only a few days earlier, a hundred or so acres burned in a blaze that had died down only when a providential shower fell.

Maybe there had not been enough rain to put it out completely. Maybe it still smouldered, waiting for the hot wind.

The northerly strengthened through the morning. The stock was uneasy, tossing heads everywhere you looked. Hemmed in by timber, Dermot could not see far, only the tops of the trees tormented by the wind that was gusting at forty miles an hour and rising with every minute.

Now he was uneasy, too. The whole day, wind and all, seemed to tremble upon the brink of catastrophe.

A break in the trees led to a crest a couple of miles away. From there he would be able to see across the treetops to Warburton, twenty miles distant. If fire were heading this way, he would spot it from there.

He left the cattle to look after themselves, rode up the trail. He was halfway to the ridge when a blink of light shone along the crest. For a moment he did not realise what he was seeing, the first golden glitter of Armaggedon. Then a great gum exploded like Guy Fawkes and suddenly flames were everywhere, a wave of devastation coming down the slope amid the roar and crackle of exploding gum crowns, racing light-footed through the branches a hundred feet above the ground. The heat was enough to pucker eyeballs.

No time to think, to do anything. He had to get out at once, evade the clutching arms of flame that even now were reaching towards him through the scrub.

Dermot's mount was shying like a loony and small wonder. He spun it around so fast it went down on its haunches, then took off down the hill with the fire demons roaring at his back.

Dermot had always envied Sean his riding skills; the way he rode now would have put Sean or any other man to shame. Down the hill, no time to think of the cattle — they'd be long gone anyway — riding for his life, the heat swarming up the scale, the air full of smoke and smuts, the sky gone.

To his left a stand of trees withered, burst into a riot of flame. Between his knees Dermot felt the thrust and pull of muscles as the horse swerved. Another swerve as a fallen log licked flame in their path.

Come off, I'm dead.

He did not come off but sensed rather than saw that the fire was raging its way through the forest on either side of him, the whole world changed to a roaring pit of heat and smoke and flame.

He twisted in the saddle, looking back with frantic eyes. A curtain of fir blotted out the slope. Despite his speed, it was gaining on him. The very air blazed with heat.

He came out of the forest like Captain Thunderbolt, the Noojie settlement ahead of him. Blazing.

Somehow the fire had got there first. Dermot was cut off.

'Agnes!'

A despairing cry wrenched from lips blistered by heat. At least she would have had some notice, enough to get out in time. Nothing he could do, either way. He spun the terrified horse, seeking a way clear. Pillars of flame a hundred feet high surrounded him. There was no way out.

There was the creek, quarter of a mile away on the edge of the blazing township. If he could get there ...

He dug his heels into the horse's flanks, rode frantically for the water across the advancing front of flame.

Agnes was in the hut when old man Magilvray came running.

'Bushfire!'

He screeched the words at her, spraying spit and terror. 'Get out while you can!'

Was already on the move.

Her own scream followed him. 'Dermot's with the cattle. What about Dermot?'

For an instant Magilvray looked back. 'Dermot gotta take his chance. Hang around here, you'll burn up, too.'

And was gone, running pell-mell while flames roared skywards above the trees beyond the creek.

'Where ...?'

Too late. She was alone, watching with appalled eyes the cavalry charge of the fire. Magilvray was right. Stay here, she would burn with the house. She fled towards the only refuge, the creek's deepwater pool a hundred yards distant.

She made it by inches. Magilvray was there and a handful of others. Their faces were so blackened by smuts that at first she didn't recognise the Hudsons, a woodcutter and his family. She crouched in the water as the flames roared up to the bank. She took a deep breath, dragging heat and ash as well as air into her lungs, ducked her head beneath the surface. Had a blurred impression of flames arching high across the creek, leaping the water as the wind tore the fire from its moorings and flung it fifty, a hundred, two hundred yards into the forest on the far side.

A roar, diminishing. An endless patter of debris sifting down from a sky black with smoke and cinders. A searing heat that raised the temperature of the creek until Agnes thought they would all be boiled alive.

On either bank twigs and branches blazed in individual conflagrations, the flames contracting at length into a core of ash and glowing embers. Ruin, as far as they could see.

Twenty yards from the bank a tangled heap of blackened branches.

After a night in the creek, waiting for the ground to cool enough for them to walk upon it, Magilvray, Agnes and the Hudson family emerged from the water. In the aftermath of the fire they were cold, arms wrapped about their shivering bodies as they drifted like ghosts through a landscape of ghosts. With the trees gone, the sky seemed to rest upon their heads. Charred stumps patterned the slopes as far as they could see.

They discovered that the tangled heap of branches was in fact the unidentifiable remnants of a horse and man. Twenty yards from safety.

Agnes, responding to some unspeaking instinct, knew.

Forest, home, man. All gone.

Two days later, trudging alone through a forest where wisps of acrid smoke still clung to the devastated ground, Agnes set out to walk to the only sanctuary that remained.

Somehow, wits scrambled in her head by the fire, by Dermot's death, she found her way up a winding track into the high country. Found a horse fair at a settlement in the forest. Met a man, tall, massive-chested, with a tangled white beard and glittering eagle's eye. Her scrambled wits remembered him, hazily. When the time came she went with him without complaint.

Carmel has been dead for years, yet always Agnes hears her voice, the endless recitation of history and abuse with which, in her lifetime, she had bruised Agnes' ears:

I have seen the vision; the world will end not in fire, but water. There will be rain, months of rain, pouring from clouds that will not be emptied. The distant seas will rise and the rivers, drowning the land as in the days of the Nephilim, a great flood to drown the summits of even these high hills. Paddocks and trees will be gone, horses and farm animals and all wild beasts. Man himself will be gone.

Thus comes the Deluge.

The vision gives me the strength to endure the daily burdens that the Lord has laid upon me in this place, far from consolation.

It is a harsh land; in winter the snow and wind are cruel, setting fangs of ice deep within the bones of those who must endure them. Few can. Families drift into the district, planning to make a go of it, but only a handful live out the first winter. With the spring, even they are gone. You need to be flint to survive here, I am married to a man of flint and have learned from him how to endure.

My husband, with his bull-like body, is a man of the soil with all the passions of the soil, a voice to quell the tempest. Were it not sacrilege, I would swear that when he stands four-square upon the earth these very mountains quake beneath his weight. He holds all — land, animals, myself — in hands that from the first filled me with loathing and a queer, sick fascination that I was helpless to subdue.

On our wedding night, they wrenched the garments from my back. I, shrinking, angry at God that He should permit me to be so abused, the anger a sin for which I have ever since made daily penance. I am not yet forgiven, must wait for that as I have had to wait for all things, all my life.

The hands were huge, clad with black hairs like wire; they handled me like the property I had become. I clenched my knees together, not in fear but anger. I knew it would avail me nothing but, by making him fight for what he had bought — three horses to my father, a keg of spirits of which he himself drank most, a shilling to the priest, that mewling man — I hoped to deny him his pleasure, at least.

I failed, as I have failed in my dealings with Jack Riordan all my life. He prised apart my legs with his great knees, his weight crushed me, I lay with frozen face and body awaiting the assault. Which, when it came, split me with its ferocity, its heat. I bit my lip, denying not pain or indignity but the wave of pleasure that arose unbidden within my treacherous body.

I would not let him see it; in my secret depths I was happy that my frigidity troubled him.

'It is your duty, girl,' he told me.

So it is, and my duty I shall perform. Nowhere in the teachings is there any word of pleasure. By denying that to us both, I work my revenge on a life that has treated me so.

God himself cannot deny that I have done my duty.

Two children born in the suffering that is woman's lot, in this kingdom of icy winds and loneliness. Both lost to me. A grandchild conceived in lust, born in pain and death, also lost. Before Dermot left, I read his future in his face: a life of sorrow; a death alone in torment and in fear.

The Lord's will be done.

I have endured much.

The African woman who beguiled my son, plunging him and all of us into the steaming vats of hell. Could she imagine I did not know what was happening in my own house?

I smelt my husband on her, that animal stench of rut and heat that I have such reason to know. I could see from the lazy glow in her eyes how he had pleasured her. My son's father. To abomination there is no end.

They went and I was thankful. Routine, my saviour, returned.

Years later, my grandson returned. I did not know him, felt nothing. With him was a young woman. This family is cursed by its appetites. They stayed only briefly. After they had gone, I returned once again to the loneliness that I had learned to welcome.

After the devastation of the great fire, my husband went to a horse fair over the mountain. When he returned, he brought with him the same woman who had come here with Dermot. The fire had scattered her brains, as it did to many. I had forgotten her name, but eventually persuaded her to tell me. Agnes. She thought she was seventeen years old. She could not tell me what had happened, only that Dermot was gone. Burned up in the fire, I suppose.

Agnes had become simple, her head filled with the flutter of birds' wings. I have read somewhere that the simple person is closest to God, in which case the wings might have been those of angels. St Agnes was the saint of chastity, but this one's body was not the body of a saint.

Lush as grass in spring, the hollows and hills, the well to drown a man's senses.

She would walk half-naked about the house, the ivory glint of breast and thigh, yet demurely, completely unashamed.

I shut my eyes to her body, the heat in my husband's face. He was old, yet still lustful. I told myself it was another burden laid upon me by God. I would accept it with humility, I would spread myself before the Lord as Agnes spread herself before my husband. The passion of my submission drowned her cries, the triumphant bull-bellow of the man savouring his animal pleasure.

What he did was wickedness, and the Lord smote him, bringing down the evildoer.

He had been down the valley to sell horses. A man there saw the mob he brought in and laid claim to one of them. My husband laughed but the man ran to the constable, who had had trouble from Jack Riordan in the past.

The troopers came after him and he got away only by riding through their line, the bullets whistling about his ears. He rode up here to safety. None of them dared follow; we could have held off an army and would, put to the test. Escape or not, he brought with him the seeds of his own destruction.

That night he was taken by a seizure of the brain. Blood ran from his mouth and his eyes rolled up. I ran to him, as was my duty, but there was nothing I could do. By morning he was dead. I washed the body while Agnes cowered in a corner, calling to the Lord in terror. I silenced her, slapping her until she fell, crawling away from me, moaning.

'Listen to me, Agnes.'

To begin with, she would not, forcing me to chastise her again. Eventually, when she was silent, I told her what we would do.

It took two days for the troopers to muster sufficient courage to come up here after him. I met them at the door, rifle in hand.

Trooper Flanagan, as Irish as myself, eyed it. 'Not thinking of using it, missus?'

'If you're come for my husband,' I told him, 'You're too late.'

'Where is he?'

'How should I be knowing where he is? He rode out of here two days gone and I've seen neither hair nor hide of him since.'

'Questions needing to be asked,' said he. 'About horses.'

I stared him down. 'Ask him yourself about that.'

'So I shall, missus, so I shall, you've Bob Flanagan's word for that. As soon as we catch up with him.' He smoothed his moustache with his finger, eyes prowling over my face. 'You'll not object if we look around?'

'Look as much as you like. You'll not be finding him here.'

Nor did they. They found the girl in the shed but got nothing out of her; she was too frightened of me for that.

When Flanagan came back to the house, I could see that he was intrigued by the girl's presence. 'Who is she?'

'A poor wight we took out of pity,' I told him. 'She helps me about the place.'

I could see he had his own thoughts about that. 'When your husband comes back, tell him I want a word with him.'

'I shall not. You want him, tell him so yourself.'

After I'd seen Flanagan's back, I went into the forest, to the place where we had buried my husband. I stared down at the grave. I told him, 'The Lord has delivered you into my hand at last. Forty years I have been your prisoner. Now you are mine, as the girl is mine. I am the instrument of God. I shall rain down sulphur upon her as did the Lord in the days of Sodom. In tormenting her I shall earn forgiveness for you and for herself. In her suffering I too shall suffer and so wipe away the sins that have stained my heart also.'

I went back to the house. The door to the shed was open but the girl was still inside, frightened of disobeying me. I had thought to drive her into the forest, to live or die as the Lord wished, but now I changed my mind. I was getting old. It was time for me to take things easy at last. Agnes would stay here and do the work that had to be done. She would eat what I chose to give her. Her looks would fade, but we would be company for each other. When the mood took me, I would lead her to my husband's grave. There I would strip her naked, so that he could see the body that he once enjoyed and that now was mine. All this place mine at last. Even the ice and the wind would be mine.

The two of us will stay here until I die. From me she will learn the mortification of the flesh that is the true road to salvation. When I am dead, she will weep for me, for I shall have been the rod to sustain her in the wilderness and without me she will surely perish.

As for the police ... I shall not give them the satisfaction of knowing their search is over.

The Lord's will be done.

Both circles rounded at last, Anneliese agreed to go on. They left Agnes to her silence, the stillness of the wind, and travelled west.

After several weeks on the road, they arrived at the rotting house, the yard overgrown with weeds, that became their home.

A few years later, Archer's father died and left him a little money. Enough to survive in poverty, to kindle the grandiose flames that were to illuminate his imagination ever afterwards. Anneliese had been seventy, but not old. Now she grew old amid the empty clatter of Archer's dreams.

Rëen and Archer had one child, Tamsin. In her heart, Anneliese knew that the child would be the answer to her secret hopes.

THIRTY-ONE

Anna had been back in Australia a week when, to her astonishment, she was invited to a reception at the South African High Commission.

She had a million things on her desk — extraordinary how they piled up as soon as your back was turned — and her first impulse was to refuse. In the end she changed her mind, her instinct telling her that it might be important.

It was the usual toffee affair: one or two people she knew, half a hundred more she didn't, most of them obvious members of the diplomatic cocktail circus. She wondered why she'd come. Then the High Commissioner, a distinguished-looking Afrikaner of the old school, grey-haired, imposing moustache, buttonholed her and she knew.

'I understand you have acquired an interest in a wine farm in the Cape?'

'Your Excellency is well informed.'

'I like to keep in touch.'

'In which case you will know that all I've done is take over the debt. I have no interest in the property as such.'

The Commissioner chewed his moustache along with the notion that she could control the debt but not the property. 'The wine industry is of great importance to the new South Africa. If we are to compete successfully in world markets, our wines have to be up to international standards. Some estates are going to need a great deal of capital. More, I would say, than they will be able to raise locally.'

Anna knew when to say nothing; she said nothing now.

'Are you planning to expand *Oudekraal*?'

'You will have to ask its owner.'

The Commissioner played with his wine glass, smiling benignly. But watching.

'There are those in the new South Africa, men of influence, who hold certain views regarding the distribution of land. They believe that justice will best be served if certain properties are re-allocated. For the benefit of the community, you understand. There has been special mention of farms that lack adequate capital resources.'

'Even where they produce award-winning wines?'

He ignored the question, pursuing his own train of thought.

'At present there are two words on people's lips. Expansion and centralisation.'

'Meaning what?'

'Expansion means that the industry has the potential to become a major hard-currency earner for the country. Naturally, it must grow if it is to meet the demands of the overseas market.'

'And centralisation?'

'There are those who feel that such expansion should be monitored centrally. To ensure the effective allocation of capital resources, you understand.'

'Surely a man should be free to run his property as he likes?'

It was a principle that the Commissioner was unwilling to concede. 'The interests of the State must always come first.'

Anna selected an olive from a tray offered by a white-uniformed steward. She nibbled thoughtfully until he was out of earshot.

'Is this discussion official?'

A frosty smile. 'Extremely unofficial.'

'Then why are we having it?'

'I understand that your ex-husband has expressed an interest in acquiring *Oudekraal*.'

She smiled. 'I never know where these rumours come from.'

'I have known Pieter Wolmarans all my life,' the Commissioner said.

'In which case you also know that Pieter kicked him out.'

'Then, perhaps. But my information is that Mr Harcourt is still interested in acquiring the property. That he has gone so far as to retain a land agent to assist him.'

'That won't help him if Pieter isn't willing to sell.'

'Those who support the principle of centralisation are aware that a high level of expertise is needed to run the industry successfully,' the Commissioner told her.

'There are plenty of experts in South Africa.'

'Not all with the capital resources that will be needed. Besides, to the people I mentioned, a foreigner might be more acceptable politically than a South African. Mr Harcourt is well known for his involvement in the international wine industry. To those people he might seem a logical choice.'

Anna laughed scornfully. 'Impossible!'

But it was not. Bizarre, perhaps — Mostyn had never been an advocate of black South Africa — but not impossible.

The Commissioner's jaws worked again on his moustache. 'I find that, in certain matters, our leaders can be surprisingly pragmatic. Which is praiseworthy, of course.'

'If you know Pieter Wolmarans, you also know that there is no way he will agree to give up his land.'

'Of course not. Given the choice.'

Anna stared. 'What does that mean?'

'If Mr Harcourt were approached, he would be in a position to name his price.'

Anna stared. If his price were *Oudekraal* ...

Bloody hell.

The Commissioner gave her a diplomat's smile, carefully crafted. 'I have been monopolising you too long. I had better talk to some of my other guests.'

And was gone, leaving Anna to her thoughts. Which troubled her, powerfully.

At the end of the reception, the Commissioner found her again.

'I enjoyed our chat,' he said.

'Perhaps we can repeat it some time.'

'With my successor, perhaps. I am being recalled.'

'I am sorry to hear it.'

He shrugged. 'The new South Africa ...'

The phrase sounded distinctly less enthusiastic than before. 'I understand you have already met my replacement.'

She knew at once, her veins tightening, but would acknowledge nothing.

'Adam Shongwe has an interesting background —'

'Is he here tonight?'

Her eyes wanted to hunt the room. With difficulty she restrained them. With these diplomats, you could never be sure how much they knew.

He said, 'He does not arrive until tomorrow.'

She gave him her most disciplined smile. 'I look forward to meeting him.'

He turned away. Paused.

'Incidentally —'

'Yes?'

'You know that Mr Harcourt is in South Africa at the moment?'

Unsure when the reception had been scheduled to end, Anna had booked into a hotel for the night. Now, as a taxi carried her swiftly through the silent streets, she thought about what she had been told.

The news about Adam Shongwe had startled her, awakening all the memories, but it was a different world now for both of them; there was no reason to suppose his arrival in Australia would affect her in any way.

Perhaps, because of her commitment to *Oudekraal*, she might need to be in touch with his office from time to time, but he was likely to have far more pressing issues on his plate than the affairs of one small and relatively insignificant wine farm. It was probable that they would have nothing to do with each other at all.

What the Commissioner had told her about Mostyn was far more important. She had thought she had Mostyn licked, that by taking over the *Oudekraal* loans she had put him out of contention. Now she was less sure. He had been in the business for years longer than she had, had forgotten more tricks than she would ever know.

She had taken him to the cleaners over the divorce; it was entirely in character for him to want to get his own back. She had told him herself how much *Oudekraal* meant to her; by grabbing it from under her nose, he would revenge himself on both Pieter Wolmarans and herself and increase his portfolio of vineyard investments at the same time.

That's why he's in South Africa, she thought. I can smell it a mile off. I only wish I knew how he was planning to go about it, that's all.

She had the uneasy feeling that, by the time she found out, it might be too late.

Mostyn had phoned Myburgh in Stellenbosch. The fool had been scared stiff because he had failed to talk Wolmarans into selling *Oudekraal*. Mostyn had never believed that the direct approach had much chance of success. No one knew better than he what a stubborn bastard Wolmarans was. It had been worth a try — the man was older now, after all, and perhaps more amenable — but he had been neither surprised nor discouraged when it had failed. Even the attempt to buy up the *Oudekraal* loans had been little more than a ploy. He had not expected Anna to leap in, the way she had, but it certainly hadn't troubled him. On the contrary; it had left her with that much less cash to play with. No, Mostyn remained confident; there were more ways than one to skin a cat, and he had come up with a good one.

Not that he was about to tell Myburgh that. Instead, he had brushed aside the broker's apologies, contemptuously, and spelt out what he wanted him to do.

'And try not to fuck up this time . . .'

Never let people forget who's boss; it was one of his favourite maxims.

Fawning, eager to please, Myburgh had come back to him the same day. The following evening Mostyn had cut short a meeting in Perth to board South African Airways flight 281 to Johannesburg.

There was an official car waiting when he touched down at Jan Smuts airport. An hour later, he was in Pretoria.

He stood on the balcony that ran along the front of the Union Building, looking southwards across the sprawl of the city to the hills on the far side. On the skyline an obelisk stuck up like a square tooth.

'The Voortrekker Monument.' The Minister's smile did not quite conceal his hatred. 'Commemorating what the Boers call their great trek into Africa. One day we shall dynamite it, but not yet. The time is not right.'

Nor would it be until the State President was gone, but Mandela was old and the day of vengeance could be tomorrow. It was one of many reasons why Mostyn had steered clear of putting money into South Africa. The reason he was here now was not because he had changed his ideas about black Africa but because his nose could smell offal in the wind. He had begun with his sights set on *Oudekraal*, but things had gone far beyond that. Why be content with a solitary carcass when the whole herd was up for grabs? If he could get the Minister to see things his way, the pickings would be enormous.

Although it was still good to know that *Oudekraal* would be part of the deal. Better than good; delightful. He gloated, imagining Anna's face when she heard the news. I said I'd fix her if she messed with me. Pull this off, and she'll know I damn well meant it.

The thought was as warming as a log fire in winter. Smiling cheerfully, he followed the Minister into the air-conditioned office and got down to business.

Chris Tembe was Minister for Agricultural Industries in the South African government. The word was that he was always in the market for deals, provided they were the right sort of deal, and Mostyn had flown to South Africa especially to meet him.

'No one else,' he had instructed Myburgh. 'Only Tembe. Got it?'

Myburgh had warned that it might be impossible; the Minister had the reputation of being vehemently anti-white. Mostyn had refused to listen to his anxious bleating; in business there was always a gulf between public rhetoric and private pragmatism. Never mind the race nonsense; Tembe knew which side his bread was buttered, and Mostyn was there to spread it for him. Nothing else mattered.

'What brings you to Azania, Mr Harcourt?'

South Africa was still its official name, but more and more hardliners were calling it Azania. By using the name now, Tembe was sending his visitor a message and trying to confuse him at the same time, but Mostyn had been in this situation a hundred times and was less easily confused than the Minister thought.

'Wealth,' he said, 'and its redistribution.'

One of the main tenets of the government's policy was the redistribution of the nation's wealth from white hands into deserving black ones. Some of which were more deserving than others, of course.

Tembe waited, dark eyes watchful.

'Taxation is one method. Nationalisation and forced takeover of assets is another. Mugging is a third —'

Tembe interrupted at once. 'Mugging is not government policy.'

'Of course not.'

It was happening on an ever-increasing scale, and they both knew it. Knew, too, that the government was doing nothing to stop it.

'The trouble with all these methods is they tend to frighten away the foreign investors that Azania' — try that one for size, he thought, '— needs so desperately.'

'We are aware of all this.' The Minister's tone asked why Mostyn was wasting his time. 'What, specifically, are your proposals?'

Their eyes met. 'Specifically, to suggest another method that will be equally effective, as well as more acceptable to overseas opinion.'

'Why should we care about overseas opinion?'

What a jerk. 'Because that is where your investment capital comes from.' And left it for him to pick up or not, as he chose.

'Go on.'

'I have a proposal relating to the South African wine industry. I think you'll like it.'

Tracy buzzed Anna. She said, 'Mr Wolmarans on the phone from South Africa.'

Frowning, Anna picked up the handset. 'What is it, Pieter?'

He was upset, barely coherent. He had received a visit, he told her. A deputation from the local branch of the African National Congress.

'They intend to take over *Oudekraal*.'

'What!'

'They say they will be buying it, but it's really confiscation.'

'How much are they offering?'

'A million rand. The house alone is worth twice as much —'

'Extortion?'

'Certainly. But it's not just a local man trying to make a name for himself. They had a piece of paper from the Ministry. This is official.'

'What did the paper say?'

'Some nonsense about people without natural heirs

having their assets stolen by the state: reallocation, they called it. Something about the need to consolidate the industry.'

'Do you have any choice in the matter?'

'Certainly. The way it looks, I can sell *Oudekraal* or have it confiscated.'

'Are you telling me it's government *policy*?'

'There has been talk of a shake-up in the industry, more government control, that sort of thing. Nothing as extreme as this. Whether it's official policy I have no idea.'

'What did you do?'

'I kicked them off my land, double damn quick, but I doubt I've seen the last of them.'

'Has anyone else received the same letter?'

'Not that I've heard.'

'What can I do from here?'

'The papers say your ex-husband has been holding talks in Pretoria.' She heard his hesitation. 'I wondered if he might be behind it.'

A surge of blood warmed her temples. 'I have no idea, but I'll certainly find out. I'll make some enquiries and come back to you.'

She cradled the phone and sat at her desk, thinking furiously. Mostyn's first move had been to try and grab the loans. She had blocked that. Now this. He had to be behind it; it had his fingerprints all over it.

She got Tracy to make some enquiries; found, sure enough, that Mostyn was still out of the country.

'I couldn't get them to tell me where he was.'

'I know that already.'

She made a phone call, got the appointment she wanted. She cancelled the rest of the day's meetings — *this is getting to be a habit* — and flew to Canberra.

The new High Commissioner's aura of physical power had not diminished since she had seen him last. The smile that glimmered briefly in the depths of his black eyes showed he had not forgotten her, either.

'Mrs Harcourt. An unexpected pleasure. What can I do for you?'

His manner was smooth and polished, where in the old days he had been as harsh as lye. Perhaps the need for harshness has passed, she thought. I hope he hasn't lost the knack; it's his harshness I shall be needing, now.

She explained. 'I know redistribution of wealth is official government policy, but —'

'The first I've heard of anything like this.' He frowned. 'I shall make a few phone calls. Come back at twelve. We shall have some lunch, and I shall tell you what I've found out.'

They ate in the private dining room at the High Commission. Silver service and all the trimmings.

'A far cry from Guguletu,' he said.

'I don't recall we had time to eat on that occasion.' Anna looked at the menu card with the South African crest. '*Spyskaart*. You still use Afrikaans, then.'

'For the present.'

'What do you have to tell me?'

'I'm waiting for a phone call. It is four o'clock in the morning in South Africa. Things take a little longer.'

While they waited they ate, chatting about this and that.

'I hear you had thought about going back into politics,' Shongwe said.

Had thought ... Anna was startled; the Premier's offer had been confidential, after all, as her refusal had been.

'You are remarkably well informed.'

'May I ask why you turned it down?'
'All that aggravation ... For what?'
'Status. Money. Power.'
'They mean nothing.'
'They would to most people.'
'Power you can use, perhaps. But for its own sake? Not to me.'
'And that is important? That what you do should be worthwhile?'
'Of course. I want more from life than money.'
'Is that why you involve yourself so much in social issues?'

It seemed incredible that he should have taken the trouble to find out these things.

'Perhaps.'

A waiter topped up her glass. She checked the label.

'Not *Oudekraal*,' she said, smiling.

'Do you want me to see if we have some?'

'It doesn't matter.'

A far cry from Guguletu, indeed, yet the essentials were the same; still the magnetism, the potent aura of physical power.

She said, 'You haven't changed.'

'I'm disappointed you think so.' He opened his jacket. 'Huntsman of Saville Row. I don't remember wearing anything like this in the old days.'

He had worn a T-shirt, the muscled arms emerging smoothly from the tight sleeves.

'I meant you, not your suit.'

'Clothing maketh man.'

'Not clothing. Manners.'

A dark smile on the dark face. 'Mine have always been bad. As you no doubt remember.'

'You had your moments.'

In one respect he was certainly different. In those days he would not have traded aphorisms with her. Clearly the diplomat had emerged from the chrysalis of the freedom fighter, yet Anna sensed that underneath was the same man she had known fifteen years before.

Another image: face contorted, hair flying, riding, riding in the cry-filled night. Seeking escape, that dark and unattainable goal.

The wineglass rang as she replaced it on the table.

A uniformed flunky came and whispered in the High Commissioner's ear. Shongwe nodded, looked at Anna.

'Pretoria,' he said.

He walked to the end of the room and took the phone. Anna tried to eavesdrop, but could distinguish no words in the soft rumble of his voice.

At last he returned to his place and sat down. 'It is true,' he said. 'The Minister has issued a directive.'

'Minister?'

'Tembe. In charge of agriculture.' He looked at her. 'It seems your ex-husband went to see him.'

I knew it.

'What happened?'

'There is a feeling that South Africa needs an expert to control the wine industry.'

'A Commissar?'

A smile tweaked the dark lips. 'If you like. Mr Harcourt's name has been mentioned. Still responsible to a minister, of course, but with a lot of power behind the scenes.' Adam frowned. 'That would have been enough for most men but not, apparently, for him.'

'What's he done?' Anna wondered, hoping for the worst.

'It seems he's jumped the gun. My information is that he has suggested forming a company to take over properties where there was no member of the immediate family to inherit.'

'Theft.'

'Redistribution of wealth,' he corrected her. 'Which, as you said, is government policy. With no one any the worse.'

'I would be willing to debate that,' she said. 'You say they're talking of forming a company. Who are the shareholders?'

'My informant did not know. Until it actually happens, you understand, there is nothing on file. But the wine industry is highly technical, so at least one would need access to the necessary expertise.'

'Mostyn has plenty of that,' she said bitterly. 'What else would they need?'

'Someone to represent the interests of those to whom the wealth is to be redistributed.'

'Tembe?'

'That is a most improper suggestion.'

'The truth.'

'Improper, none the less.' He stood. 'Leave it with me. I'll see what I can do.'

She put out her hand, letting it rest for the tiniest fraction of a second on the silk-smooth African skin. 'Do you really think you can do anything?'

He hesitated. 'I'm not sure.'

'Then I shall have to do something myself. *Oudekraal* owes me a lot of money. The agreement says I can convert the loan into shares whenever I want. Once the business is in my name, they won't be able to touch it.'

He looked dubious. 'Let me throw that at the legal boys. See what they think.'

They went to his office, where Shongwe spoke briefly on the phone. When he put down the receiver, his expression was bleak. 'They say you can't.'

'Why not?'

'You're a non-resident. Reserve Bank approval would be necessary. You would be most unlikely to get it, in the circumstances.'

'Then I reclaim my loan —'

'You should not have been permitted to make the loan in the first place. An oversight, perhaps, but the fact remains that it was illegal. They say you have no claim against the company at all.'

Shongwe escorted Anna courteously to the High Commissioner's private entrance, stood watching until she had driven away. He went back to his office and sat behind his desk, dark eyes focused not on the elegant trappings of the silent room but on the opportunities that had opened so unexpectedly before him.

Chris Tembe was an old enemy, had outmanoeuvred him when the ministries were being allocated. Tembe had ended up with Agriculture, Adam with Canberra. He liked what he had seen of Australia but, in the scheme of South African politics, it was undeniably second best. Tembe had real power, whereas he had only influence. Now, perhaps, there might be a chance to change that.

He thought of the woman who had just left him. It was the second time she had done him a favour, even if this time she hadn't realised it. She has put the gun in my hand, he told himself, with Tembe in the sights. I always hoped his greed would trip him up; now it has. All I have to do is press the trigger. I shall need to be careful, though. He has friends in high places. It would be good to have another card up my sleeve. If I decide to fire the gun, I had better be very sure I don't miss.

THIRTY-TWO

Anna kept in touch with Pieter Wolmarans but for the moment could do no more; things were out of her hands. The temptation to badger Adam Shongwe was ferocious but she would not allow it to overwhelm her. She would hear when he had something to tell her. These things took time; nagging would not help and might do a great deal of harm. So she reined in her impatience and, as far as possible, got on with her life.

She had phoned Mark as soon as she got back to Sydney to let him know what had happened. After Pieter Wolmarans's frantic phone call, she did so again; already it seemed natural to turn to him for help and consolation, for that feeling of friendship that she had sensed so strongly during their lunch together. She did not expect him to come up with any miracle cures nor did he, but keeping in touch gave them the excuse they needed to start seeing each other again. They did not need excuses for long.

For a second time, Mark became part of her life. No fireworks; a cautious progression from lunch to dinner, from meeting in the company of others to meeting alone. Later still, to being alone when surrounded by others.

They became friends, then more than friends.

Neither said or did anything that might endanger the equilibrium of their togetherness. Their memories were still tender; they had learned to value what they had, to allow it to develop at its own pace, to permit nothing to damage what it seemed they had succeeded in recapturing from the past.

One weekend they were caught by a sudden squall, found shelter in the entrance to the Concert Hall. They shook off raindrops, looked at the bills announcing a concert.

'Starts in half an hour,' Mark said. 'A string quartet. Fancy it?'

'Not my line.'

'Give it a go.'

'There may not be any seats.'

There were. They found their places, sat amid a murmuring surf of voices. Silence punctuated briefly by applause. The music began.

Anna had never been interested in music, had agreed now only because Mark had asked. She tried to make sense out of what she was hearing, found it hard going.

At the interval, Mark asked what she thought.

'Okay. I suppose.'

'Want to leave?'

Some inner stubborness would not let her admit defeat. 'I'll stick it out.'

The second half was better. She looked at the programme. Dvořák's American quartet. She had never felt any relationship between herself and music but now the mingled serenity and yearning of the slow movement sent a message directly to her heart. What the message was she could not be sure, only that it was there.

'Better,' she said as they left.

It was dark. They ate at a restaurant they knew, shared a bottle of wine, sat staring at each other across the table. She was surprised by the intensity of her feelings. 'Desire is alive and well,' she said, amazing herself.

'I'm glad.'

'The question is what we do about it.'

His smile was so faint that it barely creased his lips.

'Oscar Wilde said the only way to overcome temptation was to give in to it.'

Thoughtfully she said, 'I've always admired Oscar Wilde.'

'Absolute genius,' he agreed.

Any minute now, I'm going to make a fool of myself, she thought. Found she did not care. 'What say we put his theory to the test?'

The flippant exchange glittered, inconsequential as fireworks.

'We'll never find out if we don't,' he said, laughing.

She opened her mouth to share his laugh, found suddenly that she could not. Instead was repelled by this game they were playing. If they were serious about the relationship, they should say so. If not ... The anguish of yet another failure was too terrible to bear. With shaking fingers she held her glass tightly and was silent.

'What's the matter?'

A look of concern as he sensed something of her feelings, yet she saw that he did not fully understand, was baffled by her change of mood. She could not put into words how she felt, was furious with herself, with the doubts that had suddenly engulfed her. If the two of them were going anywhere, they had to take the next step. Without it, there could be no hope for them at all. Yet terror remained.

As though she could control doubt by movement, she stood abruptly. Astonished, he did the same. She tried to walk past him towards the door but staggered, blundering against him.

He grabbed her hand. 'We don't have to do anything. If we don't want.'

His appeal tore her. 'Please,' she begged. 'Please ...'

She waited by the door while he settled the bill. Eyes watched; Mark, the waiter, other diners. Nerves like hot wires skewered her flesh.

I am fine ...

She had to force herself not to scream the words into the speculative faces. Mark came towards her. She yanked open the door and staggered, almost running, into the street.

He caught up with her outside. 'Whatever's wrong?'

She shook her head furiously, willing the tears not to fall. 'Nothing's wrong, nothing.'

She turned and walked away down the hill towards the harbour. She found herself walking faster and faster until she was close to running, her high heels skidding on the steep pavement. She was gasping, could barely breathe at all. The warm air was stagnant, as sticky as glue. Thank God that in the inner city you were never far from water. She longed so much for its coolness, the breath of wind that, even on the hottest nights, came intermittently out of the darkness.

At the bottom of the hill, she reached it at last. She could hear the pounding of her heart as she stood between two warehouses, their blank walls blocking the glitter of the city's lights. From the jetty before her, silver beneath a sickle moon, the harbour stretched away. There was indeed a breeze; its breath cooled her skin, calmed her tormented mind.

She was aware of Mark beside her. He radiated concern, but said nothing. She was grateful, both for his presence and his silence. She breathed deeply, drawing into her lungs the salty coolness of breeze and water. She turned to him, tried to smile. 'Sorry about that.'

He shrugged it away.

She wanted to explain how frightened she was that things might once again go wrong between them. The words trembled, but she held them back. She had to make up her own mind.

'I was warm,' she apologised, 'but I'm better now.'

She hoped that he might understand her feelings; might even share them, perhaps, but could not be sure. Like herself, he was trapped in a conspiracy of silence.

They were always so polite with each other.

Nothing's wrong, nothing ...

Sorry about that ...

I was warm, but I'm better now ...

Polite phrases, signifying nothing. She felt herself drowning in a rising tide of hysteria. Does it always have to be like this? she demanded, silently. Are our hearts never to be naked to each other?

She could no longer bear the stilted silences, the words devoid of feeling behind which they hid. Emotion was a scream rising, deafeningly, to overwhelm her.

She told herself that this was what love was, the willingness to be naked before each other, in trust. I trust him, I do, but no one can forget the past. Lack of trust, of nurturing, destroyed us before. Surely it cannot happen again? Surely we have learned from our mistakes? Oh God, I am so frightened.

Frightened or not, she saw that they had to take the next step at once. Not to do so would be failure, from which the relationship would never recover.

She seized his hand, drew him to her, kissed him passionately. There was no one to watch; she would not have cared had there been ten thousand.

Her heart was pounding in terror but she forced herself to smile, tasting his lips on her own. 'Come,' she said.

Lying in darkness, in the moments before Mark came to her, Anna went over the steps that had led to this moment. The meal, the brittle laughter, the sudden avalanche of doubt. A taxi had brought them to his apartment overlooking Circular Quay. Without a word they had taken it for granted that was where they were going; Anna's house was too far, peopled by too many discordant memories.

Perhaps I shall sell it, she thought. If ... But would not permit herself to consider ifs, or the future.

For the whole journey she had sat, half-lying, while Mark cocooned her in gentle words. Now that taxi drivers had learned to cut themselves off from their passengers they had been private, almost secret in the darkness; he talked softly about nothing, kissing her tenderly before speaking again, everything so gentle that she felt herself rocked in a silken cradle of words and acceptance and hope, experienced again the yearning fulfilment of the music they had heard that afternoon.

Now, lying in the dark, she remembered nothing of what Mark had said, only the texture of the tender words. That was all that mattered, that she should understand with both love and fear the language he had spoken, that henceforth they would speak together.

A circle restored, she thought. A circle representing truth. The lost years mattered nothing now. She remembered her great-grandmother at the very end of her life, how in Anneliese's case the circle had not been closed, how her last thoughts had been of the home from which she had been driven all those years before.

From her Anna had learnt something of what truth meant, the sacrifices that truth demands. Pray God I am never put to such a test, she thought.

At the end of her long road at last, Anneliese van der Merwe, born Anneliese Wolmarans, for sixty-six years known to the world as Anneliese Riordan, was dying.

She had fought and fought, now had decided to fight no longer. It was her decision; she did not yield weakly to death but accepted it, calmly, as an equal. When she had been young, the horizons of her life had seemed boundless, filled with hope and glory and challenge. Over the years they had contracted, little by little, until all that now remained was the cessation of all things that must come soon.

For the little time that was left, as long as her brain remained alert, it was important to remember all that had happened in her life.

Because when death takes me, she thought, all the people and events that have made up my existence will cease also. It will be peaceful, like visiting friends. Or enemies. Her body had gone beyond the ability to smile, yet in her brain a smile flowered, resolute, derisive, unafraid. By all means, let me not forget my enemies.

All the buildings I have known. *Oudekraal* and *Uitkyk*. Jack Riordan's wooden house in the cold ranges; even now I can feel those splintery boards under my backside. The sugar plantation called Huntingdon. Paradise Downs. Finally this rotting house with the rags and tatters of my family about me; I, dying in the midst, as rotten as the house. The buildings, the thousands of nights on the road. A lifetime of sleeping, of lying awake. Of joy and regret, sorrow and anger. For what purpose? All roads end in death. What can joy or anger do about that?

The people, too. Dominic, so much a man in Africa, yet of little substance after he had returned to his father's shadow. Jack Riordan; that devil. Like none before or since, he had the power to draw the marrow from my bones. I was right to leave, yet the imprint of his body remains after all these years. I never loved him, hated him too much for that, but as a man of power he had my respect. Yes, indeed.

Sean is his. Never would I admit it to a living soul, I cannot prove it even to myself, but I know. Sean, my blessing and my curse. He chewed up and spat out everyone who came in contact with him. Dermot, Sylvia, Scott.

Dermot took refuge in flight, and died. There is peace in that knowledge, a cure for what had been a festering sore in my life.

Sylvia, who thought to find security by raising barriers against the world — how clearly I could read her — but ended like the rest, broken on the iron wheel of Sean's will.

Even Scott Macdonald became his victim. Scott was a hard man but, after his son died, something died in him, too. Before the end, Scott had become Sean's dog.

I did what I could; after Dominic's death, we came to each other in our loneliness. We found warmth without fire, consolation without enrichment. When, a year or two ago, I heard that a stroke had carried him off, I felt none of the desolation I had known after Dominic's death.

Dominic, whom I had threatened to abandon so many times, who in the end, through my neglect, abandoned me. After his death, I understood how full our existence together had been, rich with the juices of life. After Dominic, after Dermot, there remained only the winnowed husk of my being.

Husk or not, I was the one person Sean could not break. I had loved him more than any other and, before the end, came to hate him with equal fervour. Sean needed to destroy in order to fulfil his own destiny. I would not let him destroy me. In time he came to hate me, too, because of it.

I seldom think of my first husband, that blank page in my memory. As for Stoffel and Amalie ... There are days when I hear their voices, a silent calling without words. I shall see them soon enough, if what the preachers tell us is true. I have always doubted, but am content to wait, having no choice.

Sean's daughter was as weakened as the rest by that ruthless man. All her life she has been ineffectual, fluttering, a butterfly with a broken wing. I should not despise her, but cannot help it; I have always despised weakness, in myself and in others. As a child she was never beautiful — you need strength for that — but pretty, like a picture on a chocolate box. I called her Rëen, as I have said. To everyone else she was Margaret. Call her what you will.

She was born to be a victim. Her solitary act of rebellion was to flee from a brutal father into the arms of the weakest man in the Territory. Archer Fitzgerald, the eternal passer-by, a head rattling with dreams, devoid of the slightest ability or even inclination to put them into practice. Who in failure, eternally renewed, embraced the bottle, like so many of his kind. In drink found visions of splendour to bewitch himself.

If Margaret was born to be a slave of life, Archer has become the slave of drink and vanity. A man — if that is what he is — of petulant rages, of tears. To this have the Wolmarans come.

Almagtige God, thank you for Tamsin. This child, the last of my blood, will do what must be done. She must;

certainly I cannot. I feel the steady dissolution of the flesh, even as my thoughts burn like coals.

Tamsin is the one who will bring me back to *Oudekraal*.

My spirit must return to the mountains of the Cape. It is too hot here; in those parts the snows lie late and, in winter, the cold strikes your flesh like a brand. The morning sun casts the mountain's shadow across the vines. They are glossy green in summer, red as blood in autumn. I shall be at peace in that cold valley. This must happen, but how can it, while my body lies in another place? My thoughts whirl frantically, the sheet that imprisons my worn-out flesh clammy with anguish.

Tamsin will do what must be done. Dermot could never have managed it. Sean had the strength but not the inclination; everything Sean has ever done has been for Sean, no one else. I pitied that poor wife of his; a fine time he gave her. She's gone too, now, all her worrying over, although she's the sort who will worry even in Paradise. Another one with no strength. What's the matter with modern people? The strength is leached out of them.

The preachers go on and on about the meekness of the Lord. Don't believe it. Could He have done all He did without strength?

I have sinned, as we all have, and for my sins will doubtless find God's punishment. I do not let thoughts of hell trouble me. What's the use? Given the same circumstances, I would do everything again. I have told Him often enough. It's your own fault, God. If you didn't want me to behave the way I did, why did you make me the way I am? There is another thing I shall want to say to him. Surely, Lord, if you had been in my place, you would have done the same thing? You threw the money-changers out of the temple, and they were only doing their job. What would you have done about the Hennings?

In the end, I miss none of them. Death consumes all. The one thing we do alone in our lives: the crossing of that bridge into eternal solitude. Two things matter, nothing else. *Oudekraal*. And Tamsin. Tamsin of the dark hair and flashing eyes. Would she have burnt the Hennings, in my place? Yes, she would; my throat chokes with pride because of it.

My voice is too feeble to summon even ghosts, but I can still handle the bell beside the bed. I ring it now.

Come, child. Before my eyes close for the last time, let me talk to you again of *Oudekraal*, the white gable amid the towering hills. Let me charge you once again with your duty.

THIRTY-THREE

Nicki had always heard that divorce was one of the most traumatic of experiences, but she hadn't found it so bad. All the same, there were limits. After she'd been through the hoop twice, each one a catastrophe, she decided she was better off staying single. Why not? She had always liked to play the field, and now there was nothing to stop her.

It was great; she had a ball. No alarm bells; life was for living, youth forever. Until two events in quick succession made her think again.

Darren Thomas was the first one. Pert eyes, lacquered hair. He was beautiful; a hard, twenty-five-year-old body, a walk-on part in a couple of TV shows. She'd shown him the town, shown him a lot more than that. She came on him giggling on the phone.

'Sick of it, sweetheart. Like making love to your mother, you know? Gruesome.'

Thank God he didn't see her. She got rid of him straightaway, of course, told herself he hadn't known his good luck. All the same, *mother* ... A blow, undeniably.

The second thing happened in public. What made it worse, she was the only one who realised anything had happened at all.

Two weeks after Darren's departure, she'd been in a pub with a group of friends. They were a fair bit younger than she was but she'd always liked young people, had her eye on a quiet lad, a financial reporter with one of the papers. Quite a change from razzle-dazzle Darren. She had been on the edge of inviting him to dinner, her treat, when they all upped and left her sitting there. Smiles, jokes, no ill feelings, but it couldn't have been plainer that they were a group, members of an exclusive club to which she no longer belonged. Youth.

I've been making a fool of myself. She tossed her drink down; considered, coldly, getting thoroughly absolutely rotten smashed.

Pride saved her. She walked out, smiling at the waiter, at the other drinkers, not a care in the world. She went home, told herself she would not crack a bottle, although she wanted it more than anything on earth. Instead had a bath, kept her eyes from the mirror, went to bed. Where, amazingly, she slept the sleep of the just — or the middle-aged. All would be well in the morning.

Except it was not. She stripped, looked coldly at herself in the mirror. Saw what had been there all along, had she the eyes to see it: a woman, still good-looking, but past her prime. Way past. No more sweet bird of youth; that had flown forever.

She wondered how she could have fooled herself so long. Wondered why, come to that. Maturity was more than a line or two where once there had been no lines; it was a state of mind. Now, belatedly, she had discovered it. To her astonishment she derived a measure of comfort, knowing who she really was after pretending for so long to be something else. But there was a warning in it, too.

If she wanted to settle down, properly and permanently, she could afford to waste no more time. She had to find the right man.

Hedy Shipley's was as good a place as any to start looking. Hedy's annual bash was pretty hideous, usually; too much booze, too many nineteen-year-old cuties fancying themselves because they'd done a stint on *Home and Away*. It was the place to be seen, all the same. The cameras were always there, and the cameras brought out the beautiful people; Nicki's sort of people. So, hideous or not, when the invitation arrived, she wasted no time in accepting.

When the great day came she made up with even more care than usual, put on the dress that, with luck, would spike the guns of the opposition — so it damn well should, the price she'd paid — and went off to the party.

She'd been a regular for fifteen years yet now, as the hired limo crossed the city, her nerves were jumping. Not surprising, in the circumstances.

All the same, she took care to arrive in style, smile as wide as the Harbour Bridge. She kissed the air close to Hedy's ear as though they'd been life-long mates and wafted indoors on a cloud of bravado and thousand-dollar perfume.

The first person she saw was Mostyn Harcourt. It was a surprise, not because he was there — he usually turned up at this sort of show — but because she'd heard he was out of the country.

She walked over to him at once, feeling his eyes giving her the once-over through her clothes. Nothing there you haven't seen already, she thought. Not that she had any complaints.

'So you made it, after all?'

'Only just. I got back from Africa this morning.'

He sipped a glass of Hedy's so-called champagne, made a grimace. 'I'd fire the cellar master who served me up crap like this.'

His eyes were busy. Nicki had always been a great-looking woman; he should know that, if anyone did. She knew how to dress, how to behave in public. In private, too, come to that. A man could do a lot worse. All the same, he knew it was a non-starter.

He needed someone at his side and in his bed, someone for the long haul. That ruled Nicki out. He'd been there, done that, more times than he cared to count, and resurrecting the past never worked. No, for the long term he needed someone younger, less travelled. On the other hand, who was talking about permanence tonight?

He said, 'Feel like some supper later?'

Mostyn's innocent look had fooled millions, but Nicki knew him too well. Her eyebrow lifted. The whisper of a smile. 'Supper? That the best you can do?'

They went to a place Mostyn knew in Potts Point. It specialised in French country cooking and hearty helpings, much needed after Hedy's bite-sized junk.

He'd known Gaston for years; they went through the normal rigmarole of discussing the menu before he allowed them to order. Mostyn had s*oupe aux marrons*, — God knows where he got the chestnuts — scalloped oysters, rounded it off with *rognons de veau* and plenty of tomatoes. Good, earthy food. Nicki had a salad, joined him for the oysters, skipped the kidneys. They drank a house red, rough as a file but full-bodied, just the thing to go with the food.

It was a meal to fire up the gonads; not that they needed much firing. They took a cab to Nicki's place, had their clothes off almost before they'd shut the door, hungrier than they'd ever been in the restaurant.

They kissed, touched and, as always, something took over. It was more than hunger. For Nicki, at least, it was fear. Fear of age. She made love as though throwing up a barrier against a flood that soon, if she did nothing to prevent it, would sweep her away.

She and Mostyn ... From the beginning, there had always been something tying them together. Sex had been no more than a part of it. They were mates, confiding in each other as with no one else on earth. They did so now; the fact — although not the details — of her bust-up with Darren, the problems Mostyn was facing now things were looking dodgy in Asia.

'A rough ride ahead,' he said. 'Very rough. We'll be seeing a few worms come out of the woodwork now.'

She listened, and was content. The only time she had turned her back on him had been when she had been planning to marry Tom Neal. That was when she had introduced him to Anna, but — as she had anticipated at the time — it had proved no more than a hiccup in their relationship. They had soon got together again. Mostyn had married, too, but after a month or two that had made no difference, either.

The fact was, Nicki thought, they were meant for each other. All they had to do was accept it; afterwards, time could do its worst and it wouldn't matter.

All this from nowhere, as they lay and rolled and played. The touch and the flame. To bodies that one would have thought had experienced it all, it was an experience to shake their bones.

They had always been brilliant in bed.

Afterwards, drained, fulfilled, awash with a lazy contentment that was almost as good as what had gone before, Nicki ran the back of her fingers gently down the side of Mostyn's face.

They had always been brittle with each other, jokey, as though needing to protect their feelings from each other. No longer. She was sick of gallivanting. She was open to him and glad to be so, vulnerable as she had never previously allowed herself to be with another human being.

Impulse took her tongue. She said, 'I want us to spend the rest of our lives together.'

Nothing of love, of marriage. The simple truth. *I want us to spend the rest of our lives together.* She smiled at him, truly naked for the first time in her life.

He laughed. 'Come on, sweetheart ... I know it was good, but I never read you for the faithful type.'

The blood drained from Nicki's face, from every vein of her body. In its place came ice.

She got rid of him. That was the worst part of all; she had expected a fuss but he went willingly, eager to escape an intensity he neither wanted nor understood.

She got dressed. She made the bed. She went out into the living room. She sat and stared. At nothing; at everything. At emptiness. She poured herself one drink, swallowed it in a gulp, put the glass down again. Gathering rage beat its red drum in her temples.

Still she sat there; thought and thought. When she had decided, her mind clear, she looked at her watch. It was not too late. She went to the phone.

The following morning Mostyn turned up for his first board meeting since flying out to Africa. With the understanding with Tembe warming the cockles of his wallet, he anticipated applause, had even honed, once again, the modest smile with which he would accept their congratulations.

Things didn't turn out like that. While he had been away, currency speculators had pulled the plug on Asia. He had known about it, of course — even in Africa he had taken care to stay in touch — but the extent of the disaster had taken everyone by surprise. To make matters worse, that morning's financial press had contained an article about Heinrich Griffiths and its managing director. A highly damaging article.

'The baht is through the floor. And the rupiah.'

Hennessy had been Mostyn's protégé, had learned Mostyn's skills too well, perhaps. Now he was on the rampage. The other directors watched apprehensively from around the boardroom table. Behind an impassive face, Mostyn fumed; he had called the shots so long that any criticism was hard to handle.

Hennessy said, 'The loans are due for review in two weeks.'

Mostyn smiled easily. 'I'll roll them over. Our name's good enough.'

'Two hundred and sixty million?'

'Why not? The Indonesian investments alone —'

'Are worth nothing.'

'That's nonsense —'

'Suharto's on the skids. Everyone knows it. These investments you've put us in over the years ... Are they really all joint ventures with members of his family?'

You've put us in; as though Hennessy did not know perfectly well that Suharto and his family had been the only road to investment in Indonesia.

'When he goes, they won't be worth the paper they're written on.'

'He'll ride out the storm. He always does.'

Mostyn looked around the table, seeking support, but for once no one seemed willing to catch his eye.

'Let's hope the institutions agree with you. After the article that reporter wrote about your Indonesian commitments ... What do we do if they don't?'

It was true that the article had been damaging; he still didn't know where the little bastard had got his information. Desperate times; desperate measures. Mostyn took a deep breath. 'They've already agreed.'

That stopped Hennessy, as Mostyn had intended, but he remained suspicious. 'Have they said so? In writing?'

Mostyn smiled indulgently. 'We've been doing business for years. Hang around a while, you'll find a gentleman's agreement is all it takes.'

It was enough. The other members of the board wanted desperately to believe him; their own futures depended on his being right. The most Charles Hennessy could do was to push through a formal request that the agreements with the banks be tabled for the board's approval at its next meeting.

One week. Nowhere near enough.

It would have to be enough.

Too busy planning his campaign to win over the banks, Mostyn hardly noticed the rest of the meeting. It would not be easy. Most of their chief executives were old friends, but that meant nothing. Business was a war of strong against weak, predator and victim. The slightest vulnerability and his friends would tear him to pieces, as he would them were their roles reversed.

At last the meeting was over. With time against him, Mostyn's instinct was to leave the room flying. It was the one thing he could not afford. He hung around, smiling and chatting, showing them all how relaxed he was. He went out of his way to be especially nice to Charles Hennessy, the protégé who had turned on him. He smiled until his jaw ached, envisaging the pleasure he would have in disembowelling him once the banks were on side.

At last, cheery smile, comradely slap on shoulder, he got away. He went to his office, warned his secretary he was not to be disturbed and drew up a list of the banks he had to win over in order to survive. Only eight mattered; the rats and mice would go along with the rest, but the big boys were scattered all over the globe: here in Australia, Singapore, Hong Kong, Germany, Britain and the United States.

All would have to agree. One dissenter would spook the rest. It meant spending the entire week in aircraft, but there was no help for it; he could trust no one else with this.

He sketched out a schedule, putting at the top of the list the institutions most likely to support him, working down to the ones that might cause problems. He knew exactly how to go about it. Banks, like sharks, were motivated by greed, fear or a combination of both. Either he must frighten them into supporting him or give them a damn good inducement to do so.

He paused by the golden axe and ran his fingers over its smooth surface. As always, his instinct was to instil fear, but he had nothing to frighten them with; this time it would have to be inducement. He must persuade them, not only that their money was safe but that by deferring repayment they stood to gain a great deal more.

The root of the problem lay in Indonesia, and that was where the solution would have to be found. Perhaps there, he thought, Hatchet Harcourt might have a chance to live up to his name.

He gave his secretary the list of names. 'Re-schedule all my appointments for later in the month.'

She studied the paper. 'What if the President won't see you?'

'He'll see me. It's his neck, too.'

Years ago he had formed the habit of keeping a packed suitcase in his car; within minutes he left the office and drove to Kingsford Smith airport on the first stage of a journey that, all being well, would take him right around the world.

Later that evening he landed in Jakarta, where an official car was waiting to whisk him away into the rain-forested hills. He approved of his host's choice of venue; the air was cooler, unwanted eyes less likely to see what was none of their business.

The magnificent palace, set in extensive grounds behind high walls, was guarded by armed paratroopers in combat smocks. Mostyn was escorted up the steps and into a luxurious foyer, where the man he had come to see was waiting for him. He was not as trim as he had once been and wore a floral shirt that hung loose about his waist.

He came forward, smiling, and took Mostyn's hand.

'Mr Harcourt, welcome to Bogor,' he said. 'To what do we owe the pleasure of your visit?'

Mostyn looked at the flint-cold eyes of the army officers surrounding them. When your purpose was to blackmail someone as powerful as this, the last thing you needed was an audience.

'If we can go somewhere private, Your Excellency, I shall explain.'

They retired to an ornate reception room, all gold paint and brocade chair coverings.

The old man stared at him. 'Very well, Mr Harcourt. Give it to me.'

He gave it to him, indeed, with both barrels. He told the old boy he had to go along. Either he gave Mostyn options on every major industry in the country — forestry, mining, the lot — or Heinrich Griffiths would take their losses and pull out. If that happened, the shock waves would destroy what was left of the Indonesian economy, and the President and all his cronies would be down the gurgler.

It was no time for fancy speaking. 'The mob will tear this place apart ...' The old man put a good face on it; would have killed Mostyn if he could, but knew he no longer had the power to do it.

Mostyn whizzed around the world, as planned, but after the Bogor meeting it was only a formality. What he had to offer now would have put Ali Baba's forty thieves in the shade.

Heading back to Sydney, he was able to relax for the first time in a week. He was safe, as long as Suharto survived.

For a month or two, things looked great. There were demonstrations in Jakarta but Suharto couldn't have been too worried; he had gone overseas and left the mobs to get on with it.

'Quietly confident,' Mostyn told the press. 'No worries at all.'

Troops took to the streets but the rioting, instead of dying down as expected, grew worse. Suharto came back.

'Now we'll see something,' Mostyn said, rubbing his hands.

It was inconceivable that the general who had destroyed Soekarno all those years ago wouldn't know what to do with a mob of students. Yet it seemed that in Indonesia, too, times had changed. From one day to the next, while Mostyn was still brandishing his confidence like a tattered battle flag, Suharto was gone. Leaving Heinrich Griffiths, and its managing director, up a tree with never a parachute in sight.

The bombshell fell at the end of the meeting.

Other Business was usually made up of a grab-bag of items that did not warrant a separate place on the agenda. This time it was different.

'I've had a letter,' Harry Dann said. 'It's a personal approach, asking me how we would feel about becoming involved in an Asian venture.'

'Asia?' Harris Donnelly said sourly. 'Good God.'

His reaction was reflected in the faces of the others around the boardroom table; these days Asia was no longer flavour of the month.

'How much?' Anna asked. 'And what kind of involvement?'

'A tad under a billion dollars. Well within our reach. And a joint venture or partnership, something like that.'

'Where in Asia?'

'Indonesia, mainly. South Korea was also mentioned.'

Two of the most vulnerable economies in the region.

'Why us?'

'The letter talks about the advantages of cooperation. Economies of scale —'

'Horseshit,' Harris said.

'Who's the letter from?' Anna asked.

'I prefer to keep that to myself at this stage. Obviously the board will be told before a final decision is taken but, for the moment, I'm simply asking for your views. In principle.'

'A venture in what?'

'Mining. Finance. Property. A full spread of activities.'

'Someone who's lost their shirt and wants us to bail them out,' Harris grunted. It seemed very likely, but that was not the point.

'If that's the case, the terms are likely to be highly advantageous,' Anna said. 'I've got three questions. One; are the people who've approached us the sort we would be willing to get into bed with? Two; are the ventures sound, commercially speaking? Three; what do we feel about involvement in Asia at this time?'

'What do we feel about cutting our throats?' Harris asked.

'The people behind this would be quite acceptable to the Board,' Harry Dann said. 'No problems there. As far as the actual investment is concerned they'll be fine when the Asian economy picks up —'

'Whenever that may be.'

Harris had obviously appointed himself wrecker of the whole proposal but that was Harris, never the most positive of thinkers.

Anna refused to be distracted. 'How do we see Asia's future? Not now, but in two years' time? Five years? Ten?'

'It'll come good. Eventually.'

'Then isn't now the time to get ourselves involved?'

'Make a lot more sense to wait, I'd have said.'

Anna was fed up. 'Why?'

'Because we don't know whether their economies have bottomed yet. Unless your crystal ball is telling you.'

'My crystal ball says it makes more sense to get in when prices are low than when they're high. If we wait until the Asian economies are on their way up again, it'll be too late.'

There was a twenty-minute discussion. At the end, by a single vote, the Board agreed to follow Anna's lead.

'I hoped you'd see it like that,' Harry Dann said. He took a typed letter from his folder and laid it flat upon the table. Looked at Anna.

'It's Mostyn,' he said.

'You bastard,' Anna said.

Harry Dann polished off his drink and snapped his fingers for a refill. 'Not really,' he said. 'Like you said, if the figures stack up it's a very good opportunity for us.

But I wasn't sure you'd back a Mostyn bail-out. So I put it to you as a matter of principle.'

'Is he really in that much trouble?'

'He was very close to Suharto. Now the old man's gone, there are a hundred institutions screaming for their money.'

'Surprising he came to us, all the same.'

'You think so?'

Dann was cautious; no one knew the state of the game where Anna and Mostyn were concerned. They were divorced, but these days that didn't mean much. It was possible he still had some influence over her.

Maybe Mostyn thinks so himself, Anna thought. He's in for a disappointment if he does. What's more he's given me an opening.

'My support is conditional,' she said.

Dann looked alarmed. Anna's defection could kill the proposal before it got off the ground. 'Conditional on what?'

'You said they were the sort of partners we'd be happy to get into bed with.'

'So they are. Mostyn —'

'I know more about getting into bed with Mostyn than you do.'

Dann's mouth disapproved; some things were better unsaid.

'Mostyn,' she said succinctly, 'is a shit.'

From bad to worse. 'Who knows business backwards,' he challenged.

'Is that why he needs us? Because he knows business backwards or because he's in trouble up to his neck? If he wants our help he must pay for it. He's got something I want; I'll settle for that.'

'Your personal affairs have nothing to do with this,' Harry protested. 'It's a matter for the Board —'

'Call it a test of good faith. I'll talk to him, get back to you.'

'But —'

Anna had done with chat. She drained her glass, got to her feet.

'Either he goes along or he can jump off the Harbour Bridge, far as I'm concerned. See you, Harry.'

She went back to her office, phoned Mostyn at once. It was after nine but if he was in trouble he'd be there. Being Mostyn, he was likely to be there anyway, she thought maliciously; it was not as though he had a home to go to, any more.

He was there, all right. Frayed around the edges, by the sound of it.

'What do you want?'

'The United Minerals board met today —'

'I'm fully aware of that. I've been expecting Harry to phone me. I hope you realise what a great opportunity this is for you —'

'Asia at the moment is hardly that for anyone.'

'Couple of years, she'll be right —'

She cut off his salesman's pitch. 'We need to talk.'

'Come and talk, then. I need an hour —'

'My office. Twenty minutes.'

And put down the phone.

He came. Of course; he had no choice.

Anna looked at him across her acre of desk, now clear of all papers. It was an odd feeling to look at this man and think of the place he had once filled in her life.

Water under the bridge.

He played his bravado card, as she had known he would. 'What do you want to talk about?'

'You,' Anna said. 'And me.'

She saw from his eyes that he had not been expecting that. You're slipping, she thought. Not so long ago you would never have shown your feelings as clearly as that.

'I've been thinking,' he told her sincerely, 'what a fool I was to have walked out the way I did.' And risked a smile. 'I've always had a hot temper, you know that —'

She said, 'You make me puke. The Board talked over your proposal. It's evenly divided. Some are willing to go with it, others don't want to run a mile. No doubt you'll check it out —'

'I offered it to United Minerals as a favour. If you don't want to run with it —'

'Spare me. You'd have tried everyone else in Sydney before you came to us.' She looked him up and down. 'Whether we go ahead or not depends on me. I can swing it either way. If you want my support, you'll have to buy it.'

'Meaning what?'

'Meaning *Oudekraal*.'

He had to try. 'I don't know what you're talking about.'

'I know all about the deal you stitched up with Chris Tembe …'

'Then you know it's too late to do anything. The legislation's already before the South African parliament.'

'If you don't back off you're dead,' she said.

'I doubt it's possible …'

'Do it, that's all. Just do it.'

Impasse.

'If I agree, do you guarantee support over this Asia business?'

She smiled; she had him by the shorts, and they both knew it. 'I guarantee nothing. You'll have to wait and see.'

'Be damned to that —'

'Good night, Mostyn.'

She took a file from the tray on her side table, opened it and began to read the papers inside. Mostyn might have ceased to exist. He got up, fuming, but decided he still had to try. He smiled down at her. 'Want a bite to eat?'

She did not look up. 'I wouldn't eat with you if you were the last man on earth.'

A killing look, then. He marched towards the door, shoulders vengeful. She waited until he had almost reached it. She said, 'Harry wants an early decision. If within three days from now Pieter Wolmarans hasn't received written government confirmation of his freehold title to *Oudekraal* — in perpetuity — I shall withdraw my support on Asia.'

And went back to her papers.

Mostyn walked down the corridor to the lift. He was seething, but knew there was no help for it; he would have to buy Tembe off. This was not a town where you could count on too many good Samaritans. Things had gone rotten in Asia; he had called in all his favours but no one was interested. With Suharto gone the tide had turned again. The Board was getting ready to chuck him. Once again Hennessy was riding high. He had to come up with answers within days, or it would be too late. And, as Anna had guessed, he had tried everywhere else first.

He had to put up with Anna's crap. He even had to grin; without her he was dead. After all the years on top, he wasn't prepared to start all over again.

The bottom line was that *Oudekraal*, even the revenge he had anticipated so eagerly, was expendable.

The lift sighed to a stop. As Mostyn went out into the street he looked up at Anna's light still burning on the twenty-second floor. He would gladly have gone straight back and cut her throat but it was far too late for that. Any throat-cutting to be done, Anna would be holding the knife.

THIRTY-FOUR

The High Commissioner said, '*Oudekraal* is safe.'
'Thank God. How —'
He smiled, shaking his head. 'Don't ask.'
'I am very grateful.'
'You had a hand in it yourself, I think.'
She pretended ignorance. 'In what way?'
'From what I hear, your ex-husband is not the sort to back away unless he is forced,' he said. 'I had nothing to do with that.'
She smiled. 'It is amazing what one is willing to do when the need arises.'
'Indeed. Once all I could think about was killing and violence. I make no apologies; at the time it was necessary. But now I have changed my views. Unlike some of my colleagues, I believe true peace will come only when we turn our backs on the past and join together to build a new future.'
'I agree.'
'Unfortunately there is still one thing that stands in our way.'
'What is that?'
'Poverty.' He paused, studied her for a moment in silence. 'I want to do you a favour,' he said.

Behind his chair the zigzag flag of the new South Africa hung limply. Its colours were right for a black land, Anna thought; bold and gaudy and alive, with a hint of violence.

'A favour? What might that be?'

'You told me once that you wanted more out of life than money.'

It sounded like the glib rubbish spoken so often by the rich. She had said it and meant it, but now was embarrassed to be reminded of it.

'I'm not complaining. I do all right.'

'A pity not everyone's so lucky.'

Watching him, time seemed to be playing tricks. Instead of the Saville Row suit, the silk tie, she saw only the massive chest, shoulders bulging the thin T-shirt, thighs potent with power. She remembered his barely suppressed rage; remembered, too, their second meeting and its aftermath. Her memory of that encounter was a taste that even after fifteen years still lingered on her tongue.

'What are you getting at?'

'In the old days, no one was willing to talk to Vorster or Botha, to any of the leaders of South Africa. Now we have access to the highest officials everywhere. Mandela wants to see Clinton, the Pope, Gaddafi — he has only to ask. It's the same for the rest of us. Last month I saw the Secretary General of the United Nations.'

And paused, watching her.

She did not understand. 'So?'

'So I told him there were two hundred million starving people in Africa. More than that in Asia and South America.'

'There are agencies.'

'Of course. Voluntary agencies, government agencies, even United Nations agencies. We need something bigger, coordinated at top level. We need a World Commissioner for the eradication of hunger.'

'A big title,' said Anna, suspicious of titles.

'A big job,' Shongwe told her. 'An important job. Possibly the most important job in the world.'

'Why are you telling me this?'

'Because I think you are the right person to do it.'

She was astounded; laughed to shield herself from disbelief. 'You don't have the authority to give it to me.'

'I have access to those who do.'

'Then let them contact me.'

'Agree in principle and they will. You can't expect the Secretary General to waste time on you if you're not interested.'

She heard herself say, 'I never said I wasn't interested.'

'Does that mean yes?'

'I don't know why you think I can do it.'

'I'll tell you.' He raised his fingers, ticking off points one by one. 'You have a political background.'

'A long time ago.'

'You were offered a ministry in the New South Wales government only recently.'

'Which I turned down.'

'The political connection is there.' He flipped the second finger. 'You have top-level business contacts, worldwide. You have an interest in the disadvantaged. You have the ability and experience.'

'The UN is a rat hole of incompetence. Why should I waste my time with them?'

'Because it may be the last chance the world has to put things right.'

She was silent. The magnitude of the challenge stunned, humbling her. 'There are others better qualified than I am. Why me?'

'Because you care.'

'I am nobody.'

She heard the appeal in her voice, crying out against the terrors of what he offered.

'You are the one we need.'

She thought, I do not want this. It is nonsense even to think about it. I have my own life, the prospect of a future with the man I love. Which I have been lacking for so long. Which by a miracle I have now regained.

The fear of what she would lose made her angry. It was too much to give up. Too much for anyone.

'No,' she said.

He watched her across his desk. 'Two hundred million in Africa alone.'

She shut her mind to an image of suffering so vast as to be incomprehensible.

'I wouldn't be able to do anything. No one can. It's too huge a problem.'

'So we ignore it.'

She stared at him across the desk, seeing not the High Commissioner's dark features but Mark Forrest, watching her in silence.

'If you had asked me a month ago —'

There was a note of desperation in her voice. Was it selfish, to want her own life? To place it, and the man she loved, ahead of the suffering of millions? Of course it was, but it made no difference. Mark was more important to her than the starving hordes of Africa and Asia.

It was an appalling admission, shaming her. It was the truth.

You call yourself a humanitarian. 'If I felt I would really be able to do anything ...'

Such a feeble offering; she could have choked on her own hypocrisy. She remembered herself, two weeks before, lying in bed and waiting in fear and delight for Mark to join her. How she had thought of Anneliese.

From her I learned something of what truth means, the sacrifice that truth demands. And something else. *Pray God I am never put to such a test.*

She stared in anguish at the man on the other side of the desk. 'Please don't judge me...'

'I would not presume to do that,' he said. 'You have a life to lead, as we all have. Besides, there is no need.' Effortlessly, he set his hook in her tormented spirit. 'You will do that for yourself.'

Her expression darkened. 'That is presumptuous.'

'I apologise. For a moment, two hundred million people made me forget my manners.'

After Anna had left him, Adam Shongwe sat at his desk, thinking over their conversation. He had given it his best shot. Either she would come back or she wouldn't.

He hoped very much that she would. Get the job and, with luck, he would be able to talk her into channelling aid to South Africa, funds that would help kick-start its ailing economy.

It would be good for the country; even better for Adam Shongwe. It would give him the clout to become what he wanted more than life itself, a key player in South African politics. Even the presidency would not be beyond his grasp.

Glory beckoned. If only she took the job.

Anna caught the shuttle to Sydney and went home. She thought. And thought.

She prowled the house, the garden gay with flowers. She sat on the stone balustrade dividing the lawn from the water, stared across the harbour at the city's buildings gleaming golden in the sunlight.

Faces everywhere. Forms as silent and wistful as shadows. The spindle limbs and bloated bellies, eyes huge in wizened faces. Children, stoic, dying by degrees. Adults wasted beyond capacity for anger. Bodies stacked like firewood.

You are the one we need.

A nightmare. A reproach that, if she did nothing, would haunt her forever.

Mark came, as they had arranged. She told him of her meeting with Adam Shongwe, what had been said.

'Thank God you had the sense to say no.'

'Yes.' But hesitantly.

He looked at her. 'You did say no?'

'Yes. Oh yes.' She took two paces, stiff-legged, across the room. Came back. Two paces, and back.

'But ...?' he prompted her, frowning.

'It is such an important job —'

'In New York.'

'I think he said Geneva ...'

'What about us?'

'I said no!'

She opened her arms, despairingly, but the gulf that had opened between them remained.

'I don't understand you.' He stared at her, eyes hot. Behind him sunlight reflecting from the waters of the harbour dazzled her eyes with spears of glittering, golden light. 'All these wasted years and, as soon as we find each other, you're thinking of taking off again.'

'It makes no difference.' She sought to appease him. 'I probably would never have got it, anyway.'

'If it's not this job, it'll be another one. The point is you're thinking of moving on. Already.'

'If I went, if I changed my mind, you could come with me. Couldn't you? You said yourself you've gone as far as you can where you are now.'

'You expect me to chuck everything and traipse off to New York or Geneva or wherever the hell it is? I'm a journalist. A good one. What can you offer that'll make it worth my while going to Geneva with you?'

Like a fist in the face.

'Aren't I enough?'

From Mark's expression it was evident she was not. 'You expect everyone to fit in with your career. I've a career, too.'

'You told me yourself you'd like another challenge!'

'I prefer to pick my own challenges.'

'And so do I!'

He seized her hands. 'I want a future for us. A child.'

It was a peace offering, of sorts, but Anna was in no mood for peace offerings.

'A child? At my age? Get real.'

'Plenty of women start families when they're older than you …'

It was true, but she brushed his protest aside.

'You say you want us to have a future. We'd have that, wherever we were. But it sounds to me as though you only want it here.'

On and on, the words as spiked and painful as the spears of golden light, until at last neither of them could bear it any more and Mark drove back to his own place, which had not been part of their arrangements, at all.

Alone in the cool emptiness of the big house, Anna seethed, furiously. She had said no. For his sake and her own. What had he been so upset about?

'All I did was *talk* about it …'

That was the point. To talk implied thinking and that, of course, was the crime.

The point is you're thinking of moving on.

Yet her sense of injustice burned; it had not even been her idea, for heaven's sake. She told herself that if he had cared he would have understood. He knew how important this job was. She had said it was too big a problem, that no one could hope to resolve it, but did that mean she should not try?

At least it would give her the chance to do what she could to put right so much that was wrong in the world. How could he expect her to reject such an opportunity, to settle back into the knife-pit of the Sydney business world, to be content with the endless accumulation of wealth?

Yet that was what she had done. She had said no. Which did not mean she could not change her mind.

She would sleep on it, she decided. In the morning, she would call him, they would discuss it again, like the rational beings they were. She lay in bed, once again remembering how she had waited for him that night, the cocoon of tenderness that had enveloped her, her eager acceptance of the future. They were so much alike: both ambitious, both determined. She had welcomed their similarity, believing that it would bring strength, yet now felt only fear and desolation; fear that their unyielding temperaments would make it impossible for them to build a life together; desolation because a future without Mark would be no more than a desert of futility and loss.

In the morning she phoned him, found she did not know what to say. Instead, he said it for her.

'You've made up your mind, haven't you?'

Until that moment she had not known, but he was right. 'Yes.'

Silence, then.

'Keep me in the picture. Okay?'
'Of course. Mark —'
Too late. He was gone.
She phoned Shongwe in Canberra, got through to him straightaway.
'Yes?'
'I've thought it over.' And paused. She could hear him waiting, silently. Eventually she said, 'I will talk to them. If they truly want me. I make no promises. Afterwards, we'll see.'

A week later she had her reply, contacted Mark at once.
'They want to see me.'
'Who?'
'The Secretary General. In New York.'
'When are you leaving?'
His voice as cold as the Arctic.
'In three days.'
'You'll be pleased.' It was an accusation.
'I'm scared.'
'You'll manage it all right.'
'It's not just the job.' From somewhere she found the courage and humility to say what was most in her heart. 'Can I see you? Before I go?'
It seemed like years before he answered. 'Let's leave it till you get back. Give me a ring then. Okay?'
Despair devastated her.
'Mark?' Her voice small.
'Yes?'
'I love you.'
'I love you, too.' He spoke angrily; in her ears it sounded almost like a threat.
She said, 'Lots of people work in different countries. Modern planes —'
'Lots of people,' he repeated. 'Not me.'

Nothing, where before had seemed everything.

'I'll phone you from New York.'

He said, 'You said I could give up my job and go with you, if you got it. Tell me something...'

'Yes?' Eagerly.

'Would you do the same, if our positions were reversed?'

And put down the phone, gently, before she could reply.

She flew to New York, spent an hour with the Secretary General, a week with various officials.

A small brown man with gold-rimmed glasses told her, 'They'll hate you out there. You know that, don't you?'

'Why should they?'

'Because you'll be rocking the boat. There are empires,' he told her excitedly. 'Emperors with their own courts. Hunger is big business, let me tell you. Some people do very well out of it.'

'While others starve.'

He brushed that aside; the starving were irrelevant. 'They won't thank you for it,' he threatened.

At the end of the week, she went back to the Secretary General and presented him with a list of stipulations.

Funding. Staffing. Autonomy. Access.

'Access?'

'I have to see you, if necessary.'

He thought about it. 'Very well.'

'There has to be a formal commitment,' she told him. 'In writing. Five years minimum.'

He hesitated but in the end agreed to that also.

When they had gone through her list, the Secretary General looked at her. 'Is that it? Have you made up your mind?'

'Not yet.'

A frown flickered. 'What more can you possibly want?'

She didn't want it at all. She could see so clearly the bureaucracy, the endless politics, the graft and argument, the remorseless sniping of subordinates and media, the conspiracies of those with their own agendas ... The prospect filled her with an overwhelming weariness and, yes, fear.

Fear was something new.

All the years she had been a director of companies, conjuring millions of dollars out of the commercial air in which she lived and breathed, she had never once been afraid. Now that had changed. She thought she might welcome the fear; it measured the value of what she was being asked to do, the sacrifice that might be demanded of her.

The Secretary General was watching her, his expression strange, as though somehow he had read her thoughts.

She said, 'There's one more thing.'

She spent a whirlwind fortnight, travelling extensively. She was insulted by a Belgian doctor in Rwanda, patronised by an Earl in London, in New York was harangued by an Australian of unbelievable arrogance, who seemed to feel his prerogatives in the international aid industry would be damaged by her appointment.

'I shall white-ant you to death,' he threatened, bloodshot eye as ferocious as his blow-dried hair, his whisky breath. 'Time I'm finished with you, girlie, you'll wish you'd never been born.'

Everywhere she heard tales: handouts for mates, first class travel for hangers-on, bribes to insurgents who stole the food anyway. Politicians, police, military all looking for a cut. An English doctor plotted to procure a supply of nubile children; another a knighthood.

All this while the starving and diseased died.

'I refer you to Hercules,' an erudite Indian official warned her. 'The Augean stables would be a picnic in comparison with what you are having here.'

'Never mind stables,' Anna said, 'I shall need a tank regiment before I'm through.'

She went back to New York, spent two days sequestered in a borrowed house on the Atlantic coast. It was cold. She rugged up and walked the dunes, watched the green and grey teeth of the rollers as they crashed, smoking, upon the land. She sat for hours in the weather-tight house with its pegged floors and panelled walls.

I must be sure. Say yes and I am bound. If I take this job I shall stick with it, whatever the cost. I must be sure.

She went to bed, slept restlessly. In the morning she had to return to New York to give the Secretary General her answer.

When she woke, she was calm. For the last time she patrolled the weed-dark beach. Fear remained, but had brought back meaning to her life. Everything she had been doing until now, however competently, had been nothing, because she as a person had never been involved.

Now you find out. You have wasted fifteen years of your life. No, she thought, that is untrue. It is not the time spent in Sydney boardrooms that matters, but my failure to realise that what I was doing was ultimately meaningless.

Ben had been right. She had left her feet in the trough, not out of greed, but because she had not even realised she was doing it. The opportunity she had now was to salvage something from the years of life that remained.

The prospect filled her with wonderment, an eager impatience to get on with it. She turned back to the house, the car waiting in the driveway.

The Secretary General met her at the door of his office, escorted her to an upholstered chair. 'Have you made up your mind?'

'One final thing.' She saw his expression. 'Forgive me, but it's necessary. If I take this job, I shall need worldwide support. That will mean international promotion and the budget to go with it.'

He shook his head despairingly. 'More money?'

'You said yourself that this is the greatest challenge facing the world. We can't meet it without funding and proper promotion.'

'How do you plan to obtain this promotion?'

'I have a few ideas.'

'If I can persuade the Assembly to agree, will this be your final requirement?'

She smiled at him cheekily, risking all. 'For the moment.'

Although I still haven't said I'll do it. He hasn't even asked me yet. Maybe he won't. Maybe he's decided I'm not the right person for the job.

'Very well.' The Secretary General studied her for a moment. 'Tell me what you have in mind.'

She phoned him.

'I've got it.'

'I never doubted you would.'

She laughed, elated by success, by the challenge she had embraced. 'Then you were a lot more confident than I was.'

'Is this on or off the record?'

His voice was cold but she refused to listen to more than the words. 'Off the record. Of course. There'll be an announcement from New York. But I didn't ring you because you're a journalist —'

'You'll be based in Geneva?'

'It won't make any difference where I'm based. I'll be all over the place. For quite a while, certainly.'

'It won't work, Anna. Australia's too far —'

'I have to talk to you about that, too. I've an idea.' With a confidence she did not feel, she said, 'I think you'll like it —'

'You want me to move to Geneva?'

'It would involve that, yes. But —'

'Forget it.'

From halfway around the earth, desperately, she threw her appeal at him. 'Listen to me! Please! We owe each other that much, surely?'

Silence. Then, 'Give me a call when you get back.'

'Meet me?'

Again silence. 'We'll talk when you're back in Sydney.'

There were rumours; no avoiding them with something as big as this. When she landed at Kingsford Smith, the media was waiting. They gave her the full treatment. Cameras zoomed, jostling reporters screamed questions in her face. Somehow she kept her cool.

'I'll be making a statement,' she promised. 'Tomorrow.'

Got away, looked for Mark's face.

Nothing. He was not there.

Anna phoned Mark's office on her mobile, determined he was in, took a taxi direct from the airport.

He was in a meeting. His secretary looked down her nose, unforgiving of Anna's treatment all those months ago. Instead his assistant, who had a motherly interest in him — in Anna, too, perhaps — said she would tip him the wink. And did so, whispering mouse-like into the phone.

She beamed triumphantly. 'He'll be out directly.'

Five minutes later he was, escorting his visitor to the door, the air between them bright with laughter. He came back. No laughter now.

'Come into my office.'

He ignored the easy chairs, went and sat behind his desk. Anna felt the skin tighten on her face. She thought, Here we go.

He stared at her appraisingly. There was a flinty harshness in his gaze, in the stillness of the air that separated them. It augured badly for what she had come to say.

'You've done it, then.'

She had looked for congratulations; this sounded more like an accusation.

'Yes.'

'Based in Geneva?'

'Yes.'

He nodded, judiciously assessing the impossibility of the situation that she had created. 'So that's it.'

Resentment stabbed. 'That's not it! Or needn't be. Unless it's what you want, of course.'

Not by the flicker of an eyelid did Mark acknowledge that.

'On the phone you said you had an idea. What was it?'

She remembered what Adam Shongwe had said. 'I want to do you a favour ...'

'When people say that, I get nervous.'

Yet first and last Mark was a journalist and listened without interruption as she told him of her discussion with the Secretary General in his office high up in the United Nations building.

She had stood at the huge window, staring down at New York, the river with its bridges bright in the sun. Down there was the frenzied city; here the room was quiet as she spelled out how she intended to go about realising their shared vision of a world without poverty.

'I shall run the Agency like a business,' she said. 'Profit-orientated.'

The Secretary General's face gleamed like an Ashanti mask in the shadowed room. 'You intend to make money out of it?'

'The profit will be our results. Total accountability. So much money in, so much return. Lives saved, nutrition levels raised, dams built, soil conservation classes. Everything accounted for.' She smiled. 'Our shareholders are entitled to see what they're getting for their money.'

'What you're suggesting is impossible. Welfare, good water, good sanitation, cannot be quantified in financial terms. Utterly impossible.'

'Utterly,' she agreed, 'but I intend to do it. There will be divisional heads within each region. They will be responsible for identifying the various facets of the problem and coming up with solutions. Or suggestions for solutions.'

'It will not happen in your lifetime.'

'Of course not. But if we can create a culture of right thinking in the decision-makers, the benefits may eventually filter through to the victims themselves. One of the first things they must learn is to stop thinking of themselves as victims at all.'

'That means changing the mental attitudes of the whole world.'

'I've an idea about that, too. We have to link the donors with those for whom the money is given. We have to promote the idea that supporting the Agency is not charity, but self-preservation. Because poverty means more than starvation; it means war and pestilence. Unchecked, it will eventually engulf us all, rich nations as well as poor. The Agency is our lifeline to survival. We have to make sure we get that message across.'

'How do you propose to do that?'

'Our own television studio. Our own newspaper. Full-time, professionally trained and funded. It will compete with the top journals, it will carry the same news they do, but it will also cover everything the Agency does or hopes to do. It will spread the word.'

'And who is to run this media empire you are proposing?'

'I've an idea about that, too.'

'Me?' Mark said. 'You want me to do it?'

'Naturally. Think what a challenge —'

'You're out of your mind.'

'Of course. You have to be to take on a job like this.' She was higher than cocaine would make her on her vision. 'Think of it! No limits to what can and can't be done. It could be the salvation of the earth.'

'What you're saying is impossible.'

'It *is* impossible. So let's do it.'

The vision, perhaps the very impossibility of the vision, licked her like a flame. It burned in every part of her, gleaming in her eyes, in the molten words flowing ceaselessly from her mouth, even in the way she walked. It had taken her over completely.

So this is what she is truly like, Mark thought. I always knew it was there but never thought to see it.

The power of her vision awed him but he knew that neither now or ever would he be able to go along. The fire was not for him. It made him envious that anyone could know such passion, possess the courage and ability to take on such an impossible task. She would fail, because no one could succeed in what she had undertaken, but that was unimportant. Even failure would be glorious.

Resentment sharpened his tongue. 'A house journal. Who'd read it?'

'I'm offering you the biggest job you'll ever have. And the chance to do some good in the world.'

The vastness of the job was the problem, of course.

'People sneer at the idea of doing good but it's more fun than you might imagine.'

'How would you know?' He could not resist the gibe.

'We both know it.' She looked at him, eyes shining. 'What about it?'

He was angry with her for refusing to acknowledge the unreason of what she was asking. 'Give up what I've got here to work for the UN? Some pollie riding shotgun on every move I make?'

Yet the idea drew him more than he would have imagined. Its challenge blew his mind. This, too, he resented. 'It will never work.'

'You'll make it work! Aid covers everything. War, famine, floods, epidemics. But it'll do more than that. It will tell the story of what people want for themselves in their own lives, the lives of their children. If we're lucky it may even show humanity coming to grips with its responsibilities at last.'

She was around his desk, seizing his hands in hers. 'Please,' she said. 'Please come.'

Her heat frightened him. The vision was too bright, the challenge too great. Panic was a sour lump in his throat.

He drew back. 'No. I told you before. I like to create my own opportunities.'

'You said you wanted a child.' It was her last card, thrown down upon the table to join the rest.

'You said you were too old.'

'I've been thinking about that ...'

More than thinking. Ever since she and Mostyn had bought the house on the harbour, she had been interested in the work of Ruth Ballard, the famous author who had lived there before them. She had read most of her books, most recently a biography of her aunt, the extraordinary Dorrie, who had been such an influence in Ruth's life. Dorrie had had a child while she was active in the labour movement. She had taken him to meetings, had not permitted him to stand in the way of the work she had to do.

What was possible for Dorrie was possible for Anna Riordan. She told Mark what she had decided. 'We can always get some help, if we need to ...'

'The Secretary General would never agree.'

'He has agreed. Before I started. I told him up-front it was a condition.'

He thought about it.

'It's something I have to do,' she told him urgently. 'But you are my life. I'll keep the house. It'll be there for us, when we come back —'

'No,' he said. His voice was weary but firm. 'I don't see how it can possibly work.'

The future was ashes, the glory and the fire gone. She had not realised how much she had been depending upon Mark to join her in this. Now that he had refused, she wondered where she would find the courage to do it all alone.

She had come so close to pleading with him, trying to make him see that the impossible dream would bring them together. In the end had said nothing. If he could not see it for himself, there was no hope for them. Finally, after so much hope and despair, nothing remained.

The darkness in which I lie. It was a phrase she had read somewhere. The darkness that existed at noon as well as midnight. That filled thoughts and dreams. That drowned past and future.

In the first despairing hours, Anna had thought she would give up. What was being asked of her, what she was asking of herself, was truly impossible. If she went on, she would destroy herself to no purpose.

Now she knew differently. Destruction came from within; only by giving up would she permit it entry into her life. She had to go on because that would be her salvation.

She carried two images within her. One was the face of her great-grandmother. Anneliese had undergone so much, yet had never surrendered to anything or anyone in her life, had remained ferocious and strong to the end of her days. The second was of a great house girt by mountains, the light of flares golden upon it, mounted men setting out in frosty darkness up the winding trail into the snow-capped hills. She watched them go, those dark and fleeting figures of the past. She saw Anneliese's face and knew that with these two images she was no longer alone. The commando rode out in pursuit of its own harsh justice. Anneliese lived according to those same precepts. Anna herself was descended from both Anneliese and the giant figure of the man riding at the head of the column. As they had kept faith in what they believed so Anna, in her own day and way, would do the same.

Work. That was where the real salvation lay. In time, it might even help her to forget.

THIRTY-FIVE

She visited the High Commissioner to tell him she had accepted the job.

He nodded. 'I am glad. For you and for the world.'

'I was surprised I got it.' Even to her own ears, she sounded more dispirited than surprised.

He frowned. 'I thought you would be delighted. But I see you are not. Why is that?'

'Too big a challenge, maybe.'

'That is not the reason.'

He waited but she said no more. Once again she saw him with the mingled vision of past and present. She passed behind the suavely cut suit, the tastefully furnished office, into the tiny shoebox of the Guguletu room to which they had returned after their tour of the township.

They had travelled for hours past shabby tenements, tin shacks, choked and squalid alleyways. They had talked to a hundred people. The elderly, the maimed, the poor with patient, suffering faces. Young studs, strangers to patience, whose hating eyes stripped the clothes from her white body and despised her as they did so. She had listened while Shongwe and others had spelt out why sanctions must stay.

Now they were back in the little room. Alone. She was exhausted. More than anything she needed rest but was aware as never before of the vitality of the man burning like a remorseless fire in every fibre of his body.

Never in her life had she felt such desire.

He looked at her. He had only to lift a finger and she would go to him gladly. She waited, breathless, surrendering herself to his will.

He stood up. 'I shall get someone to take you back.'

What Mark suspected had never happened yet, in her imagination as in his, it had indeed happened with an intensity that she had never forgotten. In a sense I lied to Mark, she thought. Had Adam willed it, I would have given myself to him gladly. How can I possibly pretend that nothing happened at all?

Now she sat decorously, watching him, and knew that he, too, was remembering that moment of surrender and rejection. Perhaps it had been no more than reaction to everything she had seen and heard, perhaps not. It no longer mattered. Neither of them would ever speak of it.

'I have to thank you,' she said. *Once again*. But that she did not say.

'Do it well,' he said. 'That will be my thanks. Then perhaps, in the future, we can talk again. In an official capacity.'

One favour for another; of course.

'I shall look forward to it,' she said.

Once again she phoned Mark. 'I'm leaving for South Africa in the morning. Then on to Geneva. I must see you before I go.'

At first he refused. 'It will do no good —'

This she would not accept. 'You say you love me, yet you won't see me, even to say goodbye?'

So they met. Not for a meal — neither of them could have borne that — but for coffee. A cafe, anonymous and busy-slick, with varnished furniture and people in and out all the time. Surely, in such a place, they could meet and be cordial, wish each other well in parting, without pain?

They could not; there was such anguish in the meeting. For minutes they sat and said nothing. Only their eyes spoke. Finally, words burst from him like a grenade. 'It's impossible. I told you.'

She sat, and looked, and said nothing. Which provoked more anger still.

'You told me yourself. *You've got to be out of your mind to do this job.* Well, I don't believe I'm out of my mind, and I'm not willing to chuck everything away for nothing.'

'Is that how you see the idea of spending our lives together? As nothing?'

'That's what it would come to. Because these fantasies of yours would end up destroying us both. It would be impossible.'

'I don't accept that. It wouldn't be easy, nothing worthwhile is, but that doesn't mean it would be impossible. And at least we'd have the satisfaction of knowing that we hadn't just turned our backs.'

Anna did not know what, if anything, she had hoped from this meeting but saw now that she might as well not have bothered. Mark had made up his mind.

'We've tried twice, now, and it hasn't worked. Maybe it's my fault, maybe I don't want the challenge, but in the end that makes no difference. I'll tell you what I'm going to do. I shall stay here, do my job, try to make a new life for myself. Once again.' He clenched his fists as they lay upon the table. His despair threatened her like a club. 'I shall be content.'

Nicki saw Mostyn at a function at the Opera House. They sailed past each other like ships trailing icebergs in their wake, eyes fixed on the middle distance.

She was glad; it showed Mostyn wanted no more to do with her than she with him. More than anything she wanted to forget how she'd opened up to him. How he'd laughed.

A lifetime would be too short. Thank God she didn't need him, that was all.

Because he was dished. She'd made sure of that when she'd tipped off the journalist, that time after ...

She didn't want to think about that time.

The whole town was talking about how Mostyn Harcourt had got his comeuppance at last. Nobody knew where the rumours had come from, but there had been plenty willing to confirm them once the word was out. The great Hatchet on his knees to his ex-wife, imploring her to pull his chestnuts out of the fire.

No one came back from a humiliation as dire as that. He would stagger on, in a wounded-duck sort of way, but for a man like Mostyn it would be no more than a living death. It would be a thousand times worse, knowing that without Anna's help he would not have had even that.

Thank God I got away from him when I did, she thought. At least I'm still a free agent.

And went looking for her partner.

'It is an appropriate thing that we do now,' Pieter Wolmarans said.

He stood at Anna's side as they gazed across the open grave, the symmetrical rows of vines, to the mountains overlooking the valley. They were huge, blue, silent. Among them Anna caught a momentary glimpse of a slowly moving speck gleaming in sunlight, a great bird circling.

'I often ask myself what those hills would tell us if they could,' Pieter said. 'They have seen good people and bad. And all the rest of us who are neither, or perhaps a bit of both.'

Anna had brought from Australia the urn containing the ashes that had remained after the cremation that Anneliese had insisted upon. Archer had made up some story about cremation being contrary to God's will. Anything to avoid expense but for once Margaret had stood up to him.

'That's what she wanted, and that's what she'll get.'

As always, Archer had suckled his grievance at the mouth of a bottle but had been unable to change her mind.

Now Anneliese was coming home.

Anna opened the urn and, bending, emptied its contents upon the fecund earth.

'Maybe we should say something,' Pieter wondered uneasily.

He had wanted a dominee to bless the interment but Anna had told him that Anneliese would not have wished it. He had been dubious; Anneliese had died when Anna was only fifteen, how could she possibly know what her great-grandmother had wanted? Anna had stood firm and won. She was convinced that she was right, knew that at that moment, in that place, she was very close to her.

'*My spirit will not rest . . .*'

It could rest now.

'Say something,' Pieter said again.

The opening in the earth was chocolate brown against the bright grass, the tawny vines reaching terrace by terrace up the hillside. There had been another grave in Anneliese's life, the wound in the yellow earth that she had mentioned so often, the place where the children of her marriage had lain with other victims of that terrible war. There had been no hope that they might eventually be brought home to this valley surrounded by mountains. Their home was the earth, without name or anything to show where they lay. No one could do anything about that but Anneliese, twenty-eight years after her death, had reached sanctuary at last.

Across the valley the sunlight lay upon the tranquil hills and struck sparks of light from the tears filling her eyes.

'Welcome home,' Anna said.

Shovels rasped as two of *Oudekraal*'s workmen filled in the hole. Around them the graves of the Wolmarans lay like the roots of a stone tree. They stood for a moment, heads bowed, then walked side by side to the house.

'I shall arrange a headstone,' Pieter said. 'It is important there should be a headstone.'

The family Bible, huge, worn, its cover edged with brass, lay open upon a table in the *voorkamer*. Pieter walked over and studied it silently. Looking over his shoulder, Anna saw a list of names, many of them very old and faded and, at the bottom, the Afrikaans text he had written there.

'What does it say?'

'Anneliese Riordan, formerly van der Merwe, died Australia 14 December 1970, buried at Oudekraal 10 October 1998.'

Again Anna felt like weeping. 'That is kind of you. But the name Riordan ... They were never married, you know.'

'In the sight of God,' he said, and smiled. 'There is more.'

'What?'

He cleared his throat and read again. 'Anna Riordan, born Australia —'

Now she did weep. 'Others before me,' she managed. 'My mother, grandfather —'

'You are the one who came home,' he said. '*In the days when the keepers of the house shall tremble.* It is from the Bible.'

'I do not understand what you mean.'

For a moment he pondered. 'No trembling now,' he said at length. 'Thanks to you.'

'I did nothing.'

'You saved *Oudekraal*.'

It was, indeed, as simple as that.

'I could never have done it without Adam Shongwe. He put the boot in with the State President, got that fellow Tembe sorted out.' She smiled. 'They sent him to Paraguay. Would have made it Greenland, he said, but apparently there is no legation in Greenland.'

'I have named *Oudekraal* for you in my will,' Pieter said.

She frowned. 'There is no need …'

'There is a need.'

'But I have commitments. I won't be able to live here. Who will look after the place?'

'Nico Walsh is a good manager. Good winemaker, too. He has done more to run the place than I, these several years.'

'Would he be willing?'

'Why not? It is his home, too.'

'That quotation from the Bible,' Anna said. 'How does it go on?'

'I'll read it for you.' Pieter's gnarled hands turned the pages of the Book until he reached the place he was seeking.

'*Or ever the silver cord be loosed, or the golden bowl be broken, or the pitcher be broken at the fountain —*'

'Not what you'd call cheerful, is it?'

'There is more.' Again he read. '*Then shall the dust return to the earth as it was: and the spirit shall return unto God who gave it.*'

Quietly he closed the book.

'I don't understand,' she said for the second time. 'What does it mean?'

'It means life. Endless renewal. A circle, on and on forever. That is what immortality is. What love is.'

She paid a courtesy visit to the State President and his new wife, then flew out to Geneva. An official car drove her from Cointron airport to her offices overlooking the lake.

Over the next days, the grinding weight of her new job descended upon her. It was proving impossible, indeed, but it was the impossibility that made it worthwhile. She worked herself and her aides to exhaustion so that at night, what there was of it, she slept. But it was not good sleep and each morning, when she awoke, her first thoughts were of all the things in her life that might have been and were not.

She remembered what Pieter Wolmarans had said about the keepers of the house. He had talked about a circle going on and on forever, symbolising immortality and love. Where were the love and immortality in her own life?

A month after her arrival; a morning like any other, clouds hanging above the lake. She got up, dressed, had a